Rake *in the* Regency

BALLROOM

Bronwyn Scott

Mills & Boon, an imprint of Harlequin (UK) Limited,
Eton House, 18-24 Paradise Road, Richmond, Surrey TW9 1SR

RAKE IN THE REGENCY BALLROOM
© Harlequin Enterprises II B.V./S.à.r.l 2013

The Viscount Claims His Bride © Nikki Poppen 2009
=The Earl's Forbidden Ward © Nikki Poppen 2009

ISBN: 978 0 263 90677 6

052-1113

Harlequin (UK) policy is to use papers that are natural, renewable and recyclable products and made from wood grown in sustainable forests. The logging and manufacturing processes conform to the legal environmental regulations of the country of origin.

Printed and bound
by CPI Group (UK) Ltd, Croydon, CR0 4YY

Bronwyn Scott is a communications instructor at Pierce College in the United States and is the proud mother of three wonderful children (one boy and two girls). When she's not teaching or writing, she enjoys playing the piano, travelling—especially to Florence, Italy—and studying history and foreign languages.

Readers can stay in touch on Bronwyn's website, www. bronwynnscott.com, or at her blog, www.bronwynswriting. blogspot.com. She loves to hear from readers.

In The Regency Ballroom Collection

Scandal in the Regency Ballroom – Louise Allen
April 2013

Innocent in the Regency Ballroom – Christine Merrill
May 2013

Wicked in the Regency Ballroom – Margaret McPhee
June 2013

Cinderella in the Regency Ballroom – Deb Marlowe
July 2013

Rogue in the Regency Ballroom – Helen Dickson
August 2013

Debutante in the Regency Ballroom – Anne Herries
September 2013

Rumours in the Regency Ballroom – Diane Gaston
October 2013

Rake in the Regency Ballroom – Bronwyn Scott
November 2013

Mistress in the Regency Ballroom – Juliet Landon
December 2013

Courtship in the Regency Ballroom – Annie Burrows
January 2014

Scoundrel in the Regency Ballroom – Marguerite Kaye
February 2014

Secrets in the Regency Ballroom – Joanna Fulford
March 2014

The Viscount
Claims His Bride

Prologue

London, June 1820

Valerian Inglemoore, the Viscount St Just, had a secret, a dreadful secret that caused him to tremble in guilt and self-loathing as he stood alone on Lady Rutherford's veranda, gazing at the paper lantern-lit garden beyond the balustrade, but not really seeing it.

His secret was all consuming, too consuming to spare a glance for the elegant town garden with its fountains and well-laid paths that wound through knot gardens and small privet hedges.

Under normal circumstances, the garden would have been quite enticing. But tonight, his secret was nearly too much to bear. He was twenty-one and he was in love with Philippa Stratten, Baron Pendennys's daughter, and she was in love with him. She was to meet him here tonight.

But nothing would ever come of it.

That was the secret.

Tonight, he was breaking it off with her, at her father's request. Tonight, he had to convince her after two months of stolen kisses and clandestine meetings that his affections were nothing more than a young man's fleeting fancy. He didn't know how he'd manage. He loved her so much.

After tonight, he'd never take her in his arms, never feel her run her fingers through his hair, as if it were the rarest silk. The last two months had been heaven. He'd danced with her at her début in April and every night since. They'd made a habit of heated kisses in curtained alcoves, and taking long walks in gardens during Venetian breakfasts and afternoon teas. It had been simple enough to manipulate time alone with her. He was an avid botanist as well as a horseman. It was plausible enough to say they were going off to look at a certain variety of flower or to see a new colt in the stables.

Oh, yes, they'd fallen madly in love with each other. One could almost say it was love at first sight except that he had known Philippa for years. She was his best friend Beldon's sister. The threesome had spent school holidays roaming the Cornish coast together. He'd known since his first visit home with Beldon that his heart could belong to no other.

Behind him, the Rutherfords' ballroom played host to three hundred of London's finest dancing away the night in their silks and satins, champagne never more than a footman's tray away. But he cared not a whit. His heart was breaking.

'Valerian.' A familiar, dear voice spoke his name in the darkness. He drew a final breath, praying for the strength to give her up. It would be for her own good, although she'd never believe it.

He turned towards the sound of her voice, letting her beauty overwhelm him as it always did. The effect was no less devastating tonight. This evening, her beauty was at its zenith, shown to perfection in the pale blue fabric of her gown. In the moonlight, the fabric appeared to shimmer when she moved. A soft summer breeze drew the thin fabric of her gown against her body, reminding Valerian of the fine figure beneath the filmy layers of summer chiffon.

'Val.' She whispered his name in response, moving towards him, her hands outstretched. 'I could hardly wait.' She wore a gentle smile on her lips, a soft look for him alone in the blue depths of her eyes. It was intoxicating to think the excitement that simmered beneath the surface of that gentle smile and soft look were all for him.

He savoured it. After tonight, he would not feel such joy again.

She slipped her gloved hands into his, expecting him to take her in his arms as he usually did. He swallowed hard against the temptation. He'd come out here to do his duty to her family, a family which had loved and harboured him since his adolescence. They'd asked him to give her up for sake of their finances and her future. It was a difficult task at best. Her merest touch, her slightest affection, made it Herculean.

The embrace did not come. He could not give it to her as much as he desired to take her in his arms and feel her against him. To do so would be to fail the family in the only thing they'd ever asked of him. As a man of honour, he owed them more.

She looked up into his face, reading him aright, unconsciously warning him to better school his features if he was to carry off his task believably. 'Aren't you happy to see me?' Philippa began.

'Of course I am happy to see you. I am always happy to see a dear friend,' Valerian said, hoping Philippa didn't hear the unspoken lie. He'd always seen her as much more than a friend.

'Then kiss me. I've waited all day for you, for this moment.' She flirted, trying to press up against him, to make him take her in his arms.

He was too skilled for her untutored efforts. 'Philippa, stop. We have to talk.'

'Here?' She glanced around curiously, disappointment evident on her features. Valerian wondered what she'd been expecting that this location was not suitable. Certainly, she wasn't expecting what he had to tell her. Her father, Baron Pendennys, had indicated that Beldon and Philippa were completely in the dark about the family's situation.

The balcony was mostly empty, but there were a few couples strolling about. It wasn't nearly as private as he'd hoped. Valerian shook his head. 'No, not here. Come walk in the garden with me.'

They found a bench settled among rhododendrons in full bloom and sat. Valerian kept her hand. He nodded towards a bower of roses across the pathway. 'The roses are lovely. I hear Lady Rutherford has imported a special yellow rose from Turkey.'

He was stalling and he knew it, putting off the news as long as he could, storing up every memory of her—beautiful, innocent Philippa, believing in the purity of his love when he'd come to prove her beliefs ill founded and her heart played falsely. It would be years before she would understand this was a sham designed to protect her family.

'What is it, Val? You didn't come out here to show me roses,' Philippa coaxed.

'I spoke to your father earlier this evening.'

Her face lit with joy. A little cry of delight escaped her lips. She clapped a gloved hand over her mouth. He replayed the words in his head the way she would hear them. He knew he'd mis-stepped. She thought he had come to propose. He must be more careful, more convincing.

Valerian shook his head in warning. 'No, Philippa, it

is not what you think. Your father has told me of your betrothal to the Duke of Cambourne. He accepted an offer for your hand this afternoon.'

Philippa furrowed her brow, disbelief and confusion warring across her face. His words had achieved their goal. This pronouncement was so far from what she'd expected she couldn't even be angry. She couldn't get angry with him until she put the pieces together. The poor girl hadn't even known Cambourne was interested, although the betting book at White's had been full of wagers over when the widower Duke would make his move. The men about town had privately acknowledged Cambourne's interest in the Season's finest débutante weeks ago. Valerian had hoped to wait out the storm. He might have succeeded if the Baron's need for funds hadn't been so desperate.

'Cambourne? You must be mistaken, Val.' She was all naïve logic, standing up and shaking out her skirts, convinced she only had to march into the ballroom and explain the situation to her father. 'He loves you. Nothing would please him more than to welcome you into our family. He would want this for me, for us.'

'Wait, Philippa.' Valerian kept his voice even and cold, not betraying the emotion threatening beneath his hardening veneer. 'I came out here to encourage you to accept Cambourne's offer.'

'What do you mean? You want me to marry Cambourne?' Philippa exclaimed, horrified. 'He's old enough to be my father! I don't love him. Beyond a few dances, I hardly know the man at all.' Her infamous temper started to show now that the initial shock had passed. Valerian did not relish being on the receiving end of her sharp tongue.

'You have the rest of your life to get to know him, Philippa.' Valerian dismissed her argument with callous disregard. 'He's an excellent catch for you, if you think about it.' Valerian made a show of ticking the other man's merits off on his gloved fingers. 'He's from our part of the world. You'll still be close to home and your family. He's wealthy. He loves horses as you do. He's not a cruel or unattractive man. You could find happiness with him. He will offer you stability and security.'

'But not love,' Philippa fired back. 'Here you are, laying out his assets like a business merger. But the only one I care about is love. He can't possibly love me. He doesn't know me. You know me, Val. If those criteria are so important to my father, then why won't you suit? You live in our part of the world, you love horses, you're kind and attractive, you have money. Under those conditions, I don't see why your offer isn't as good. What was wrong with you, Val? Let me talk to my father. We'll be engaged by midnight. You'll see.'

Valerian looked into the azure depths of her beseeching eyes. It was deuced awkward playing the jilt. If he was successful, she'd walk out of the garden thinking he was unaffected by the turn of events. She'd never know he'd carried a ring in his pocket for the last two weeks, hoping against hope that Cambourne's suit would come to naught.

The ring was still there, in the left pocket of his evening coat. And there it would remain. He strongly doubted he'd ever give it to another. It was slow torture to outline Cambourne's merits to her, to offer her reassurances that all would be well when in fact he didn't think he'd ever be well again. His stomach was churning.

'What was wrong with me?' Valerian echoed with feigned flippancy 'For starters, I don't want to be engaged by midnight. Secondly, I didn't ask.'

More lies. He had asked anyway, even knowing the situation. Her father had explained plainly that the young viscount didn't have enough money—at least not until he was twenty-seven and came into his inheritance. But Baron Pendennys couldn't wait that long. It had hurt enormously to realise his dreams had been sold for golden guineas. He would be a wealthy man for ever living without the one thing his money couldn't buy.

'What? You never asked?' Her eyes filled with tears, her voice full of disbelief. 'I don't understand.'

God, she was beautiful. Valerian fought the urge to pull her against him. She stood so close it would hardly be an effort to do so. He could smell the light fragrance of her lemon-scented soap rising from her skin, the lavender rinse of her clean hair.

She sat down hard on the stone bench, grasping at the logic of it all. 'I thought you loved me. I thought you wanted to marry me.'

Valerian fought the urge to follow her down, and take her hands in comfort. He had to stop touching her or she'd know it was all a lie.

'Keep your voice down. We don't want to draw attention,' Valerian scolded, covertly casting his gaze about the area. 'The last thing we need now when it's all over is to be compromised.' He'd meant it to be a setdown. She seized on it as the answer to their troubles.

'That's it!' Philippa said wildly. 'If you compromise me, Father will have to let us marry and Cambourne will have a gracious out. Everyone would understand he couldn't marry me then.'

Valerian felt himself rouse at the very idea. It would be easy enough to compromise her, but he loved her too much not to warn her of the consequences—consequences she couldn't fathom through the lens of her innocence, but with three years of town bronze on him, Valerian could. 'Philippa, no one in London would receive us. We'd live a life of exile and I could not doom you to that. I could not doom myself to that,' he added selfishly.

Philippa could not be fooled, and her face tilted, perplexed by the incongruous statement. 'Do such things matter to you? I thought if you had your horses and your gardens and me, it would be enough.' She rose and moved into his embrace, her head finding its way to his shoulder.

Valerian let her, although he held himself stiff, his arms wooden at his side. He was tired of fighting on all fronts. It was inevitable now. He was down to last things. He would not see Philippa after tonight. He'd decided already that he could not go back to his home in Cornwall and watch her become the wife of a neighbour. It would drive him insane to know she and her husband lived only a day's ride away. He'd known when he met her tonight what he had to do. He'd known she would try to argue against her father's choice. He'd known he would have to resist her entreaties no matter what form they took. He had not known how painful it would be.

In her desperation, Philippa was arguing with all the tools at her disposal, even her body as she was doing now. Early on in their relationship, he'd revelled in teaching her about a man's body. There was something heady about tutoring one's beloved in the sensual arts. He'd never dreamed he would not be the one to teach her the ultimate love lesson. He fought back the wave of nausea sweeping his form.

Philippa raised her head from his shoulder, a lock of her long hair falling from its loose coiffure. Valerian involuntarily reached out to brush the russet strand back from her face. How many times had he made that gesture in the past months?

'If you won't marry me or compromise me, at least give me one night of passion. Let me be with you, as we intended to be together,' she whispered.

Just hearing her utter the words completed his growing erection. A small moan of regret escaped his lips as he shut his eyes, gathering his strength. With her head on his shoulder, thankfully she could not see the torture on his face, although he knew she could feel his desire straining against her stomach. God knew how much he wanted her. He made no attempt to hide his arousal. She knew how she affected him and he her. But he was a man of honour. He'd promised to let her go.

'That's a very unwise suggestion, Philippa,' he heard himself saying in a steady voice that sounded as if it came from another man who watched the vignette unfolding with great uninterest.

'Please, Val,' Philippa cried, clutching his hands. 'I love you and you love me, I know you do. I can feel it.'

He had to end this scene soon. She was on the verge of breaking and his restraint was failing. If this went on much longer, his reserve would crack and they would spend the rest of their lives paying for the foolishness of a few mad minutes. He would not do that to her.

'Don't beg. I can't stand to see you grovel,' he said in a low voice close to her ear. Then he released her and stepped back, preparing to say the most difficult words he'd ever uttered, but he had to make her believe them. 'I do love you, but perhaps not in the same way you love me. I am sorry if you've misunderstood my intentions when we started our little experiment in *l'amour*. We are finished now, you and I. Whatever we had is done, a fair-weather fling. That is how it is for a man.'

He could feel the nervous tic jump in his cheek as a silent curtain fell between them. A tickling bead of sweat ran its slow race down his back as he waited on her next words. His heart warred with his mind. His mind wanted her to see the practical logic of ending their *affaire* and accept his hurtful fabrication. His heart wanted her to see the words for the farce they were.

He watched coldness steal over Philippa's face as her features changed from desperation back to anger. An unchecked fury raged in the depths of her eyes as her mind raced towards the conclusions he'd wanted her to draw. When she spoke, he could hear her voice tremble with emotions.

'A fair-weather fling? This was all a game to you? Everything was a lie?' she cried as the truth spread across her face, like clouds across the sun, as she began to acknowledge the import of his words. He wished he didn't know her so well as to guess her thoughts. In her pale face he saw her doubt and pain. He knew that she believed that every knowing look, hot kiss and searing touch had been little more than seductive perjury of the worst kind. He'd played his part well. She believed those gestures had meant nothing at all to him while they had meant everything to her.

'I thought you were a man of honour, Valerian.' Her voice trembled. Her heart was breaking.

Valerian tightened the reins on his resolve. 'I am a man of honour. That's why I feel I need to call a halt before our sweet interlude goes any further.'

'Interlude?' Philippa was incredulous. 'You make it sound as if our *affaire* is nothing more than an intermission at the theatre! Something to occupy your time between activities!'

Valerian held himself stiffly, ready to deliver the *coup de grace*, the last stroke. 'I am to leave tomorrow to join my uncle on the Continent, something of a belated Grand Tour now that peace has been restored.'

'Valerian, this is not like you. You're playing a cruel game.' There was reproach in her voice for both of them. Reproach for his despicable behaviour and self-chiding for her rashness. She was wrong, of course, he loved her very much, but there was no honourable way out of the situation. Perhaps it was best if she believed the worst, that his love was a fraud, that she was an extended exercise in dalliance. Valerian said nothing in his own defence. Instead, he gave her a neat bow. 'I'll leave you here. I can see you need a moment to collect yourself before returning to the ball,' he said with polite coldness and turned to leave.

Philippa called to him one last time. Her anger was perilously close to giving way to tears as she spoke in a strangled whisper. 'Tell me you loved me, that it wasn't all false coin.'

Valerian stopped, but did not look back. Like

Orpheus, it would be his undoing. 'Miss Stratten, I cannot.' He comforted himself with the fact that it was the truth. He was too choked with emotion to utter the words she wanted to hear. Worse, he knew the reason for his silence would be misconstrued as heartlessness. In reality, to say the words would be to give her false hope. If she thought there was any window of opportunity for her case, she'd not give in. Philippa was tenacious. He was counting on that tenacity to help her through this crisis and build a new life for herself.

Valerian closed his eyes as loss swept through him. It was better that the words went unsaid, no matter what cruel conclusions she might draw. His logic was cold comfort when Philippa spoke again, her emotions mastered, her quiet parting words piercing him like a venom arrow to the heart. 'I will not forget this, Valerian.'

Miserable and heartsick, Valerian squared his shoulders, intending to find Philippa's father and tell him the deed was done. He'd no longer stand in the way of the family's financial stability. He'd tell Beldon to take Philippa home. Then he'd leave—it was the only truth he'd told tonight.

In the other pocket of his evening coat was his uncle's letter, inviting Valerian to join his uncle's family on the Continent where he served as one of Britain's premier diplomats. The letter had come yesterday in response to Valerian's own inquiries. Valerian knew he could not stay in England and watch Philippa's new life unfold. Instead, he would go and serve England against whatever threats arose and try to exorcise the memory of Philippa Stratten from his hot blood.

Chapter One

30 December 1829

An icy wind blew steadily through the poorly sealed post chaise, keeping its two occupants chilled in spite of their caped greatcoats and the hot bricks they'd installed at the posting inn. But it had been the best they could do at the time. The west country was not known for its luxuries. The newly returned Viscount St Just didn't mind. He'd been in far less comfortable situations over the past nine years and he was simply glad to be home.

'What are you smiling about?' Beldon Stratten, the young Baron Pendennys, groused, stamping his feet in a futile attempt to generate some body heat.

'Am I smiling?' Valerian asked. 'I was unaware of it.'

'You've been smiling since the inn at St Austell. I can't imagine what about.'

Beldon was right. There wasn't much to smile about. Their journey had become a comedy of errors. Nothing had gone right since they'd left London after celebrating the Christmas holidays in town. They'd hoped to sail down the Cornish coast to St Just-in-Roseland, Valerian's home on the peninsula, and avoid the roads. But foul weather on the Channel had scotched those plans. So they'd set out on horseback, hoping to make better time than a lumbering coach. Valerian had a yen to be settled in his home by New Year. But weather again played them false, turning too cold for safe passage on horseback. They'd abandoned the horses at St Austell and hired the only post chaise available.

It went unspoken between them that they'd get no farther than Truro today. If they wanted to try for St Just-in-Roseland by New Year, it would have to wait until tomorrow.

'Do you believe in serendipity, Val?' Beldon asked, stretching his long legs out across the small space between the seats.

Valerian looked at him queerly. 'I am not exactly sure what you mean.'

'You know, making valuable discoveries by accident.'

'Ah, coincidence,' Valerian corrected. 'You think it is merely a fortuitous happening that I ran into you in London.'

'Definitely luck since you'd sent no word ahead of your return.' There was a censorious note in Beldon's

voice. Valerian did not miss it. He had not said goodbye
to Beldon properly when he'd left London so abruptly
years ago and he had not written over the long years with
the exception of one short letter early on. It was a credit
to the depth of their friendship that Beldon had felt his
absence so keenly and forgiven him so readily.

Beldon's tone softened. 'Perhaps you will explain to
me some day why you all but vanished into your uncle's
household overnight. I am your friend. I would understand, whatever your reasons. We all missed you, even
Philippa. I think she had always admired you from afar.'

Valerian started at that. Had Philippa kept their
secret all these years? He'd expected her to blurt it all
out. He'd imagined her crying on Beldon's shoulder in
the garden that last night, sobbing out how her heart had
been broken by her brother's cad of a best friend.

He'd known this moment was inevitable. Hearing her
name would be just the first of many such moments. He
knew in his heart that was why he hadn't written ahead
to Beldon to tell him of his return. Of course, he hadn't
known until the last moment that he would be assigned
to the team of negotiators sent to London to pound out
a peace treaty to end the latest conflict between the
Turks and Russia. Even when he'd known with a certainty he'd be coming back, he still hadn't sent advance
notice of his return. It was a stalling mechanism and a
desperate one at that, designed to put off any encounter
with Philippa until the very last.

His tenure on the Continent had not outlasted his own broken heart. He had stayed on in Europe as long as he could, volunteering for myriad diplomatic assignments that lingered in the wake of the Napoleonic Wars. Napoleon's efforts had left their mark on old and new regimes alike and Valerian had quickly learned that there was always someone to fight.

Treaties may have been signed, but Europe, particularly the Balkans, was not at peace. There was still plenty for Britain to worry over as countries fought to define themselves and empires sought to expand in the power vacuum left by Napoleon's defeat.

Valerian had watched modern history play out before his very eyes as Britain and the rest of Europe fought to corner the fledgling Balkan markets.

After years of pointless victories and disappointments, Valerian found he had no stomach for a fight motivated by greed and avarice, thinly cloaked in a facade of ideals, and he could not stay away from home indefinitely. He had gardens and an estate to manage. He could not rely on his steward for ever.

While a broken-hearted young man of twenty-one could be forgiven for impetuously leaving his inheritance, a grown man of thirty years, who knew his duty, could not continue to shirk it. Yet it was difficult turning for home when he knew it would mean facing Philippa and Cambourne. But duty and honour beckoned, two ideals he had always held dear even when his country hadn't.

'How is your sister?' Valerian inquired, hoping to sound casual.

Beldon nodded. 'She's doing well. I see her often. You just missed her in London. She spent the holidays with a friend in Richmond before heading out here. If I had known you were coming, I could have persuaded her to stay in town.' Beldon paused, seeming to consider his next words before speaking them. 'It's hard to believe she's twenty-seven and already through her first husband. Here I am at thirty and I haven't been married, not even close. It makes me feel "behind" somehow.'

Valerian felt his body tense. 'Through her first husband?'

'Yes, didn't you know? It was in all the papers, quite a newsworthy death.'

'I wasn't exactly holed up in Vienna the entire time,' Valerian said wryly, thinking of the rugged Balkan territories he'd journeyed through with their mountains and sparse populations. There were places in Europe the mails didn't reach, places with names like Voden and Negush. Places that didn't appear on a map unless you were a Turkish Pasha charged with keeping the Christian millet in line.

'Cambourne died three years ago in a mining accident. There was a cave-in while he was touring one of his tin mines. It was a freak incident. A shaft support gave way. The miners pulled him out, but he died of his injuries three days later at home.'

Philippa was a widow. The implications were not lost on him. Valerian's emotions ricocheted from a morbid elation that Philippa was free to a sadness that she'd had to bear the loss of a husband, set adrift in society as a dowager so early in life.

'I hope Cambourne left her well provided for,' he said quietly, knowing that the Pendennys's fortunes had rested so completely on Cambourne's welfare. Valerian didn't like to think that her marriage had come to naught.

'Absolutely. He had a cousin who inherited the title and the other estates, but Philippa has all she needs or wants. Of course, the principal estate went to his heir, but Philippa has the house in Cornwall where they spent their marriage. To my mind, she got the better end of the deal. Coppercrest is a much more hospitable dwelling. Even Cambourne himself preferred it.

'"The heir" isn't much on going up to town, so Philippa has free run of the town house. Cambourne also bequeathed her a substantial interest in the mines and the associate businesses. He owned a tin smelter and a small gunpowder works.'

Valerian only half-listened to Beldon's itemization of Philippa's situation. The first line had caught most of his attention—a cousin had inherited. Ah, there were no children. Another delicate question answered. Valerian wondered if Beldon had shared that information on purpose or if it had been accidental.

Beldon chuckled softly. 'I forget that you haven't seen her recently. She's much changed since you saw her last. She's not a budding débutante any more. She's a sophisticated woman now, as comfortable in town among the leading hostesses and politicians as she is in the country, tramping over the cliffs and riding neck-for-nothing at the hunt. When she's in town, her house teems with politicos. Everyone seeks her endorsement and asks her opinion. She's a leading supporter of mine reform these days, and with justifiable reason.'

Valerian smiled thoughtfully in the gathering gloom. The grey afternoon was turning towards evening. Truro couldn't be more than a few miles in the offing. Beldon's revelations were enough to fill the time. Valerian turned his mind inwards, pondering all Beldon had shared.

Philippa was free. In a fairy-tale world, he would have a second chance. But his world was far from a fairy tale. They had parted badly nine years ago. Philippa's final words to him were still achingly clear. And now there was all he had done during those years to contend with as well. His years in the Balkans had left him with another set of nightmares, another set of people he'd failed in their hour of need. Those failures hung like an invisible millstone about his neck, even when he was able to subdue the more physical reminders of his futile efforts.

He'd been surprised in London to know how much

people had heard about his antics on the Continent. Of course, no one had known the depth of such shenanigans, but they knew the gist. He'd led a flamboyant lifestyle in Vienna during his brief time there, playing the role of a womanising diplomat. It had been the perfect foil for something darker that took him to the sinister underbelly of the rebellions popping up across Europe. He'd been nothing short of an expert spy and negotiator, engaging in the kind of diplomacy that *never* made the broadsheets.

'We'll stop tonight at Lucien Canton's place just outside Truro. It'll be much better than an inn. He has an excellent cook and an even better cellar,' Beldon broke into Valerian's ruminations.

Valerian nodded, only half-engaged in the conversation. 'It won't be an imposition, I hope?' He didn't remember this friend of Beldon's from their early days as young bucks on the town. 'I don't believe I know him.'

'He's Viscount Montfort's son and heir. He was close to Cambourne before his death. Since then, he's been Philippa's strong right hand.'

Valerian couldn't quite read Beldon's expression. It didn't seem that Beldon was precisely elated about the man's association with his sister, but had resigned himself to it. Beldon's conversation was moving on. 'It will be a party before the party, the three of us together again like old times. With luck, Philippa is there already. Lucien asked her to act as hostess for his New Year's gala since she's the best hostess in the neighbourhood and his sister couldn't come down from London to do it.'

Now Valerian was fully engaged. 'Philippa will be there?' Regardless of Beldon's assurances that Lucien Canton was a grand chap, Valerian doubted he'd like the man very much. He was inclined to dislike any man who had a claim on Philippa's attentions and this Lucien clearly did. No one played hostess for someone they didn't know well. They must be good friends indeed and perhaps something more.

Beldon grinned and leaned forwards in his growing excitement. 'Yes. She will be beyond surprised to see you.'

She would indeed, Valerian reflected wryly, although he and Beldon would likely disagree about her reaction to that surprise.

Philippa Lytton, the widowed duchess of Cambourne, glided down the curved staircase of Lucien Canton's Truro manor at half-past six, consciously aware that she would be the last one to the drawing room and that she'd be the only female present. What had started out as a small *en famille* supper with Canton and the bachelor vicar from down the road had turned into a supper party with three unexpected guests.

One of them was her brother, Beldon, who had arrived unannounced just two hours ago and a guest he'd brought with him. Beldon's arrival was understandable given the terrible weather and the fact that she was already in residence. The third guest's presence was less clearly explained. Lucien knew him only through the acquaintances of others. He was a Mister Danforth, a well-to-do shipping merchant from Liverpool who hoped to start a provincial bank. He was not someone they would normally associate with. He was a rich Cit who'd made most of his money during the war, making his fortune somewhat speculative as to the legitimacy of its origins. But the underpopulated wilds of Cornwall in mid-winter and his tenuous connection to Lucien made it difficult to turn him away.

Philippa stopped at the foot of the stairs to draw a deep breath and square her shoulders. She stole a glance in the hallway mirror as a final check. She looked fine with her hair piled high and threaded with pearls. The heavy satin folds of her skirts fell neatly to her ankles into a deep Van-dyked hem. She liked the quiet shushing of the satin skirt as she walked.

Indeed, she loved this gown for its textures and feel as much as she loved it for its look. The cream skirt was set off by the deep blue velvet of the round bodice that fell low over her shoulders and into a plunging vee in the back. She fiddled with the simple choker of blue Kashmir sapphires that set off the expanse between her neck and the delicate cream-lace trim of her bodice.

She looked well. Not that she wanted to attract any attention. She wasn't dressing for a man's approval, not even Lucien's, although he'd readily give it. Being in high looks boosted her confidence, a security blanket of sorts. In a room dominated by the male species, one could never have too much confidence if one was going to hold one's own.

She stepped into the wide doorway of the drawing room, her eyes quickly assessing the gathering. Lucien stood at the carved-oak fireplace mantel, dressed in dark evening clothes, looking slender and elegant with his usual immaculate perfection. He was doing his host's duty by chatting with the unworthy Mr Danforth. Across the room in a little grouping of chairs situated beneath an expansive Gainsborough landscape sat her brother, the vicar and apparently the guest her brother had brought with him. The guest's back was to her, affording her only a glimpse of broad shoulders and dark hair, sleek in the evening light of candles.

Beldon saw her first. He gestured that she should join them, saving her from joining Lucien and his odious guest at the fireplace. Philippa smiled warmly at her brother and moved towards the group. She was always glad to see Beldon. They had been close as children and become even closer with her marriage to Cambourne. He'd supported her as she had learned to navigate London society and after when she had to re-learn the treacherous paths of society as a new widow.

He and the little cohort under the Gainsborough rose as she approached. 'Beldon, I am so happy to see you!

We weren't expecting you, but it's delightful all the same.' She gave him a sisterly kiss on the cheek, having to reach up only slightly to do so. They were nearly of a same height, both of them tall and built for grace. Anyone seeing them side by side would not doubt their similar genetic origins. Both had sharp blue eyes and russet hair the colour of chestnuts, each strikingly attractive in their own way.

The vicar leaned forward to take Philippa's hand in greeting. 'I am pleased to see you again, your Grace.'

'And I you, Vicar. How are your plans for a miner's school coming? I believe you had plans drawn up when we spoke last.'

'Very well, thank you. It is kind of you to remember.' The vicar beamed. 'I hope we'll have time to talk about its progress later tonight. I would love your opinion on a few things.' He gently inclined his head to indicate the third gentleman in the group.

The vicar was right. It would be unseemly to jump into conversation before all the introductions were made. Philippa turned her attention to the stranger immediately, small talk coming easily to her lips. But the man to her right was no stranger at all and the small talk died a quick death.

Chapter Two

Valerian Inglemoore was the last man she'd expected to see in Lucien Canton's drawing room. Philippa mustered all her aplomb. 'Viscount, this is indeed a surprise.'

Surprise didn't even begin to cover it. What was he doing in Truro? How long had he been back? A thousand questions rioted through her mind. She mentally tried to tamp them down, telling herself she didn't care about such information. But it was like fighting the Hydra. The more she tried to squelch the rising tide of questions, the more questions came forward—worse questions because they didn't deal with the basic information of who, what and when, but with more intimate concerns—had he thought of her at all during his absence? Had he realised what he'd termed a mere dalliance was something far stronger? Did he have feelings for her yet? Did she, in spite of her efforts to deny it?

Her pulse was certainly racing as if she did, as if she'd forgotten why she'd foresworn any connection to him years ago.

'It is a surprise for me as well, and a pleasant one at that, I might add.' Valerian bent over her gloved hand with an elegant bow. *'Enchanté, Duchesse.'*

The warmth of his touch sent a powerful *frisson* up her arm, so sharp she had to control herself not to snatch her hand back as if burnt. She told herself the reaction was due to the strength of his grip. The reaction had nothing to do with still being attracted to him. She had hardened her heart against Valerian Inglemoore years ago and rightly so.

Time had proved her choice a good one and her escape from his seductive clutches a lucky one. Reports from Europe during his sojourn abroad reached her circles, portraying him as a splendid diplomat with a talent for seduction. From captain's wives to Continental princesses, no woman was safe from the dashing viscount's wiles and no woman wanted to be. He'd become a much sought-after commodity.

It was easy to see why. She was doubly glad she'd given him up years ago. He was far too handsome for his own good now that he'd come into the fullness of his adulthood. Anyone less wise than she would be easily distracted by the silky sleekness of his dark hair. She knew from experience how simple it was to spend an evening thinking about running hands through those ebony skeins.

If the hair didn't distract one thoroughly enough, there was the trap of his piercing jade eyes, the angular planes of his chiselled face, the sensual promise of his lips, the caress of knowing hands, firm and confident as they learned the contours of one's body and the pledge of his own body, all muscles and hot strength beneath superbly tailored clothes. Ah, yes, Valerian Inglemoore was a walking minefield of passion— promising pleasure but delivering heartache to the unsuspecting miss. It was good she knew better. That was one trap she would not fall into again.

Valerian gave her a slight nod, a smug smile playing on his lips. She felt herself blush. He'd caught her looking. She hadn't meant for that to happen.

The butler entered and intoned the announcement for dinner. Philippa felt herself breathe again. She started towards Lucien, eager to escape the scrutiny of Valerian's gaze. A warm hand on her arm stayed her.

'Would you do me the honour of allowing me to escort you into dinner?' Valerian asked, his voice low next to her ear, his message just for her.

Philippa shot a look at Lucien, but he would be of no use to her. He'd already acquiesced to the situation, a hard look in his eyes that belied the friendly tenor of his words. 'You've got her then, St Just? I remember now that the three of you grew up together.' It was said pleasantly enough, but Philippa didn't miss the tightness of Lucien's smile or the covert scrutiny in his eyes.

Valerian seated her at the foot of the table and put himself promptly on her right, leaving Beldon and the vicar to juggle Mr Danforth between them.

Philippa couldn't decide if she preferred Valerian next to her or next to Lucien. Both positions offered their own forms of temptation. She could either have him next to her and struggle with his physical nearness or spend the entire evening fighting the distraction of his handsome visage down the table. But it hardly mattered, she reprimanded herself. He didn't affect her either way. Her current reaction was merely the shock of seeing him again without warning.

She wished she could read Valerian better. It would be a small measure of comfort if he was struggling to adapt as well. Did she have any effect on him at all? All at once, she vividly recalled the hardness of his erection, the feel of him pulsing through his trousers in their youth, how he'd taught her to caress him. Was he hard now? Or entirely immune? No matter that he'd once claimed only the shallowest of feelings for her, he'd roused to her none the less.

She had to stop! Philippa reached for her wine glass and took a generous sip. These were unseemly thoughts. They were base in nature and had no place at the dinner table, especially coming from a woman who had spent the years putting the memory of his kisses behind her.

The footmen removed the soup and served up the fish course. Conversation lagged as they performed their duties. Once the course was settled, Lucien picked up the threads of small talk. 'St Just, are you home for good or has the Continent enchanted you?'

Valerian patted his mouth with a fine linen napkin before speaking. 'I am home for the duration and proud to say it. I terminated my affiliation with the diplomatic corps while I was in London over Christmas. I can now devote my time to my estate, my much neglected gardens and my nursery.'

The statement was ambiguous. Anyone knowing Valerian as she did would wonder if he meant his flower nurseries or perhaps a nursery of another sort. No one was ill bred enough to ask for an explanation, but apparently such probing was not beyond the pale for Mr Danforth, who hadn't known Valerian for more than the time it had taken to eat the soup.

With a smug masculine tone to his voice, Danforth said, 'You mean to marry and beget an heir. Very good thinking. I hear you've quite a fortune. You'll need an heir to look after things.'

At the head of the table, Lucien nearly sprayed a mouthful of wine at the tactless comment. It was practically an art form to make such a *faux pas* as mentioning 'begetting' *and* money in the same poor comment.

Valerian met the rude comment evenly. 'In fact, I do mean to marry as soon as possible. Enough time has been wasted, I think. I find myself eager to embrace matrimony. With the right woman, of course.'

'Naturally,' Danforth agreed, oblivious to the social *faux pas* he'd committed. 'A wife must have certain qualities. She must be pretty, biddable, malleable, open to a husband's training and all that. No man wants to spend his life leg-shackled to an opinion-spouting shrew, no matter what her dowry.'

Philippa stiffened at Danforth's belittling remarks. 'I think finding a wife is altogether different than shopping for a brood mare, Mr Danforth. At least it is for those of us who hold marriage as something more than servitude.'

Beldon coughed and the vicar looked nonplussed. There was more she'd liked to have said to the sputtering Danforth, but Valerian's hand pressed heavily on her thigh beneath the damask cloth in warning. She fought back a smile. Was he remembering her infamous temper?

Valerian smoothly intervened with the honed skill of a diplomat. 'For myself, Mr Danforth, I am looking for different qualities in a wife. I prefer a more mature woman, a woman who can speak for herself, who can hold her own in an argument. In short, a woman of independence.'

Danforth bristled. 'Yes, I've heard that about you.' His beady gaze met Valerian's directly in a surprising show of spine.

Everyone at the table stopped eating. Philippa wondered how Valerian would confront his 'reputation', as it were. Would he deny it? Part of her wished he would.

Valerian smiled. It was not a friendly smile, but a wolfish one that suggested he was not, nor ever would be, the prey. 'Then you will have also heard that I am not afraid of a woman's opinions, that I am not a man who will cower behind old-fashioned thought and conventions when it comes to the suppression of the fairer sex. Much would be missed in our world if we neglected half the population. Take, for example, the excellent champagne our host is serving from his excellent cellar tomorrow night.'

Valerian turned to Canton. 'Pendennys mentioned you'd be offering a Veuve Clicquot, an outstanding champagne thanks to the revolutionary efforts of Clicquot's widow. Did you know, Danforth, that she is responsible for inventing the *remuage* process? We have a woman to thank for clear champagne. Without her efforts, we'd have nothing more than a cloudy, fizzy novelty.' Valerian raised his glass. 'Here's to Madame Clicquot.'

In a few short sentences Valerian had eloquently smoothed over Danforth's uncomfortable claims and moved the conversation into the safer realm of wine. Danforth did not venture out to play with verbal fire again.

Dinner went smoothly after that if Philippa did not count the unnerving sensation of Valerian's body in such close proximity to her own. In all the numerous dinner parties she'd attended, she had not ever noticed the intimate closeness she was now exceedingly aware of with Valerian next to her. His knee touched hers; she dropped her napkin and his hand brushed her skirt as he bent to retrieve it, beating the footman to the task.

* * *

By the time dessert was served, Philippa's nerves were jangled beyond reason. She stood as soon as it was politely possible. 'Gentlemen, excuse me. I'll leave you to your port and cigars.'

Lucien rose and protested. 'Please stay, my dear. You are welcome to stay.' He directed the comment at her, but his hazel stare was directed at Valerian. The look in his gaze was sharp and penetrating, meant to send a message.

So he had noticed Valerian's casual touches, Philippa thought, and he'd found them as unsettling as she did, but for altogether different reasons. She could feel Valerian's eyes read every message, spoken or not. She had no desire to stay in the dining room and become a prize to be fought over. 'Really, I would prefer to retire and give you gentlemen some privacy,' she insisted, not waiting for permission to leave the room.

Philippa collected a shawl from her bedroom and then made good her escape to a quiet veranda where she could let the cold air do its work. She needed a clear head. Valerian was back and he would have to be contended with. His presumptuous behaviour at dinner suggested he wasn't the least bit penitent about breaking her young girl's heart, nor was he disinclined to live down the rumours regarding his profligate behaviour abroad.

Certainly, she didn't want to be petty. What had

happened between them had occurred years ago. They were both adults now. She should put the past behind her. He obviously had if his behaviour at dinner was any indication. He apparently thought she might welcome his advances. But he would have to take her for a fool if he thought she would disregard his well-taught lessons after one flirtatious encounter.

Would she disregard his harsh lesson in love? The thought that she might re-think her position on Valerian was startling. In her mind, she'd often played out an imaginary encounter. In that encounter, she'd been an aloof lady with grand manners, icily polite to a fault and he would know that his attentions had come too late.

Funny how in her imaginings she always assumed he'd care what had become of her. Maybe that was because she could not fathom how he'd gone from a dedicated suitor with words of undying devotion on his lips to that of a cold jilt in the span of a day. Undisputably, he'd broken her heart, but she'd never quite convinced herself it was for the reasons he'd cited. None the less, in the end, the results had been the same.

Valerian would drive her mad! Perhaps it was time to think more seriously about Lucien Canton's offer. There had been no formal proposal, but much was implied in their long-standing relationship. She did expect a proposal soon. Perhaps Valerian was the impetus she needed for getting on with her life.

Lucien was exactly the kind of man she needed and

he'd spent the years since Cambourne's death proving it. He'd overseen the difficult tangle of financial matters and entailments until she'd learned to manage them on her own. He'd been the one to ride out to the mines and keep the Cambourne industries running while she was in mourning. Besides herself, no one knew the extensive Cambourne holdings better than Lucien. He was competent, handsome, well mannered, comfortable to be with. He was reliable and steady, a constant companion.

'Philippa.'

All thoughts of Lucien vanished. She didn't need to turn to know it was Valerian. 'I came out here to be alone.'

'Then we have something in common. I came out here to be alone with you, too.' Valerian took up a position next to her at the railing, leaning on his elbows. 'I wanted to talk to you. There are things I want to explain.'

Philippa shifted her body to face him. 'I don't think that's a good idea unless you want to start explaining why your hand spent most of dinner on my thigh. We are finished. You made that clear nine years ago.'

Valerian would not be put off by her harsh words. It was disappointing, but not unexpected that he could not be handled like the ballroom beaux. A set-down from her usually sent them scrambling for apologies.

Instead of begging forgiveness, Valerian laughed softly in the darkness, a beautiful, sensual sound that promised indecent pleasures. One would have thought she'd spoken love words to him instead of a scolding.

'You are more sharp-tongued than I remember.' He paused to look at her, his voice lowering. 'And more beautiful. You've done well for yourself.'

If he refused to be scolded, then she would refuse to be taken in by his flattery. 'St Just, if you intended that as a compliment, your skill is diminished greatly. I am insulted by the idea that my beauty has done well for me as if my looks were an industry designed to turn a profit. My looks have bought me a few houses and financial security. While those are not unpleasing things, the price for them has been my personal happiness. To think that my looks have done well for me is to be misled by the shallow mind you apparently possess. You show yourself poorly by believing I would settle for so little.'

There, such a scalding set-down should drive even him from the veranda. But Philippa was supremely dissatisfied with the results.

Valerian's face broke into a wide grin, showing all his white teeth. His voice was low and private, laughter lurking beneath the surface. 'I am glad to see that along with selling your hand in marriage, your parents didn't succeed in selling your soul.' He chuckled, enjoying his humour.

'You've a black sense of humour, St Just.'

Valerian reached for her hand where it rested on the

railing, caressing it idly with his fingertips. 'My dear, when have I ever been St Just to you? Call me Valerian as my friends do, as you once did.'

Philippa snatched her hand away. How dare he come out here to insult her and then expect that he could take liberties? 'Let me set you straight. I am not your "dear" or your friend. Nine years ago, I paid the price for what passes as friendship with you. I shall not make that mistake again. I have a new life now and there's no room for you in it.' It was important that she define the rules first before he had a chance to worm himself into her good graces. He could be charming and she must be wary of letting her guard down, of letting him pretend to be her friend.

His face flushed at her words. She did not think the flush was from her candour, but rather from a rising anger. Valerian gripped her by the arms, his soft sensuality of moments ago replaced by a hard envy. 'A life that includes Lucien Canton? What is Lucien Canton to you? Is he your lover?'

'Take your hands off me. I don't answer to you.' Philippa looked him squarely in the eye. Something dangerous and erotic lurked in their emerald depths. In an unfair moment she thought Lucien's hazel eyes merely pretended towards greenness.

He ignored her request. He crowded her against the hard iron of the railing. Somewhere in the far recesses of her mind she thought she should have minded the invasion. But his hot envy had transmuted into molten seduction.

'Your body answers to me, Philippa. My hands were made for you and you alone. No one has ever felt like you do, Philippa. I've not forgotten how your skin feels like rose petals.' He pushed back the shawl from her arms and trailed the back of his hands down their length, removing the long gloves as he went until her arms were completely exposed.

'I have not forgotten what it is to span the width of your back with my hand and pull you against me.' Warm skin met warm skin where the plunging vee of her gown bared her back and she trembled against her will.

'And you've not forgotten either,' Valerian whispered against her mouth, his lips moving to seal hers, his hands moving to crush her against him, one hand finding the firm mound of breast beneath the velvet bodice. He palmed it, caressed it reverently until she cried out in his mouth from unwanted pleasure.

It was all coming back to her in a rush, how he felt against her, how he could make her body come alive, how she loved the exquisite sensations he could coax from her. How could she have forgotten *this*?

Philippa burned. Every part of her body was on fire. Heat licked at her from the inside out. Pressure built at her core until she wanted to scream. Valerian was the sum of her world in that moment. He was everywhere— his hands on her body, his scent in her nostrils—and she didn't want him to stop. She wanted this moment to go on for eternity. She hated herself for it.

She pulled away with the greatest of efforts, panting and desperate. Valerian looked dismayed at her retreat. That was some gratification. 'Have a care, St Just. Lucien will not tolerate playing the cuckold.' She gave a slight nod to the empty room beyond the French doors, where Beldon and Lucien had just arrived. She hoped she didn't look as dishevelled as she felt.

'Philippa—' he began in a ragged voice.

She didn't give him a chance to beg, to explain, to persuade. 'You have gravely overstepped the boundaries of polite society.'

'I didn't do it alone,' St Just responded, his eyes hot, gleaming dark with unslaked need.

'How dare you try to implicate me in your base conduct?' Philippa flamed. 'Let me remind you that this is not some decadent European court filled with women who are dying of lust for your attentions.'

'You're just angry because you liked it.' He had the audacity to give another throaty laugh.

Philippa's nerves were stretched to breaking. She raised her right hand and slapped him hard across the face.

'What was that for?' Valerian put a hand to his red cheek, stunned.

Philippa inhaled deeply, squaring her shoulders. 'That was "welcome home."'

Chapter Three

Welcome home indeed, Valerian thought sourly, watching Philippa disappear inside. Through the glass panes of the French doors he could see her sit down at the polished cherry-wood pianoforte and arrange her skirts.

Lucien Canton slid on to the bench next to her, ready to turn pages, acting the devoted suitor to perfection. From the looks of him, the man did everything to perfection. He was immaculately turned out and not just his clothes, Valerian had noted. Canton's nails were trimmed and buffed to a healthy sheen, his face freshly shaved. Valerian looked at his own nails, just as neatly kept. He too was fastidious in his personal habits. He had learned quickly in his time abroad that women responded to two things, cleanliness and sincerity, both of which were in short supply in many parts of the world. But from all appearances through the window pane, Canton possessed both qualities in abundance. Through the panes, Philippa smiled and laughed at something Canton had said.

Primal envy sparked in Valerian. He didn't want Philippa laughing with Canton. He wanted her laughing with him. He hadn't come home expecting to woo her. He hadn't even known wooing her would be a possibility until Beldon had mentioned Cambourne's death in the coach. But now that the chance to win her back was present, he could see no other course of action.

He'd meant what he'd said at dinner about taking a wife and starting a family—as long as that wife was Philippa. He still desired her and she still responded to him, if that ill-conceived interlude here on the balcony was any indication. He only had to convince her of that. She'd had nine years to nurse her grudge and she'd always been far too stubborn. The sting of her slap suggested the job in front of him would not be an easy one. The passion of her body's response to his said the task would not be without its rewards. She might have struck him, but he was not convinced she'd slapped him out of anger about his advances. Given her response to him, she'd struck him out of anger over her own behaviour. He was merely a convenient target.

However, he was willing to acknowledge that it had been the height of foolhardiness to seek her out alone, knowing that his emotions were ruling his better judgement. The thrill of seeing her again, of feeling her presence next to him at dinner, of watching her deal with Danforth, combined with the surge of jealously that coursed through him at seeing Canton lay claim to her, was too potent a mixture to swallow without consequence.

He'd meant to confess his feelings to her, to declare his devotion and even to explain away the events of their last evening together as the poor decisions of youth. He'd got nowhere with his agenda. Instead, he'd no doubt affirmed all the sordid rumours that had trickled back to London about him. Within moments they'd been sparring and then, his blood hot, he'd taken her in his arms and silenced her the only way he knew how. But his reckless kiss had been more consistent with the behaviour he wanted to refute than the man he wanted to convince Philippa he was, and had always been, in spite of actions to the very persuasive contrary.

The only thing more senseless than kissing Philippa was standing out here in the cold, allowing Canton to hold Philippa's attention uncontested. Valerian pushed open the door and went inside. The battle was joined.

Lucien spied his return to the company as Philippa finished playing a pretty country piece. The small group clapped politely. 'Let us play our duet for them,' Lucien suggested to Philippa, sorting through the sheets of music until he found the one he was looking for. He gave Valerian a challenging look that could not be mistaken for anything other than what it was—a silent dare. Valerian returned the stare with a short nod of acknowledgement.

They executed the duet flawlessly. Valerian had known Philippa was a dab hand at the pianoforte, but Lucien was the stronger of the two players. He wondered if Canton knew he played as well. The piece flowed seamlessly, the four hands following each other to Lucien's trademark perfection.

Amid the brief applause at the end, Canton tossed him a smug look of satisfaction. Philippa caught him at it and gave Canton a hard look. Valerian was hard pressed to smother a laugh. Lucien didn't know Philippa well if he thought such masculine antics would go unpunished. She would make Canton pay and, he noted ruefully when her quick stare censured him as well, he would pay too.

'Anyone else care to play?' Lucien asked, once more the congenial host. Valerian doubted any of the other guests were aware of the currents flowing between the little triangle. It was tempting to play, but it was also petty. Valerian opted to refrain, but Philippa had different ideas. She caught his eye. 'Viscount St Just is quite accomplished if I remember correctly. Do you still play, St Just?'

'Yes, I do. It would be an honour to perform on such a fine instrument.' Valerian took the bench and flexed his hands experimentally.

'I have some music…' Canton began.

'I won't need any music,' Valerian said shortly and

launched into a complicated scherzo that left the audience mesmerised.

'Magnificent! You've been training,' Beldon enthused afterwards. 'I'd forgotten how good you were.'

'Thank you,' Valerian said, rising from the bench. He tossed a covert glance towards Canton, making sure the man understood he'd picked up the gauntlet.

The tea tray arrived, but no one lingered overlong. There would be much to do on the morrow to be ready for the evening's festivities. As everyone retired, Valerian stopped off at the library to select a book to read. A few minutes later there were muffled footsteps on the Axminster carpet. He didn't need to turn around to know the newcomer was Lucien Canton. He'd expected as much. The problem with perfection was that it was often predictable.

'I thought you and I should talk, St Just. Have a seat.' Canton sat down and motioned to the chair across from him.

'You have an extensive collection of books,' Valerian said glibly.

Canton waved away the attempt at small talk. 'I am not here to trade banalities with you. I came to make sure you understood how things stand between myself and Lady Cambourne.' His eyes glittered like hard gems.

Valerian steepled his hands. 'I understand from Pendennys that she is acting as hostess in your sister's stead,' he said, deliberately misinterpreting the implications of Canton's message. If the man wanted to stake his claim, he'd have to do it directly. He would not get away with subtlety.

'She is more than my hostess. We have discussed the possibility of a more permanent arrangement between us. I mean to propose marriage to her and I have every reason to believe that my suit would be met favourably.'

'Why are you telling me, a mere stranger, this?'

'You know very well why—you didn't take her into dinner for the sake of old friendships renewed and all that. I did not know the depth of your former relationship was quite so, ah, developed. It is clearly much more than a friendship. No one looks at an old friend the way you looked at her tonight.'

'And how is that?' He'd been more transparent than he thought, or perhaps Canton was simply more astute.

'Like a starving man looks at a feast,' Canton said acidly.

Valerian raised his eyebrows, ready to strike. 'Is that cliché the best you can do?' He liked Canton less and less by the moment and not all of it had to do with envy. All his instincts said Canton had ulterior motives regarding Philippa. A man in love and certain of his affections being returned would not feel a need to stake such a blatant claim. Canton's next statement confirmed Valerian's suspicions.

'I know you didn't go to the drawing room to study

the Gainsborough when you left the dining room,' Canton said, referring to the facile lie Valerian had used to excuse himself and to follow Philippa. 'My footman reported the two of you were out on the balcony, intimately engaged.'

'Spying on your guests? That's quite an admirable trait,' Valerian said drily. 'I wonder how the Duchess would feel if she knew you had her followed. Do you do it regularly?' He rose, book in hand. 'I've had enough of this gentlemanly conversation. Goodnight, Canton.'

Lucien rose with him. 'I mean to have her, St Just. She's mine. I'm the one who has been here through the years when she was in mourning. You can't waltz into my home after a nine-year absence and undo in the span of a few short hours what I've worked years to accomplish.'

Valerian stopped at the door, his hand forcefully gripping the knob as he reined in his temper. He'd faced down Mehemet Ali, the renowned Egyptian naval commander. By God, he would not suffer the threats of a viscount's top-lofty heir whose only pretension to greatness was his father's title. 'You're wrong, Canton. If a stolen kiss and a dinner among others are all it takes to "undo" your hard work, it was never "done" in the first place.'

He strode purposefully up the stairs to his chambers, fitting pieces together in his mind. He knew now what he didn't like about Lucien Canton beyond the simple fact that he coveted Philippa: Lucien Canton was dangerous.

Behind his polished perfection was a lethal streak. He'd seen men like Canton during his years abroad in the highest levels of covert intelligence and diplomacy, catapulted into such positions because of their cunning and arch-shrewdness. To these men, attainment of their goal was everything. Nothing was too sacred to escape sacrifice. There was something Lucien Canton wanted and Philippa was a vital link in his ability to get it. He speculated that Lucien Canton would be willing to do more than marry to secure it as well.

The man had portrayed no signs of lover-like affections, but had instead acted like a man in possession of a great treasure around which he must place guards and fences. It didn't take a large amount of speculation, even knowing as little as he did about the state of Philippa's inheritance from Cambourne, to surmise Canton had his eye on some aspect of her estate.

Beldon had asked him in the coach if he believed in serendipity. Absolutely not. He had not survived the dark side of diplomacy by luck. He'd survived because he believed a man made his own chances. From the looks of things, Lucien Canton believed that too. That made the man more dangerous than he might have been otherwise.

He wondered if Philippa knew Canton didn't love her, but what she owned. If not, he'd be sure to call it to her attention by showing her the depths of his own passion for her. It looked like he wouldn't make Roseland Hall by New Year after all.

31 December

The dancers whirled about Valerian in a dervish of luxurious winter velvets and satins to a rowdy country dance played by the five-piece orchestra seated above the crowd in the small balcony at the top of the ballroom, designed for just such a purpose. The guests were in high spirits as midnight approached. Philippa had done a splendid job playing hostess, making sure everyone had partners for dancing. No one went unnoticed, from the plainest of girls to the quietest of matrons.

He and Beldon had done their parts to ensure her success in that pursuit. They'd danced with the matrons and charmed the local wallflowers until they blossomed.

But for the most part, Valerian had spent the evening listening to the rhythm of Cornwall. What did people think about these days? What was the lifeblood of the Cornish economy? Where did people think their future lay? The answer repeatedly came back to mining.

It was not surprising. Mining had been an ongoing consideration in the region for literally centuries. Valerian's own family had mining interests upon which the family fortunes were built. He knew the Duke of Cambourne had invested heavily in tin and copper mines as well as the ancillary businesses that accompanied the industry of mining: smelting, furnace parts and mining equipment.

What *did* surprise him was the growing competition. Mining had not yet reached its apex, but the foundations for managing those future interests were being laid now. Mining had become a full blown industry and much more highly politicised than it had been before.

Valerian had caught snatches of conversations regarding mining-related legislation. House of Commons members, home from the Michaelmas session of Parliament, and members of the House of Lords, debated the need for safety laws that ensured a quality of life for the miners and their families.

More intriguing to Valerian were the conversations he overheard regarding the merits of importing metal ores from British settlements in Chile and Argentina. The capitalists of the group argued importing would certainly help meet growing industrial need, while other, cooler, heads argued for caution; glutting the market with copper and tin would drive the price down, which in turn would affect the domestic market's ability to turn a profit.

Canton sided with the capitalists, avidly arguing for aggressive expansion in South American mining. Valerian's earlier suspicions about Canton coveting the assets brought to him through marriage to Philippa were finding substantiation in Canton's avaricious stance on the economics of mining. Valerian made a mental note to ask Beldon about the extent of Philippa's mining assets.

'Fifteen minutes until midnight!' The cry went up from the orchestra conductor, who urged everyone to find a partner for the 'last waltz of the year'. There was an excited flurry on the dance floor as people laughingly paired up.

Valerian strode purposefully towards the group Philippa stood with. Other than acting as a willing dance partner for her wallflowers, Valerian had stayed apart from her. He preferred to study her movements and behaviour from afar—a certain kind of exquisite torture he'd imposed on himself as punishment for the prior evening. In hindsight, he acknowledged that he had not handled himself well on the balcony. He'd rushed his fences without knowing his quarry.

Tonight, she sparkled among an already glittering crowd. The deep gold of her gown was an elegant foil for the mass of burnished hair piled on her head and coiffed in strands of gold, woven through the coils like other women wove pearls. Her long neck was shown to advantage with the upsweep of her hair and Valerian was seized with the urge to kiss her nape as he came up behind her. He settled for putting his hands on her shoulders as if he were settling an imaginary cloak about her. He bent close to her ear, saying, 'I believe this dance is mine.'

It was a proprietary overture on his part and he knew it well. Most women thrilled to such a seductive, possessive claim. Odds were that Philippa wouldn't. But neither would she be able to politely refuse without looking like a shrew in front of the others.

Whatever scold she had in store for him would be

worth the feel of her in his arms. Waltzing was something they'd done often and well in the old days.

'Viscount,' Philippa said, recovering from having been caught unaware by his gambit, 'I thought you'd forgotten. You've left it until the last minute.' She gave a smile, forced to cover for his presumptions.

'My apologies.' Valerian swept her a gallant bow and escorted her to the dance floor, knowing he wouldn't get off that easily. He had no sooner fitted his hand against her back when she showed her displeasure.

'Don't ever handle me like that again,' she began.

'I am afraid it would be rather difficult to dance without touching you,' Valerian said obtusely.

'That's not what I meant and you know it. You put me in a position where I could not refuse you without looking rag-mannered. Moreover, you insinuated claims on my attentions that you do not have.'

'Haven't I?' He couldn't resist the temptation to flirt with her.

The music started up before she could fire another insult at his head. Valerian swept her out into the centre of the floor, effortlessly creating space for them in the crowd. He was confident her pique wouldn't last long. Philippa could not resist the lure of the waltz. It had always been her favourite dance.

He had waltzed women across dance floors from the Black Sea to St Mark's Square in Venice, but no partner could rival the beauty of Philippa in his arms. Her long legs matched his stride with ease; her body answered the subtle guidance of his hand. She was all fluid grace as they moved through the turn at the top of the ballroom, her anger at him erased in the exhilaration of the dance.

They turned swiftly and tightly, giving him a reason to bring her up close to him instead of holding her at arm's length. She gasped at the change in contact, then threw back her head and gave an honest laugh. 'You waltz scandalously, St Just. Is this how they do it in Vienna?'

'It's how *I* do it.' He wondered how long he could keep her like this. The sight of her smile was breathtaking. In that moment, the smile was all for him. It was not her hostess smile, or her duchess smile, just *her* smile. A smile he'd known for years. It was the smile she'd given him when they raced neck or nothing, the smile she'd given him when they'd danced at her début, the smile she'd given him the first time he'd kissed her, deeply, thoroughly, and she'd recognised him as a man of powerful urges.

He laughed back and whirled them about at a faster pace, heedless of convention. The dancing halted promptly at midnight in order for the ballroom to cheer in the New Year. Both of them were laughing and breathless. Valerian had his arm about her waist, keeping her close at his side, enjoying her unhampered good humour.

All her masks were off and she was Philippa Stratten beside him once more. His masks were off too. He was simply a young man again, in the throes of a first and true love, untouched by the rougher edges of life. A giddy elation fired his blood at the final stroke of midnight. As the raucous cheers went up, he recklessly pulled her to him and kissed her full on the mouth. Her arms wound around his neck and her head tipped back to take his kiss completely. There was an unequalled sweetness in knowing she felt the fire, too, and had given herself over to it. In that moment Valerian swore a silent resolution to himself in the fashion of old English tradition. By this time next year, he would have her. He'd already lived too long without her.

The orchestra struck up a tune for another waltz before the guests headed in for the New Year's supper. Valerian swung her into the dance without asking. She protested with a laugh, 'We've already danced once tonight.'

'That was last year,' Valerian parried easily, his elation only partially dampened by the stare of an infuriated Lucien Canton, who watched them from the sidelines, rage emanating from every pore of his impeccably groomed form.

Lucien viewed the pair waltzing with abandon and a disgusting amount of apparent ease in each other's arms. They were beautiful to watch as long as one wasn't also watching one's opportunity to marry one of them decreasing exponentially. Valerian Inglemoore was most definitely an unlooked-for complication in the progress of his plans. He had meant to propose to Philippa in the spring when he could do it in high style in London among the haut monde. Watching her with the newly returned viscount, Lucien knew without doubt he couldn't wait that long.

He had to strike *before* the iron was hot, as it were. Most people who knew him believed him to be a keen judge of human nature. Lucien knew his accuracy in guessing people's motivations and desires was partly his own intuition, but also partly because he spied on everyone in his milieu. The duchess was not exempt.

His spies indicated that the viscount was besotted with her, stealing away from the dinner table last night to steal kisses on the veranda. It was no balm to Lucien's concern that his spy also reported Philippa had slapped the bastard across the face. At the moment she might be conflicted over her response to the return of her curious friend, but hate ran a close parallel to love. From what Lucien had seen, if he waited until spring, the lovely and pivotal duchess would no longer be interested or available.

Without the Cambourne mines, his hopes to corner the tin market and establish an elite, profitable tin cartel, with holdings in Britain and South America, would become an idle dream. And without access to the Cambourne finances, he'd be hard pressed to cover some of his investments. It didn't take any amount of genius to know that if St Just claimed Philippa's affections,

Lucien's own friendship with her would come to a quick end. St Just was not the type of man who'd allow his wife to keep a close male friend.

Lucien's hard gaze followed St Just into the last turn of the waltz. He'd ordered murder done before to get what he wanted. He wouldn't hesitate to see it done again.

Chapter Four

'He made you look the whore last night,' Lucien bit out crisply over breakfast late the next morning in the library.

Well, there it was. Philippa had expected as much when she'd received the note requesting they privately break their fast together, away from the other guests. Lucien was a stickler for propriety. Not one of his more desirable traits. Apparently, he was covetous too. She'd not had reason to notice that before. But no one had ever posed a threat to his claims on her time.

Philippa buttered her toast calmly, unbothered by Lucien's pique. 'You can hardly be jealous because I danced with an old friend.' That wasn't to say she was pleased with her behaviour the night before. She had indeed let her guard down with Valerian, a behaviour she did not indulge in with anyone. But Valerian's enthusiasm had been contagious and in his arms she'd felt the responsibilities of her world lift for a moment.

'Old friend? The word is too tame,' Lucien scoffed, reaching for his coffee. 'I've never danced with the sister of an old friend the way he waltzed with you. He desires you, Philippa. One cannot *not* notice. He makes no effort to hide it. Such behaviour is better suited for a brothel than a ballroom.' Lucien set his cup down and looked at her squarely. 'St Just needs to understand in specific terms that his attentions are not welcome, even if they were encouraged in the past.'

Philippa met his stern gaze evenly, bridling at his in-sinuations about her virtue. She was the Dowager Duchess of Cambourne. She would not be commanded in such a high-handed fashion. She chose to ignore Lucien's subtle probe into her past. Whatever had trans-pired between she and Valerian was their business alone. Lucien could speculate all he wanted. She hadn't even told Beldon.

'Are you suggesting I am forbidden to see him?' This possessiveness was exactly the kind of behaviour she'd been trying to avoid in a relationship with any male acquaintance of her circle since Cambourne's death. She didn't need to take direction from well-meaning men who thought she couldn't manage the reins of her estate or social life on her own. In Lucien, she'd thought she'd found a liberated man who would tolerate her independence.

It had been the basis of her attraction to him. Lucien had been a welcome friend during a difficult transition period for her. He'd been a loyal escort and adviser when she'd begun rebuilding her social circle after Cambourne's death. She'd believed they complemented one another well and had a comfortable companionship between matched intellects and interests.

She'd helped him too in a myriad of ways, like acting the hostess when his busy sister wasn't available. It had been the least she could do in return for the assistance he'd given her throughout the years.

'What right do you have to make such a demand of me?' Philippa flicked him a tight glance.

Lucien's eyes flashed. 'What right? We have been together for years.'

'We are hardly married, Lucien,' Philippa warned. They'd not explicitly talked in such terms before, although it would be unfair to say the issue had not arisen in other ways in the last year.

'Perhaps we should be. Married, that is,' Lucien said coldly.

'Is that a proposal? Your lack of enthusiasm makes it rather hard to tell,' Philippa shot back. Damn Valerian for this, Philippa thought hotly. Lucien's proposal, if one could call it that, was all his doing. He had to come rushing in and wreck everything with hot kisses and knowing caresses, making her remember the possibilities.

Philippa put down her napkin and rose, leaving her

toast untouched, but it didn't matter. Her stomach couldn't tolerate a bite of food now. 'I regret to inform you that I have no intention of accepting a proposal articulated with such lacklustre ardour. It bodes ill for the marriage.' She tinged her voice with exaggerated ennui. The sooner she was out of the room the better. She hoped she made the door before she gave full vent to her temper.

Lucien rose, the glacial calm that usually accompanied his demeanour, melting at her comment. 'My displays of "ardor" have been quite acceptable to you right up until St Just began stealing kisses on the balcony right under my nose.'

Philippa stiffened. How could he have known? But to accuse him of spying on her would mean admitting he had the right of it. She turned to face Lucien before sweeping into the hallway. 'You've shown yourself in a poor light this morning, Lucien. Jealousy does not become you.'

Wrapped in a heavy wool cloak against the damp weather, Philippa stormed out to the gardens. No one else was about in such inclement weather. She was glad for it. She would make terrible company. She would be hard pressed to behave politely when all her thoughts were focused on less than polite behaviour.

Valerian and Lucien were worse than two stallions in season fighting over a mare and now Lucien had proposed, no doubt prompted by his sense of honour and apparently the belief that she needed protection from the likes of Valerian. In the three years of their association, Lucien had never once pressed her for a discreet affair. There had been nothing beyond a few private, dry kisses, a gentleman's touch on the dance floor or helping her in and out of carriages. *Nothing at all to compare with Valerian's very public seduction.*

Lucien's kisses were preludes to nothing. They inspired no wish to lose control, to cross over the boundaries of propriety. Valerian's kisses lit a raging fire in her, forced her to abandon her grip on control. Valerian's kisses were an invitation to decadence.

The very thought of Valerian's audacious assumptions brought colour to her wind-whipped cheeks. Lucien was right. Valerian made no secret of his sensual habits. The differences between the two men could not be more clearly illustrated if she drew a line in the dirt. On one side there was Lucien with his icy good looks and restrained passions to match his rigid sense of honour. On the other, there was Valerian, all devil-dark hair and hot eyes, flouting honour and convention at every turn. If the disparities were so obvious, why did she hesitate?

The answer gnawed at her. She was no longer sure Lucien's companionship would be enough for either of them. She was hard pressed to believe Lucien was happy with the dry affection that passed between them.

Certainly, he must wish for more. Surely there must be another reason why he'd forgo physical pleasure. She wished she knew what he'd gain to make the sacrifice worthwhile. She could understand if he openly declared he needed to marry for money. But she did not appreciate hidden motivations. They were usually dark and dangerous and wrapped in lies.

Valerian leaned on his cue stick in the billiards room, pretending to watch Beldon take a shot. In reality, his gaze was fixed on a point just beyond Beldon's shoulder, through the window. Philippa was walking in the garden, alone. He'd been disappointed to learn she and Canton were taking breakfast privately when he'd come downstairs late in the morning. He could imagine what they'd talked about. Canton was none too pleased with him.

Beldon cleared his throat. 'Val, it's your turn.'

'So it is,' Valerian returned, but his interest in the game had waned. 'Beldon, would you mind if we finished our game later? I suddenly remember some pressing business I need to see to.'

Valerian didn't stay long enough to let Beldon quiz him on his sudden business. He slowed his pace only when he neared Philippa. It wouldn't do to appear the over-eager swain. She needn't know he'd interrupted his billiards game to rush after her the moment he'd glimpsed her.

She looked lovely, her colour high and her hair less than perfect from the wind. Desire surged in him, raw and elemental like the weather. She turned and spotted him at the gate.

'Nice day for a walk,' Valerian offered drily, striding towards her.

'I found the house a bit stifling,' Philippa said shortly, bending to study a dormant plant.

'The house or our Mr Canton?' Valerian pried shamelessly. 'I heard the two of you were closeted together over breakfast. I hope he wasn't angry about last night.' The last was a lie.

'You are too bold, St Just.' Philippa straightened, her eyes flashing as they studied him. He liked the feel of her gaze on him. Let her look and see that he desired her.

'But yes, Lucien has asked that I make our relationship clear to you.'

'So to speed my departure,' Valerian mused aloud uncharitably.

'Be fair, St Just. Lucien has done nothing to earn your enmity besides stand my friend.'

Valerian studied her. 'Is he your friend? I did not know him from before. He must be a new friend.'

'Why, of course he's a friend and he's perfectly acceptable. He's the oldest son of a viscount with excellent prospects of his own. He's not a new friend, not to me anyway. I've known him since John…' she hesitated here and then corrected herself '…Cambourne's death. He was with John the day of the accident and he's been with me ever since.' Her sharp tone had softened at the mention of her husband.

Valerian matched it with a quiet tone of his own. 'Beldon mentioned the accident briefly. Cambourne lived a while afterwards,' he prompted, liking the quiet intimacy that had sprung up between them.

Philippa turned bittersweet eyes on him, her gaze far away with her memories. 'Lucien got him home and arranged for a physician, even though he was hurt himself. We stayed by John's side for the next few days.' She shook her head. 'The doctor had known immediately that there would be no recovery. I was afraid to leave him out of fear that he would slip away the moment I was gone.'

Valerian took Philippa's hand, stroking her knuckles with his thumb, pleased that she hadn't snatched it away. A queer pang jabbed at him. He was both grateful that Philippa had cared for her husband and yet envious that those affections had been given to another. 'You cared for the duke, then?' he asked curiously, wanting to know the nature of the relationship she'd shared with Cambourne.

'I grew fond of him. He was a good mentor to me and he denied me nothing. He let me use his wealth and his name to build a model school for miners' children in the village. It's the one the vicar is modelling his own school after. He was a good and tolerant man. I sincerely missed him when he was gone.'

'But Lucien was there,' Valerian prodded.

'Yes. He helped with all the details of transferring the estates to me and to John's heir. That can be tedious work and Beldon was so busy settling the Pendennys estate in those days it was a relief not to burden him with my worries as well.' Philippa sighed.

The bastard knows how much she's worth to the farthing. He's had an intimate look at her holdings. The thought was unworthy, but it was the first one that came to mind. How convenient everything was for the man. That raised an alarm for Valerian. He no more believed in 'conveniences' than he believed in Beldon's blasted 'serendipity'. A man made his own luck. Lucien Canton appeared to have manufactured quite a lot of it.

Valerian's talk with Philippa in the garden did not go unremarked. Mandeville Danforth let the length of curtain drop in front of the library windows. 'Look at them, close as courters. He's holding her hand, damn it. Canton, how could you let him upset things so quickly and so thoroughly? He's turning her head.'

Lucien pierced the man with a cold stare. 'I didn't know he was coming. He and her brother arrived unannounced, much like yourself,' he said pointedly. 'How was I to know that he was more than her brother's best friend?'

'You could tell the minute he saw her,' Danforth groused.

'We *all* could tell. It's amazing the house didn't spontaneously combust. But by then it was too late. I could hardly expel him from the house. We have to be careful with Pendennys. We need his blunt. Where he invests, others will follow. Giving his friend the cold shoulder won't help our cause, especially with Pendennys still sitting on the proverbial fence where the bank is concerned.'

Danforth huffed in concession to Lucien's wisdom. 'Winning the Dowager Duchess of Cambourne's affections would be enough to bring her brother into the fold. It's a bad time for a kink in the works. Did you read your father's letter? I hope it was important enough for me to hare down here from London.'

Lucien felt some inward satisfaction that Danforth didn't know the contents of the letter. The man was getting above himself to think he could scold a viscount's son. He had not missed Danforth's barb about the need to win Philippa's affections. But Danforth was wrong to assume his only role in this scheme was to play the suitor and woo Lady Cambourne.

While the thought of finally having Philippa in his bed after all this time was pleasant enough, he'd invested the last three years of his life for a far more lucrative gambit than a roll in the ducal bed. He had an empire at stake.

Lucien gave Danforth a cold smile. 'My father writes that the London investors are in place. We may go ahead and officially announce that the Provincial Bank of Truro is open for business, with you, of course, as the nominal head.' It went unspoken between them the reasons for that choice. A viscount or his son might sit on an executive oversight board of a bank, particularly if the bank was in his own area of the country, but he would never overtly sully himself with such work as the daily running of the bank.

Danforth rubbed his hands together in delight. 'I am glad to hear it.'

'As am I. The sooner we can begin loaning funds to the smelting companies and the mining corporations, the sooner we can have our cartel.'

'And the sooner we have our cartel, the sooner we control the market. Everyone will be in our pockets,' Danforth remarked shrewdly.

'Not just the market, but the world,' Lucien said meaningfully. He didn't expect Danforth to understand. The man's financial acumen was daunting on a domestic scale, but he had yet to grasp the implications of the new British mining colonies springing up in the Bolivian and Argentine territories. That was Lucien's gift to the venture—futuristic foresight.

His eyes strayed to the window. His foresight and exquisite planning would come to naught if he couldn't control the Cambourne interests. The strength of his cartel and its ability to regulate tin and copper prices would be minimal if the Cambourne mines and other associated industries remained outside the cartel's umbrella to compete against it with prices.

St Just was an unfortunate distraction, but not insurmountable. He would have to send to London for news about the returning viscount. With nine years in the diplomatic corps, there must be dirt on the man somewhere—real scandal beyond his rakish reputation with women.

Lucien had yet to meet a diplomat who couldn't be bribed to shape foreign policy. Not that there was anything wrong with greasing palms. Lucien was man enough of the world to know it took a bit of well-placed oil to keep that world running smoothly. But Philippa was another sort altogether. She believed in ideals, like the miners' school the late duke had let her open.

Lucien rather thought she'd take badly to the news that the dashing St Just was not only a womaniser—a fact openly known in certain London circles—but a man who'd been involved with darker dealings, selling 'opportunities', as it were, to become involved in the great British Empire for a price—things like rights to waterways or trade commodities. Those were things that quietly went to the highest bidders and not necessarily those who deserved them most. Such injustice would not sit well with Philippa.

However, until he could manage to tarnish St Just's sterling image a bit, he'd follow the old adage of keeping one's friends close and one's enemies closer. It was time to pay a visit to the garden.

Chapter Five

Philippa didn't see Lucien approach, but was instead alerted to his arrival by the sudden tenseness in Valerian's pose and the feral light that lit his green eyes. She tried to slide her gloved hand discreetly from Valerian's grasp, but the effort was nothing more than an afterthought. The stormy visage Lucien wore made it clear that he had already seen her hand in Valerian's.

She resented the intrusion. For a short while, she and St Just had been companionable, simply Philippa and Valerian again, like they had been on the dance floor. She'd liked the soft, intimate tones between them as they discussed her marriage to the duke. She'd liked the absence of witty repartee designed to spear the other, the social politics of claiming and possession. With Lucien's interruption, all that was back, and back in force. The moment Valerian had spied Lucien, he'd become all St Just again—the rakish diplomat who would not be cornered or made to feel guilty for his actions by any man.

'Philippa, it's freezing out here,' Lucien said, rubbing his hands together for good effect and trying to minimise Valerian's presence by ignoring him. 'What could possibly bring you outside?'

'We're reminiscing, catching up,' Philippa offered smoothly. It was true. They'd been talking of the past, nothing more.

'My dear, that is why we have a dozen sitting rooms, expressly for the purpose of talking.' Lucien forced a laugh.

'Is that true or is it merely an example of hyperbole?' Valerian put in, shielding his eyes against the wind and making a great show of surveying the manor as if he could count all the sitting rooms and doubted the manor was large enough to uphold Lucien's boast.

Philippa couldn't decide what she wanted to do first: laugh at Lucien's bluff being called—the manor was large by Truro standards, but there weren't twelve sitting rooms unless one counted the small salons attached to a few of the larger bedchambers—or strangle Valerian for poking at Lucien's pride so deliberately and with no greater purpose than to antagonise the man.

'St Just has an interest in gardens. I thought he'd enjoy seeing yours,' Philippa interjected quickly.

Valerian smiled beside her. 'Yes, the family seat has extensive gardens over on the Roseland Peninsula. I am eager to get back to them.'

Lucien smiled back. 'I hope you aren't in such a large hurry to get back that you won't stay on with us for a while? Perhaps I could entice you with a visit to some excellent gardens nearby?' Lucien offered magnanimously. 'I've heard rumour that the new vicar in Veryan, just a few miles from here, has been rebuilding the vicarage and has plans to expand the gardens. I could arrange for you to ride over tomorrow and talk about plants and whatever else you gardening types enjoy talking about.'

Philippa turned to Valerian. 'Please say you'll stay. I know the vicarage. It's lovely and you would enjoy meeting Samuel Trist, the vicar. He's an avid landscaper. The two of you would have much in common.' The thought of Valerian leaving, after having only discovered he'd returned was suddenly unpalatable. But he wouldn't stay if he thought he was beholden to Lucien in any way.

'Who knows what other pleasant surprises might crop up if you stay long enough?' Lucien put in, playing the expansive host to the hilt. 'With luck, you could be one of the first to congratulate me on my good fortune. I have proposed to our dear Duchess this very morning. I thought it was best to start the year off on the right footing, beginning as I mean to go on and all that.'

Philippa felt the colour go out of her cheeks. How

dare Lucien call his angry, jealous retort a proposal. She was keenly aware of Valerian's probing stare.

'Has our "dear Duchess" accepted?' Valerian asked of Lucien, although his eyes didn't leave her.

'She has—' Lucien began glibly.

'She has *not* accepted the proposal,' Philippa broke in angrily. Who knew what kind of fiction Lucien would fabricate? If he was willing to risk portraying their quarrel as a proposal, he might be willing to go so far as to say her storming out of the library was akin to 'thinking it over'.

Philippa stared hard at each of them. 'I will not stand here and be talked about as if I am invisible. That goes for both of you. However, since my presence is not intrinsic to this conversation, please feel free to stay out here and continue. I'm going in.'

She must have been momentarily mad to think she wasn't ready for Valerian to leave. *Valerian.* That was another thing. Some time between his arrival two nights ago and this afternoon, she'd started thinking of him as Valerian again instead of St Just. Out in the garden, he'd been her friend, so reminiscent of the old days, and then he'd become St Just. On an instant's notice, the mask had slid into place as assuredly as the one he'd worn to the ball last night.

Was that what it was? A mask? Why she was so certain the mask of cold, sharp wit was the facade? It could just as well be that the friend was the front instead.

* * *

Up in her room, Philippa threw her cloak onto the bed and paced in front of the window, her thoughts in turmoil. For a woman who'd thought herself well armed against the dubious charms of Viscount St Just, her defences had proven to be woefully inadequate. Already, she was willing to cast off what she empirically knew to be the truth for the old fantasy he'd spun once before in her girlhood.

Why was it so easy to fall back into believing those old myths? Especially when she *knew* they were myths. Inspiration struck. She would prove to herself that Valerian Inglemoore was not to be trusted with her affections. Yes, if she could visually see the proof with her own eyes, it would be harder to stray from the truth the next time he held her hand or led her in a waltz.

Philippa drew out a sheet of her personal stationery from the escritoire and sat down. Purposefully, she drew a line down the centre of the paper, dividing it into two columns: one for myths, the other for realities.

When she was done filling in the columns, she had three myths and five truths. Myth number one: he had loved her in their youth. Myth number two: he'd meant to marry her. Myth number three: he'd returned and hoped to woo her, to atone for bad behaviour in the past. Yes, those were the things she wanted most to believe about Valerian.

Then there were the dismal truths. Truth number

one: he'd blatantly acknowledged their little *affaire* was nothing but a young man's fleeting fancy.

Truth number two: he'd never meant to marry her. He'd known that very night he was leaving for his uncle's diplomatic residence. What else could explain such a rapid departure? He must have been planning it for months, perhaps for even longer than their short-lived infatuation.

Truth number three: he'd never asked her father for permission to court her and certainly not permission to ask for her hand. If he had, her father would have told her, she was sure of it.

Truth number four: he had made no effort to contact her or Beldon in his absence.

Truth number five: he'd come home with a reputation to match the behaviour he'd shown her that long ago night in the Rutherfords' garden.

The bottom line of her analysis convicted him. With the exception of a few fleeting moments, nothing corroborated the behaviour she wanted to see in him. Nothing supported the items listed in the myth column. Everything supported the facts both past and present. The stark truth was that Valerian Inglemoore was a seducer of women—a very good one at that. So why was it so hard to resist him, even with the truth staring her in the face? And why was it so hard to accept that truth?

Was it possible there was another side to Valerian

that he deliberately kept hidden? Perhaps there was a side that he couldn't afford to expose. There might be reasons for his tightly tied mask, reasons that had to do with his work for his uncle. Philippa drew out another sheet of paper. She had friends in political circles who could find out. All wishful thinking aside, it suddenly seemed of paramount importance she knew the truth about Valerian Inglemoore.

Philippa sanded the letter and set it aside, nagged by a growing sense of guilt. She didn't feel right about the inquiry. It felt too much like spying, going behind Valerian's back. No, she wouldn't send it, at least not right away. Now that her initial anger was waning, she was beginning to recognize she had done little to get to know the man Valerian had become.

Before she sent off a letter of inquiry prying into the man's background, she should try to exhaust more direct routes available to her. After all, she sat at the same dinner table with him and there was the outing to Vicar Trist's in Veryan tomorrow if Lucien's request was accepted. Those were prime opportunities to reacquaint herself with Valerian and determine the truth on her own.

The evening was a relaxed contrast compared to the prior two nights. Many of the guests who had stayed over after the New Year's ball had departed late in the afternoon for short journeys home. In addition to Beldon and Valerian, only two couples remained, a Lord

Trewithen and his wife, and the ageing Baron Pentlow and his wife from the Penwith area, who were friends of Lucien's father and had come to the ball en route from London on their way home.

With the exception of the queer Mr Danforth, Philippa knew the other guests as regular acquaintances from the Cornwall community during her marriage. It was a simple task to make conversation over dinner and have a congenial time with the two ladies after the meal in the music room while the men took their port.

Afterwards, the men joined them for a short night of cards. She and Beldon offered to play whist with the Trewithens. At the far end of the music room, Lucien already sat at the cluster of chairs and sofa, talking avidly with Danforth and Pentlow, to the exclusion of all else, leaving Philippa to consider what to do with the elderly Lady Pentlow.

Unlooked for, Valerian rescued her admirably. 'Duchess, would you mind if I played the pianoforte this evening? I haven't a desire for cards at the moment or for business.' Valerian gave a quick nod to Lucien's group deep in discussion, his tone indicating how inappropriate he felt such a topic of discussion was in this setting.

'It would be delightful to hear you play again, my lord,' Philippa said, inwardly laughing at the formality of their exchange, so bland and perfect compared to the heated, more imperfect exchanges they'd exchanged in private.

Valerian inclined his dark head in a gracious nod.

'Lady Pentlow, if I might impose on you to turn the pages for me? I recall at dinner you said you enjoyed the country pieces. Canton has a decent collection of music, perhaps you could sort through it and select a few.' Valerian offered Lady Pentlow his arm and escorted her to the pianoforte, bending his head low to catch the woman's excited chatter.

Philippa watched them go with gratitude. How deftly Valerian had managed the situation. Lady Pentlow was a dear, sweet lady and Philippa hadn't wanted her to feel left out or in the way. Valerian had sensed the need and adroitly stepped in. *Unlike Lucien.* For a man she'd considered eminently eligible marriage material, she'd certainly had a lot of uncharitable thoughts about him recently.

Philippa shot a glance at Lucien's coterie, wondering what they could be talking about that would raise such an interest that Lucien would forgo his guests? Typically, Lucien was an excellent host with an eye for details, showing every guest the utmost courtesy due them in polite society. Tonight, he'd left that task entirely to her. She didn't mind. She was there to play hostess, after all. Still, such behaviour wasn't like him and it seemed odd that he would commit such a *faux pas* in order to talk to Mr Danforth, a man whom Lucien had claimed not to know two days past.

'Are you coming? We're ready to play,' Beldon called from the card table.

Philippa smiled and took her seat. 'I hope my brother has warned you how competitive he is.'

Their game was lively and they rotated partners at the end of each rubber. The Trewithens proved to be capable players, demanding all of Philippa's attention. Usually she was quite good at cards, whist and piquet being two of her favourite games. But tonight, too many distractions competed for her attention, not the least being Valerian's quiet ballads coming from the piano-forte. On occasion, she caught snatches of Lady Pentlow's trebly voice singing a few lines.

At last the tea cart arrived, signalling the end of the evening. Philippa poured out and then went to stand with Beldon as the group congenially sipped their tea. 'What do you suppose has Lucien so interested?' she asked quietly.

Beldon gave a soft laugh, part-teasing, part-cynicism. 'I see the privileges of being a male prevails here. If you'd been allowed to stay at the table, you would have been treated to Mr Danforth's announce-ment that he was opening a bank here in Truro, the Pro-vincial Bank of Truro or some such nonsense.'

'Nonsense?' Philippa queried. 'Why would you say that?'

'You know what these country banks are really like, Phil. They're investment firms.'

Philippa nodded in agreement. Cambourne had done

business with Praed and Co., a bank in Truro that invested in high-risk ventures such as inventions and new technologies. If one was clever, these investments paid off. Cambourne had had good luck with them, but it was no surprise that these country banks went bankrupt far more often than the style of bank one would do with business with in London.

She better understood Lucien's potential interest now. Lucien was always interested in money. 'Does Lucien think he'll invest?'

'More than that. Mr Danforth has offered Lucien a place on the bank's board of directors.'

'For a sum, I'm sure.' Philippa offered thoughtfully.

'Definitely for a sum. But Lucien would be in charge of directing the investments. He seems quite taken with the idea.'

'He'd be good at it. Lucien is no fool when it comes to money.'

'But not women, at least not you.' Beldon eyed her over his teacup.

'Valerian told you?'

'Hmm. Rather cowhanded of Lucien to think you could be politely coerced, if not into an actual betrothal, then at least as far as a publicly announced engagement. Are you thinking of accepting?'

'I haven't given it much thought,' Philippa murmured vaguely. Marriage to Lucien Canton had been a foregone conclusion until the very unsuitable Valerian had arrived. Now, she believed she'd been rather naïve not to have thought about it more deeply, to look beyond the simplicity of an arrangement between two friends who enjoyed each other's company. What other reasons could there be for a man with Lucien's looks and prospects to choose to marry a childless widow when there were so many eligible débutantes available to him?

Beldon looked as if he would press her for more details. She stalled him with a shake of her head. 'This is not the place for such a discussion.' Lady Pentlow was starting to nod off in the middle of her conversation with Lady Trewithen. The evening was coming to a close. Her guests would want a good night's sleep before beginning their respective journeys in the morning. They would look to her for the sign to retire.

Beldon assented. 'Promise me we will have that discussion soon.'

Philippa smiled at her brother's protectiveness. Even with childhood long behind them, he had not forsaken his role as a doting brother. 'I promise. There is something I want to ask you, too, something about Valerian.'

Chapter Six

Beldon returned his empty cup to the tea trolley and said his goodnights to the group as they began to depart upstairs. He wasn't as ready for sleep as the rest of them. His agile mind was alert, pondering the little dramas of the holiday, and Canton had excellent brandy in the library.

In general, he found people to be an interesting area of study. Younger men of his acquaintance dreaded the routine of a house party unless hunting was involved, but he found them to be intriguing affairs. The gatherings were a constant source of amazement to him, full of the dramas of intersecting lives.

Even in a group as small as the one here tonight, the web was tightly woven—Lucien and that merchant-cum-banker Danforth establishing a business tie together; he and Lucien, friends established through their common tie in Philippa; Lucien and Philippa and the budding drama of Lucien's proposal; Lucien and Valerian, enemies on first sight. Why? The two men did not know each other. They had only Philippa in common between them.

Philippa was the only possibility. Did Valerian have a liking for Philippa? It was fantastical to think Valerian had fallen in love with his sister at first sight, and yet Val's animosity towards Lucien had seemed palpable the moment he'd walked into the manor. A hypothesis began to take embryonic shape, events of the past starting to form connections to one another instead of existing as isolated occurrences. But Beldon was interrupted before he could decipher what the link was that bound them all together.

'A farthing for your thoughts.' Valerian strode into the library as if conjured from Beldon's own mind. He'd removed his jacket and waistcoat, shirt sleeves rolled up.

Beldon shifted in the comfortable chair he'd taken up residence in. 'My thoughts are worth far more than a farthing, old chap. Pull up a chair. Canton has a superb brandy collection.'

Valerian gave a short chuckle at that. 'Is that his chief requirement in being your friend? Since I've met him, his cellar seems to be his primary recommendation.'

Beldon waved his snifter. 'Well, you have to admit

the Veuve Cliquot was superior at New Year.' He paused, stopping to consider the play of firelight on the amber liquid swirling in the snifter's bowl. 'In truth, I'd thought Canton was quite an amicable fellow, a bit aloof at times, but otherwise acceptable, until you showed up. Why do you think that is, Val?' Beldon studied his friend closely, watching him adopt a comfortable slouch in the opposite chair, his feet resting negligently on the fireplace fender as he pondered the question.

'Do you want me to answer that question or is it rhetorical? I seem to recall you made a habit of telling us what to think in school.' A teasing smile hovered at Valerian's lips before he sipped from his glass.

'*Touché*, I am wounded,' Beldon said. 'The accusation is true. However, in all fairness, you must admit most of our friends *didn't* think. I did them a grand favour by doing it for them.'

'Then carry on. Clearly, you have ideas.'

Beldon set his drink on a small side table next to his chair. He leaned forwards in earnest, elbows resting on thighs. 'Tell me the truth, Val. I don't have all the angles worked out yet, but I think you have a penchant for Philippa.'

It was telling that Valerian didn't meet his eyes, but chose to look straight ahead into the waning fire. 'Philippa is an attractive young woman who is intelligent and confident. I am certain many men desire her. She would be an asset to any peer's household—'

'More to the point,' Beldon broke in, not swayed by the general terms of Valerian's response, 'you desire her *and* you have for some time. This is no incident of love at first sight. You're both past the first blush of such fantasy. How long have you carried feelings for her, Val?' How had such a thing as his best friend's affections escaped his notice? Beldon felt a twinge of betrayal. He and Val had been closer than brothers and yet Val had not confided in him. Still, such an omission from Valerian was apparently not amiss. He'd not shared his plans to join his uncle until the night of his departure.

Valerian straightened and turned to face him, this time not avoiding his gaze. 'I've loved her since we were young together. I was head over heels for her by the time she made her début.'

'You didn't tell me,' Beldon said slowly, his mind whirring to adjust the pieces of this puzzle, how it fit against the backdrop of what had transpired. 'Did she return your affections?' There was a pit growing in his stomach. It was a horrible feeling to know that the two people he was closest to had fallen in love and he hadn't known or been told.

Valerian must have sensed the direction of his thoughts. His answer was simple. 'Yes.'

There it was. Valerian had not kept the secret alone. They had conspired together to keep the secret from him. 'Why didn't you tell me?'

Valerian shrugged. 'How could I? Cambourne had offered for her.'

'And you stepped aside?' Beldon asked sharply. 'That doesn't sound like your typical behaviour at all.' The Valerian he knew had championed the underdog at school, standing up for the principle of right, even when the odds were against him. He'd earned more than a few bloody noses for not knowing when to back down. In fact, the Valerian he knew didn't believe one ever backed down. What had changed that when it came to Philippa?

Valerian tossed him a warning glance. 'Beldon, I must ask you to stop your inquisition right now. The hour is late. In my experience, late hours are good for confessions between friends, but not necessarily for understanding them. Be satisfied to know that I have loved Philippa for years from afar. Be satisfied also to know that I would still claim her if she would have me.' Valerian rose, putting an end to the conversation.

Beldon put out an arm in a restraining motion. 'You can't leave me on tenterhooks, Valerian.' He gave a snort. 'No wonder you were such a fine diplomat.'

'Go easy on me, Beldon,' Valerian said wistfully. 'I have the utmost confidence in your mind's ability to solve the rest of the riddle in short order and I will be waiting to confirm your conclusions. You know I value our friendship too much to ever cheat you out of the truth.'

Beldon nodded. 'I know. Sleep well, Val,' he said in all sincerity.

'Aren't you coming up?'

'No, I want to sit a while longer.' Beldon held up his half finished snifter. 'Wasting fine brandy is a sin of the highest order.'

'Enjoy,' Valerian said from the door. 'Remember, I did answer your question.'

'And gave me a hundred more to think about in return.' Beldon offered him a sardonic toast. He would sleep shortly. Valerian was right in one respect. Part of the riddle in terms of Valerian's dislike of Canton was appeased. They both wanted Philippa.

Beldon would wager it was for vastly different reasons. Valerian loved her. And, well, love was not a commodity Lucien Canton was known to trade in. Canton wanted her for something else.

For a long while, Beldon had entertained the idea that Canton appreciated the intelligent companionship Philippa offered. She understood the man's talk of finances and business since she'd been well groomed by Cambourne for appreciating that aspect of the Cambourne holdings. The duke had believed a woman should understand her worth and seen to it that Philippa had.

After watching Canton and Danforth tonight talking over the new bank, Beldon had to wonder if Canton's interest in Philippa was and had been financial. He'd not thought of it before, since Canton was not without his own wealth or the ability to increase it on his own. Canton had no obvious need to find a wealthy bride.

Valerian's sudden reappearance had certainly acted much like a clarifying solution, throwing the muddied depths of their lives into sharp relief. If it was up to him, Beldon much preferred that Philippa married Valerian.

Valerian was a man of honour, a man who could be trusted to do right even in the most dire circumstances, which brought his thoughts for the evening full circle.

Why had Valerian stepped aside when Cambourne offered for Philippa? What would Valerian have seen as a more honourable pathway than the chivalry of fighting for his heart's desire? Who or what had Valerian been protecting that would have compelled him to set aside Philippa and leave his own country? They had not spoken of his abrupt departure, but Beldon felt certain the two were connected.

Beldon smiled to himself in the near-darkness. The fire had died down to mere embers. He loved a good mystery and this was proving to be an excellent one. He'd need his sleep in order to be fresh for the trip. He could hardly wait. Who would have thought such a seemingly innocuous jaunt to view plants at a vicarage could provide so much drama? Oh, yes, the morning promised to be very interesting indeed.

Cornwall could always be counted on for oddities when it came to weather. When the rest of Britain's estuaries froze, the streams near Truro and Falmouth were full of migrating eider and goldeneye ducks. When many parts of Britain thought the dark winter would go on end-lessly, the sheltered south of Cornwall celebrated an early arrival of spring. So it was that the weather for the trip into Veryan was mild for January, even though the day before had been plagued with bitingly cold winds.

The last of the guests were gone by eleven o'clock after a late breakfast that would preclude the need for lunch, and the group of four was seated comfortably in Lucien's shiny black coach with large glass window panes by half-past the hour for the short trip. Philippa would have preferred to ride, since the distance between Veryan and Truro was negligible and the weather promised to remain true. But Lucien insisted on the coach.

'What's the point of having such a splendid vehicle at one's disposal if one does not make use of it?' Lucien said.

Philippa secretly thought it more likely Lucien pre-ferred the attention the elegant equipage drew as the coachman tooled through Truro. 'Still, there aren't many days in the winter when the weather holds for a long ride. It seems a shame to waste one of them,' Philippa replied.

'Ah, but that's just it, my dear. I doubt this weather will hold.' There was a slightly condescending tone to his voice. 'Certainly, the skies appear safe at midday. But I predict clouds and rain before tea this afternoon.'

Valerian stirred in his seat across from them, a glint in his eye that made Philippa uneasy. 'You sound quite sure of your prediction, Canton.'

'I am, St Just. I've spent the better part of the year these last few years living here,' Lucien boasted.

Valerian nodded, gesturing to Beldon and Philippa, 'I've spent, as the rest of us present have, the better part of our lives living here, and I say the weather will hold.' Valerian glanced out of the window and tilted his head to catch a view of the sky. 'In fact, I would go so far as to say the sun will show itself by two o'clock.'

'Care to wager on that?' Lucien responded.

Philippa stifled a groan. The weather was supposed to be the one safe topic of English conversation. Wasn't that the rule one learned growing up? Somehow, Valerian and Lucien had turned the weather into a competition as if either of them could control it. Although, if she had to place her bets, she'd bet on Valerian. Lucien knew mining, but Valerian knew the climate. His estate on the Roseland Peninsula contained some of the rarest plants and flowers known to grown in Britain.

'Twenty pounds,' Valerian said. 'The sun shines by two o'clock with no rain until after five, I win. Canton here wins if the sun fails to shine *and* it rains by tea at four o'clock.'

Beldon broke in, drawing his attention away from the window where it had been riveted for most of the trip. 'Who wins if the sun doesn't shine and it doesn't rain? Or the sun shines, but the rain comes early?'

Oh, lord, not him too? Philippa sent her brother a beseeching stare. Worse, Lucien and Valerian looked as if they were seriously contemplating the developments. By the time they reached Veryan, the two of them would have concocted such an elaborate wager it would be impossible to determine a winner.

'A draw then,' Valerian declared resolutely. 'If there's any discrepancy, it becomes a draw.'

'Fair enough,' Lucien concurred.

Philippa shook her head and shot Valerian a scolding glare. He fought back a smile and discreetly turned his head to look out of the window at the passing landscape.

The vicarage was a place of organised chaos when their coach pulled in. Samuel Trist, the new vicar, broke away from a cluster of workmen and strode through the soft mud and dirt to greet them, smiling excitedly. 'You're here! This is a great pleasure. I was delighted to get your note yesterday.'

Philippa liked the man immediately. He was tall and lean, moving with a loose-limbed gait. Even though he'd known they were coming, he still wore the cotton flannel clothes of a workman and mud-spattered boots. He stripped off his gloves and ran a hand through the shock of flax-coloured hair that stood on end. She recognised his type immediately. He was the kind of man who forgot all else when set on a project dear to his heart.

'It was kind of you to let us come on such short notice,' Philippa said, giving him her hand as she stepped down, glad for her sturdy half-boots and short-skirted walking dress of simple merino wool. She'd guessed correctly that anything more formal would be out of place, although Lucien had quietly disapproved of her informal attire.

'Watch your step there. Some of the mud is a bit squishy yet,' Trist advised.

'Reverend Trist—Viscount St Just. He enjoys horticulture. I immediately thought of your place,' Lucien said, making the introductions. Lucien surveyed the scene. 'Quite the ambitious project you've got going.'

'Yes, this is just the beginning. The vicarage had become seriously run-down during my father's last years. I took over as vicar and decided the place had to be brought up to standard. I want something more fashionable, more up to date.' Samuel gestured for a man to join them. 'This is my foreman on the project. He can show you the plans while I show the viscount around. There's not much out here yet in terms of a formal garden, but I have my hopes.'

Reverend Trist turned to Philippa, seeing that Beldon and Lucien were already poring over the new plans for the house. 'Your Grace, will you join us?'

Trist walked them through the garden, talking of plants and herbs. He stopped to check the tight, close-budded rhododendrons. 'Will only be a month and these beauties will pop open.' He stopped at the edge of the garden. 'Now here is where I've planned a lane of trees.'

He gestured to lines of seedlings strategically placed. 'There's copper beeches and evergreen oaks.' Something twinkled in his eye. 'Look over there.' Samuel Trist pointed. 'That is my pride, a Chilean Pine.'

Valerian was immediately taken with the tree. 'What a curious species. May I?' He strode towards the tree, studying it intently with gentle hands. 'Philippa, come see this!' All formality was forgotten in the wake of his excitement over the exotic tree.

The tree was indeed a curiosity. Dark green in colour and covered with stiff needles, the tree had arm-like branches that stuck out haphazardly, becoming a complex tangle of maze-like arms that took up vast amounts of space. 'Why, I think it would puzzle even a monkey to climb it!' Philippa exclaimed, laughing at the intriguing shape of the tree.

'Perhaps that's what I'll call it,' Samuel Trist said, joining in her merriment. 'A monkey-puzzle tree. That certainly sounds more exotic than "Chilean Pine."'

'I've not seen anything like it,' Valerian said, his tone nearly reverent.

'I might boast enough to say that if I can get it to grow, it'll be one of the first planted in Britain,' Trist said.

'I'd like to get a cutting of this and have a go at it myself,' Valerian said. Philippa didn't miss the excited sparkle in his eye as he contemplated a new plant.

Trist nodded, glad to have found a fellow enthusiast.

'I need to get back to the vicarage, but feel free to walk farther. There's a grotto I am currently filling in to make a folly and I've got stakes laid out where there will eventually be a man-made lake. The walk is a bit rough this time of year, your Grace. You're welcome to come back with me,' he added.

Philippa flashed a look at Valerian. She should go back. Returning to Beldon and Lucien was the safest path to travel. There was no temptation there, just polite conversation. Valerian had proved to be the opposite. In the short time since his return, he'd managed to tempt her passions and her temper, two irreconcilable forces.

It was something of a mystery to her how she could resent the passion he awoke so easily and yet she had continually courted opportunities for him to stoke those same flames.

Valerian's sharp gaze seemed to sense her hesitation as she weighed her choices. 'Come with me, Lady Duchess. The weather promises to remain fine and you remarked in the carriage how much you wished to be out of doors. If the path proves too hard, we can turn back.' He held out his arm in a gesture that brooked no refusal. How could she gracefully decline a gentleman's arm without turning it into an outright rejection?

Reverend Trist was staring at her, confirming her suspicions that she'd contemplated her situation too long.

She smiled and said with forced brightness, 'Thank you, St Just. I think a walk is the perfect idea.'

She took Valerian's arm, telling herself that the bachelor vicar couldn't see her inner turmoil over the decision or even that he suspected anything amiss. Women took a man's arm all the time. But it did not escape her notice that the vicar glanced from one to the other before he set off towards the house, trying to understand what had really transpired. Philippa wished him luck with the conundrum, although she doubted he'd succeed where she had failed.

'Shall we?' St Just turned them towards the stone-strewn path leading to the folly site, which Philippa thought was aptly named in light of the fact that she'd had very little luck with Valerian when it came to gardens. The last time she'd been alone in one with him, he'd left her with a broken heart that had taken years to patch. She wondered what he'd leave her with today. She could already feel the seams of that patch starting to unravel against all logic and her better judgement.

Chapter Seven

'You hesitated, Philippa,' Valerian said matter of factly, guiding her around a large stone in the centre of the path. 'Did you fear being alone with me?'

'Don't overestimate yourself.' Philippa fought the urge to give an unladylike laugh. 'I recall the last time we were alone, you ended up with my hand across your face. If either of us should fear being alone with the other, it should be you.'

Valerian tossed her a sideways glance. 'I must correct you. *That* wasn't the last time we were alone. Yesterday, I thought we did very well together. I thought our conversation was quite civil. As for the other time you are referring to, I am still not sure if the slap was meant for me or if I was merely an available target for your own personal frustration.'

The man's arrogance was phenomenal. But she was

thankful for it. Fighting with him was better than wallowing in silence with her fantasies about the man she wished he was. 'Enlighten me. What would I be frustrated about, if not your outlandish assumption that I was inviting your attentions out there on the balcony?'

They called an implicit truce while Valerian helped her over a small pile of scrim. The path smoothed out and argument resumed. In a detached part of her mind, Philippa thought the scene would be quite funny if played out on stage—their courteous behaviours being interspersed with the contradiction of the verbal spears they hurled.

'Outlandish?' Valerian repeated with calculated incredulity. 'I believe "outlandish" refers to being odd or strange. My dear, I regret to inform you my "assumptions" were anything but "outlandish". You did not find my "assumptions" strange or odd in the least. Perhaps you're looking for a different word?'

'I don't know what that would be,' Philippa snapped.

Valerian gave a shrug and a sigh. 'I don't know either. Perhaps a word denoting "liking" or "appreciation"? After all, you did like my kisses. Point of fact, you liked them so much, you managed to kiss me back quite thoroughly *before* you managed to slap me. By the way, I find that deuced unfair—slapping *me* for *your* kissing.'

'No gentleman would ever speak to a lady in such a manner!' Philippa fumed. The man was more than arrogant. He was a positive boor. 'How dare you make such assumptions!'

'Oh, that word again, "assumptions",' Valerian parried with feigned blitheness. 'I think before we go any further we should define precisely what you mean when you say "assumptions". I'm starting to believe you and I use the word differently.'

Philippa's temper flared again. 'If this is your idea of diplomacy, Britain is lucky not to be engaged in a conflict of major proportions.' She regretted her words instantly. Valerian's face went strangely blank for a moment, his eyes giving the impression that his thoughts were suddenly far away. The impression was so fleeting that the next moment Philippa wondered if she hadn't imagined it.

'But this is not a diplomatic mission, my dear, it is a walk to a folly with an old friend who, frankly, seems a bit confused about her feelings.'

'You dare too much.' Philippa stopped and withdrew her hand from his arm, her voice as stiff as her spine. The cad had gone too far. She would argue with him about stolen kisses or 'assumptions' or whatever he wanted to call them, but she would not countenance this effort to make their past history her fault. Neither would she let him portray her as a wanton widow eager to bed down with any handsome house guest.

'You cannot come back into my life after what you did and expect to be forgiven on two days' notice. Neither can you expect me to engage in whatever kind of *affaire de coeur* you are used to carrying on with women of your acquaintance.' She knew very well the kind of women who peopled Valerian's diplomatic circles.

To her satisfaction, Valerian did have the decency to look penitent. 'Are you finished?' he said quietly, the toe of his boot digging out a muddy hole in the ground.

For a moment Philippa felt awful. She'd been too harsh. She'd let him get the better of her. But she found her resolve. She would not be won so easily. He had to be accountable for his actions. It was best for both of them to know how she felt. 'Yes, I believe I am finished.'

Valerian's voice was subdued. 'Suffice it to say, I didn't want things between us to end that way.' He shook his head as if to dispel unpleasant memories. 'I didn't want to make you cry. I don't expect you to forget what passed between us. However, I would welcome any forgiveness you'd be willing to offer. Over the years, have you ever thought once that maybe I had my reasons and those reasons had to remain secret? After all, you knew me to be a man of honour, Philippa.'

Philippa shook her head in denial, her voice matching him in despairing softness. 'No, Valerian, I know no such thing.'

'So be it,' he said quietly in tones that passed for the barest of whispers. He offered her his arm again and they trudged forth in silence, but Philippa was not immured from the hurt that had flitted across his face at her words. She was not a cruel person inherently or by design and she regretted her words, although she did not regret thinking them. They represented the empirical truth as she knew it. Still, a part of her did not welcome hurting Valerian, and that part worried her very much.

They did not speak again until they reached their destination. 'Ah, there it is, Trist's folly, or what there is of it,' Valerian said with a modicum of gallantry to cover the silence that had sprung up between them.

'Yes, there it is.' Philippa offered half-heartedly. She wasn't thinking of the stone grotto slowly being renovated, but of a different folly; this one being a handsome man with broad shoulders who was busy stripping out of his expensive coat and rolling up his sleeves a few feet away from her to better explore the rocks that lay haphazardly about the grotto.

Philippa found a flat slab of granite and sat down, to wait and to watch. *Handsome is as handsome does.* The nursery-room warning clanged in Philippa's head. Valerian had certainly proved the adage true. He'd stolen her débutante's heart with hard, full-mouthed kisses and soft promises that roused her budding sense of passion. Then he'd disappeared from England without a backwards glance or even a letter. Still, the old memories, memories that predated heartbreak and harked back to a better time, persisted, a time when she'd believed differently.

She'd enjoyed watching Valerian in gardens before. He would wander around in silence and then suddenly remark, 'wouldn't this be a lovely place for a fountain?' or 'a maze would be a splendid addition here'. In their youth they'd often used the pretence of looking at landscapes to steal a private moment. Only, it hadn't been so much a pretence since Valerian made a regular habit of mentally rearranging everyone's garden.

The recollection made her smile now while she watched him stroll about the grotto. Watching him, so absorbed in his study, she could almost believe time had stood still. Errant strands of his hair were being blown in his face by the light breeze. He bent occasionally to study the stones that seemed to intrigue him. The expensively cut shirt moulded his strong physique to perfection across the expanse of his shoulders and the exquisite muscles of his back.

Valerian turned towards her, a hand pushing his hair back from his face. 'Come and see this prospect. The view from the north-west corner is outstanding. I think I'll tell Trist he should build rockeries, too. The quartz-veined rock from Carne Quarry at Nare Head would be handsome here.'

At his words, a stab of yearning speared through Philippa, causing a near-physical pain. Hot words and devastating past aside, in that moment he was the old Valerian, the one she'd thought she'd loved, and she wanted him. This was no lustful coveting of his body.

No, she wanted more than sex from him, although she wanted that, too. She wanted Valerian Inglemoore body and soul, the way she thought she'd had him when they were younger. She wanted to know what he was thinking the moment he thought it. She wanted to anticipate his every desire. It had been years since she'd felt a longing so complete, so intense, and never with anyone but him.

Time stood still, then fractured into a kaleidoscope of half-forgotten memories. She was in his arms, although she hadn't the faintest idea how she'd got there or when he'd moved. His lips were on hers, full and demanding. His mouth possessed her and she returned it with a possession of her own. Someone was crying, and she had the vague impression it was her own sobs. Valerian's hands were rough on her body and his breath was ragged as he ravaged her mouth. She did not care. They were both frantic.

He was a master at this, kissing her with insistency, his tongue probing her mouth, his teeth nipping her bottom lip and sucking hard. His hands moved from her waist to expertly cup and caress her breasts, kneading them through the fine wool of her gown until they were erect with need.

Philippa caught fire. All she could do was wrap her arms about his neck and press into him until she couldn't tell where she ended and he began. But it wasn't enough. She wanted to throw off her clothes and let his hands range free on her body no longer hampered by the fabric of her gown and the undergarments beneath.

She could feel his body rise, burning hot and hard. His erection was full and insistent against the folds of her skirt. His hands had moved to gather up the material of her dress and she could feel his body, taut with desire and anticipation. No wonder he'd had half of Europe on its knees.

All reason fled. She cared not a whit for the hardness of the granite slab beneath her back or for the painful ghosts of the past. She cared for nothing save the heat of Valerian's body as it covered hers in an attempt to assuage the need that coursed through them both.

Valerian, green eyes forest-dark with desire, hesitated for a moment. 'Philippa, are you sure?'

'Val, I want…' She met his eyes, searching for what it was that she so desperately sought—that her Valerian existed, that this moment was the moment she'd thought to claim so many years ago. But it wasn't there, not really. This was wrong, no matter how right it felt. And she remembered why. She had loved him. He had shared her passion, but not her depth. He'd scorned her and sent her off to marry another man.

'Yes, what do you want?' Valerian panted.

'I want to believe,' she said softly, her arms twining around his neck, pulling him down to her in mute apology. 'But I can't. Not yet.'

'I can make you believe again, Philippa,' Valerian vowed. 'Let me try,' he pleaded, every ounce of his muscle straining in desire as he held himself in check.

She held him there, full against her. She couldn't deny that she wanted him, but she didn't want him, not as a fiction. 'Don't do this. I won't have it. You had your dalliance with me years ago. I won't be played for the fool again.'

'You were never my fool, Philippa.' He raised himself up on his arms, drawing back from his seduction only slightly. His eyes shut as if in an attempt to hold back the memories. 'We had a great passion between us once. We can have it again,' he coaxed. 'I want you, Philippa.'

Philippa felt the old animosity flare against her passion. 'I was the one left crying in the Rutherfords' garden. I thought you were going to propose and you *knew* I thought that.' When she had him, *if* she had him, it would be with an understanding of the truth of who he was. It was the only way she could protect herself from being hurt a second time. If she learned nothing else today, she'd learned that being hurt again was a distinct possibility.

A distant 'Halloooo!' reached her ears and the reality of their situation hit her. She'd done the most foolish thing of all—she'd almost let Valerian make love to her in the open, where they were no doubt visible to all sundry passers-by.

Valerian groaned a miserable 'Oh, God,' as he moved to stand, fumbling with his clothes. 'We have company.'

Philippa struggled up to see Beldon and Lucien tramping towards them. Good lord, how much had they seen? She and Valerian had been kissing in plain view of anyone coming in that direction. That was the problem with follies and prospects. They thrived in wide open spaces.

'I don't think they saw anything,' Valerian whispered reassuringly in her ear as if he could read her mind. Out loud, he called to them, 'What brings you out here?'

'Lucien's come to concede!' Beldon called back good naturedly.

Philippa's cheeks went scarlet. She didn't need a mirror to know her face was burning with mortification. *They had seen.* Beldon's reference made it perfectly clear.

'Steady, love.' Valerian chuckled. 'I don't think Lucien's coming to concede on that point.'

He made a show of pulling out his pocket watch and flipping it open. 'Concession accepted, Canton. It's two o'clock and the sun's been out for ten minutes.'

If her cheeks could have reddened further, they would have, this time from anger. While Valerian had been seducing her with sweet words and kisses, half his mind had been on the ridiculous wager and she'd lost half of hers for falling temporarily to his seductive efforts—further proof that Valerian Inglemoore was no more than the sum of rumours and her past experience made him out to be.

* * *

'How's the prospect from here?' Beldon asked, striding to the area marked off with string where the folly was slated to be.

'It's lovely. You can see all the way to Truro,' Valerian said vaguely. 'Philippa hasn't seen it yet. Now, we can all see it together.' He led the way to the outcropping, very much aware that Philippa lagged behind, shooting not-so-subtle daggers at his back.

He could imagine with a fair degree of accuracy what she was thinking: how like a man to turn the situation so adroitly. One would never guess he'd been lying on top of her, proclaiming to be in the throes of passion and making impossible promises literally moments ago. Here he was, playing tour guide and looking for all the world like a man whose sole interest in coming up here had been to see the sights.

Well, she was wrong about that. He'd seen the opportunity to get her alone when the vicar indicated he had to go back. That had been the end of his inspiration. He'd taken the opportunity, but done nothing with it except compound Philippa's distrust. He'd meant to tell her Beldon knew about their past romance. He'd meant to confess the reasons for leaving her. But events had taken a different direction and they had ended up on the granite slab, apparently against Philippa's better judgement.

Her 'better judgement' rankled. It was one thing to

know, to suspect, what she thought of him. It was another thing entirely to hear her articulate those ideas out loud. She thought he wasn't a man of honour. She thought she couldn't believe in him again.

And maybe she was right.

Valerian fought back a wave of self-doubt. He'd failed to help those people in Negush too, failed to find a way to peace before all revolutionary hell broke out. People who believed in him notoriously came to bad ends. It was not an accomplishment he was proud of.

Valerian cautioned himself to control his dark thoughts. He could not give in to the megrims that accompanied his guilty moods. This was not the place for it, on top of an overhang on a house-party outing. It would be the height of bad form to come down with one of his devastating headaches—compliments of the Phanariot revolutionaries.

Gathering his concentration, Valerian had to admit that the prospect did not disappoint. Once the actual folly was built, it would have a breathtaking command of the Truro area. The vicar would be pleased with the results. Beside him, Beldon took a deep breath and exhaled expansively. 'Ah, there's nothing like clean Cornish air. I swear there's no place on earth as grand as this.'

Valerian smiled at his friend's Cornish pride. It helped to lighten his mood. He too had loved growing up and living here. But Lucien seemed inclined to argue, suddenly much less 'Cornish' since he'd lost the weather bet.

'I think I prefer the Lake lands with their mountains. Much more rugged, more challenging. Makes the mountains here look like rolling hills.'

Valerian raised an eyebrow, indicating that he disagreed wholeheartedly. 'While I was away, I saw many different terrains—mountains, seaboards. Some places were blistering hot and others were cold enough to freeze a man's thoughts. When I couldn't tolerate the climates, I would think of Cornwall.' His eyes strayed to Philippa as he spoke the last. He had meant more than 'Cornwall' in the comment. The startled look on her face suggested she guessed as much.

Encouraged, he went on, blurring out those around them. 'I would think of the gardens, especially the gardens at Pendennys Hall and Roseland and all my plans for it. I'd imagine walking in the gardens in those places, sometimes making plans, other times finding peace.' Did she remember their walks? Their talks? They'd shared many secrets in their time.

Philippa broke away from his gaze and turned to stare out over the land. He hoped she'd heard the hidden message: *I thought of you; I treasured memories of our time together.* Most importantly, *you and you alone sustained me when I kept no hope for myself.* Although he doubted she'd fully comprehend how dark his life had been, how far from the light he'd wandered.

Beldon coughed discreetly, drawing his attention with an over-loud voice. He must have drifted off in his thoughts. 'Contemplating the weather again, Val? Lucien and I were wondering how you knew it wasn't going to rain.'

Valerian gave a negligent shrug of his shoulders, all glib aristocrat once more. 'Well, for one, I didn't say it wouldn't rain, only that it wouldn't rain before tea time. As for that, I do believe it will rain after six tonight and before nine o'clock. Double or nothing on that, Canton?'

Canton eyed him suspiciously and Valerian knew he'd be packing his bags tonight. It was a sure sign it was time to leave when one was reduced to the subterfuge of wagering on the weather in order to distract the host from the reality that his guest was bold enough to seduce his hostess right under his nose. Oh, yes, it was definitely time to go home.

Chapter Eight

Philippa was going home. Danforth's stultifying conversation at dinner decided it by the time the duck was served. She would leave in the morning. From the looks of things at the table, she wouldn't be the only one.

Immune to such uncharitable thoughts, Mr Danforth held forth ceaselessly about his bank throughout dinner, although it was exceedingly obvious no one was paying him serious attention except Lucien. But even Lucien appeared to have his mind on other things. Philippa didn't want to dwell too long on what those things might be for fear of discovering she was at the heart of them.

She was certainly at the heart of Beldon's absorption. Beldon, who was normally very adept at dinner conversation, seemed lost in his own thoughts, letting his gaze drift between her and Valerian.

Valerian had apparently used up his quotient of good

behaviour the night he'd squired Lady Pentlow. It was clearly not in evidence tonight. Valerian was in one of his blacker moods, not even making an effort to follow the conversation beyond sprinkling it with an occasional pointed comment regarding the risky nature of country banks. 'Venture capital is all well and good, but let's call it that instead of calling it "banking",' Valerian drawled over the last course.

Lucien took offence, which was probably what Valerian had been planning, Philippa thought. 'Exactly how is it *not* banking, St Just? We do what any other bank does. We loan money to those who wish it. We hold money for those who wish to deposit sums with us.'

Valerian sipped his wine thoughtfully. 'With the exception that you invest deposited sums in high-risk ventures without the benefit of safe investments to act as ballast should the risk fail. Frankly, you and I both know there is a significant chance people could not get their money back. It's why folk of our status bank in London at Childs or Coutts. Don't you find it telling that certain classes of people are rather limited in the banks they have access to?'

Philippa didn't like the gleam in Valerian's eye, but could find no way to intervene without giving the impression she was championing Lucien. For starters, Lucien didn't need a champion. He could handle himself well enough in a financial conversation. For the rest, she didn't want to give any impression to Mr Danforth that she'd be willing to invest in his provincial bank.

'St Just, are you implying that I would deliberately swindle investors by making promises I could not uphold?' Lucien was all cold ice, piercing Valerian with a stare that said he was merely a comment away from pistols at dawn. Philippa stifled a groan. The Provincial Bank of Truro was about to erupt into scandal and the doors weren't even open. She shot her brother a quick plea for help, but Beldon was enjoying himself too much.

'I am suggesting that there is something of a history of short-lived provincial banks, that's all,' Valerian said easily, his long fingers caressing the stem of his wine goblet. 'Their limited livelihood comes from the tendency to invest in risky enterprises. Odds are usually against them. It wouldn't be the first time something went amiss.'

'It would be for me, Viscount,' Lucien said evenly. 'I have yet to invest foolishly. Those who follow my lead reap the profits of their trust. Don't they, Pendennys?' He looked down the table to Beldon for confirmation, putting Beldon in a tight spot.

'That is certainly true, in my experience,' Beldon acquiesced. But Philippa noticed he didn't bother to elucidate further on the point. She could tell Lucien was disappointed. She knew Lucien had hoped Beldon would expound on the British-Bolivian mining colony in the

Americas that the two of them had invested in. Beldon had sold his shares a few months back, reaping an enormous profit. It was left to Lucien to blow his own horn.

'Pendennys and I had a lucrative opportunity in Bolivian silver. We took a large sum in the proceeds when we sold. I'd be glad to guide any investments you might consider making as well, St Just. Your man of affairs is welcome to contact my secretary any time,' Lucien said with cold magnaminity.

He turned to the rest of the table. 'Since it is just the four of us, I'd like to suggest dispensing with cigars and brandy. It's been a long day with departing guests and the trip to Veryan. Perhaps, gentlemen, you would enjoy a game of billiards. St Just, if you'd like to play the pianoforte, feel welcome. Make free with my home. I find I have business to discuss with my gracious hostess. If you will excuse us?'

It was all skilfully done and moments later everyone was dispersed, leaving Philippa and Lucien to talk alone in his library.

The meeting was not at all what she was expecting. The last time they'd spoken, Lucien had been angry. Since then, they'd only spoken in the company of others. She'd anticipated a continuation of their former conversation. She'd anticipated an angry, self-righteous Lucien Canton. What she encountered was a very different face.

'Sherry, my dear?' Lucien solicited from the sideboard, pouring himself one of his special after-dinner wines.

'No, thank you. I have packing to oversee, so if you don't mind, I'd like to keep this short,' Philippa insisted, taking a seat in a deep-wing backed chair near the fire.

'I am sorry to hear that. My valet reported you were preparing to leave. I'd hoped you would stay on after everyone had left. We haven't had much time together this week,' Lucien said in sincere tones, taking the seat opposite her.

He drew a deep breath and exhaled, relaxing. 'This is nice, sitting with you by the fire. Two chums, taking their ease together, eh, Philippa?' He gave a charming smile, looking and acting more like the Lucien she'd known over the past three years than the arrogant man of the last few days. 'We are still friends, aren't we?'

'Of course, Lucien,' Philippa said quietly. In truth, as upset as she was about Lucien's behaviour, she could not logically throw out years of steadfast friendship with him over the matter of a few days and events; events she was responsible for. She imagined she might behave quite the same as Lucien had if she'd been in his place. No one liked being usurped in one's own house and there was no denying that Valerian hadn't hidden his dislike of Lucien Canton.

Lucien cocked his head to one side, studying her intently. 'My God, you're a beautiful woman, Philippa. The shot-blue silk becomes you.'

Philippa blushed. 'Thank you. But I am sure that isn't what you called me in here for,' she prompted gently. She wanted to be in her room, watching the maid pack her things. When she'd returned from Veryan, she thought some of her things had been moved, that her escritoire had been looked through, gently, of course, but still it felt like a violation. The letter she'd written, but never sent to London regarding Valerian was in a different spot than she'd recollected. For an unexplainable reason, the incident felt like more than just negligence on the part of an unobservant maid cleaning the room.

'Yes, our business.' Lucien nodded. 'I need to thank you for acting as hostess. Everything went splendidly, as I knew it would. I had time to talk business with my guests and you took care of the rest.

'I also need to apologise. I have not looked after our relationship as I should. I was reckless and self-centered. Such behaviour caused me to jump to poor conclusions.' Lucien reached for her hand and closed his fingers around hers.

His hand was warm and she thought the gesture was meant to convey reassurance. But she wasn't reassured at all. She had the distinct feeling they were being watched, and coupled with the fact that Lucien was not a man who would admit to such shortcomings, something was afoot, although she couldn't put a finger on it.

'You have nothing to apologise for,' Philippa offered,

hoping quick absolution would end the conversation. But Lucien wasn't finished.

'I have everything to apologise for. I didn't understand how close you and St Just were, that he was your friend as well as your brother's. I misunderstood your desire to simply spend time with an old friend. He had your time, Philippa, and I didn't. It made me a bit jealous and jealousy can cloud a man's judgement, make him see things that aren't there or put incorrect constructions on what is there. I am guilty of doing that. I spoke harshly to you on New Year's Day. You were right. Jealousy does not become me and, indeed, there is no place for jealousy between us.'

Lucien ended his pretty speech and reached inside his evening coat. 'I have something for you, Philippa.' He took out a square, blue velvet box and opened the lid to reveal a sapphire pendant on a thin gold chain, tasteful and expensive. It had not come from a local jewellers. 'I made a shambles out of things New Year's Day. No woman wants to be asked to wed in a haze of anger.'

'You don't have to do this. You don't need to atone for anything,' Philippa began to stall. Right now would be the perfect time for Mr Danforth to burst in and start babbling about his bank. The odd man hadn't bothered to follow any protocols of polite conversation at the dinner table, why not put all that lack of couth to good use and barge in now, when it would be useful?

Lucien was prosing on about his growing sentiments

for her and she supposed she'd better pay attention. 'Although I regret my behaviour during St Just's visit, I do not regret what his visit has caused me to see. That is, I want to spend my life with you. We are well matched in status and intellect. In you, I see more than a wife and mother to my heir. I see a partner. Would you consider doing me the honour of marriage?'

He was even down on one knee. Philippa was struck by how different her response to this scene might have been had it occurred a month earlier. She might have said yes immediately, as a logical conclusion of their long-standing friendship. Companionship was worth marrying for, even in the absence of passion. Her first marriage had been based on mutual companionship and it had not been a poor experience. But now, everything was somehow different.

Still, she was not foolish enough to toss away a modicum of happiness and security on a whim. Neither was she so much of a sapskull that she would ignore the assets of marriage to Lucien Canton. As her friend, he deserved more from her than an out-of-hand dismissal.

'Lucien, you pay me a great honour. It deserves thinking about. Rest assured that your proposal will be in the forefront of my thoughts as I return home to Cambourne.'

'Then take this pendant as a token of my esteem and my affection, Philippa. It will serve as proof that I am in your thoughts.' Lucien was too gallant to refuse as he fastened the sapphire pendant around her neck. 'Now, off to your packing, my dear. Rest well. I will be up to see you off in the morning.'

The wall panel to the left of the fireplace slid open and Mandeville Danforth came out of hiding. 'That's quite a room you've got back there,' he chortled. 'Right out of Bonnie Prince Charlie's time.'

'That went well, I think,' Lucien said, uninterested in Danforth's thoughts on the priesthole.

'Yes, indeed. Although, she could have said "yes",' Danforth was quick to point out.

'At least she didn't say no. St Just has turned her head, but how far is hard to say. We're not the only ones making inquiries in London. She's thought about it. My valet found a letter in her room. Still, her doubts about St Just are enough for us to exploit if we must.'

'We must. It is a foregone conclusion,' Danforth corrected. 'She must marry you or sell you all her mining rights and ancillary companies. You have to control the Cambourne interests. I don't see her selling.' Danforth's eyes narrowed in thought.

'We could stage another accident, perhaps several of them, that would convince her to sell.' He began to plot.

'No.' Lucien cut him off sharply. 'Properties with accidents don't inspire investors to cough up their pounds. It would do us more harm than good in the long run.

Besides, she's stubborn and sabotage would take too long. We need those properties by late summer.'

'Then it looks as if the Duchess should reconcile herself to being a June bride,' Danforth said in a tone that suggested Philippa Lytton would find herself at the altar, whether she wished it or not.

Lucien raised his glass. 'Here's to the end of my bachelor days.'

Chapter Nine

She was glad to be home! Philippa put down her pen and looked up from her ledgers, taking a moment to stretch her back and survey the glorious view spread before her through the long windows of the library. Not even the fine mist that blurred the landscape could dim her appreciation. The vast lawns spread before her, green even in winter. The pond floated on the horizon, filled with ducks. In good weather, she would have been tempted to throw open the windows in order to hear their squawking.

In all, she'd been gone two months; first up to London for the Little Season and the Michaelmas session of Parliament, wanting to support some early discussions on mining reform; then to Richmond for Christmas and Lucien's for New Year. Now she was home for three months before she'd need to return to London after Easter.

Home. Her kingdom where she reigned supreme. She did the ledgers, she oversaw the transactions of daily business, she visited the tenants, the fields, the home farm, the mining interests. Here, she was not ruled by any man.

Philippa knew how rare her situation was. It had not come easily, but at the price of sacrificing a youthful dream. She'd wanted to marry for love, the passionate romantic kind of love found in fairy tales and Minerva Press novels. Instead, she'd married the man of her family's choice and found a quiet companionship with him.

Perhaps that was better. Her experience with Valerian had been quite illuminating about the quality and strength of romantic love. It had its limitations. But companionship had its limitations, too. Cambourne had been kind and generous with a giving that extended far beyond his purse. He'd educated her in business and finance, delighting in her interest in his estates.

In the beginning she'd become interested to keep her mind off Valerian's desertion. She had to do something to fill her life. Later, she'd seen the genuine need to take an active part in the life of Cambourne's holdings. She'd built the school for miners' children and it had become one of her favourite projects.

Then Cambourne had died so suddenly, firing her involvement in legislation concerning mine safety. Oh, yes, there was no disputing that her life was full these days. She'd remade herself admirably as the young Duchess of Cambourne and then again a few short years later as the Dowager Duchess. But re-fashioning oneself was hard work and she had no desire to do it again.

Philippa fingered the sapphire at her neck. She'd worn Lucien's gift today out of a need to honour her word. There was no one to see her, no one to hold her to her commitment. But *she* knew. She'd told Lucien she'd consider the offer. Wearing the pendant was a reminder of what she'd promised. She owed at least some consideration of his offer. Although, if he could read her thoughts, he'd probably wish she hadn't felt so obliged. Marriage to Lucien would definitely require some re-fashioning.

Most likely, she could get her solicitors to design a betrothal contract that would protect her property, but it would be difficult. Not even a dowager's possessions were safe from a new husband's rights. She would have to give him something. It wasn't that she didn't trust him precisely. It was more the issue of having to give up the control she was so used to having.

Control would be given up in other areas, too. Lucien would expect her to stay with him wherever he went. The year would be divided up between Truro, London, his father's estate, and then Cambourne. There wouldn't be time to live as she liked. Her interests would give way to his and when his father eventually died, Lucien's responsibilities would increase. Becoming the future viscountess to Lucien Canton would require quite a lot of re-fashioning, leaving very little room to be the Dowager Duchess of Cambourne—obliterating it, in fact.

And for what?

Security? She didn't need security. She had it aplenty with her own holdings.

Finances? She was far wealthier now than the Pendennys family had been during her growing-up years. Marriage to Lucien didn't enhance her wealth in any meaningful way.

Companionship? Certainly they rubbed along well together, but that was already something she enjoyed with him, not something she needed marriage to gain.

Love? Definitely not. In spite of his protestations the night before she left, Philippa knew without question that Lucien didn't love her any more than she loved him. She appreciated him, but one didn't marry for appreciation. She wasn't sure Lucien was capable of a great love, the kind of love you married for, because you knew with a pure certainty that this was the one person in the entire world whom you could find fulfilment with.

There were none of the usual reasons that women typically married for. She couldn't think of a single reason why she would want to marry Lucien and give up all she had. It all provoked the question—why Lucien had asked in the first place? Surely he knew?

But Lucien needed the one thing she didn't. He

needed an heir and he was approaching thirty-five in a couple of years, the magical age when heirs finally decided it was time to start their nurseries and look to their futures. Perhaps he'd looked about for a wife and decided she would be better suited for him than one of the débutantes peopling London's marriage mart.

That was a conclusion she could understand. Lucien would not tolerate an insipid wife. He would want someone with intelligence and social skills. It was the only conclusion that made sense. Like her, Lucien didn't need additional wealth. Being a man and his father's heir gave him inherent security. He didn't need to marry for companionship.

Philippa sighed and took off the necklace, carefully laying it in a desk drawer for the time being. She'd take it upstairs later. Lucien would be disappointed in her answer and it could very well scotch their friendship. He would want to know why. He would try to resolve her misgivings with promises he'd mean to keep, but that social pressure wouldn't allow him to—like the right to live her own life. He would say, laying out his assets like a balance sheet, 'Why not me? Do you think someone better will come along?'

In fact, she did. At least she hoped. She'd married once for the sake of her family. If she married a second time, it would be for her. For someone who considered herself to be fairly conversant in the realities of the world, she was hard pressed to let go of her romantic notions.

It didn't mean she had someone specific in mind and it absolutely didn't mean she was holding out to see if Valerian could be brought to heel. He'd already proved he couldn't be. But his kisses were hard to forget and served as potent reminders that one did not have to settle for the convenience of lukewarm companionship.

Philippa rose from the desk. The drizzle had stopped. She would change into a habit and take a ride between showers. When she came back she would write to Lucien and tell him of her decision. There was no sense in waiting. Bad news didn't get better over time and the longer she waited to dispel him of his matrimonial notions, the more likely it was that he'd build up his expectation of being accepted.

Expectations being what they were, Lucien was not all that troubled by the arrival of Lady Cambourne's letter at the manor in Truro the first week of February. In fact, he was precipitously jubilant. The New Year had got off to a perfect start.

Danforth's bank had been well received by local men with money to invest. Cornwall was rich in many resources and not all of them came out of the ground. Industry bred invention. Plenty of men like Dabuz, Bolithio and Williams had seen the need for other industries like tin-smelting and gunpowder. Dabuz and Fox swore that smelters and gunpowder works were more profitable than the actual act of mining. From the amount of funds at their disposal, Lucien was inclined to agree with them.

It had been the simple work of a few dinner parties to corral the financial resources needed to start investing and buying. These men were as avaricious as he was. They immediately saw the merit in banding together to form a cartel that controlled the outside world's access to tin and regulated the prices at which that outside world would have to pay for the commodity.

They'd also seen how important it was to control the mining interests in Britain's new South American colonies. If those resources were allowed to compete against the cartel, it would diminish the profit. But if those colonies were controlled by the cartel, then the prices would be controlled as well.

Lucien had hand-picked the men who would serve on the new bank's board of trustees and all had agreed buying up shares in the largest British mine in South America would be the first place they'd start with the building of their overseas control. Monopolies and cartels were tricky things. It wouldn't do for there to be a large broadcast of their intended plans until they had some leverage.

So with his finances firmly in hand, Lucien had complete confidence that all else would fall into place, too. The letter from Philippa had arrived as if on cue. Just that morning at a bank meeting someone had asked about the Cambourne mines. He'd given the man an enigmatic smile and said vaguely something to the intent that he hoped to have more concrete news to share shortly. Then, like magic, the letter had arrived.

Lucien ripped open the envelope and scanned the contents, reading it twice and then again a third time to make sure he understood its contents correctly, his blood turning to ice.

Damn Valerian Inglemoore.

Lucien crumpled the note in one angry fist. The man's name hadn't been mentioned once in the missive, but he could read between every line. Although Philippa would deny it, St Just had turned her head. Whatever the man had once been to her, whatever claims, spoken or unspoken, had lain dormant between them during her marriage and his long absence, they had been awoken once more.

The man had kissed her at least once since his ill-timed return, making Lucien highly suspicious that St Just's tenure away from fair Albion's shore could be directly linked to Philippa's marriage. Lucien didn't like surprises. It galled him there was something of that nature he didn't know about Philippa.

Lucien's secretary knocked and asked for the day's correspondence. Lucien sent him away. 'No letters to write today. Take time to work on cataloguing the library.' The door shut on the office. Alone again, Lucien took out a sheet of crisp paper. There was one letter to write, but it was too private to entrust to another pair of eyes.

Lucien dipped his pen into the inkwell and began to

write. St Just stood in the way of his bid to build a mining empire; for that, the man must be ruined.

Something had ruined the relationship between Valerian and Philippa, Beldon mused, and not for the first time since he'd parted ways with Valerian at Roseland three weeks ago.

After seeing Philippa off in her coach bound for Cambourne, he had ridden with Valerian to Roseland, stayed a few days to see his friend settled and then turned for the Pendennys lands outside St. Mawes.

Today, as he rode home from his weekly visits with the tenants and his meeting with the vicar, the subject dominated his mind, perhaps because he had little else to think of. He was a social creature and this was a lonely time of year for him. There was small need for him to be in London and Philippa was busy with her own interests before she had to be back in town.

It wasn't that he didn't have options. He could go up to London anyway and Philippa would always welcome him at Cambourne. Roseland was close by and now that Valerian was home, he'd probably ride over to Roseland on occasion to ease the isolation he felt rambling around alone in the big Pendennys country house.

Certainly, he had options, but, in truth, his own estate needed his attention too. He'd worked too hard to save it from genteel poverty in the years since his father's passing. Of course, he couldn't take all the credit.

Without the generous loan from the Duke of Cambourne, all the effort in the world could very well have been useless. When he'd first starting going over the ledgers, that fact had become glaringly apparent. Cambourne's wealth had kept the Pendennys family afloat. He'd silently thanked the fates Philippa had married well, if precipitously, and at such a fortuitous time.

Beldon drew sharply on the reins, bringing his horse to a rather sudden and jarring halt. The answer to his riddle hit with full force. Cambourne's money had been the 'something' that had come between Philippa and Valerian.

He kicked his horse into a hard gallop, covering the remaining distance home as fast as he dared. Once home, he raced into the estate office, pulling down old ledgers from the shelves. Beldon didn't even wait to take off his coat, only taking time to strip off his gloves so as to turn the ledger pages better.

Hours later, when he'd finally removed his outer wear and his jacket, rolled up his shirt sleeves and eaten sporadically from the tray the housekeeper had sent up after she realised the young baron would not be swayed from his task long enough to eat in the dining room, Beldon had his answer.

The office was a mess, with books open to various pages strewn across any available surface. Ledgers from nine years ago had simply been a starting place. He'd had to go back further to determine why the Pendennys barony had needed the funds so badly in the first place.

What he found had been devastating. The office had paid the price of his sleuthing and so had his memories. It was almost like learning the life he thought he'd had was only an illusion. His father had not confided in him, not really.

He'd known about the loan from Cambourne, naturally. But he'd thought very little of it beyond the exorbitant expenses of a few years. Philippa's Season and début were costly affairs coming on the heels of supporting his time away at Cambridge with Valerian. At the time, his father had only said that the wars with Napoleon had placed the economy under undue stress.

Beldon had believed him. When he'd taken over the reins of the barony, he'd not looked back far enough in the ledgers to see that while there was truth in what his father had offered as an explanation for Cambourne's loan, there was also much else. The Pendennys finances had been in a slow decline for years. He could trace a string of investment losses and a decline in the production rates of the mines. Too much money had gone out and too little had come in to cover the losses.

The loan had been used to shore up the failing coffers and Beldon had used part of the funds later to diversify the family holdings. In anticipation of a future where the copper and tin mines wouldn't produce as much ore, never dreaming that future was already coming to pass,

Beldon had bought a tin smelter. Later, he'd invested wisely with the Perran Industries gunpowder works. Both had paid off handsomely. A tin smelter was to the mines what a miller was to farmers. Grain needed to be ground into flour and tin—well, tin needed to be smelted. The smelter would continue to pay out long after his own mines had exhausted their resources.

Beldon pushed a hand through his hair, leaning back in his chair. It was all embarrassingly clear now. They had been in dun territory and Philippa had been married to Cambourne in order to save the family—in order to save him, really. He was the heir. Without her marriage, there would have been little to inherit but trouble. All his life, he'd thought he was protecting his younger sister, watching over her at balls to see that she didn't dance with the wrong sort of gentleman, making sure she went nowhere unescorted, and all the while she had been protecting him. There was a certain amount of guilt that went with that realisation.

Had she known? He remembered vividly the night he'd found her in the Rutherfords' garden. She'd been crying although she wouldn't admit it. At the time, he thought it had been the shock of the sudden engagement to Cambourne. Had she known why their father had favoured the match?

Beldon remembered too his brief encounter with Valerian that night. Valerian had been brusque and out of sorts. His friend had paused only long enough to tell him that Philippa was in the garden. The next weeks had been chaos. Valerian had gone and Philippa's wedding had to be planned. He'd had little time or reason to ponder the turn of events or even to see his friend's disappearance in connection with the wedding.

In retrospect, Beldon began to think it was highly plausible that Valerian and Philippa had met secretly in the garden and that she was crying for a different reason. He couldn't quite puzzle out that bit yet. Still, on one hand he had more answers. Cambourne's money had likely come between them. Cambourne's money had not been a serendipitous godsend as he'd always believed, but rather a calculated move on his father's part to save the barony.

Beldon took stock of what he had: some answers, more questions, and one damning hypothesis beginning to form—if the move to woo Cambourne had been planned, then Valerian had to have known, otherwise he would not have willingly stood down from his claims on Philippa's hand.

The mantel clock struck midnight, late hours for the country. It was time for bed. He had a long day ahead of him, beginning with a ride over to Roseland.

Chapter Ten

Valerian was in the greenhouse, working with his new rose hybrids, when Beldon arrived the next day. He looked up from his pots and cuttings in glad surprise. He had been alone too much with his thoughts lately in lieu of any available company. 'I'm hoping to get a yellow rose with pink highlights,' Valerian said, brushing off his hands on a towel.

'It's good to see you. What brings you over so suddenly? I hope everyone is well.' For a moment his stomach tightened. He hoped the news wasn't about Philippa. A hundred images of all the things that could go wrong raced through his mind. She could fall from her horse on uncertain terrain, she could take ill with a winter cold, she could have accepted Lucien's ridiculous marriage proposal.

Apparently, his concern was obvious. 'At ease, old

friend,' Beldon chuckled. 'Everyone is well. Philippa's well, if that's what you're worried about.'

'Would you like to go inside?' Valerian offered.

'No, don't let me stop your work.' Beldon waved the offer away, pulling up a tall stool next to the long work table. 'I came to talk. Some things about our riddle were niggling at me,' he confessed.

Valerian nodded, pushing a wooden crate across the table. 'You can sort seeds while we talk.' He knew precisely what Beldon meant by the riddle and he could guess with approximate accuracy what Beldon had unravelled and what he hadn't.

Beldon grabbed a packet of seeds and starting sorting the menagerie by flower type. 'Good lord, what are all these for? There must be a hundred packets in here, Val.'

'They're all wildflowers. I want them for the south garden. Sort them by type, not colour,' Valerian instructed.

'You're making plans. That must mean it feels good to be home again,' Beldon said.

Valerian looked up from his clipping and smiled gently at his friend. 'First, yes, it does feel wonderful to be home. I am finally starting on the plans I once had for this place. Second, you don't have to ease into it, Beldon. We've been friends a long time. I'd like to think you could ask me anything and our friendship would not suffer for it.'

Beldon snorted at that and Valerian knew he was

thinking of the irony of that statement, thinking that Valerian had not felt he could tell Beldon his own great secret years ago. 'Perhaps you'll think differently about why I didn't tell you, when you're done with your questions,' Valerian said softly, apologetically. There was so much he had to account for. Today would be a start.

Beldon drew a deep breath. 'All right—what do you plan to do about Philippa now that you're home to stay?'

Valerian chuckled, intent on the plant before him. 'It's not so easy as what I intend to do, Beldon. Philippa's a stubborn woman. She'll do what she pleases and I am afraid she's not convinced I am in her best interest.'

Valerian looked up in time to see Beldon's brows furrow as he tried to work through his statement.

'I don't really understand the difficulty,' Beldon began. 'The two of you were in love once, she's free to pursue her own interests now and you're still in love with her. Beyond a little wooing, I don't see the problem.'

Poor Beldon, Valerian mused. He knew so much and yet so little of the details. Valerian took mercy on his friend. He set down his garden shears and leaned across the rough-hewn work table. 'Listen, Beldon. The night you found her crying in the garden, she wasn't crying because she had to forgo me and marry Cambourne. She was crying because I purposely broke her heart. She thought I was going to propose that evening.

'Instead, I told her I wanted her to marry Cambourne, that what we shared together was nothing more than a young man's dalliance.' Valerian winced at the last. Surely, Beldon would forsake his seed sorting and send him a rounder across the jaw. He deserved no less.

Beldon stopped his sorting, his fists hardening into tight balls, white at the knuckles. 'Why would you do that?' His voice was that of an angry older brother. 'Philippa was never anything but good to you. She adored you and apparently in a way far deeper than I guessed. You were her hero.'

Valerian nodded his assent, countless images of Philippa as a young girl, hair still in braids and skirts still short, tromping beside them during the long summers; Philippa slightly older, still coltish with her long legs, begging him to partner her during dance lessons.

Oh, yes, Beldon could not be more right. He'd been her hero. Once upon a time, he'd revelled in her adoration. There had been a type of strength in knowing that someone believed in him so thoroughly. The power of her young girl's adulation had got him through the darkest year of his life—the year his parents had suddenly died in a tragic hunting accident up in Scotland and he'd become the young Viscount St Just at the age of fifteen.

Philippa had been a rock, listening to him grieve

when he gave in to his blacker moods. Beldon had been the consummate friend, just as Beldon's parents had been loyal to their son's young friend. Valerian owed the family fiercely for what they'd done. They'd sheltered him, protected his inheritance when there had been concern over his young age, and, most of all, they had loved him. He'd no choice but to return that offering in kind when the time came, even if it meant hurting Philippa for the larger good.

Valerian sighed, moving to a tomato plant he was growing indoors. He began checking the leaves for any fungus. 'I've felt guilty enough over the years for what happened. I've wondered if I should have handled it differently. Mostly, I blame myself for starting it in the first place.' It was easier to talk if he kept busy.

'I am not so interested in how it started, Val, as to why it ended with a broken heart,' Beldon encouraged.

Valerian heard the unspoken message. Beldon understood how deuced awkward it was to talk about romancing one's best friend's sister. Those memories were too intimate, too private, memories that rightly should be only for him and Philippa.

'Philippa was not wrong. I had meant to propose that evening. She'd only been out a little over a month, but I'd known long before her début how I felt about her. That afternoon, I went to speak to your father.' Valerian hazarded a quick glance at Beldon.

'My father refused you?' Beldon's reaction was incredulous. 'He loved you.' But something else was working in Beldon's mind. 'The money,' Beldon said quietly. 'I came today because I spent most of last night going over the Pendennys's accounts. We would not have survived without the generous loan from Cambourne.'

Valerian gave a slight nod. 'Your father asked me to step aside. He said he was entertaining an offer from the duke.' He didn't need to say any more of the difficult words. Beldon was quickly piecing the rest of that interview together.

Beldon's voice was full of disbelief when he spoke. 'What my father did was dishonourable. He sold his daughter in marriage when she loved another and that other was willing to marry her and give her a respectable life—'

'Don't be angry with your father,' Valerian broke in. 'I didn't tell you this to drive a wedge between you and his memory. He was a good father to all of us. I do not think it is a sign of dishonour to try to protect your family from ruin.'

Beldon protested. 'It's not as if you were disreputable or poor or untitled. You were Philippa's equal in all ways.'

'He did what he thought was best,' Valerian said with finality. 'I must take some of the blame. I knew Cambourne was interested. The betting book at White's attested to the fact. But I went ahead and put your father in the position of having to refuse me. It might have been better for all if I had just let the romance dwindle, or I hadn't started it at all.'

Beldon shook his head. 'It is so typical of you to bear the burden of another's choices. At school, you were so quick to champion the underdog and to protect others, even when they should have shouldered their own responsibilities.'

'Still, it had to be done. You know I couldn't access my full inheritance until I was twenty-seven,' Valerian reminded him. 'If the family could have lasted five years, I would have thrown every pound I owned into seeing the family redeemed, but your father could not wait.'

Beldon went back to sorting the packets. 'I understand.' But his tone suggested otherwise. Valerian knew it would take Beldon a while to come to grips with the realities of the past. He appreciated that, for Beldon, the past was being rewritten.

'Your father asked me to break it off with Philippa in a way that didn't place him as the villain or jeopardise her willingness to marry Cambourne. You know Philippa. If she thought there was any chance of coercing her father into changing his mind, she would have tried. She could not know about my offer.'

'So you played the cad and told her this "*affaire*" meant nothing to you.'

'Essentially,' Valerian admitted, then added, feeling the need to clarify that there were limits to how much of cad he'd been willing to be, 'It wasn't an "*affaire*" in the truest sense of the word, Beldon. I left her untouched. You needn't assume the worst about me, whatever the rumours have asserted about me since then.'

'Rumours aside, I've always found you to be a man of honour,' Beldon said, meeting Valerian's gaze evenly.

'Yes, well, you might, but consequently Philippa does not. The past and the present—the way she understands them—fit together all too well. My performance that night in the garden was quite convincing. Perhaps you can see for yourself the implications that now impede any courtship I might conduct with her at present.'

Beldon tossed the last packet into a pile of violet wildflower seeds. 'I absolutely see what a mess you've got yourself into. She thinks you really are a cad for using her so poorly in the past and now doubts that your affections are sincere.'

Valerian gave him a wry smile. 'It's worthy of a Drury Lane farce.'

'I don't know if "farce" is the right word,' Beldon replied. 'Do you think your efforts will be in vain?'

'If they are, we'll call it a drama. If I am successful, we'll call it a comedy. It can't be a comedy unless the ending is happy.' Valerian was glad for a bit of levity. The conversation had been far too serious, but necessary. If his time abroad in diplomatic circles had taught him anything, it was that the past always came back to roost. He'd known the choice to come home would mean facing his old demons. But he'd chosen to do it anyway. There was only so far a man could run and only so long.

Valerian set aside his work. 'Let's go up to the house and see if Mrs Wilcox can set out tea for us.'

'I agree with the going up to the house part, but tea, Valerian?' Beldon raised his eyebrows. 'I suspect we'll need something stronger before we're through.'

Valerian gave Beldon a chary stare. What else did his friend want to winkle out of him today? Certainly there were more secrets to impart, but he'd shared all he was capable of sharing in one day. Professing one's soul took a lot out of a man.

Beldon came around the table and slapped him on the back, laughing. 'From the look on your face, you'd think I was the Spanish Inquisition, Val. I mean, we have plans to make. The way I see it, we have to convince Philippa that you were play-acting that night and all for a good cause, paint you as the noble fellow you are, and convince her to put her trust in you again.'

'You make it sound so easy,' Valerian groused, shutting the greenhouse door behind them. The weather seemed exceptionally cold after the humid warmth of the orangery.

'Well, it would be easy if she was here to be convinced,' Beldon drawled, stopping to stare at the back side of Roseland, looming impressively in all its sandstone majesty. They began the short trek to the back terrace. Beldon stopped shy of the granite steps. 'Aha! I have an idea.'

'Oh, no, your ideas—' Valerian began.

'Are good ideas,' Beldon finished for him, fixing him with a stern stare. 'Listen, here's your "situation" as it were: you've just returned from years away and have never really lived here since you came of age. You find there is much to be done to make Roseland liveable, modernised.' Beldon pitched his voice dramatically. 'But, alas, you are a feeble man with no brain for interior design. If left to your own devices, you'd have striped chintz curtains with polka-dot-satin bed comforters.'

'I see where you're going with this.' Valerian glared. 'You want me to ask Philippa to redecorate Roseland.'

Beldon shrugged. 'She'll do it anyway if you marry her. Might as well get a jump on it.'

Valerian laughed at his friend's practicality. 'You're an optimist.'

Beldon sobered from his earlier jocularity. 'I mean to see you both happy. She doesn't have to choose you unless she wants to. It's a bitter pill to swallow, to know all that happened, happened for me. I was the heir. You can't sugarcoat the bottom line, Val. I was the one who benefited most from Father's choices.

It's been a hard discovery, finding out that your sister and best friend gave up their personal happiness for your benefit.'

'She doesn't know,' Valerian put in, foolishly thinking for a minute that might ease Beldon's guilt.

'Ah, but she will. To win her, you'll have to tell her everything,' Beldon said. 'Making a clean breast of it will probably make your road with her easier to travel.'

Valerian scuffed his foot in the dirt in mild protest. 'Since when did the shortest distance between two points become confession?'

'Since confession was good for the soul,' Beldon laughed, stomping the mud from his boots as they mounted the terraced steps of Roseland.

Beldon was right. He did have to tell Philippa. He'd seen how painful the story had been for Beldon and he did not relish going through it again with Philippa. But it would go a long way in explaining things to her.

However, Valerian was acutely aware that it might not go far enough. He acknowledged what Beldon had not yet realised. He'd led a very different life the nine years he'd been gone and he had a reputation to contend with from that life. Mr Danforth had made that blatantly clear at the dinner table. But there were other 'pigeons' too from his time abroad that would come home to roost, pigeons far more damaging than his wenching. It would only be a matter of time before they migrated north.

* * *

Reputations could be damnable things, Lucien Canton reflected, rereading with ill-concealed glee the extensive missive that had arrived in the mails from London. He splayed his hands wide on the smooth surface of the cherrywood desk that denoted his power at the Provincial Bank of Truro.

He came in daily to read the post and the week-old Times financial section and to conduct private business for the bank. The local squires and gentry found it comforting to apply directly to him for a loan. It lent an air of status to know that they were able to do business with a viscount's son. Lucien traded on that cachet liberally and often.

Danforth knocked and stuck his head in Lucien's elegant, private office. 'Good news, I hope?' he asked solicitously.

Lucien smiled and said only, 'Yes, very good. Thank you for asking.' He'd learned the power of information was a highly prized commodity. He had no intention of letting anyone, especially not that status-sucking, tailcoat-riding, self-fashioned banker, Danforth, in on his latest *on dit*. Technically, it wasn't an '*on dit*' yet, but it would be when he chose to let it out. And really, the gossip would be the aftermath. All the action would have occurred already.

It was all Lucien could do to refrain from rubbing his hands together in unabashed joy. He re-read it a third time. It seemed the Viscount St Just had participated in an ill-fated rebellion in a town called Negush. There'd been a massacre, the town had burned. Women and children had died brutally. St Just had failed to quell the rebellion before such atrocities occurred.

Lucien had no idea where Negush was and since he had no mining interests there, he cared very little what part of the map it was on. But St Just would care a great deal if such information got out. If the tale was told in just the right way, St Just could be made out to be a murderer of innocents, which he likely was, even indirectly. If Lucien spun the tale skillfuly enough, he could have the *ton* thinking St Just capable of treason for his part in the uprising. At the very best, St Just would hang. Not even peers were immune from treason, especially not if his father and cronies at Whitehall decided to make an example of them. At the least, the man would hang in a different way. The *ton* would not countenance a man capable of such actions either from his own negligence in quelling the rebellion before it got out of hand or from actual participation in such meaningless bloodshed.

St Just would pay and Philippa would come running to him. Really, Lucien thought, he couldn't lose. Philippa would shun Valerian and congratulate herself on avoiding being taken in by such a monster, or, if she had fallen for the man, she'd come running, willing to bargain all she had for his clearance. Lucien would be in a prime position to offer that protection, to call off his father's watchdogs.

Maybe he would look up Negush on the map after all, since apparently he owed the success of his future to the little speck. Lucien walked to the small sideboard and poured himself a brandy and toasted his imminent success.

Chapter Eleven

*T*he conflagration was spreading rapidly. Soon the flames and smoke would reach the unprotected villagers caught between the oncoming Ottoman army and the burning remains of their homes. Surprised and unsuspecting, women and children had run into the night, giving no thought to where they ran, thinking only of immediate escape from the scorching inferno that consumed their village.

A child fell. A woman screamed. The carnage of Turkish retribution had begun. Under the cover of darkness, Valerian did what he could to protect a few of them. In the heat of battle, who could say with any certainty that it was he who had killed an Ottoman soldier or a Phanariot revolutionary fighting desperately with whatever weapons were at hand?

Through stealth and a warrior's skill, Valerian made

his way toward the burning huts, yelling her name. After all, he'd promised Dimitri he'd do what he could. The smoke sucked the very breath from his lungs, rendering his voice hoarse, the flames licking dry the cold sweat from his body. Someone cried out his name, barely audible above the roar of fire and the screams of panic.

Valerian turned towards the sound. There she was, as foolish, as selfless as ever, a sword in one hand, her eyes wild, holding off two soldiers, using her body as a shield to protect the three children with her.

She did not stand a chance. If she was lucky, the soldiers would cut her down before realising what a prized prisoner she'd make, sister to one of the Phanariot leaders. She deserved better. She'd not asked for any of this. She'd pleaded with her brother to take the peaceful surrender the Ottomans had offered.

Valerian hefted his knife and drew his other dagger. He would need them both along with speed and surprise. He began to run, issuing a hoarse roar with the remnants of his voice. It was enough. The soldier closest to him looked in his direction. Valerian threw his knife, taking the man in the throat. He covered the distance, leaping over the fallen man's body, and made quick work of his comrade.

His hands were soaked in blood, but he took no time to wipe them off. Fire was his biggest enemy now. 'Help the children. Give me the baby,' he yelled hoarsely over the flames to Natasha, who had already grabbed the oldest child's hand so as not to lose him in the tumult. The girl gave him the baby she'd so diligently cradled and took Natasha's other hand. Valerian put the baby in his left arm, leaving his knife hand free. He needed it twice before they gained the dark sanctuary of the forest.

The horrors of the night were not over. Ottomans burst into their safe harbour, skewering Natasha in the side with a wicked curved blade. The beautiful young woman fell. Valerian charged like a bull, taking one man down by sheer force, his blade ripping into him in ret-ribution. He fought like the devil himself, stabbing, slicing, killing, aware only briefly that the boy had picked up Natasha's blade to help him. When he was done, the ground ran red from his efforts, the last Ottoman fighter slain from his beserk rage. But some time in the fight, the boy had fallen too and lay deathly still not far from Natasha. He had failed Dimitri. One of the children was already dead.

He pushed down his grief and crawled to Natasha's side. She lived yet, but it would be only a momentary condition.

He took her hand, feeling her clutch at it with a last mad strength. 'Save the children.' She gasped. 'Find Dimitri.' Then her eyes widened with terror. 'Val, behind you.'

He had the disturbing sensation this had all happened before. He was losing her again. She deserved better than a bloody hand holding her own as she slipped away. He wouldn't lose her. He called her name.

No, not the darkness. He didn't want the darkness, not yet. He hadn't saved the others. He wasn't ready.

Valerian woke in a sweat, his head throbbing, his body trembling. Breath choked in his throat. Bile rose. He groped blindly for the bowl next to his bed, set there in anticipation of just such a purpose, and retched until the trembling subsided.

The dream again; the night in Negush that he never wanted to relive, but seemed doomed to do so. Valerian steadied himself, drawing deep breaths. It was the first time he'd had the nightmare since returning home.

Valerian threw back the covers and got out of bed, slipping into a robe. He lit the lamp, knowing he wouldn't sleep again that night. The fear of the dream coming back was too real. He couldn't do anything about the dream, but he could minimise the headache.

Valerian poured himself a glass of water from the carafe on the bedside table and rummaged in the drawer, looking for a small vial. He pulled the stopper and put a few drops into the glass. He drank it down and sighed with relief. In twenty minutes, his headache would numb to a dull throb thanks to his special herbal potion. He went nowhere without it. Until then, he'd have to sit and tolerate it.

Valerian sank into a chair near the cold hearth in his private sitting room. He hated the dream. More, he hated what the dream represented: his failure to protect people he cared about.

It had been his job to help the Turks negotiate a peaceable surrender after the Negush district had rebelled against Ottoman rule. The district had actually succeeded in temporarily liberating themselves. It had spread to neighbouring villages, but eventually the revolutionaries were no match for the Turkish army. He'd been sent to advise the revolutionaries to lay down their arms. But they'd not relented. They'd been shown no mercy by the Turks, who'd slaughtered the soldiers, rounded up prisoners, sold them into slavery and relocated any who had escaped those two fates deep into Macedonia. The district of Negush had been effectively erased from the face of the earth.

But he'd known the Phanariot rebels. He'd feasted at their tables, stayed in their homes. They were regional aristocrats. Natasha had been like a countess, her brother an earl of sorts. They'd reminded him intensely of Beldon and Philippa.

Originally, Britain had charged him with the mission of befriending the Phanariots, but then switched sides when it became apparent that a weak Turkey needed British support if Britain wanted to stand against Russia in that part of the world.

Even now, eight years since the disastrous 1822 uprising, the whole event filled Valerian with self-loathing. Britain had changed sides, seen innocents slaughtered all for the sake of maintaining British-friendly waterways to India.

There were no ideals behind what they'd ordered him to do, simply pure capitalist greed. Britain liked having a weak Turkey in its pocket. It did not like the idea of people throwing off the Ottoman yoke to form a new, powerful Christian nation that might compete against England.

Natasha, Dimitri and Dimitri's gallant young son had died for their ideals of freedom all because Britain couldn't countenance the emergence of a new, large Christian nation that might unite eastern Europe into a competitive force.

Valerian fought against the grief that rose up at the thought of the loss: Natasha bleeding to death in the copse; the boy fighting futilely against men twice his size; Dimitri executed with the other leaders two days later in a gruesome display of Turkish revenge.

He supposed he'd technically committed treason that night, stabbing the ally Turks as he fought to save Natasha, but he could hardly care when the reasons for supporting the Turks had been so mercenary on England's behalf to start with. He'd done his duty by attempting to negotiate peace. Then he'd done his duty by Dimitri and got the two other children to relative safety. He hoped it had been enough.

That had been the beginning of a stalemate in the region between the Great Powers, each checkmating the other in their bids for dominance. It had also been the beginning of Valerian's own disillusionment with diplomacy. Diplomacy was not, as he'd originally believed, a chance to participate in history, to leave one's mark on the world.

The remainder of his time in Europe had been marked by a constant shifting of allegiances as Britain attempted to pre-empt Russian control and pull Ottoman strings. Towards the end, the balance of power was shifting again. Britain had gained control of Cyprus and no longer needed to control Turkey in order to control waterways. Further proof that Dimitri had died for nothing, not even for the posterity of the waterways. The cause for which Dimitri's dream had been pushed aside had been fleeting. The Turkish alliance had only held for a few years until Britain had achieved its objective.

Valerian had come to the conclusion that if he wanted to leave a legacy, it would best be done in the beauty of his gardens, where the focus was on living and peace, and in his nursery where he could raise a child. But he needed a wife for that. He needed Philippa.

She would be here at Roseland by tomorrow afternoon. She'd responded to his request affirmatively, no doubt because of his promise to have Beldon on hand. He'd promised many things in that letter, anything that would get her here and give him a chance to prove his worth to her.

He was a man of action, but in his desperation to claim her, his actions had all been wrong. He'd rushed his fences. He knew the whole of his story, but she didn't. She needed time to know him again, believe in him again as she once had.

Philippa sighed and carefully refolded Valerian's letter, placing it back in her reticule. She was twenty times a fool for coming. She was inviting all kinds of madness. She and Valerian had proved they could not behave rationally in one another's presence. The few times they'd been alone had led to all sorts of mischief. Yet here she was. There had been something plaintive about the note, a personal plea of one friend to another, that she found she could not refuse.

Philippa looked out of the window of the coach. She was nearly there, if memory served. The tall, square tower of St Justus Church was coming into view and Roseland was a mile down the road after that. She'd only been here once, right after Valerian's parents had died. Her family had come over to help settle the estate. She had been twelve at the time, but she remembered the journey with remarkable clarity. The road veered south past the church's lych gate, past the tidal creek that ran alongside the building and up one last hill to the vast park and gardens of Roseland.

At first glance, Roseland looked no better than it ought for a place that had been masterless for nearly a decade—even longer if one counted the years after Valerian's parents' deaths. The magnificent gardens that had once been Roseland's fame were overgrown, rhodo-dendron bushes crowding out old woody hydrangeas, and bluebells growing wild where they willed.

But at second glance, Philippa could already see Valerian's expert hand at work as the coach tooled up the long drive toward the house. Gardeners swarmed the lawn with long scissors, trimming and shaping the ragged edges and uneven patches of lawn. The gardens closest to the house teemed with workers digging re-straining walls and clearing flower beds.

The coach pulled into the circular drive in front of the house and Philippa marvelled at the elegance that greeted her. The cobblestoned circle was free of any in-trusive weeds that might grow between the stones. The stones looked freshly paved, smooth and evenly laid one against the other without any uneven ground between them that might trip an unsuspecting guest.

Philippa dismounted, staring in wonder at the centre of the driving circle and its *pièce de résistance*, a magnifi-cent stone fountain spilling water into a pool at its base. To add colour to the centre, the fountain base was sur-rounded by a bed of flowers in bright blues, whites and reds.

The fountain was done in the classical style to com-plement the architecture of Roseland and reminded Philippa of something one might see in an Italian piazza.

She could not resist the lure of splashing water.

Thinking she was alone, Philippa gave into the temptation to put her hand beneath the spilling water, laughing as she did so.

A man's chuckle answered her laughter. She swiftly pulled back her hand and gathered her dignity, looking around.

'Your Grace, welcome to Roseland.' A dignified man walked down the stairs leading up and to the front door. 'I am Steves, the Viscount St Just's butler. He instructed me to watch for you.'

Philippa stifled a groan. What an image she must paint. Steves would think her quite gauche for engaging in such childish behaviour.

'The viscount will be pleased to know you liked the fountain. It is new. Milord put it in just this past month. He laid the cobblestones himself.'

Philippa could very well imagine Valerian doing such a thing. If Steves thought the news would surprise her, he would be disappointed. 'His craftsmanship is excellent as always,' she said.

Steves nodded and said meaningfully, 'Indeed it is. He hoped you'd like it.'

She blushed and fought the urge to ask Steves to clarify. It would show too much eagarness to probe. Instead, she asked. 'Where is the viscount, Steves?'

'He's out on the back terrace, my lady. If you would follow me? A footman can see to your trunks.'

'Out on the back terrace' was something of an understatement, Philippa realised shortly. *She* was on the freshly swept terrace with its sturdy wicker furniture. Valerian was engaged with four other men in the process of moving an enormous planter containing a type of tree Philippa had never seen.

Apparently, the gigantic container was to go on the edge of the terrace, situated so that it could shade the cluster of wicker furniture grouped on that side. Valerian caught sight of her and waved, motioning that she should take a seat and wait.

He looked glorious. His hair shone in the sunlight and he wore only his shirt, the sweat of his efforts plastering the thin material to his back so that Philippa could plainly see the play of his muscles as they strained to set the planter into place.

The men gave the planter a last push and Valerian stepped back, satisfied with its placement. 'Perfect. It's exactly what I was hoping for,' Valerian explained, stripping off his thick workman's gloves and coming to take a chair next to Philippa.

'It's a marvellous tree, Val.' The old nickname slipped off her tongue before she could catch herself. She bit her lip. To his credit, Valerian did not comment on it.

'It's a Chusan Palm. I sent a seedling back from Italy several years ago. My head gardener saw to it and here it is today.' Valerian rose and walked over to study the mop of green fronds that topped the palm, estimating its height. 'I don't imagine it will get much taller than this. The gardener I talked to in Italy said the plant stays shorter in colder climates because of the winds bothering its top leaves. Of course, in the Mediterranean regions it grows much taller.'

'I didn't know you were in Italy,' Philippa said in surprise. She was just starting to realise it was only one of many things she didn't know about him.

'Just briefly. It was a trip only, nothing permanent.' Valerian shrugged. 'I took full advantage, though. I visited every garden I could. I even went up to Florence when my work in Rome was concluded so I could see the Boboli Gardens.' Valerian laughed suddenly, looking very young and very happy, if one ignored the tell-tale dark circles under his eyes. 'I've been in the dirt so long, I've lost my manners. Here you are, newly arrived, and I am rambling on about plants. My apologies, Philippa. I am glad you're here. Do you think you're up to the task?'

'You don't need to stand on ceremony with me.' She smiled back, lost in the wondrous moment of being with her friend. This was the Valerian she missed. 'The place looks good. I like the fountain.'

'It will look better once you and I are through with it,' Valerian said. 'I want the gardens to shine again, on equal with Trewithen and Trebah,' He cited two large, nearby estates famed for their botany. Valerian sobered a bit. 'I was gone a long time and this place shows it.'

Philippa sensed he was scolding himself. She wanted to say something to ease the guilt she heard in his voice, but what could she say? She had no idea why he'd stayed away so long. She'd always thought he'd liked being away, that it had been a choice. Now, something in his tone indicated it might have been otherwise.

Valerian shook himself and his smile returned. 'Would you like to see inside? See what you're up against? Beldon won't be back until supper.'

Valerian had been right—the house did need a lot of work. Philippa made mental notes as they strolled through the large, airy rooms of Roseland. Beeswax and lemon could only do so much. Wallpapers were faded and needed replacing. Curtains were dusty. She wouldn't know how deteriorated they would be until they'd had the dust beaten out of them. Carpets were thin with wear over time. But she was up to the challenge. She'd cut her teeth on Cambourne's townhouse in London and had turned it into a showcase for his works of art by the time she was finished.

Valerian threw open the double doors leading to the ballroom. Philippa was not ready for the rush of memories the empty room evoked. The room itself was not special. The floors were scarred from years of hard dancing, the polish having worn away. The paint was faded, chipped in places. Curtains hung limply at the long Georgian-style windows that lined the far side.

The niches where enormous crystal vases could stand, filled with flowers from Roseland's hothouses, were empty. The room's only piece of furniture, a long pianoforte, was covered with a dust cloth in the far corner.

No, the room was nothing spectacular. In fact, it was just short of shabby. But to her eye, she was twelve again, seeing the ballroom for the first time. 'I remember you bringing me here,' Philippa said softly, drifting into the centre of the room.

Valerian followed her in. She was acutely conscious of his presence behind her. He gave a warm laugh. 'You declared this your favourite room in the house. You told me that yellow was the best colour for a ballroom.'

'And I was right,' Philippa teasingly protested. 'Look how well it has weathered the years.'

'You tried very hard that day to cheer me up,' Valerian said quietly.

'I don't remember.' Philippa replied awkwardly. She didn't want him to do this—to be so nice, so kind, to make her believe she hadn't imagined the man she'd once known. Of course, she did remember, quite vividly, what she'd done to cheer him up.

'I remember.' Valerian swung her around to face him and swept her into his arms. 'You danced with me, you talked the whole time about all the parties we'd hold here later, how Roseland would be a happy place again.'

'I must have been very annoying,' Philippa said, startled to find herself in his arms, his body moving them into the opening turns of a silent waltz. Good lord, he was irresistible. How was she to stop her heart from loving him in spite of her better judgement?

'Val, is this wise?' Philippa asked, letting him whirl them down the length of the ballroom floor at an exhilarating pace.

'We won't run into anyone. We're quite alone.'

'Don't be glib, Val. I am well aware that we're alone. That's what has me worried. We can't fall in love again, or whatever you want to call it.'

Valerian brought them to a hard stop. 'What are you saying?'

Better to eat her pride now rather than later, Philippa thought. 'If you invited me here to help with decoration efforts, that's all right. However, if you invited me here with other intentions, perhaps those of a—a—a—romantic sort…' Philippa paused, groping for the right phrasing. But there wasn't any. 'If you invited me here to seduce me or romance me, or to relive an *affaire* of your youth, I'll have no part of it.' She shook her head. 'I understand what constitutes a relationship with you and I can't do it. I loved you all those years ago and I fear that I could love you again. I would be devastated when you left. I wouldn't survive such heartache again.' She gathered the courage to meet his eyes after her foolish speech, feeling much more like an eighteen-year-old girl than a full-grown woman of twenty-seven.

'Shh.' Valerian put a finger to her lips, his voice a

mere whisper. 'What if I told you I loved you, that I never stopped loving you? That the night I played the jilt, it was all a lie? That is what all your worries are based on, isn't it?'

A wild hope surged in her, raising all kinds of confusion. Did she dare to believe these fantastical claims? Then she remembered and her hope fell. 'And the women, Val? Was all your wenching on the Continent a lie too?' she asked in a sad, teasing tone, trying for a brave smile.

'They were a fool's stratagem to try to forget what I had left behind,' Valerian whispered, his eyes pleading for a chance.

Philippa tried to pull away, but he held her tight. 'Let me tell you my story, Philippa. Let me give you permission to love me again.'

Chapter Twelve

'I don't know what to say,' Philippa said after Valerian's account of their fateful evening came to an end. His revelations left her at sea, awash in uncertainty. She'd built her mental fortress on the foundations of that evening, that he'd spoken the truth when he'd jilted her, cast her off as no more than a dalliance. The reasons for her distrust and harsh words stemmed from that night.

In the single telling of the tale, Valerian managed to make those foundations unstable. If she believed him entirely, her foundations were reduced to nothing more than rubble. Her world had shifted. Everything had changed. She could love Valerian again. Her one reason for attempting to withhold her affections had been swept away.

'Say you believe me, that you find me to be a man of honour.' Valerian answered quietly.

His hands held hers tightly. They had long since given up standing and had seated themselves on the floor of the ballroom. The shadows had lengthened into early evening, the bright room growing darker. The floor was a hard seat, but Philippa would not have moved from the dusty wood floor for anything. Valerian's tale had riveted her from the beginning. It had made sense, why she'd found such incongruity in his statements that evening. All that nonsense about needing society's approval had not sounded like the Valerian she'd known.

A voice from the doorway caused her to turn her head. 'I'll vouch for him, Phil. The Pendennys's ledgers support all he says. We needed Cambourne and Father arranged for it to happen.' Beldon pushed off from the door jamb and strode towards them.

'Beldon, you know?' Philippa stood up awkwardly, shaking out her wrinkled skirts.

'I suspected as much.' Beldon gave a short laugh. 'I started thinking how serendipitous it was that Cambourne's money came along just when we needed it. The pieces started to fall into place. I searched the family ledgers and I discovered there was nothing lucky about the appearance of Cambourne in our lives. He was Father's last great campaign to save us.'

'I wish you had told me.' Philippa turned to Valerian, quiet censure in her voice.

'How could I tell you? You were desperate enough

that night. If you'd thought there was any chance of undoing your father's plans, or if you thought I could be won over, you would never have agreed to marry Cambourne.'

'So you decided for me?' Philippa's temper began to simmer. 'You decided it would be better to let me believe the worst about you, about my own judgement, for nine years?' She saw Beldon slip out the door, trying hard not to be noticed. Very well, this was between her and Valerian.

'Your father asked it of me,' Valerian answered with a rising anger of his own. 'If you knew, we'd have ended up running off to who-knows-where with nothing but the clothes on our backs.'

'It was my life.' Philippa stomped her foot in irritation. She was tired of having men decide what was best for her. First her father, then Lucien and now Valerian's disclosure. Did all men think women were such sapskulls? 'I expected better from you, Valerian.'

Righteous indignation fired Valerian. 'Better? In what sense?' He should have known this would be Philippa's response. For once, why couldn't she be like other women? Other women would be won over by the romance of his sacrifice and the long constancy of his affections. But Philippa challenged the realities of the situation.

Her sharp eyes studied his face, testing his reactions for truth. 'You should have trusted me instead of trying to bear that burden alone.'

Valerian pushed a hand through his hair in frustration. He'd bared his conscience, confessed the greatest sin Philippa knew him capable of. And, yes, he'd expected to be believed. More than that, he'd expected to be accepted. He'd rather thought—and foolishly so— that her heart would welcome him back on the spot. It seemed quite unfair to be treated to her scolding instead and he'd had enough of it.

'Regardless, it was done with your best interest at heart. I regretted hurting you. I regretted denying myself happiness. But I won't stand here and be tongue-lashed for upholding your father's wishes and doing what was best for the family. There were no easy answers or choices, Philippa.' He was aware he'd raised his a voice in his agitation. He controlled it, bringing it down a notch. 'I feared if I told you, you would hate me and then your father would know that I had failed him.'

'I ended up hating you anyway,' Philippa said sharply. Her hands were knotted into fists at her sides, her voice full of impotent frustration. 'Nine years is a long time to hate, Val.'

'It's also a long time to love,' he said softly, walking towards her and taking her hands in his, uncurling them from their tight fists. But he knew what she meant. She could not be expected to change course suddenly. The news was too raw, too unfiltered. She had the permission she needed to trust in him again, to see him as the friend she'd once known, but it would take time. She had her permission. The rest was up to her.

Valerian relished the thought of that challenge. He would woo her gently. While she was at Roseland, he would court her as sincerely as he had once dreamed of doing. The idea of Philippa thrilled him enormously. This time there would be no sneaking off under the facade of excuses to steal hasty kisses, there would be no fear of being caught. He would court her openly, starting with this kiss.

Gently, he tipped her chin up and captured her face between his hands, taking a chance to drink of her countenance, the creamy skin, the brilliant blue of her eyes, the tremulous smile that played uncertainly at her lips while she waited, her own gaze searching his. Then he brushed her lips with his, softly, tenderly. This kiss lacked the roughness of their heated engagement at the folly, but was no less intense for that absence.

Slowly, he could feel her body soften, the rigid posture with which she'd held herself in her anger relaxing against him, arms finding their way around his neck as he took her weight. He'd waited his entire life for this. He'd come back for this. The darkness of his world receded in the wake of the peace that flooded through him from the simple act of holding her tight against him.

'I will not be so foolish as to let you go again,' he vowed, pressing a kiss to the top of her head.

'You may have to for dinner,' Philippa joked, her voice muffled against his shoulder.

'Well, just for dinner, then.'

The next days were heady ones for Valerian. True to his word, he hardly let Philippa out of his sight. They rode in the early morning along the coastal bridle path between St Just-in-Roseland and St Mawes. They picnicked with Beldon in the hilly meadows above the St Justus churchyard, watching the small wildlife run through the fields. They took long walks beside the tidal creeks that bordered Valerian's property. It seemed that he talked endlessly of his plans for the future in those days: plans for his gardens, his landscapes, his stables. He couldn't help it. Life, full and pure, coursed through his veins again. There was purpose everywhere he looked. He was young and fit with the wealth he needed to bring his plans to fruition…and the woman.

Philippa was intoxicating. Her very presence in the same room could steal his attention for minutes at a time. The curve of her neck when she bent over a book during their quiet times after dinner drove him to distraction, making his hand itch to gently massage her exposed nape. The lilac scent of her light perfume lingered in the air long after she'd passed through a corridor. Her soft music at the pianoforte lent a cultivated feel to the house, filtering through the halls from the music room.

There were signs of her presence everywhere, from the cut-crystal bowls filled with colourful flowers placed on tables throughout the house to the very obvious redecorating efforts. Painters had come to paint and others had come to hang the drawing-room walls with a damask silk of deep crimson. It was more than simply noticing the difference a woman's touch made in transforming a house into a home. Valerian was struck afresh daily that it was his home, his woman.

She smiled easily these days, she laughed, she stared at him with a dreamy look in her eyes when she thought she had him unawares. Most of all, she'd found her ease with him again. They roamed the hills, comfortable in their conversation and in their touch. She'd take his hand or reach out to brush a strand of hair back from his face without thinking.

If he were naïve, he'd say it was like the old days of their youth. But those days were gone. Only a fool would think they could be reclaimed in their entirety. These were new days, new times for them, and Valerian was not careless with that reality. He treasured each knowing look, each shared laugh as spring came to his beloved Cornwall. He'd lived too long in places where life changed at a moment's notice to discard the simple pleasures he found in Philippa's company. As the days passed, he had reason to believe she felt that way also. Her own life had not been without the pain of loss that had come too early.

On St Piran's Day, they rode down to St Justus to put flowers on the graves of miners and to join in the village celebrations. The weather was fair for March and everyone for miles around had turned out for the festivities honouring the legendary hero-saint who, legend held, had imparted the wisdom of tinning to early Cornish miners a thousand years earlier.

Valerian found himself to be something of a celebrity. Although several tradesmen and day workers had been tramping up the hill to Roseland since his return, he'd not spent much time in the village re-establishing ties yet. He was proud to make his entrance with Philippa at his side, looking splendid in a rich brown riding habit trimmed in black with a small hat to match, her russet hair twisted into an exquisite knot at the back of her neck. He wanted people to get used to seeing her with him. She would be his countess soon. Valerian thought of his quietly sworn New Year's resolution and smiled. All he'd ever truly wanted was within his reach.

Philippa did not disappoint. At the village, she dismounted from her horse, immediately engulfed by a group of children with daisies in their hands. She took the little bouquets, some already wilting, exclaiming over each one in delight until she'd compiled one big one. The children were charmed. Two little girls seized her hands and led her to the village green where preparations for celebrations were just finishing. She tossed a smile back at him as the children merrily towed her away.

Valerian lifted his arm in a brief wave and followed at a slower pace behind the excited children, stopping to talk with a few men as he progressed. Booths were set up around the perimeter of the green and he caught up with Philippa and children at a booth selling Cornish pasties.

'We were deciding if we were hungry or not,' Philippa called out.

A little girl with dark curls piped up. 'We've decided that we are.' Excited cheers went up from the little coterie and Valerian found himself handing over coins for nine pasties filled with savoury beef. He was starting to think the children might be with them all day, when a handful of mothers bustled up to claim them.

'We're so sorry, your lordship, milady. I hope they didn't bother you too much,' one woman said in apology, casting a stern look at her three youngsters.

Valerian assured her it had been no trouble. But the children's eyes began to fill with tears regardless of his reassurances. Philippa knelt down swiftly, taking their hands. 'Come and see us this afternoon. I think I heard there are to be games.' Her offer dried their tears and Valerian thought he could literally feel his chest swell with pride at her kind efforts.

'That was very generous of you,' he remarked as they began a slow stroll past the booths.

Philippa shrugged. 'Children make the world brighter. It's a shame the world doesn't do more for them in return other than to force them to grow up too fast and assume adult responsibilities.'

'Perhaps that will change. I hear there is legislation in Parliament regarding child labour.'

'I hope it goes through. I have thrown whatever political clout I have behind promoting such laws. Perhaps you will too?' Philippa cast him a cautious sideways glance.

Valerian raised her hand to his lips and kissed it, his eyes returning her gaze. 'Absolutely.' For a fleeting moment he thought of Dimitri's young son forced to be a warrior, forced to flee from a village that had become a war zone. He wished Dimitri's children could have had a village like this one, a day like this one, and the security of knowing there would be other days.

'What is it, Val? You're miles from here,' Philippa asked with concern.

He pushed his sad thoughts aside. Today was about the future. 'An old memory, that's all. There's a vendor with some good lengths of ribbon over here.' He tugged on her hand and the moment passed.

They shopped the rest of the morning. Philippa bought several lengths of ribbon and cakes of soap. At the last booth she bought a bag of peppermints.

'Sweet tooth, my dear?' Valerian inquired teasingly.

'They're for the children,' Philippa protested and Valerian smiled. She hadn't forgotten her promise.

Valerian spread out a blanket on the green near where

the games would take place that afternoon and went to assemble a luncheon of sorts from the different stalls. By the time he returned, Philippa was surrounded by her court of children again. She sat placidly in their midst, weaving daisy necklaces for the girls and crowns for the boys.

The scene made his heart lurch, not this time for the boy who had died fighting beside him, but for the children that might be—his children with Philippa. Yes, six or seven little ones seemed just about right.

After lunch, he let the children talk them into playing some of the children's games. Philippa was quickly snatched up to partner one of the girls in a three-legged race. One small boy shyly asked him to play too. The little boy's name was Geoffrey and he barely came up to Valerian's waist. It would be a terribly difficult race with the difference in their heights, but Philippa was already at the starting line, smiling her approval. In the end, he and Geoffrey took third and the vicar's wife awarded them a shiny white ribbon that made Geoffrey's eyes light up in delight.

'He'll remember that for ever,' Philippa commented as they left the children to admire their prizes. 'The day he raced with the local viscount in the three legged race and took third on St Piran's Day.' She looked at him with a wealth of meaning in her eyes. 'Old wives say there's a lot of good in a man who has such joy in children, Val.'

That did it. He'd been wanting her all day and not

just because of how lovely she looked in her habit or the graceful way she'd moved, but because of her easy way with the children, the way everything at the simple fair had pleased her, the way she made people feel good about themselves when they were with her, even him. That had always been her gift and he loved her for it.

Valerian drew her round the back of a wide tree. What he intended was meant to be private, out of sight of children and families.

'What are you doing?' Philippa whispered, picking up on his need for secrecy.

'I want to kiss you,' Valerian confessed, his eyes falling on her lips. 'I've wanted to kiss you all day.' His tone was playful. He felt like a young boy with his first miss. He bent to kiss her and all boyishness faded. There was no mistaking that he was all man with a grown man's urges. At the brush of her lips, he felt himself go hard, passion and want surging through him in an irrevocable tide of longing. He'd held himself in check since that day in the ballroom, giving her time to accept him again. But his grip on those reins was starting to slip.

Philippa gave a little moan of pleasure and pressed against him, a hand going to his hard length where it jutted against his buckskin trousers. Her palm found the sensitive head of his manhood through the fabric and she gently rubbed her hand over it.

Valerian groaned, deepening his kiss, desperation to

have her flooding him. He wanted to rip off all his clothes and lie naked in the grass with her. 'We must have more than this, Philippa. I don't think I can survive on kisses alone much longer.'

'Nor me,' she breathed, her eyes full of a pure desire that shook him to his core. This was not the calculated gaze of a woman who wanted him solely for his looks and bedroom skills. He'd seen that assessing gaze far too often in his years abroad. Philippa wanted him body and soul, heart and mind, perfection with imperfection, and he'd never felt more complete in his life.

'Tonight,' he whispered, kissing the column of her neck.

'Tonight,' she affirmed.

The rest of the day held a heady tension for him, the activities of the fair acting as a form of exquisite foreplay, knowing that each hour moved him closer to the moment he craved.

Reluctantly, he gave into Philippa's cajoling and joined in the knife-throwing competition. He won easily, to which Philippa remarked, 'I had no idea you could throw a knife like that.' He shrugged and said nothing.

The paper lanterns were lit, surrounding a squared-off space for dancing. Shadows lengthened. Night was coming. Valerian felt his anticipation ratchet up another notch. They'd be expected to dance, of course. It would be wrong to leave before the dancing was underway and he found he wanted to dance. Tonight it would be all country dances and polkas, furries and scoots in the Cornish fashion. It would be thirsty work. The taverner had already set up barrels of ale on the perimeter.

He and Philippa led off the first dance, a rowdy, hand-clapping country dance. Philippa danced the next polka with the greengrocer's son and Valerian took to the sidelines to watch. Her hair had come loose and she'd given up any attempt of putting it back in place. Now, it hung in a heavy chestnut sheet down her back, flying behind her as she and her partner took a turn. She threw him a joyous smile as they passed and he smiled back.

'She's a wonderful woman, milord,' the vicar's wife said at his side, following his gaze. 'Should I be so bold as to set aside a date at St Justus for you?'

Valerian chuckled, his confidence high. 'I have hopes in that direction.' If he had his way, he'd marry her tomorrow. That being an impossibility, he'd like to marry her at the summer's end, after the hubbub of the London Season.

The dance ended and he went to claim Philippa for his turn. She was light in his arms. If he hadn't known what awaited him at the end of his evening, he might have been convinced to dance with her all night. But he did know. They'd both pledged it and, from the look in her eyes, she knew it too. There was no reason to wait any longer.

The dance ended and he leaned towards her to whisper one simple word. 'Home.'

Chapter Thirteen

Philippa shivered on the threshold of Roseland. Her anticipation had grown to a fever pitch on the short ride home in the dark. Valerian was beside her, lighting a candelabrum left on the entry table, taking her hand, leading her up the stairs to the master's chambers.

Inside, he set the brace of candles on a small table and turned to her. He held up his hand. It trembled in the candlelight. 'See how you affect me?' His voice was husky. 'I want to please you so badly. I've thought of nothing but this for longer than you can know. Most of my adult life, really.'

Philippa smiled at his confession. She went to him, slowly removing the cravat wound about his neck. 'I know.' They'd come close to this on a few occasions, reckless with hot youth. Her hands moved down to his shirt. She unbuttoned the shirt and pushed it back, his shoulders flexing to push it off. She ran her hands down the length of his chest, exploring the sculpted torso and the sensation of smooth, male skin. Her fingernails lightly raked his nipples, causing Valerian to gasp in sensual delight.

Empowerment swept through Philippa. She reached for the waist of his trousers and the rigid length of his manhood. At her touch, everything transformed. They came alive as lovers, no longer tender friends but something much more demanding, more animate.

Heat engulfed them. She felt Valerian's hands on her body, caressing as they made short work of her clothing until she was entirely naked to his hot gaze. His green eyes burned with an incinerating desire. In a fluid motion, he bent and grabbed her up in his arms and carried her to the bed. He followed her down on to the mattress, surrounding her with his taut body, aroused and ready for love.

She offered up her body and he took it, suckling at one breast, then the other, worshipping with every kiss and caress. Philippa arched against him, caressing his hair, his shoulders, anywhere she could reach. The man who rose over her was magnificent and wild, treating her to pleasures she had not imagined existed. She parted her legs for him, feeling herself growing unabashedly damp from his efforts. He sank between her thighs, taking himself in hand and manoeuvring smoothly to her entrance. He tested her readiness. She felt herself stretch at the fullness of his member, accommodating, taking, begging for more until she felt his sex pressing against her very womb, so deep was he inside.

He moved and began the ancient rhythm, his breathing coming in ragged pants. She closed her eyes and gave herself over to the sensations surging through her. She felt as if she was standing on the edge of a cliff, each step taking her closer to an edge where something wonderful awaited if she would only jump.

She wrapped her legs about Valerian's waist, urging him on, to help her jump. Her hands clung to his muscled shoulders. She could feel the unbridled strength of his arms as he kept his full weight from pressing down on her. She started to shudder.

'Open your eyes, Philippa.'

Her eyes flew open at the last moment. She heard herself gasp in pleasure as she plunged over the cliff, soaring and falling at the same time. And Valerian was with her, shuddering his own release, his eyes dark with his passion, his body slick with his exertions. He collapsed against her, spent. She could feel the fast thump of his heart and knew her own pulse was racing in the glorious aftermath of what they'd done.

Valerian shifted to his side and she snuggled into the nest of his body, revelling in the safety and warmth of his strong arms. Nothing could hurt her here, nothing could reach her. 'Val?' she whispered.

'Hmm?' His hand tightened around her waist.

'I never hated you. I couldn't bring myself to do so, not really.' In her drowsy state, she recognised it for the truth it was. She'd wanted to hate him, she'd forced herself to it. But it had been a hard battle and tonight she was glad it was one battle she had lost.

Philippa awoke late the next morning, giddy with her realisations. She was free to love Valerian. For the first time in years, she could follow the dictates of her heart and never mind the doubts her mind tossed up as facts. Valerian's arm was still around her waist. When had she ever slept so soundly that she hadn't moved an inch? But when had she ever felt so secure that she could lay down her burdens long enough to sleep undisturbed?

Behind her, Valerian began to stir. She squirmed experimentally and felt the jut of his straining morning erection against her buttocks. Wanton desire rocketed through her, along with a healthy measure of curiosity. Could last night be repeated or was the intensity of her feelings unique? Would she feel that way each time she made love with Valerian? She was out of her depth here. It had never been like this with Cambourne. She'd not known how powerful a coupling could be until last night.

Valerian nipped at her earlobe, whispering love words as he positioned himself. Dear lord, he was going to take her from behind. Such a strange position caused her a moment's panic. She tensed. 'Val? What are you doing?' She knew, technically, but she wasn't sure it worked in practice. 'Does this actually work?'

Valerian gave a low, sensual chuckle and hugged her close. 'Yes. Relax and let me show you. I won't hurt you. This is new to you?' His free hand gently rubbed her shoulders, massaging away the tension. 'This position is a woman's gift to a man. She is at her most vulnerable here,' he explained softly. 'But it allows a man to penetrate her more deeply than other positions.'

He gave a gentle thrust. Philippa gasped. There was something exceedingly decadent and yet wondrous about the position. There was no doubt that she had all of him and she revelled in the feel of him so completely entrenched inside her. It didn't take long for either of them to reach their pleasure, Valerian holding her tight as he poured his warm seed deep inside her.

He held her close, letting his release shudder over him in waves. She was silent, a sure sign her mind was rampant with questions, thoughts.

She dared her question once the initial wave of ecstasy had subsided. 'Is it supposed to be like this all the time?' She turned in his arms to face him, pushing hair back from his face.

'No, not always.' Valerian answered carefully. It was inevitable she'd ask, wonder about the rumours that had floated back to England, most of them clear exaggerations of a truth only he knew. He rather wished she hadn't asked at such an inopportune time, though, when he'd rather lie with her in peace instead of fencing with her dragon of a temper.

She seemed to contemplate his answer. 'Has it been like this for you before?'

An even worse question than her first one. 'Not really.' How could he explain to her that a man could enjoy such a release on a purely physical level without the emotions that had accompanied what passed between them? How could he make her understand that there was a different sort of satisfaction to be had, but that it didn't compare in the least with what he'd done with her? Nothing ever would.

She was poised to ask another question. Valerian raised himself up on one arm. 'This is neither the time nor the place for such an inquisition, Philippa. There is not room enough in this bed for anyone else you'd care to drag in here.

'However, since you have raised the topic, I will tell you this—I was not a monk those nine years, but most likely the reports of my licentious behaviour were greatly overestimated. Those women meant nothing. They were a poor excuse to forget what had happened in England. They wanted my body and they understood that was all they'd ever get from me. My heart was engaged elsewhere—with you—and it always has been. I'd prefer to put paid to that part of my life.'

Philippa smiled her assent. 'I didn't mean to pry. I was curious. That was all.' She blushed and looked away. 'I never knew…' she stammered, shy in her embarrassment.

'Not with Lucien?' Valerian knew he was pressing her, but he had to know. She'd had her inquisition and he had things he needed to know too.

She shook her head. 'No, Lucien and I have never been together and Cambourne…well, that is to say, Cambourne and I didn't achieve…'

Valerian pressed a forefinger to her lips. 'Shh. You needn't say any more.' He understood perfectly what she meant and it thrilled him, deep down in some primal core of his being, that while he hadn't been the first, he'd been the one to bring her true pleasure. And he'd be the last. If he'd had any doubts on that score, he would have used a sheath to prevent a child.

The Jezebel! Lucien Canton was furious. The man standing in his office at the Provincial Bank of Truro looked away anxiously and Lucien tried to remember it was bad form to kill the messenger.

It was not the messenger's fault that Philippa had not been at Cambourne Hall when he'd arrived to deliver the note. It was not the messenger's fault that he'd followed her to St Just-in-Roseland and caught her in what seemed an obvious case of *in flagrante delicto* with her hand on the viscount's bloody cock. The messenger had assured him the little moment had been done in privacy and good taste. He'd been the only one to see them. Such assurances didn't change the fact that Lucien wanted to hit someone and since Valerian Inglemoore wasn't available at present, the messenger just might do after all.

Everything had been going well. He should have known that was when the bottom usually dropped out from beneath you. Philippa had rejected his marriage proposal out of hand so that she could go traipsing around Cornwall with the viscount. Good lord, she'd been seen at a peasants' fair fondling the man's private parts. It didn't matter that the messenger had been full of assurances that no one else had seen them. They'd been discreet. She'd refused his proposal because she'd felt he'd had nothing to offer her. That was about to change. She would discover shortly he had something she wanted quite desperately.

He would not be played as the cuckolded suitor. Everyone in London knew he'd been her strong right arm these past years. Everyone expected something to come of it. His reputation would suffer if he turned out to be nothing more than Lady Cambourne's jilt, to say nothing of his finances when the bank's board of trustees understood that he did not control the Cambourne mining interests.

He would confront St Just with his treason, force Philippa to barter for the man's freedom and then make sure there would be no happy ever after for them. St Just would not forgive Philippa if he believed it was by her hand that such treasonous issues had been brought up.

Fortunately, Lucien had the letter to infer such a thing. He would have his bank, his revenge and a wife too. Not a day would go by that Philippa wouldn't be reminded of the favours he'd done for her and how much she owed him. He would start by going to her as a wolf in sheep's clothing.

Philippa sat in the small sitting room she'd commandeered as a lady's parlour at the back of the house. The windows gave her a view of the back terrace where she could watch the men working on the new flower beds Valerian had designed. She could look up from her writing at the elegant escritoire Valerian had moved in there for her and see him at his labours on the lawn. All in all, it was a very domestic arrangement.

She was seldom disturbed in this room. She used it primarily when Valerian was out, as he was today, working in the ravine garden on the edge of the estate. And Beldon had taken himself off on long visits and explorations these last few days to give her and Valerian some privacy. Knowing this was her preferred time of day for correspondence, the maids left her alone as well. No one bothered her here unless something was wrong. Which was why she was surprised to see Steves at the door.

'Is something wrong with the dinner menus?' she asked with a pleasant smile.

'No, milady. This letter has arrived for you. It came by special messenger. I thought it might be urgent.'

Philippa looked at the envelope. It was from Truro. Her initial worry that something drastic was wrong at Cambourne eased. She didn't know anyone in Truro well enough to warrant a letter by special messenger. In fact, the only person she knew in Truro of any real significance was Lucien. But Lucien had no reason to send such a letter. The regular post would do for any business they might have.

Philippa opened the letter, reading the back first to see who it was from. Lucien.

Philippa flipped the paper over and began to read.

My dearest Philippa,

Thank you for your kind words and polite refusal of my proposal. I appreciate your considerate words as much as I regretted your need to decline. As for me, I shall remain your obedient friend and servant in the hopes that my offer might meet with your fondest reconsideration.

It is my sincerest hope that any impetuosity on my part might be forgiven. It is also my sincerest hope that you keep yourself safe. To demonstrate that sincerity, I feel compelled to bring you news of great concern regarding your family friend, the Viscount St Just. Lately, it has come to my attention that he is suspected of having dealt in some behaviour of a treasonous nature while serving Britain in the Balkans—something to do with a little town called Negush.

I do not know all the details or even how true such claims are. But I thought you should know. You know him better than I and are perhaps best placed to help exonerate him should these charges become more than speculation and rumours at Whitehall.

I would encourage you to be vigilant on your friend's behalf. Look for anything that might prove him innocent if need be.

I was surprised to discover you had gone to Roseland. Do have a care with your reputation. I would not wish to see you suffer simply by association should St Just be branded a traitor.

As always, I stand your true friend,
Lucien

Philippa clenched the paper, wrinkling the fine linen bond with the strength of her hand. Treason? What nonsense was this? But it wasn't exactly 'nonsense'. There was no reason for Lucien to make any of this up and, really, one couldn't fashion charges of treason out of whole cloth and expect to get away with it. If Lucien didn't think it was the truth, he'd hardly have bothered writing about it and sending the news by special courier.

That worried her. The letter had been sent with all haste possible. The letter had been written with the express intention of sharing that news with her. He'd made no mention of the bank or of any local news. In the past, the letters they'd exchanged had been full of such events. It was unlike Lucien to write an entire letter without making a single financial reference. She'd not known he was capable of it, in fact.

Worry twisted in her gut. Philippa looked at the little clock on the wall. Eleven. Valerian wouldn't be back until tea time, four hours away. Four hours to search the house, looking for some proof that it was all balderdash, whatever those charges might be. But she had no idea what she'd be looking for.

She was suddenly struck with the thought that she didn't know anything about what he'd actually done during his time abroad. In order to look for clues, one usually had to have something to start with. Philippa had nothing but the name of a place she'd never heard of.

She would start with that. There had to be an atlas in the library. Then she could practise how she'd ask the man she loved if he'd committed treason.

Chapter Fourteen

In the end, Philippa elected to say nothing. Valerian had returned late, barely in time for supper, out of sorts over a retaining wall in the ravine garden that had collapsed. A day of hard labour had hardly made a dent in the damage done to the eroding hillside.

Valerian's bad mood aside, Philippa reasoned she'd be better off waiting until she had proof of something before she brought the subject up. Otherwise, she'd have to confess her interest in the topic stemmed directly from the potentially spurious letter Lucien had sent. Knowing how Valerian felt about Lucien, she felt it best to leave Lucien's letter out of the situation. If she wanted to investigate Lucien's concerns, she needed to do it under her own power.

Philippa let Beldon carry the dinner conversation. He was animated about a meeting with an inventor by the name of William Bickford. 'He's created a method for inserting a strand of yarn into rope fuses that makes the fuse more predictable.' Beldon paused long enough to take a sip of wine. 'The funny thing is, Phil, he's from your area. He lives in Tuckingmill, outside Cambourne. He's just here on a visit with friends. You should meet him, help him get established. Can you imagine what this might mean for promoting mining safety?'

Of course she could imagine it. The tubes of reeds currently used as fuses for blasting were erratic. On several occasions they were known to go off too early, and on other occasions they went off after a long delay. Either way, men were hurt or killed by the faulty fuses. 'I should like to meet him,' Philippa said noncommittally.

Tonight, her mind had difficulty concentrating on business, her thoughts already occupied by Lucien's disturbing letter. Every time she looked down the table at Valerian, the thoughts kept creeping in. Had he committed treason? She knew very little of what he'd done in the diplomatic service of his country. This was difficult territory to navigate. He was a man of honour. His sacrifice for her family's greater good proved her initial instincts about him had not been wrong. However, she also understood that he valued honour above all things, including her opinion and her desires and his own.

From what she knew of her own experiences in political London, loyalty to one's country or party often conflicted with one's sense of honour. It was entirely possible that what Valerian viewed as the honourable path had, at some point, become a treasonous path. That particular juxtaposition concerned her gravely.

Before now, she'd always imagined traitors to be deceitful spies out to make a quick pound for selling out one's country. She was starting to see where that interpretation might be a bit limited in its scope. If the charges proved to be founded, how would the public see it? Would they share the same latitude she was willing to give or would they paint Valerian with a traditional traitor's brush? More than his reputation would be tarred. She knew very well the price for treason. Being a peer would not protect him.

She shuddered at the last, drawing a strange glance from Beldon. 'It's just a chill from the sorbet,' she said lightly, forcing her mind to push away such dire thoughts.

She was putting a very big cart before the horse with her suppositions and conclusions. She had taken the afternoon and discreetly searched the house, looking for any information that might help her understand Valerian's post and service. But she'd found nothing. She couldn't even find the place called Negush on any of the four maps of Europe Valerian possessed.

'Are you sure you're all right?' Valerian asked, too.

'Yes, both of you are old mother hens,' she teased and dipped her spoon into the sorbet to prove it.

Convinced, Valerian and Beldon returned to their

conversation about Bickford's fuse. 'Invention is one thing,' Valerian was saying, 'production is another. It won't matter how incredible an invention is if it can't be produced in quantities.'

Beldon waved his hand in a dismissive gesture. 'That's what has impressed me so much about Bickford. He's thought of everything. He's in the process of finishing his design on a machine that performs the task of winding rope around a central core of gunpowder, then winding a second strand of rope in the opposite direction to keep the fuse from untwisting. He's already talking about ways to waterproof the rope by using a special varnish. He's got the plans with him. He'll be in St Mawes for the rest of the week. We could ride over and see him, Val.'

'I'm free tomorrow. The materials for repairing the retaining wall won't arrive until the day after so there's nothing more I can do. Philippa, would you like to come?' Valerian inquired.

'I would, but the men are coming to hang the silk in the music room tomorrow. I should be here for that.' It would also give her a chance to look around the house to further assuage her fears. Perhaps it was a good sign that she couldn't find anything. Perhaps his diplomatic work had been as bland as all the reports indicated. Maybe he had spent all his time hosting parties and squiring around delegates' wives. That might not be all bad.

She was suddenly less jealous of his parade of

women if they'd kept him from harm. After all, how busy could he have been? He'd had time to visit Italy and study gardens. He'd mentioned at Lucien's that he'd been actively studying the piano. Those didn't sound like the hobbies of someone who had time to hatch a treasonous plot against the crown.

'You can advise me as to the wisdom of helping this Bickford with his invention, whatever he is calling it.'

'Safety rods,' Beldon put in.

'Safety rods,' Philippa repeated. 'If you like, you can write to Lucien and tell him about it. It might be the type of investment Danforth's new bank is looking for.' She made the offer to be helpful. It did indeed seem to do both sides a favour. Bickford would need funds to build a factory and Lucien needed Bickford's type of business to make the bank thrive.

But Valerian clearly disagreed. He pushed back his silver-stemmed sorbet dish and all but glared at her down the length of the table. 'I'd be very careful what I sent Canton's way.'

'He has money and good business sense. What could be the problem with that?' Philippa protested, not so much out of a need to stand up for Lucien, but out of dislike of having her judgement questioned.

'Too good, if you ask me,' Valerian said pointedly. 'Have you ever wondered why the financially savvy Mr Canton has his fingers in so many pies?'

Philippa leaned back in her chair and folded her

arms, entrenching. 'No, I have not thought about it beyond the simple fact that he understands wealth is based on diversified holdings. Apparently, you think otherwise?'

'I do think otherwise. I suspect he wishes to corner the market, as it were. From there, he could regulate the prices to his whim and squelch any budding competition.'

Philippa laughed. 'Hah, that is theoretically how such a manoeuvre works, but, realistically, it would be almost impossible to perform such a feat with mining. It wouldn't be enough to control the mines, you'd need the other industries too, the smelting and the gunpowder. And I don't see how it would be possible to regulate the new mines in South America. They'll always provide some level of domestic competition to keep the price of ore fair. Valerian, not even Lucien could pull something like that off.'

Valerian quirked an eyebrow. 'Really? Why do you think he was so interested in Danforth's bank? I rather suspect Danforth's arrival was less spontaneous than you might have been led to believe.'

'You're spinning out of whole cloth now, Val,' Philippa said. 'He'd have to control Cambourne to at least make a start and I am not sure I am interested in the merits of a cartel at this point.'

Valerian pushed back his chair with a rough shove, his eyes glittering like sharp, cutting emeralds. 'Why do you think he wanted to marry you?'

Philippa rose out of her chair, horrified. 'Why are you attacking him in this manner?'

'Why are you defending him so vigorously?' Valerian shot back.

Beldon rose, eyeing each of them charily. 'Let's take some time and think this through,' he said slowly. 'Somewhere along the line we stopped talking about Bickford's safety rods and started talking about something else. I am not convinced we're really talking about Lucien Canton's bid to establish a tin cartel.'

'My apologies,' Valerian said stiffly. 'I'll be in the music room.'

Philippa watched him go with a sigh and sat back down, suddenly weary now that the fight was over. Beldon was right. The fight had been about something else. 'He's upset about the garden wall,' Philippa said by way of a facile explanation for his outburst.

Beldon relaxed into his chair. 'Don't play me for a fool, Phil. Has something happened between the two of you? I thought things were going rather well.'

Philippa toyed with her spoon, drawing it through the melted remnants of her sorbet. 'Things were going well, but it is to be expected we'll have some rough times. Nine years is a lot of time to account for. We have to learn about each other again.'

Beldon would not be put off. 'Something has happened to make you question him again.' He shook his head. 'Certainly there are events in his life that you do not know about. But you know him and you know how Valerian would handle those events. You know that he can be trusted to act with honour at all times.'

'That does not reassure me,' Philippa said quietly. 'It is what concerns me the most. I had a letter from Lucien today.'

'Does Valerian know? That would explain his pique.'

'He might.' Philippa could see how that would be possible. Valerian may have asked Steves if there was any correspondence and Steves could have reasonably answered that there had been none but a letter from Truro for the Duchess. 'I never thought of Valerian as the jealous sort.'

'Of course not. Valerian is the least covetous man I know. But he's also the most protective. He doesn't trust Canton. Protection is honourable. Coveting is not. That's the difference between him and Lucien—one of them, at least.' Beldon shrugged.

Philippa stared at her brother. His insights, as usual, made perfect sense. When it came to people, Beldon was a genius. 'I think you could have been a splendid fortune teller, Beldon. You see people so much more clearly than the rest of us do.' She rose, laying her napkin on the table. 'Excuse me, brother. I have to go mend fences with Val.'

The music drew her down the hallway. Valerian was an exquisite musician, his playing both technically perfect and emotive. Tonight, he played a quiet nocturne.

She listened for a while at the doorway, unwilling to interrupt. 'The piece is very soothing,' she said softly.

'That's why I chose it. I hoped it would help clear my head and my heart,' Valerian said, his fingers still on the keys, his back to her.

'Has it?' Philippa moved to stand behind him, her hands on his shoulders, gently kneading away the tension there.

'To a certain extent.' Valerian sighed. 'That feels good. I think I will feel better once I apologise for my boorish behaviour.'

'I came to apologise for mine. I didn't mean to defend Lucien. He assures me that he remains my friend, but I think my refusal of marriage has fractured that friendship regardless. I have not sought him out, even in correspondence, since I declined his second proposal.'

'His second? I hadn't known.' Valerian stiffened, leery of such news.

'He asked again the last night in Truro. But I have refused him. He has no reason to hope that my feelings will change. However, he wrote today, citing his prolific friendship for me.'

Valerian nodded, confirming what she had suspected. 'Steves mentioned it in passing.' He put off her hands and stood. 'I am sorry for the way I behaved at supper, but I am not sorry about my motives for doing so. May we speak reasonably for a moment? Do you think our anger has subsided enough for that?'

Philippa took his arm and they began to stroll the halls, coming to the long portrait gallery that ran the length of the second floor. Their anger had indeed passed and the peace between them was a balm to her earlier agitation.

'What shall we talk about?' Philippa said after a while, sensing Valerian's reluctance to break the quiet.

'In all honesty, have you considered why Lucien felt compelled to offer for you?'

'I did think about it, but I could not come up with a reason beyond his need for an heir.'

'I did not say it well at dinner, but have you considered that the reason is that he would gain control of Cambourne when you married? Marriage to you would solidify the cartel's success. Without the Cambourne mining interests, the cartel is nothing but businessmen with venture capital. Without Cambourne, they can't regulate prices or control the supply and demand in the marketplace for ore.'

Philippa took a deep breath. 'No, I had not thought of that. I overlooked the issue of holdings simply because he had no obvious need for my wealth. He has plenty of his own.'

Valerian gave a deprecating snort. 'A man like Canton always wants more. He's greedy and ambitious. He can never have enough. I fear that that avarice puts you in danger, my dear.'

'I can handle Lucien,' Philippa said. 'You forget I've

been on my own for some time now. I know how to take man's measure.'

Valerian stopped their strolling and turned to face her directly, placing his hands on her shoulders. 'If you will not be guided by your lover, be guided in this by your friend and listen to my advice as that friend. Canton will not brook your refusal lightly, not because his feelings are hurt—I doubt the man has any—but because it now puts his purse at risk. He *must* have Cambourne or give up his dreams of a cartel entirely. Your refusal has put him in an untenable position. Short of trying to coerce you into selling out or breaking up the unentailed holdings, he has no options left.'

'Coerce?' Philippa said. 'I am far too intimidating to be forced.'

'Coercion doesn't have to be obvious, Philippa. It could be sabotage.'

Sabotage. Philippa blanched at the word. Surely Lucien would not betray her in such a way? He'd been a steady friend, someone she'd counted on in numerous ways. Friends didn't sabotage each other, they respected each other's decisions.

'You mean like causing accidents to happen at the mines?'

'Possibly.'

'Well, I wouldn't worry on that account. Accidents now hurt his profit, if he later acquired the mines.' No, she felt confident that Lucien would not resort to such ridiculously extreme tactics.

'What did Lucien write to say?' Valerian said, veering on to another topic of conversation.

'Only to reassure me of his friendship,' Philippa said, glossing over the letter's contents. She was more than glad she'd waited to discuss Lucien's concerns. Tonight was definitely not the time to mention them.

She had too much to think about. Valerian's comments had placed Lucien's letter in an entirely different light. She *had* thought that the letter seemed odd, not Lucien's usual style. Now she wondered if the letter hadn't been a strategy of some sort. Lucien would see Valerian as an obstacle. If Valerian were out of the way, perhaps Lucien believed she might reconsider his offer. But the consequences were too terrible to think of. She couldn't believe even Lucien would see a man dead or ruined simply to achieve a goal.

A shiver ran down her spine.

'Are you sure you're not catching a cold? That's the second time tonight,' Valerian inquired.

Philippa smiled up at him, playing the flirt. 'Perhaps I am a little chilled, after all. Why don't you take me to your chambers and warm me?'

Valerian flirted back readily. 'I do know a clever trick they use in the Danubian provinces during the cold winters for warming up people.'

Philippa gasped in mock modesty. 'Do tell!'

'Well, they take off all of their clothes and crawl beneath a blanket and hold each other.'

'It sounds scandalous.'

'Not scandalous, *scientific*. The belief is that the body of the warm individual is passed to the colder recipient. With clothes, so much heat is lost in the transfer.' Valerian made a great display of shaking his head. 'A shame for so much heat to go to waste.'

Philippa laughed for the first time since Lucien's awful letter had arrived. She put her arms about Valerian's waist. 'What are we waiting for? Do you by chance know a cure for lightheadedness?' she asked, teasing heavily.

'Why?' Valerian looked wary.

'Because I think I might swoon.' Philippa passed a dramatic hand over her brow and let Valerian take her full weight.

'Minx, you just want me to carry you to our room,' Valerian laughed at her theatrics.

With a quick sweep of his arm beneath her legs, he hefted her up, making it seem so easy. Philippa rewarded him with a kiss. 'I hear kisses heal almost anything.'

Valerian held her gaze, his eyes merry, but his voice soft. 'I've heard that about love, too.'

Philippa was glad he was holding her or she might have really swooned, so powerful was the effect of his simple words. He loved her. And the very knowledge of that held her fears at bay, like a night fire against the wolves.

Chapter Fifteen

Philippa was in the music room overseeing the hanging of the wallpaper and new curtains when the summons came. The usually unflappable Steves appeared to be slightly winded as he delivered his message. Philippa thought it highly likely he had run all the way from the front door.

'My lady, there is a woman here to see the viscount,' he puffed, trying to hide his rapid breathing.

Philippa began untying the apron she wore, her mind working quickly. The caller was unexpected. If Valerian had had an appointment, he would not have agreed to ride out with Beldon to talk with the fuse inventor. The caller was also a stranger. If she'd been from the area, Steves would have recognised her and have been less flustered.

'I shall see her, Steves. Did she have a card?' Philippa

said calmly. In spite of the spontaneous nature of the call, it was not beyond the realm of acceptability. There could be any number of reasons that a chance visitor had stopped at Roseland: a broken carriage part, a desire to see the gardens, or an old acquaintance passing through the area. Those things had happened often enough at Cambourne. The Duke had had an enormous number of acquaintances and they had on several occasions dropped by.

But Valerian hadn't been home long enough for that, nor had he publicly announced his return. She'd sensed he was waiting to make his return official once the Season was under way in London.

'Where did you put her? Does she have a name?' Philippa asked, smoothing her skirts and catching a glimpse of herself in a mirror to make sure she didn't have a bit of plaster in her hair. It wouldn't do to meet the caller, whoever she was, looking like the housekeeper.

'I put her in the small receiving room downstairs. She said her name was Lilya Stefanov.'

Worry came to Philippa for the first time. She started to understand the source of Steves's unease. The woman's name indicated she was foreign. Was she someone, then, from Valerian's past? She fought a sudden wave of nausea at the implications. Was this woman one of his reported lovers? Perhaps more than a reported lover? Surely they had shared some substantial connection if she felt she could call on him.

'Did she say what she wanted?'

Steves shook his head and said quietly, 'No, your Grace. However, she does have a young son with her.'

Philippa's stomach roiled again and she was doubly glad only toast and tea had appealed to her at breakfast. She chided herself. She was not acting like the Dowager Duchess of Cambourne. The Duchess would regally sweep down the stairs and take charge of the situation. She would not be standing in the music room letting nerves get the better of her.

The problem was, she hadn't thought of herself as the Dowager Duchess for more than a month. In the six weeks she'd been at Roseland, she'd been Philippa Stratten again, a woman in love and resident lady of the manor. She'd not thought of herself as anyone's duchess, widow or viscountess; she'd rather liked defining herself as a person instead of a title.

Now it was time to put the cloak of official authority back on. Philippa straightened her shoulders, reminding herself that it wasn't appropriate to show emotions or weakness in front of the servants. Loving Valerian had made her more careless than she'd realised over the past weeks. 'Have Cook send a tea tray to the parlour, Steves. We'll show our guest the best of Roseland's hospitality, whatever her mission may be. Tell Cook to put some of her special sugar biscuits on the tray and a cup of milk for the boy.'

Steves smiled his approval. 'Yes, your Grace,' he

said crisply, his relief evident that someone other than he was about to handle the delicate situation that had arrived on Roseland's doorstep.

Philippa drew a deep breath and headed downstairs. The parlour had been one of the first she'd re-done. She just hadn't planned on using it so soon to receive callers. Soft voices in a language she didn't recognise drifted out into the hall. Philippa was struck with a fresh thought. She hoped the woman hadn't come to tempt Valerian with any more treasonous activity. Philippa checked her thoughts and amended them. Assuming he'd already been tempted before.

'Good morning, Miss Stefanov.' Philippa swept into the room. 'Viscount St Just is not at home right now, but perhaps I can assist you.' She was the consummate polite hostess.

The woman on the new yellow striped sofa rose, smiling her relief. 'You are too kind to receive us.' The boy beside her stood stiffly at her urging. 'This is Constantine.'

'How do you do, Constantine?' Philippa greeted him. The poor boy was terribly uncomfortable, trying hard not to fidget in his suit of clothes. He was a handsome boy with thick, dark hair and dark eyes. She judged him to be seven or eight years of age. He was old enough to be Valerian's son, a child fathered a few years into his tour abroad. But the girl didn't seem old enough to be the boy's mother.

'Please, be seated. A tea tray will be here shortly

and you can refresh yourselves. Have you been in England long?'

The girl, for that was what she was now that Philippa had a moment to study her, shook her head. 'We arrived two days ago. We came straight here. We know no one else in this country.'

The tray arrived and Philippa used the time to assess the girl while the servants laid out the tea things. She looked to be in her mid-teens and uncommonly beautiful. Like the boy, she had ink-black hair. She wore it twisted up in a tasteful hairstyle with a pretty jewelled comb to fasten it. Her skin had a slight olive cast and was flawlessly smooth. And her clothes were well made. These two were not country peasants. Wherever they hailed from, they were people of means.

The boy was delighted with the milk and sugar biscuits. The girl smiled her thanks at the thoughtful gesture. 'Our journey has been long and we have not eaten as well as we should.'

She was brave and proud, Philippa thought, watching her over the rim of the tea cup. 'Where are you from? Your English is very good, but I detect an accent.'

The girl blushed. 'Please call me Lilya.'

'Is that a Russian name?'

'No.' There was a hint of defiance in her 'no'. Philippa wondered where that came from. 'It's a Balkan name, a Macedonian name.'

Philippa maintained her smile, but a slow coldness

began to spread through her. She could guess where this girl was from. 'I don't know terribly much about the Balkan region.'

A shadow of sadness passed over the girl's face. 'I am from a village that doesn't exist any more. It was called Negush, but it was destroyed. Since then, I've lived wherever there was peace.'

Philippa started at the mention of the village. She recognised it from Lucien's letter. Her stomach lurched. Was Valerian in true danger from something that had happened there? Was Lucien serious about what he'd uncovered? A thousand questions rioted through her mind. It took a large amount of self-control to keep from quizzing the girl. The truth about Lucien's claims likely sat across from her. Her curiosity raged. Philippa tamped it down, opting instead to be selfless. The girl had undergone a difficult journey and was now in foreign surroundings. She needed empathy, not an inquest.

'I'm sorry.' Philippa offered quietly. In spite of her concerns for Valerian, she felt her heart go out to the girl. Her phrase, 'I've lived wherever there was peace', spoke volumes about her struggles. Philippa could hardly begin to comprehend what that must have been like. She'd grown up during the wars with Napoleon, but that was different. The war hadn't been fought, thank God, on English soil. She'd been able to remain insulated from a first-hand encounter with the terrors of war.

Philippa set down her tea cup. 'I confess, I have a thousand questions for you.'

'Please, you may ask us anything,' Lilya said. 'But first, would you tell me your name?'

Philippa had the good grace to laugh at her oversight. She'd been so worried—still was worried—about what these newcomers would mean to Valerian. 'I'm the Dowager Duchess of Cambourne, but you may call me Philippa.'

Lilya's eyes widened with something akin to excitement. 'You're the one who has the brother, Beldon.'

Philippa was caught entirely off guard. That was the last thing she'd expected the girl to say. 'Yes. How do you know about my brother?'

The girl seemed to relax for the first time. 'Valerian used to tell us stories about the three of you.'

'Valerian.' She was quite free with his name. She did not call him by a title or his surname.

'I hope the stories were all good,' Philippa said wryly. 'Perhaps we should start with how you came to know the viscount?'

The girl's reserve was back and she sat straight as she told her tale. 'The viscount was a regular visitor at my father's house. We lived in the Negush district. We were Phanariots. Do you know the word?'

Philippa shook her head.

'The Phanariots were high-ranking Christians in the Ottoman system. Our family held an important position in the government. I suppose you could say we were a type of ruling elite. We had wealth and power and we controlled huge portions of business, especially in the area of shipping.'

Philippa nodded her understanding, noting how the girl spoke of these Phanariots in the past tense.

'Valerian came to our home to talk about British shipping and trade. He was a diplomat. He'd been charged to discover whether or not it would be profitable to establish a business relationship between us and the British government.'

The pieces were starting to come together. Philippa knew how valuable shipping routes were to the British government. But this charge seemed rather straightforward to carry out. It sounded as if the Phanariots had British sympathies.

'Valerian visited us often. I've known him since I was a little girl. I would practice my English with him. Languages were important in our house.' A wistful look passed over the girl's face and Philippa could well imagine she was recalling a happier time.

'Valerian befriended my father, Dimitri, and my Aunt Natasha. He stayed with us even after the negotiations proved to be unsatisfactory.'

'Unsatisfactory? In what way?' Philippa seized on the words.

'I was only eight, as young as Constantine is now. I hardly know exactly. But my father was furious. I do remember him shouting, "By God, we have six hundred ships between the Black Sea and Venice!"'

'But Valerian remained your family's friend?' Philippa pushed, wondering what would have caused him to pursue a personal tie.

'Right until the end. He risked everything for us. We would have died without him that last night.' Her face grew cloudy.

Philippa felt guilty for bringing it up. Perhaps she'd pushed too far on such short acquaintance. She wanted to ask more, but refrained. 'You're tired. Valerian won't be back until later in the day. He's gone to see an inventor with my brother. Perhaps you'd like to rest?' She did a quick mental inventory of the bedchambers upstairs. One of them had just been completed a few days earlier with fresh linens and paint. She would have the day maids Valerian had hired open up the nursery wing for the boy. He might enjoy the chance to be the master of his domain.

Lilya looked relieved at the suggestion. 'It has been an exhausting set of weeks.'

'Do you have trunks or any baggage?' Philippa inquired. No matter what this girl or boy were to Valerian, she could not send them away knowing they had nowhere else to go.

Lilya nodded. 'I left them at the posting inn in the village.'

'I'll send a cart for them. You will have them by

dinner. Until then, ask for anything you need,' Philippa offered graciously, leading them up the stairs.

The newly finished pale green room at the end of the hall was perfect for Lilya. A small sitting room opened on to a large, airy bedchamber that overlooked Valerian's prized herb garden. Philippa threw the long windows open to let the scent of lavender waft up from below. Lilya was enchanted.

'I'll have the nursery wing ready for you, Master Constantine, in a few hours, if you'd like,' Philippa said to the boy. Her curiosity was killing her. Was this solemn young boy with his dark hair and the beginnings of a broad-shouldered build Val's son? If so, there were a hundred other questions burning in her mind, not the least being who and where was his mother?

He nodded his thanks and Lilya quickly explained that his English was not that good. She gave an elegant shrug. 'I've taught him what I could, but…' Her voice trailed off and Philippa suspected that life spent running away from war zones allowed little time for formal schooling. It also struck her that times had changed for this apparently ex-class of ruling elite. Speaking any language other than the local tongues might call unwanted attention to two people who had their own reasons perhaps for remaining inconspicuous.

Philippa left them in the chamber. She glanced at the clock. She couldn't expect Beldon and Valerian for another two hours at the earliest. She felt a bit fatigued, too, after the interview with Lilya. She'd have liked to have lain down as well, but there was too much to do before Valerian returned.

She knew herself well enough to know that if she laid down she wouldn't sleep at all. All the thoughts rolling through her mind would keep her awake. She would be better off keeping busy. Philippa concocted a mental list in her head.

She would check on the workmen in the music room and tell them to be done by four o'clock. She wanted all the peace she could find for Valerian's return home. On that note, she stopped to report briefly to Steves and suggest he send a groom out to find Valerian. She penned a quick note to send with him. Valerian might appreciate being forewarned.

With that done, Philippa went to the kitchens to let Cook know there would be two more people for dinner. She left instructions for the table to be set with the best china and the good wine to be decanted for the occasion.

Finally, she went upstairs to see how the maids were progressing with the nursery. In hindsight, she'd wished she'd put the nursery wing higher up on the priority list for redecorating. But it had ended up one of the last, there being no hurry with it at the time.

Fortunately, it was not in bad shape. The paint was faded, but a good dusting and beeswax had made a lot of difference in a short time. Like most nurseries, this one contained a large centre room used for playing and for school work. Off the big room were a series of smaller bedrooms.

Philippa helped the maids remove the holland covers shrouding the chairs and tables in the playroom and then wandered on to take stock of the bedrooms. Some were empty, some were partially furnished. They'd probably never been completed. Valerian had been an only child. There'd been no need.

Philippa selected the largest of the four bedrooms for Constantine and called for a maid to help her move some furniture from the other rooms. When they finished, the room looked presentable, with a small chest of drawers and a bookcase to hold personal items.

The housekeeper brought fresh linens for the bed, and clucked appreciatively over the change in the quarters. 'This used to be young Master Valerian's room. You've done well in a short time. It looks very respectable.'

'I didn't know it was his room,' Philippa said thoughtfully. By the time she'd known Valerian he'd moved out of the nursery and she was too old to be in the habit of visiting boys' bedchambers. Thinking of Valerian playing here brought a smile to Philippa's lips. It would have been a cheery but lonely nursery.

'A sad thing it was too that there weren't brothers and sisters to fill the other rooms,' the housekeeper said briskly to cover the little catch in her voice. 'But he found you and the young baron. You've done well for him.'

Philippa coloured a bit at the housekeeper's praise. 'Thank you.'

'The viscount will be proud of what you've done today. It can't have been easy to be so kind to those people. But you've done it anyways. It's what the master would have wanted if he'd been home, I think.'

Philippa nodded. The staff was probably abuzz with speculation. Perhaps the housekeeper thought Philippa might share some information with her that she could take back to the staff. But Philippa knew no more than they did. Her own curiosity remained as unsatisfied as theirs.

Philippa went back out to the main room and turned about, studying their efforts. They had done well. Improvements could be made later, but, for now, the room was inhabitable. Still, she felt as if something was missing. Her eyes fell on the long window seat and the empty cupboards below. She knew what it was.

'Mrs Wilcox, are there any of the viscount's toys left somewhere?'

The housekeeper's face brightened. 'Yes. They're packed away in the attic. I'll send some footmen for them right away.'

Philippa was delighted with the crates brought to the nursery. She spent the remainder of the afternoon unpacking boxes, dusting off toy soldiers, a wooden chess set, and other myriad treasures for a boy Constantine's age. Soon, the cupboard beneath the window seat was filled and a few books lined the small bookcase in the bedroom.

* * *

She'd left strict instructions that she was to be notified the moment Valerian and Beldon were sighted, but the nursery windows overlooked the front drive and she saw them coming long before a footman could race up the three flights of stairs to tell her.

Careless of her appearance, Philippa sprinted down the stairs. Her note had been short, saying only that two unannounced guests had arrived from far away.

Valerian came through the door in a rush with Beldon close behind, his face anxious and his hair wind-tossed, evidence that the groom had found them. 'Is everything all right, Phil?' He gripped her hands hard, searching her face.

'I think so. It's hard to say,' Philippa said slowly. 'I've put her up in the green room and opened the nursery for the boy.' Now that he was here, she wasn't sure precisely what to say.

Valerian looked perplexed. 'A girl? A boy? Do they have names?'

'She says they're from Negush, that you knew their father.' Philippa cast about for the name. The girl had mentioned the man's name. 'Their name's Stefanov. Dimitri, that was the man's name. Yes, Dimitri Stefanov.'

'My God, they're here?' Valerian looked unsteady. Philippa couldn't tell if it was from genuine surprise or fear.

A young voice called out from the top of the stairs

in blatant delight. 'Valerian, we've come. Oh, thank heavens we've found you!'

Valerian looked beyond her shoulder, his eyes blazing with emotion, his grip quite shattering on her hand. 'Lilya! Constantine! You're safe. Thank God.' He moved past Philippa, his throat working hard and his arms wide open. The pair flew down the stairs to meet him and he enfolded them in his embrace.

Philippa watched the teary reunion. She'd seldom seen Valerian so deeply moved and the sight of it caused her own eyes to blur. He held them tightly, then Lilya stepped back slightly and Valerian knelt down eye level with the boy, his hands on the boy's shoulders. He was speaking the language Philippa had heard them speak in the receiving room earlier.

There was no mistaking the tears on Valerian's cheeks for anything other than joy as he spoke to the boy. Seeing them together, Philippa was overcome by the sensation that she was watching a father being reunited with his son.

Chapter Sixteen

Valerian rose from his crouch to face Beldon and Philippa, an arm around each of the visitors. 'I am pleased to introduce Beldon Stratten, Baron Pendennys, and Philippa Lytton, the Dowager Duchess of Cambourne.'

He was glad to see Lilya make a nice curtsy and that Constantine had manners enough to sketch a light bow. He gave Lilya credit for that. It was unbelievable that they were here. Even with Lilya's resourcefulness, the journey was an arduous one. For a young girl and a boy alone, the journey was almost beyond comprehension. They would not have had the means to travel easily in private coaches or the funds to stay at quality inns. He started to note how thin Lilya was, although it did not detract from her delicate beauty. It didn't matter. They were here now and he would take care of everything for them from now on.

Valerian had to slow his mind down before plans ran away with him. He'd do well to finish his introductions. 'Philippa, Beldon, this is Miss Lilya Stefanov and her brother, Constantine. They are my wards. Their father was one of my closest friends during my time in the Balkans.' He knew he was beaming with ridiculous joy but it was completely overwhelming to know they were here after years of separation.

He watched Beldon and Philippa's reactions. Beldon was normally a dab hand with manners, but he seemed quite tongue-tied as he greeted Lilya. Philippa's response was harder to gauge. She seemed relieved? Shocked? Then her eyes met his above the exchange of pleasantries and a warm smile lit her face especially for him. Whatever worries she'd had would have to wait until they were alone. For now, there were questions to answer and stories to tell.

Beldon had already begun. 'How did Valerian come to be your guardian?' he was asking Lilya.

Lilya looked at him for direction and Valerian felt guilty for not having mentioned if before. 'I am their guardian in the absence of any of their countless aunts and uncles,' Valerian offered, glossing over the fear that had prompted Dimitri to place the children in his care. Dimitri had been afraid the Turks would wipe out the entire family, leaving the children orphans if they lived at all. And Valerian had known in that part of the world, orphans were as good as dead.

Lilya inserted herself into the conversation. 'My aunts and uncles have generously taken us into their homes these last years, but now there is a new war between the Turks and the Russians. Nowhere is safe. This war won't be the last and it won't change anything. Not for people like us.' She turned dark, pleading eyes on Valerian. 'I know there is talk of peace, but upheaval takes many different forms. I had to try to make a better life for us.' She gestured to the silent Constantine.

'You are welcome here,' Valerian assured her. He knew all too well what the aftermath of so-called peace brought. Peace in the Balkans would net the Western powers a chance to insert their own economic revolutions into the area, which was exactly why the West had been meddling there in the first place. There would be 'upheaval'—as Lilya called it—of the social and economic type for years. But perhaps the bloodshed would be less and, after a while, perhaps even the quality of life would be better. A man could make himself a fortune in post-war economies, but such places were not safe for a woman or a child.

Philippa gently ushered them upstairs and suggested everyone change for dinner. Valerian was grateful for her thoughtful intervention. In the midst of all the excitement, he'd forgotten they were still standing in the middle of the wall.

* * *

Valerian washed and changed as quickly as his valet would allow it. He wanted a chance to speak to Philippa before dinner. It could not wait until tonight, when he would share her bed.

Philippa was sitting before her dressing table, letting the maid do her hair when he came in. She wore a pale sage-coloured dressing gown of silk that fell softly over the full swells of her breasts, reminding Valerian of how delectable her body was. He felt his own body stir in longing. He wanted to dismiss the maid and take his ease. Was that a trick of the mirror or did her breasts look fuller? He had an irresistible urge to palm them and test them himself.

'Val.' Philippa turned from the mirror and murmured a few words to the maid.

'You saved me the effort of doing that myself,' Valerian joked, taking a seat on the bed as the maid shut the door behind her.

'I assumed you needed to talk.'

Valerian nodded. 'I need to thank you for all you did today. My valet insisted on regaling me with all your efforts. According to him, as he heard it from Mrs Wilcox, you left no detail overlooked, from the dinner menus to getting chambers opened up, even the nursery.' Valerian paused here and reached for her hand. 'My valet says that you behaved honourably and denied the guests nothing, not even when there was speculation the boy was my bastard son.' He said it in kindly tones. But Philippa tensed.

He'd had to drag that confession out of his valet. His valet had suddenly fallen silent at some point in their very one-sided conversation, aware that he'd said too much. But Valerian had not let him stop. It explained the odd look on Philippa's face downstairs. She'd thought it was possible.

'His dark hair and age made it a distinct possibility,' Philippa answered. 'But, Val, I did not condemn you for it. If Constantine had been your son, I could not blame you for that. I had no claims on you during those years. It is not realistic to expect you would form no attachments.'

'You are too kind, Philippa. I hardly deserve it.' Especially, Valerian thought, knowing that she understood him to have been a very different man during that time, thinking that he'd truly shunned her.

'Do you have any more secrets, Val?' Philippa queried.

'None I can think of at the moment.' Valerian drew her to him, settling her on his lap. 'But thinking is deuced difficult when I am so distracted.' He kissed her neck, his hand working at the belt of her robe. His need for her had intensified to the point he knew he couldn't control himself for the duration of the evening. If he didn't have her now, he'd be sneaking off with her for a quick tumble on the billiards table.

Philippa laughed between kisses. 'Do you think there's time?'

'Steves won't serve dinner without us.' Valerian grinned and rolled her on to her back.

If they were twenty minutes late coming down to the drawing room where the others patiently waited, or if anyone noticed that Valerian's cravat was tied in a less than complicated knot, no one said anything.

Conversation hovered around Lilya's journey and news of acquaintances Valerian knew. Occasionally, he'd lean over to Constantine, who sat on his left and say something in Koine, the language spoken by the Phanariots. He would have to see to tutors for the boy immediately so that Constantine could start learning English. He wondered where he'd find an English tutor who spoke one of the Balkan languages. Constantine spoke some Turkish and Russian. Surely there was someone in London or at one of the universities who would be able to converse with him?

'You still remember!' Lilya was delighted to hear Koine. She directed the rest of her comment to the table at large. 'Valerian has the most wonderful command of languages. He learned Koine while he was with us, but he also speaks French and German and some Russian and Turkish too.'

Valerian felt uncomfortable under the aegis of her praise. Philippa was smiling at him. 'I had no idea, aside from the French,' she said.

'It seemed the best way to accomplish my work,'

Valerian said shortly. 'One can hardly be assured of fair negotiations, even with a translator present, if one doesn't know the language.' Beside him, a tired Constantine yawned. Valerian was thankful for the well-timed interruption.

Philippa and Lilya rose. 'Let's get Constantine settled for the evening while the men have their port,' Philippa suggested. 'Don't take too long,' she instructed as she led a sleepy Constantine from the room.

For a moment Valerian let his mind fantasise that it was his son and his wife heading upstairs. Those kind of domestic fantasies had taken up a considerable amount of his time lately. Whenever he saw Philippa in her little office or talking to the housekeeper about menus or arranging flowers for the many vases sprinkled about the house, he could not imagine Roseland without her.

'German? You learned German?' Beldon was saying.

'Yes. It wasn't that hard. English came from German, you know.' Valerian dragged his thoughts back to the present.

Beldon was thoughtful for a moment, studying his friend. 'Is that why you were in London at Christmas?'

'Whatever can you mean?' Valerian schooled his features into a look of utter confusion, as if he could not grasp the connection between his fluency in German and being in the capital in December.

Beldon wasn't fooled for a moment. 'It was. There had been a rumour that the Russians and the Turks were willing to negotiate peace. Britain and France were to broker the treaty. Those talks are in process right now. The papers are calling them the "London Protocols".'

'One would hardly need to speak German for that,' Valerian said, pushing the remark aside as he reached for the decanter of brandy. Talk about his diplomatic skills always made him self-conscious. He didn't want people making the mistake of thinking he'd been a modern-day knight, dashing around broken kingdoms and restoring peace with his diplomacy.

Beldon toyed with the stem on his brandy snifter. 'Unless, of course, one was talking with Prince Otto about overseeing an independent Greek kingdom. Then German might come in handy.'

'Yes, well, perhaps I had a small hand in that. The German delegates needed an escort and it seemed as good a time as any to return home.'

Beldon chuckled. 'You're positively astounding, Val. Why so shy about your accomplishments? Why did you let the gossip paint you in another light?'

'It suited my cover at the time. It's not all untrue, at any rate. In the beginning, my uncle needed me to act as a host and I needed to learn quite a lot about the business of international politics. I spent a vast amount of time at parties, listening and learning; becoming self-educated about alliances and the people behind them. I'm sure from the outside, it appeared that I was doing little but enjoying myself.'

'Well, I am proud of you and Father would have been too,' Beldon said charitably.

'I think its time to join the ladies.' Valerian swiftly redirected the conversation. He didn't want praise. Beldon couldn't realistically give it to him anyway. Beldon only knew a tiny portion of what he'd been involved in. Beldon only knew that he spoke several languages and had participated in a few high-profile negotiations. Beldon didn't know about the diplomacy conducted at knifepoint, gunpoint, or sword point. Beldon didn't know about the men he'd killed.

He wondered what Beldon's reaction would be if he knew about the night in Negush when Valerian had turned his blade on British allies to save rebels. For that matter, what would Philippa think?

In the music room, Philippa was chatting easily with Lilya and it did Valerian's heart good to know that Philippa and Lilya had taken to each other so well. He hoped Philippa would be able to guide Lilya through a Season next spring. Lilya would be eighteen and it would be high time to help her find a husband and settle her life in England.

Valerian played the piano for a while, letting the ladies talk. Beldon read quietly, casting a furtive look at Lilya every few moments. Valerian had never seen his friend quite so taken with a woman before and he found it amusing. Beldon spent so much time studying others and watching the drama of their lives unfold; he seldom gave his own life the same consideration. It would serve him right to finally have some drama of his own. Perhaps while Philippa was matchmaking for Lilya, she might do a little matchmaking for Beldon.

This time next year was promising to be very interesting. Valerian stumbled over a stanza, recognising certain assumptions about that claim. He was assuming Philippa would be married to him. This time next year, she'd be the Viscountess St Just and in a position to help his young ward come out. It was time to ask her. There was no more reason to put off proposing. Her actions today proved that she had no further reservations about him.

But he should wait a few days, let the excitement of Lilya and Constantine's arrival wear down. She needed to see the proposal as something between them, born of their love. He didn't want her to think for a moment he wanted to marry her because he needed help with his wards. Lilya would shortly move on to be mistress of her husband's home. But Constantine was young. He'd be a long-term responsibility. Valerian knew such a responsibility would be asking a lot of Philippa, but she'd been generous with the boy today and she'd genuinely enjoyed the children at the St Piran's Day fair.

The situation with his wards wasn't the only reason for delay. There was one last secret to share with Philippa before the path was clear to claiming her. And he had to share that secret soon.

He smelled lavender and knew Philippa was behind

him before she laid her hands on his shoulders. 'Your playing is lovely, but it's been a long day. Lilya and I are going to bed.'

Valerian stood to wish them goodnight, noting that Philippa did look fatigued tonight. She was usually so energetic, but the day's exertions had left signs of weariness about her eyes and she seemed paler than normal. It was all understandable given the demands of the day.

'May I come to your room?' Valerian asked, *sotto voce*.

Philippa gave him a wan smile. 'I think it would be best if you didn't.' She gave a slight nod, indicating Lilya. 'I'll want to be available if she or Constantine need anything during the night. Sleeping in new places can sometimes take getting used to.'

'I will miss you.' Valerian covered her hand with his where it rested on his sleeve.

In part, he was relieved by her decision. He feared the nightmare. He'd not dreamed it since Philippa's arrival. But all the talk of the past at dinner and seeing the Stefanov children again had brought those concerns to the fore. Before he could propose to Philippa, he had to tell her about the night in Negush. It would only be a matter of time before Lilya confided in Philippa. He wanted no secrets between himself and Philippa when they wed. Tomorrow, he told himself. He would find a way to tell Philippa tomorrow.

* * *

Philippa's maid woke her at nine o'clock the next morning, under Philippa's strict instructions. She'd been in the habit of oversleeping lately and was determined not to laze the morning away. In Philippa's opinion, nine o'clock was late enough. She'd prefer getting up at seven or eight. A note, and a yellow rosebud tinted with pink at the edges, waited for her on the small table near the window.

'What's this?' Philippa asked, crossing the room to look at the envelope.

The maid giggled. 'It's from his lordship. He had me bring it in so you'd have it when you woke up.'

Philippa smiled and opened the envelope. 'He wants me to join him for breakfast on the back terrace.'

'It's a beautiful morning for it,' the maid said, throwing back the curtains to reveal the sun. 'Shall I lay out the jonquil muslin?'

'Perfect. A sunny dress for a sunny day.' Philippa's pulse raced at the prospect of a breakfast with Valerian. Something was afoot, she could sense it.

She arrived on the back terrace thirty minutes later almost breathless from her flight down the stairs. She stopped to gather herself at the French doors. The sight that met her gaze almost undid her, so moved was she by it.

A white-clothed table set with breakfast china and crystal glass sat under the Chusan palm, looking like something out of an Italian painting. But what held her abject attention was the man standing beside it, his back to her as he surveyed the lawns.

She'd thought Valerian handsome as a youth, but none of that compared to the manly beauty he exuded now. This morning, his hair was brushed forward on to his forehead in raven-black waves, the way she liked it best. He'd been for a ride and was still dressed in his tall boots and riding jacket, looking like a prince of the world.

Philippa went to him, wrapping her arms about his lean waist and laying her head against the broad strength of his back. 'Good morning, Val. This is lovely.'

Valerian turned and kissed her gently. 'Good morning—did you sleep well?'

'Yes. I feel much recovered.' Philippa smiled easily and sat in the chair he held out for her. 'And you, did you sleep well?'

'As well as a man can when he has so many things on his mind,' Valerian confessed.

Indeed, he looked slightly ragged about the edges, Philippa thought after a good look at his face. His jaw was smooth, evidence that his valet had been up early this morning, but there were the beginnings of tired circles beneath his eyes. 'You should have come to me.'

'I needed time alone to think.' Valerian shook his head. 'I needed time to think about us.' He passed her a basket of warm toast covered with a cloth napkin.

'You've been at Roseland for nearly two months. I

can't imagine this place without you. You've been generous with your time. I know Cambourne is a large estate. But I can't accept the idea of you leaving here.'

Philippa lifted the napkin and reached for a slice of toast. She furrowed her brow. There was a small box of sorts beneath the piece she'd taken. 'What's this?' She took the square box out.

'Something I should have given you years ago. I had it with me the night of the Rutherfords' ball,' Valerian said quietly, motioning for her to open it.

She flipped the lid up to reveal a ring set with a tiny band of diamonds surrounding an emerald. 'It's beautiful.' She shot him a questioning look. 'What does this mean, Val?'

'It means I want to marry you. But there is something I need to tell you first so that you can make a fully informed decision about whether or not you want to marry me.'

The last bit took some sparkle off the proposal. It made her think of Lucien's letter. Was he going to confess to something terrible or was there a logical explanation behind it? Perhaps Lucien was just grasping at straws because he felt he'd been jilted.

Philippa set down her toast and folded her hands. 'More secrets, Val?' she tried to tease.

'Something like that.' Valerian looked pained as he took a moment to collect himself. Philippa's heart lurched. She wanted to comfort him and she feared the worst.

Valerian drew a deep breath and began. 'Lilya's father, Dimitri, was part of a rebel force that tried to throw off Turkish rule. They were successful at the start. The rebels were organised and the district of Negush was liberated from the Ottomans in 1822. That victory was followed by another in the Voden district, but the Ottoman army was too large for the rebels to stand against for long.

'The Turkish army sent delegates to speak to the rebels. The rebels were offered terms of surrender and a peaceful return to Ottoman rule. I was with the delegation that went to meet Dimitri's group. I had two years' experience in the field by then and was considered more than a junior aide. After the first few months in Vienna, my experience had been beyond the ballrooms, in the little villages where the real living took place. I was selected to go because I knew those men. I spoke their language. For their sakes and their families, I hoped they would be guided by my influence. They were not.

'The retribution the Ottoman army meted out to them was horrific. Villages were plundered, women and children were killed. The army finally advanced to Dimitri's village in Negush. He'd been taken prisoner earlier and I had seen him just once. He made me swear to look after his family. He knew what was coming and that he faced certain death.'

A sound at the door intruded. Philippa looked away from Valerian, startled by the noise. Steves rushed forwards, a thousand apologies falling from his lips. 'My lord, they would not wait to be received. My lord…'

A large group of men flooded on to the terrace behind Steves, led by none other than Lucien Canton.

Valerian rose, placing himself as shield between Philippa and Lucien. His face was grim, set in threatening lines. But Philippa rose beside him, lacing her hand through his. Fear lanced through her. She wished she'd told Valerian about the letter. Lucien wasn't here to squabble over her. He was here for Valerian. 'I love you, Val,' Philippa whispered hastily. His hand tightened around hers in response and then he let it go.

'What is the meaning of this, Canton? You cannot just invade a man's home at will.' He crossed his arms, looking imposing and making the most of his two-inch height advantage over Lucien.

Canton thrust forwards a legal-looking document. 'I find anything is possible when one has a warrant for arrest,' Canton said icily. 'The rules no longer apply to you, St Just. You're under arrest for a crime of the highest order.'

Valerian managed to not look surprised. He merely raised his eyebrows and said, 'What would that be?'

Lucien met him with a level stare. 'That would be treason, my lord.'

Chapter Seventeen

'Treason? On what grounds?' Valerian responded in a tone that suggested he found the claims laughable.

Lucien was not appreciating the humour Valerian found in the situation. Philippa fought the urge to warn Valerian not to toy with Lucien's temper overmuch. Valerian might not be concerned, but Philippa was scared. This was her fault. She should have been more discreet when refusing Lucien's proposal. She should not have come to Roseland so soon after rejecting Lucien, giving him the impression she'd chosen Valerian over him. She should have told Valerian about the letter. He would have been prepared.

'I do not care for your naïve claims of innocence, St Just. You know exactly what you've done. And I know it too. You killed British allies at the Negush Uprising in 1822 for the express purpose of assisting the rebellion,' Lucien spat out.

Philippa felt Valerian stiffen beside her. 'How convenient it must be to label someone a traitor for unproved suppositions that occurred eight years and two thousand miles away,' Valerian snapped. 'I had no idea it was so easy to paint someone with the traitor's brush these days,' he mocked. 'Now, get out while you can. My footmen will not hesitate to use force.'

'And neither will we.' Lucien gestured to the men with him. 'I've brought a few of his Majesty's finest to ensure that you come with us in one way or another. Although you think the claims are flimsy, there are those in power who believe the claims are well substantiated,' Lucien said with a sneer.

'Did your father get you the warrant?' Valerian would not be cowed by the Lucien's assertion. Philippa would have laughed if the situation wasn't proving to be so dire.

One of the soldiers stepped forwards. 'I am sorry, milord, for the inconvenience. You will have to come with us and explain yourself to the justice system.' He held out cuffs. 'If you would please come peaceably.'

'Where are you taking him?' Philippa stepped around Valerian, cold horror knotting in her stomach.

'To London. It is where all good traitors are tried. And hung,' Lucien added.

'Stop this right now, Lucien. You've gone too far and you have no proof, only suppositions,' Philippa tried vainly to reason. She could not believe Lucien would do this. The wonderful, sunny morning was turning nightmarish.

For the first time since he'd intruded on to the back terrace, Lucien seemed to notice her. Philippa did not drop her gaze from his intense stare. She was not certain what Lucien would do in regards to her. She expected he might rail at her in his jealousy. She thought he might bring up the damning letter he'd sent warning her. But Lucien did something worse than what she anticipated.

'Gentlemen, if you would excuse me. I would like a private word with the Duchess.' He was all politeness and manners. 'Perhaps we could step inside?' he suggested when she hesitated.

Valerian looked ready to tear Lucien to bits. 'If you harm her, I will see you dead.' Valerian's eyes flashed with menace as Lucien offered her his arm.

'Dig a little deeper, St Just,' Lucien snarled before raising his voice. 'Did you hear that, gentlemen? The viscount is threatening me with bodily harm.'

Once inside, Lucien faced Philippa with an inscrutable expression. 'Philippa, I am sorry you had to be here for this. I would have spared you if I could have. I did try to warn you.' Lucien was all sympathetic friend.

'Don't take him. You don't need to do this,' Philippa pleaded, hoping for a moment his guise as friend was sincere.

'I cannot forgo a clear duty to my country,' Lucien

countered. 'In some way that would make me a traitor too, wouldn't it? A type of accessory to treason, I think. Dishonour comes in many forms in this world, Philippa. There are those who commit the acts and those who stand by and watch them without doing anything.' Lucien smiled and reached out a hand to touch her hair. 'You look lovely today. I've missed you.'

Philippa swallowed hard and fought the urge to flinch. How could she ever have thought this man was her dear friend? But Valerian needed her and she would gain him nothing if she lashed out at Lucien now. She did not miss the import of Lucien's message. He had not been talking about his obligations. He'd been talking about her. If he dared to come into a man's home and arrest him in front of friends, he would not hesitate to haul her off too.

She saw clearly the choices he was presenting her with. She could fight for Valerian and find herself facing scandal if not worse, or she could keep quiet.

'I will protect you, Philippa,' Lucien said, divining her thoughts. 'I won't tell St Just about the letter I sent you.'

'He knows about the letter,' Philippa snapped out, but it was a weak play and she knew it.

Lucien easily called her bluff. 'Yes? And the contents of the letter? Does he know those too?' He shook his head. 'I didn't think so. How do you think St Just would feel if he knew? Perhaps he would feel betrayed. Perhaps he'd even think you had a hand in this, that whatever feelings you professed to have were a lie simply to get close to him and steal a confession.' Lucien sighed heavily.

'This will not go down as the best day of his life. I almost pity the man. He's lost his freedom, his dignity—I am sorry about the cuffs, but they are necessary, my dear—and he's lost the woman he loves.'

Philippa's anger sparked. She'd never wanted to do violence to another person as much as she wanted to hit Lucien Canton at that moment. She was no fool. She saw all the implications of his subtle blackmail. She'd been right on the terrace. Lucien was doing this because of her. This was all her fault. But she could say nothing without ruining any hope she had of seeing Valerian safe again.

'I will protect you, Philippa,' Lucien repeated.

She wanted to scream out she didn't need his protection. She wanted to scream that she knew why he wanted to keep her separate from this travesty he was wrecking on Valerian. He wanted her mines and he couldn't have them without a legally binding commitment from her and Lucien Canton couldn't be associated with someone under the cloud of scandal. It would be bad for business. But she could say nothing.

The implicit devil's deal was struck and they returned to the terrace. Philippa was glad to see Beldon had made his way through the crowd and now stood with Valerian in soft conversation. Apparently, without

Lucien to goad them, the men had been unwilling to forbid Valerian to speak with anyone.

Valerian caught sight of her immediately, his gaze roving her face, looking for something. But Philippa had nothing to show him. She kept her face as blank as possible. Her little part in all this was embarrassing. As for the rest of what had passed inside, Valerian didn't need to be told. He would be able to piece it all together soon enough. He'd been right from the start about Lucien's avaricious nature.

'Thank you, gentlemen. The lady is understandably overwrought,' Lucien explained glibly to the soldiers. 'Now, if Pendennys will step aside, we can get on with our unpleasant business. It's a long trip to London. I want to make the most of the daylight.'

'Lay out your proof, Canton.' Beldon spoke up this time. 'You cannot haul a man out of his home without a legitimate case.'

'I don't need to answer to you, Pendennys. I have already offered sufficient proof to those in power. I wouldn't have been granted the warrant otherwise.' He motioned to the men. 'Take him. I am done with all this stalling.'

A soldier stepped towards Valerian. Beldon threw a fist to the man's jaw, sending him reeling backwards. It was all the tension on the terrace needed to light the fuse. Beldon was in the thick of it with Valerian, swinging hard rounders. Footmen joined the fray.

Philippa stepped backwards, removing herself from the fight. The last thing Beldon and Valerian needed was for her to get in the way. That was when she saw Lucien draw out a gun. There was no doubt who his target was.

She couldn't let it happen. She would not let Valerian die on his beautiful back terrace under his Chusan palm. Philippa screamed a warning. It was enough to halt the fray for an instant. 'He's got a gun!' The words rushed out in a hurry.

Valerian took a look at Lucien, immediately taking in the danger. But his fear was for her, not himself. Beldon started towards Lucien. Valerian shook his head. 'No, Beldon. I think I'd best go with them. I won't have you or Philippa hurt on my behalf.'

Philippa ran forwards, but Beldon grabbed her, whispering, 'No, Phil. We can't help him, not yet.'

Beldon was right, but it was a bitter task to stand by and watch Valerian roughly imprisoned in handcuffs and marched from his lovely home to be stuffed unceremoniously inside the dark coach that waited in the drive.

On the stairs in the hall, Lilya watched the scene, pale faced and frightened. 'His cloak,' she whispered as Beldon and Philippa followed the last of the soldiers outside, unwilling to let their friend out of their sight until the last possible moment. Philippa looked up blankly at the girl. Lilya nodded and thrust the cloak into her hands.

Beldon took it from her and went down the steps, having the forethought to lay it across Valerian's lap in the carriage. Philippa was glad for his quick thinking and for Lilya's. At least now he'd be warm. With any luck, the soldiers wouldn't think to search the cloak and perhaps Lilya had had enough time to put a few things in it.

As for herself, Philippa had to get her thoughts well in hand. She would be of no use to Valerian if she gave into the guilt and panic that threatened to swamp her. She watched the unmarked coach disappear on to the road, thinking of Valerian alone, surrounded by his enemies and no way to defend himself.

'Lucien means to see him dead in some fashion or other.' The thought hit her all at once and it was all it took to galvanise her into action.

'We won't let it happen,' Beldon said staunchly beside her. But she noted he didn't bother to contradict her with soothing claims.

Lilya joined them on the front steps. 'Valerian is a strong man. He is resourceful.'

Philippa turned to the girl. 'I am sorry this happened. It's not much of a welcome for you. You did well to think of his cloak.'

Lilya shrugged and met Philippa's gaze meaningfully. 'In my country, this happens often. We are always ready.'

'You were with him that night in Negush,' Philippa said. It wasn't really a question. She was starting to see how the disaster had unfolded. 'Come inside and tell us about it. Perhaps there is something there that can help us.'

They rang for tea out of habit. None of them were particularly hungry, but it gave Cook something to do and the household a way to return to normal after the brawl on the back terrace. Everyone was anxious and Philippa knew the best way to beat anxiety was to keep busy.

'My father had been taken prisoner in earlier fighting. Valerian had been allowed to see him once. He promised my father he'd protect us. The army was coming. There was no way to escape it. I was nine, I think. Constantine was a baby, and my brother Alexei was twelve.' Lilya stopped here, struggling for composure.

Philippa shot Beldon a confused glance. She had not heard of the older brother before. 'Did Alexei stay in the Balkans?' Perhaps the girl was homesick for her family.

'No.' Lilya said quietly, staring into her teacup. 'He and my Aunt Natasha were killed that night. We'd all have been killed if Valerian hadn't been there.' She went on with her story, telling of the fire and the fighting, how her Aunt Natasha had held off two Ottoman soldiers with a sword, how Valerian had arrived, slashing and killing like a berserker.

Valerian had got them to the relative safety of a copse, but the fighting had drawn too near and their hideaway had been invaded by Ottomans intent on blood. 'Natasha fell and Alexei picked up her sword. He fought back to back with Valerian. He fought well, but he was too young to fight with such a heavy weapon for long. Valerian killed several soldiers before the others fled the copse. Then he found our relatives who saw us to safety. He went back, though. The army was expecting him. I imagine he went back to the embassy shortly afterwards. His work was done on that mission.

'He didn't forget us. When he knew where we were, he sent clothes and food. He even came to visit us a few times when his work brought him into the area. On those visits, he gave us money. He kept us alive. Our circumstances had been greatly reduced after the uprising. We learned later that he had seen to a decent burial for Alexei and our aunt and that he was with my father at the last.'

After hearing Valerian's part of the story that morning, Philippa could accurately guess what the 'last' had been. Of course Valerian had done all that at personal risk and expense to himself. There was never a man more true to his friends than Valerian. He did not deserve to suffer for his kindnesses.

'But it is true, he killed Turks,' Beldon put in.

Lilya nodded. 'To save us.'

'The Turks aren't even our allies any more, which is what makes the situation so damnable,' Beldon huffed. 'There should be a statute of limitations on these sort of things the way alliances shift these days. After eight years of no one noticing, no one caring, it seems ridiculous that one good man should be brought to task for such a thing.'

'Lucien wouldn't care if it wasn't for me.' Philippa put in softly. 'He's doing this for spite.'

'More than spite, Phil. You can't take all the blame. Lucien believes Val stands in the way of his progress.'

'I think we have to go after Lucien,' Philippa said after a while. 'The charges of treason won't stick. Val has friends in the government who won't allow this to go very far once they hear of it. It's too bad his uncle is still abroad. But even so, there are people who can appeal once we're in town. No one is interested in calling a hero a traitor. Lilya will tell her story, we'll manage a few people in high places and the charges will go away accompanied by a nice public apology. Lucien must surely know this. The charges will stir up a short scandal but nothing more. In the end, they're only a red herring.'

Beldon nodded. 'I agree. Lucien does know all this. He is just buying time. A trial would be laughable. Perhaps he can manage a hearing, but he knows the charges are too frail for a full-blown trial. He means to see Valerian dead long before the charges are heard. Once Val is in prison, any number of unfortunate incidents can occur without anyone paying close attention to them.'

It was as she feared. Philippa felt her body grow cold. Her fingers became ice. Lucien meant to do murder. What could she do to stop him? To change his mind? She'd do anything, give anything to protect

Valerian. She cast about in her mind for an offering. 'I will sell him the mines if needed.' It was all she could think of.

Beldon gave her a black look. 'While the sentiment is heartfelt, Phil, I dislike the idea of dishonour prospering. There's no guarantee that will stop Canton in the future. We don't want him to be able to blackmail you or Valerian in the future.'

'I have a plan, then, Beldon. You go to London and keep Valerian safe. I'll go to Truro and see if I can find anything that might be useful to pressure Lucien. I'll meet you in London after that.' It wasn't much of a plan, but it was a start.

'Agreed.' Beldon turned to Lilya. 'Will you be all right here?'

She was white-faced, her hands clenching the tea cup so tightly it was in jeopardy of shattering. 'I am coming with you. I will go to Truro with the Duchess. Valerian is my friend. He protected my family and now it is my turn to protect him.' Her voice was firm, but her gaze wavered in the direction of Constantine.

Philippa smiled approvingly. 'I will welcome your company. The housekeeper will delight in looking after Constantine.'

'I will leave right away.' Beldon rose. 'On horseback, I can catch the coach by nightfall. No one can deny me the right to stay at an inn of my choice. So be it, if it happens to be the same one Lucien is at.'

'I'll send a note for you to give to Valerian. There are things he must know,' Philippa said quickly. 'Lilya, start packing our things. We'll leave after luncheon for Truro.'

An hour later, Beldon hugged them each goodbye in the drive and vaulted up on to the back of his hunter, a horse named Hercules, known for its endurance over long distances.

Philippa had no doubts about the horse's ability to catch up with the coach.

Beldon carried with him a valise strapped to the back of the saddle and a letter in his pocket that confessed the contents of Lucien's letter and one last secret.

Philippa raised her hand to wave as her brother clucked Hercules into motion, the sunlight dancing off the brilliant emerald she wore on her finger.

Chapter Eighteen

Valerian kept his gaze fixed on a spot on the carriage wall, his hands surreptitiously gripping the cloak Beldon had passed to him at the last moment. The day was mild, but come evening he'd be glad of the cloak's warmth. He had no reason to expect any courtesy from Lucien, who seemed committed to playing the righteous patriot to the hilt. The iron cuffs were an indignity that could have been done without, but Lucien was intent on making the experience as degrading as possible. He was meant to be put on display as a dangerous prisoner.

A man sat opposite him in the carriage, the other men and Lucien rode on horseback outside in the crisp spring air. Valerian ignored the man, keeping his gaze on the mark on the carriage wall, his thoughts fixed elsewhere, so that his mind was free although his body was trapped.

It was a trick Dimitri had told him about when he'd seen him that last time in prison before the execution. It seemed ironic that he was ostensibly facing the same end as Dimitri and just days after Dimitri's son and daughter had arrived.

For the first part of the journey, he allowed himself to think about Philippa and the promising start of the morning. He stored up images of her, of Roseland, of Lilya and Constantine, and all the things he loved. Night would assuredly come and sleep would not. He did not dare let it, for fear of the nightmare, for fear of giving Lucien some evidence that could be twisted into incriminating proof. He needed the peace of those memories to see him through the night. He'd spent many lonely nights practising that same technique in the Balkans.

They stopped briefly for a stretch around tea time, then headed on, making the most of the daylight. For the second part of the trip, Valerian thought about Lucien's game, keeping his mind active by trying to match wits with Canton. It was clear to him that while Canton wouldn't mind seeing him tried as a traitor, it was unlikely that anything would come of it beyond an initial hearing. Canton probably wanted to use the opportunity for something else.

It occurred to Valerian that Canton would have ample time alone with him to carry out any dastardly plans. Canton would have plenty of chances to kill him on this trip alone. Cuffed and confined, Valerian was at the man's mercy. What he didn't know was how much of a coward Canton was. Did Canton have the temperament to kill a man outright? Or was he the sort who favoured 'accidents', preferably those that were ordered by him, but carried out by others?

Accidental occurrences had certainly played a lucky part in Lucien's life in recent years. The accidental appearance of Mandeville Danforth at Lucien's home in Truro led directly to a seat on the bank's board of directors. An accident at Cambourne's mines had offered him a direct connection to the Cambourne inheritance and a chance to use Philippa's friendship for his nefarious schemes.

That gave him pause. He'd seen all the angles Canton had decided to play so far. But he'd not looked past the present. How involved was Canton's scheme? Had it incorporated the planning of Cambourne's death? Was this plot so detailed that he'd been willing to invest three years in setting it up? To wait until Philippa was out of mourning and able to legitimately remarry? The potential depth expanded the parameters of the situation. This was no longer an opportunity to exploit a plum that had fallen into Canton's lap on happenstance. It was much more defined than that. If his suppositions were correct, then Canton had known all along what he was doing. It explained why Canton would be willing to go to such lengths to remove him from the equation.

He'd unknowingly put the entire scheme at risk and Philippa too.

He hoped Philippa was holding up. She'd looked devastated after her discussion with Lucien and she'd been pale after the fisticuffs. But she was tenacious and he had no doubt that she was planning some way to assist him. He rather hoped he'd find a way to resolve his situation before Philippa could leap into action. He didn't want her endangered and Lucien was a more perilous foe than she realised.

He fingered his cloak, taking comfort in the fact that someone had had the foresight to slip a few things into his cloak, probably Lilya. She would have been the only one able to do it. Beldon and Philippa had been on the terrace with him.

If he wasn't mistaken from the feel of things, there was a small knife, some money and a tiny vial. He could imagine Lilya racing to his room and seeing the vial on the bedside table. She'd probably grabbed it in hopes that if it was medicine he needed, he'd have it. If he lived long enough to see the inside of Newgate, the money would come in handy. He hoped he wouldn't have to use the knife. But he thanked Lilya silently for her efforts.

Dusk was falling when they stopped for the night at a wayside inn. An hour ago, they'd driven through a larger village. But Valerian could see now why Lucien had chosen to stop here. It was less likely to be frequented by travellers, less opportunity to call attention to their party. Such a choice supported Valerian's thoughts that Canton had other plans than a trial for treason in mind.

'My hands, please,' Valerian said as the coach rocked to a stop. He held them up to be unlocked.

The man riding with him shook his head. 'Sorry, I've got orders not to under any circumstances.'

'Very well. My cloak about my shoulders, then, if you don't mind,' Valerian ordered. 'The clasp is in front. Fasten it well, I don't want it sliding off in the dirt.'

Uncomfortably, the man did as Valerian asked, grumbling about being treated like a 'bleeding valet'. Valerian took some petty pleasure from the man's complaints. Perhaps the man would tell Canton he didn't sign on to be a 'bleeding valet' and get permission to remove his cuffs. It wasn't as if Valerian wanted to engineer a prison break, or in this case a coach break. Running away only enhanced the look of guilt. He simply wanted to stay alive long enough to reach London and put Lucien's case to rest.

The inn was rough, but empty of guests with the exception of a few locals. Lucien sneered at him as he clumsily took a seat at one of the benches. One of the men was allowed to remove his cuffs for eating. Dinner came shortly afterwards, greasy fare of lamb stew and overcooked carrots. But Valerian had eaten worse.

Lucien apparently hadn't and pushed his plate away in disgust. He eyed Valerian malevolently over the plank table. 'Probably wise of you to eat what you can now. Can't say as how there'll be much food or opportunity to eat where you're going.'

Valerian met his gaze evenly and said nothing. He had no intention of saying a word to Canton. Lucien looked away, his attention drawn to the door and the newcomer. Lucien's eyes went hard.

'Pendennys, what a surprise to see you here,' Lucien drawled coldly.

'Ah, yes, who would have thought, out of all the inns to choose from, we'd have the same taste?' Beldon returned in a jovial tone, sounding as if he'd just walked into the finest gentlemen's club on St James's. 'St Just, I trust you're well?' Beldon came over to the bench and sat beside him.

Valerian stifled a laugh. 'Whatever are you doing here?'

'I'm journeying to London on business, much the same as you, I am guessing,' Beldon said off-handedly. 'Is the ale here any good?'

Lucien stalked outside in anger, barking an order to keep a close eye on the prisoner.

'We're going nowhere,' Beldon said cheerily, lifting his tankard in a salute. 'At ease, gentlemen, I am simply here to keep an old friend company. There's no crime about that in your law books, is there? Here...' Beldon slapped down two coins on the table '...innkeeper, ale for everyone and keep it coming. These boys have had a long day.'

Valerian shot Beldon a quick look. He was up to something. Surely he realised 'rescue' or 'escape' was out of the question? Beldon merely smiled.

After the first round, the men had gathered around the table where they sat. After the second, they were comparing battle scars from the morning's fisticuffs, more like comrades instead of enemies who had been on opposite sides of the fray. When the third round arrived, Beldon asked congenially, 'So, how much does it pay to take a facer from a viscount these days?'

'Enough,' one of the men replied. 'Double what we'd earn in a week on half-pay.'

'I'm not sure the wages are enough, considering the beating we took from you and the viscount today.' A man called Johnny gingerly touched his black eye, courtesy of Beldon's fist.

Beldon nodded in empathy. 'Sorry about that.'

'You and the viscount don't fight like sissified dandies,' Johnny put in.

'We're old friends,' Beldon said, throwing an arm around Valerian. 'We go way back. We've been in more than one scrape.'

For the next half-hour, Valerian sat back and watched Beldon charm the group of rough soldiers He saw his friend's ploy. Beldon too realised that escape was moot. But there were benefits to having one's captors on one's side. Valerian wouldn't be surprised if he'd be allowed to remain uncuffed during the ride tomorrow or if Beldon would be allowed to sit with him in the carriage. Little pleasures meant a lot in these situations. And perhaps, too, Beldon was trying to establish an ally to use once they got to London, someone who would prove to be sympathetic to their cause.

Eventually it was time to bed down. Lucien had arranged for a private room upstairs for himself. The others were expected to bed down in the common room on pallets, Valerian included. Men were appointed to stand watch in shifts in case Valerian tried anything foolish.

It was an immense relief to have Beldon with him. 'You sleep first,' Beldon said quietly, gesturing to a pallet. 'I'll stand watch for us.'

Valerian nodded. Beldon implicitly understood his concern that Canton would not be beyond murdering someone in his sleep.

'How is Philippa?' Valerian asked in low tones.

'She is well.' Beldon looked around him at the room of men. 'Tomorrow in the carriage, I'll tell you more. Not now. I have a letter from her.'

A man shouted over at them to stop talking. Beldon raised his hand in acknowledgement. 'Sorry to disturb you.' But both of them knew the ale had paid off. They shouldn't have been allowed to exchange even those few sentences. The shout had been for good form alone to keep up appearances.

Valerian lay down with his cloak about him, his hand closing over the handle of the small knife. The setting reminded him of many evenings spent in uncertain circumstances in the Balkans—the only difference was that he'd been alone then. Valerian glanced over at Beldon, who was already deep in a chess game with the soldier appointed to the first watch. It had been more than he'd expected to see Beldon come through the inn door. Beldon's presence was a good sign, too, that Philippa had not been revolted by the charges laid at his feet. For the first time since Canton had dragged him from Roseland, Valerian felt the foreboding recede.

Philippa could not quell the sense of foreboding that infiltrated her thoughts. The carriage ride to Truro had been interminable, although Lilya had done her best to keep up a stream of conversation in the hope of taking her mind off the circumstances.

Philippa only followed the stream of chatter in snatches, her mind fully riveted on Valerian. Was he safe? Had Beldon reached him in time? She worried for her brother too. Perhaps it had been a fool's madness to throw her brother after Canton. She'd never forgive herself if anything happened to Beldon.

But Beldon was adept in the art of protecting himself. She'd seen him box and handle a sword on occasion. It was quite telling to think of Lucien as someone who was capable of harming another. But Beldon had gone after Valerian because he agreed with her that Lucien wanted Valerian dead. Beldon's presence might act as a shield, at least until they got to London. She desperately hoped by then she'd have something else to act as a shield, some proof of Lucien's unethical behaviour. But it would be difficult. Valerian had technically committed treason. Technically, Lucien had done nothing wrong. How did one prove nefarious motives?

Philippa grappled with the conundrum throughout the afternoon until the carriage finally rocked to a halt in front of a respectable inn in Truro. It was too late to do anything tonight, but in the morning she and Lilya would pay a visit to Lucien's Truro manor. She hoped she could gain entrance based on the servants' familiarity with her, but if not she was prepared to use force and intimidation.

In the morning, she dressed in her best day gown. Lilya dressed as her maid. They went straight to the manor. The butler recognised her immediately.

'Your Grace, milord isn't home,' the butler said, flustered by her sudden arrival. 'Surely you knew of his plans?'

'That's why I'm here,' Philippa said, quickly moving into the story she and Lilya had concocted. 'Mr Canton has forgotten some items he needs. He asked me to come back for them. It's quite desperate. He fears his new contracts can't be signed without them.' Philippa wrung her hands for good measure.

'Do you know where he left them?'

'He thought they were in his office or maybe in his bedchamber,' Philippa said.

'I'll help you look,' the butler offered.

Philippa declined the offer, gesturing to Lilya. 'I brought my maid, so as not to bother you. I know you have responsibilities.' She swept into the hall and began making her way up the stairs to the room Lucien used as his office before the butler could muster up any other concerns.

'What are we looking for?' Lilya whispered once she'd closed the office door behind them.

'Anything incriminating. I don't know beyond that. There might not be anything here at all,' Philippa said. It had been something of a victory to get into his house. They would have to be quick. She had no idea how long it would be before the servants began to suspect something was wrong. How much time they had would depend on how much Lucien had told the staff about their estrangement. She hoped Lucien had remained true to his arrogant character and not lowered himself to share their relationship with the staff.

Their luck held in terms of discovery. No one bothered them beyond an occasional inquiry. But luck was against them in unearthing anything of merit that might indicate Lucien was capable of such deceitful conniving.

'We'd better try somewhere else. I don't think anything is here,' Philippa said when they'd exhausted the office.

'I'll check his bedroom,' Lilya offered.

'I'll check the library.'

In the library, Philippa gazed at the walls of bookshelves. She'd never be able to check each of those books in a reasonable amount of time. Even if she had time, it would take more than a day to check them. She supposed it would not be beyond the realm of possibility that a book was hollowed out or that the cover masked the book's true contents. But she didn't have time to make that check. She also thought it would draw undue suspicion from the staff if they found her looking through books.

Philippa checked the small desk that sat in the corner, but it was virtually empty. Flummoxed, she sank down on the sofa. It was hard to believe a few months ago she'd received a marriage proposal in this very room from someone she had believed to be her friend. She remembered the incident quite clearly. The room had felt awkward, as if she were being watched.

She stood up and started to pace in front of the fireplace. Given all that had happened in the past months, she was starting to feel that it was not unbelievable that she had been watched. Perhaps there was a hidden panel somewhere.

Philippa shot a furtive glance at the doorway, then back at the fireplace. The portrait above the fireplace had given her a strange feeling the night Lucien had proposed. Perhaps there was a switch in the fireplace that led to a secret room.

She didn't have to feel for long before her hand felt a knob in a place no fireplace typically had one. Philippa held her breath and pressed. A panel slid open. Elation coursed through her. She'd found a secret room! She cautioned herself. A secret room didn't mean anything was in it. Lots of houses had such rooms left over from the Civil War, and further back in time.

Philippa stooped and stepped inside. The room was far larger than she'd anticipated. A table and chair sat against one wall with a few books stacked on the table. A rug was on the floor. A small spiral stairway led to a little alcove big enough for a person to stand in. Philippa grimaced. She'd bet there were peepholes through the queer portrait.

She went to the desk and picked up one of the books. Her hand stopped. There were crumbs on the desk. This room had been used recently. Hurriedly, she sat down at the desk and opened the drawers. They weren't locked. She supposed there was no need to lock drawers when they were in secret rooms.

Her heart raced a bit faster. Her letter to Lucien, rejecting his proposal, was there in the top drawer. It was proof Lucien used this room. But not any proof that would do Valerian good.

In the last drawer, she found a set of three diaries dating from the last three years. Philippa leafed through the first one, noting the date. The diary had been begun a few months before Cambourne's death. In fact, the diary seemed focused on his relationship with Cambourne to the exclusion of all else. No other events were recorded, no mention of any of the mundane issues that usually made up diaries.

Philippa flipped faster through the pages. She stared in horror at an entry one month before Cambourne's death.

I believe I have the duke's trust and his wife's too, after two months in their social circle. It is time to set the scheme in motion.

Philippa stifled a gasp at the entry written on the day Cambourne had been injured. It had been no accident that the Duke had been caught in the shaft. The accident had been planned. Lucien had deliberately seen to John's murder.

Philippa steadied herself and forced herself to glance through the other two diaries. They were even worse. In them, Lucien outlined his plan and subsequent progress in currying her friendship. At the sight of one entry, Philippa felt physically ill.

After a year or so of marriage, a horrible death will claim my dear beloved, leaving me a wealthy widower and next of kin when it comes to dividing up her estate.

Shock threatened to claim her. Her hands shook as she stared at the pages. Lucien had fooled her entirely. Never once had it occurred to her that Lucien was contemplating premeditated murder. She'd never suspected he'd been connected to the mine incident or Cambourne's death in anyway. *She had nearly married a murderer.*

She had to get out of the house. There was no telling how much the servants knew. Philippa forced herself to stand and gather up the books and carefully re-enter the library. Her legs trembled beneath her skirts. She gathered her strength. She had to look normal! She went back to the study and stuffed some paper in a random folder to create a decoy. If anyone asked if she'd found anything, she could show them the folder. Lilya was coming down the stairs, shaking her head in disappointment.

Philippa gave her a little smile as the butler came into the hall.

'There you are, your Grace. I've been looking for you. Did you find what you needed?'

Philippa held up her hastily assembled folder. 'Yes, we'll be on our way. Lucien will be anxious for us to catch him up.'

'You've found something!' Lilya exclaimed as they settled in the carriage.

'Yes,' Philippa said grimly, waiting for her racing pulse to slow. The discovery had shaken her and it had been all she could do to get them out of the house without acting suspiciously.

She handed Lilya one of the diaries. 'Once we get to London, we'll have something to bargain with. In his arrogance, Lucien has given us enough rope to hang him.'

Chapter Nineteen

After the long coach journey with far too much time to ponder the desperate situation she faced, Philippa was glad to see London. London meant Valerian and London meant action. She'd been idle for too long. A day out of Truro, the weather had conspired against them with a fierce deluge that managed to flood the roads and wipe out a bridge. They'd had to cool their heels at an inn, waiting for the roads to dry out. When it was possible to travel, they'd had to detour quite a way in order to find a serviceable bridge.

The three-day journey had turned into a long week. Now they were here. At last, she could do something.

She directed the driver to take her straight to Pendennys House instead of the Cambourne townhouse. She and Lilya would stay with Beldon. There would be safety in numbers and comfort too.

Night was falling and lights already burned their welcome from the Pendennys's window when the coachman opened the door and helped her down. Lilya followed her out, gazing about, wide-eyed at the magnificent homes lining the street. Philippa linked her arm through Lilya's. 'You'll come to know London as your own city. By next year, these houses will be well known to you.'

'I can hardly believe that. I never expected to be surrounded by mansions,' she breathed in awe, letting Philippa guide her up the steps while she stared.

Beldon was at home. At the knock, he came to the door himself. 'I thought it might be you. I've been on the lookout since yesterday,' Beldon said, wrapping Philippa in a genuine embrace. 'Are you well?'

'Yes, just tired. Lilya has been a great support. How is Valerian? Where is he? Did you petition for a house arrest?' Philippa stepped back, the questions that had occupied her mind during the slow journey tumbling out of her mouth.

'Come and sit. I'll ring for tea and tell you all the news if you're up to it. Are you sure you don't want to change first?'

Philippa shook her head. 'I've thought of nothing but Valerian for days now. I must have some news.'

Beldon led them to the music room and the three settled on the cluster of chairs near the fireplace. The room was warm and intimate. It eased Philippa's nerves simply to be there in a room full of long-ago memories of time spent here with her family, with Valerian.

'How was the journey?' Philippa asked the moment she was settled to Beldon's satisfaction.

'As good as it could be. He and I took turns keeping watch in the night. I bought kegs of ale to keep the guards affable. During the day I rode in the carriage with him. I didn't leave his side for a second out of worry that Lucien would take any opportunity.'

'I wish I could see him now,' Philippa whispered, staring at the pianoforte in the far corner. Valerian had spent hours at the instrument, playing for them after family dinners.

'No, Philippa,' Beldon said sharply. 'Valerian insists you don't visit.'

'I can't support that,' Philippa said. 'I want to see him. I cannot sit around in the house all day doing nothing.'

'You can send a letter. I'll take it when I go. Newgate is a filthy place even with my blunt greasing every step of the way.' Beldon was firm on this.

'Newgate!' Philippa exclaimed, horrified. She hadn't known. She supposed in her mind she'd speculated about the possibilities of where Lucien would take him, but she hadn't allowed her mind to grasp the full import of those speculations. Of course Lucien would push for Newgate. It was lawless and all the better suited for an accidental death, a stabbing, a poisoning. The guards would hardly care if there was enough money to blind them with.

'Yes,' Beldon said quietly. 'I've done everything I can, bought him every convenience they'd sell. He has his own small chamber. He has food from this house every day that I personally deliver myself. Cooky fixes all his favourites. I've taken him clean clothes.'

Philippa studied her brother, seeing the signs of strain around his mouth and his eyes. Beldon had only been in London a week ahead of her, but it seemed an eternity separated them. In that time Beldon had been immersed in a dark world of experiences neither of them had ever thought to endure. She heard the unspoken 'but' at the end of his litany of activities. 'What is it?'

'There's an initial hearing scheduled for tomorrow to determine if there's any substance to the charges. Valerian's friends in the government are outraged. At least they've managed to make it a very quiet affair. It'll be at Whitehall. Lucien's father is on the committee.'

Lilya gasped beside her. Beldon reached across to place a comforting hand on the girl's arm. 'We will be vigilant, Miss Stefanov. Valerian has a friend on the committee as well.'

'We haven't come this far to be thwarted now. I have faith in English justice,' Philippa assured her. She better understood Lilya's life after spending so much time with her on the road. She understood Lilya's reaction. In the girl's country, it was unlikely someone survived prison or hearings or trials. They were all slow precursors to the gallows.

Philippa wished she felt as confident as her brave words. She grasped the full import of Beldon's news. A hearing would bring everything to a head. If the committee dismissed the charges, Lucien would have to act quickly if he meant to have Valerian fall victim to an accident while in Newgate. If the charges stuck, then there was a very real chance Valerian would stand trial.

'Can we attend the hearing?'

'I might be able to arrange it,' Beldon said.

'How is Valerian taking all this?' Philippa asked. It was the question she wanted answered most, but the one she wanted to ask least. How had he taken the letter? Did he blame her?

'He is doing as well as can be expected. He stays on guard constantly. He knows what the real danger is at this point. But it is wearing on him. I stay as long as I can each day so that he can sleep. Sometimes we play chess, we talk. I've engaged a discreet, highly recommended barrister and he's come to meet Valerian several times in case he's needed. But at night, I have to leave. He doesn't sleep at night for fear Lucien will send his assassins in the dark. I can't say the fear is unfounded. And I think, too, that he fears what he may dream.'

'I wish I could help him.' Philippa felt tears fill her eyes. It was dark now outside and she wanted to be with Valerian, to throw her arms about him and take his worries away. Right now, across town, he was beginning his long, lonely night vigil, wondering if this would be the night he had to fight for his life.

'You do help him, Phil. He was appreciative of your letter,' Beldon said cryptically.

Lilya took the cue. 'I think I'll go on up and unpack. I'll find someone to show me my room. You go ahead and talk to your brother, Philippa. I'll be fine.'

'A baby, Phil? Are you sure?' Beldon whispered fiercely as the door shut behind Lilya.

Philippa nodded. 'I didn't want to wait to tell him in case I waited too long. It seems Valerian and I have an unfortunate habit of holding off on sharing until it's too late.'

'Valerian was thrilled, but anxious,' Beldon said honestly. 'He doesn't want his child born under the banner of such nasty events.'

Philippa's hand went to her flat stomach. 'These events will be long past when this child arrives.'

'Let's hope so. Did you find anything in Truro?'

'More than I wanted to find, I think,' Philippa said sombrely. 'I have diaries Lucien kept about Cambourne, and about me. He's schemed to get control of the Cambourne mines for years and he's willing to stop at nothing to get them.'

Beldon nodded grimly. 'Then we have something to bargain with when the time comes.'

Philippa dressed carefully the next morning in a dress of flowered blue delaine. True to his word, Beldon had secured the right for them to be present at the hearing. She wasn't sure how he'd done it. But she'd heard him leave last night to go 'out' and he hadn't been home when she'd retired at midnight.

The carriage ride to Whitehall took twenty minutes. They were expected and an escort hurried them inside into a basement room hidden deep in the building. Philippa doubted she could find her way out on her own. She and Beldon were given chairs at the back of the room and told to remain silent. They were in no way to interrupt the proceedings.

The committee came in and took their places. Three of them were ministers from various departments of the Foreign Office. Philippa recognised Lucien's father, Viscount Montfort, among them, an older, chiselled rendition of Lucien at sixty. She didn't know the other two members, but Beldon whispered they were from the Home Office, one of them a particular friend of Val's. Valerian's barrister was there as well. Even though it wasn't technically a legal proceeding, Beldon had insisted.

Valerian was brought in at five minutes past the hour and Philippa's heart was in her throat at the sight of him. He was dressed well for a man who'd had to dress without his valet. His clothes were clean, and his hair was well ordered. But his features were haggard, his skin pale. For a man who loved the outdoors, she was starting to realise just what an agony the week in Newgate had been.

But his eyes were sharp as they swept the room, assessing the committee, taking the measure of each man present. His roving gaze fell on her in the back of the dim room. Philippa sat up straighter, fighting the urge to acknowledge him in some way. She didn't dare call out for fear of being dismissed. But she did hazard a wave of her hand in hopes that he would see that she wore the ring he'd given her. In fact, she hadn't taken it off since Lucien had come to take him away. She thought she saw the minutest of smiles pass across his lips.

Philippa was here. Her presence shocked him utterly. Valerian had not expected it. Indeed, he was beleaguered by conflicting emotions at the very sight of her. He'd hungered for her steady presence all week, filling his lonely night-vigils with the mental pictures he had of her and the new ones he conjured up of her growing big with their child. That news had overwhelmed him with joy in spite of the darkness he faced.

This morning, he thrilled to the sight of her serene beauty lighting up the back of the room, knowing that such loveliness was a mere foil for the intelligence and temper that lay beneath the surface. The sight of his ring on her finger meant more to him in that moment than she could probably guess or understand.

But now that she was here, he'd rather she not be subjected to what the hearing would reveal. She would leave here firm in the knowledge that he was a tarnished hero, if a hero at all. He'd done his country's bidding, but it had often been grim work. He hoped it had been worth it, that his services in all their forms would be enough to offset the death of Turkish soldiers by his hand.

Valerian knew how important it was that he fight these charges with everything at his disposal. The longer he remained in Newgate, the longer Lucien held the upper hand. He didn't worry so much for himself. In a fair fight, he could manage Lucien's henchmen. It was Philippa for whom he had the most concern. The longer he was imprisoned, the longer she was un-guarded. Of course, she had Beldon, but Beldon could not be in two places at once. Beldon could not watch them both.

He sat straight in his chair, refusing to look ashamed of the charges as they were read.

'What do you have to say to these charges?' the chairman of the committee asked, setting down the papers.

Valerian speared him with a sharp glance. 'I rescued two innocent children from certain death, one of them a babe only a few months old. Since when is it England's policy to make war on women and children who have no say in the politics and treaties of men?

'I for one could not countenance such wanton and unnecessary violence. They were of no threat to us or our ambitions in the region. Yet the Turks were allowed to destroy their homes and take their lives. I do not believe any of you gentlemen would stand by and watch that type of slaughter take place if you had the means to stop it.' Valerian looked each of them in the eye. 'Am I wrong? Has English chivalry been bought for gold and trade routes?'

The men shifted uncomfortably in their seats. He'd hit a mark with them. No one would want to be branded a coward and they'd certainly appear less than saintly if they argued it was acceptable to slay women and children, all for the sake of a passage to India.

Viscount Montfort blazed at the insinuations. 'You paint the truth too lightly, St Just. You didn't save random children on a battlefield. The children you saved were the get of rebel leader Dimitri Stefanov. He worked hand in glove with the secret society, Filiki Eteria, to fight against the Turks. You befriended Stefanov's family and remained in contact with them after British negotiations with the Phanariots ceased.' Montfort pointed an accusing finger at him. 'You were the last visitor to see Stefanov alive before his execution. You stand as guardian to his surviving children.'

'I was,' Valerian answered smoothly. 'Children are children, it hardly matters who their fathers are. They are all worthy of our protection.'

The chairman glared at Montfort. 'These proceedings must be managed in an orderly fashion. We will get to everything in time, but we must not resort to outbursts.'

Valerian's barrister intervened. 'Viscount St Just has an exemplary record of loyal service to England in the discharge of his duties abroad.' The man skillfully began laying out Valerian's career. 'He was responsible for critical negotiations in Morea that mitigated the civil war there…'

The list was long and Valerian was well familiar with it. From his work in Port Navarino to prevent an Egyptian invasion of Morea, to the sinking of the Egyptian navy, which ended Egypt's bid for power in the area, to the Phanariot issue and ultimately his latest participation in the London Protocols, he'd participated deeply in what had once seemed to him a noble calling.

Even after the harsh realities of his work had become apparent to him, he'd stayed involved, no longer for the sake of lofty philosophical principles, but in the hopes that he could do something practical. He no longer ascribed to the battle cry of 'make the world England' but to his own heartfelt calling—make the world better.

The barrister had set down his list. 'I submit to the committee that this is a man who hasn't a dishonourable bone in his body, who has spent his life serving England most nobly. To even suggest that what happened on the battlefield in Negush is akin to treason is an absurdity and waste of our time.'

Valerian watched the group for a reaction. Beldon had found a deuce fine barrister. He almost believed his work had been useful once the man had finished with the list. The group seemed to think that, too, except for Montfort.

'We are splitting hairs over an issue that can only be black and white. We cannot start forming grey areas where national security is concerned,' Montfort began. 'We cannot begin establishing different standards for different situations. He killed allies who were acting in British interests. He did it deliberately in an attempt to protect the enemy. By doing so, he put a rebel's concern above the needs of his country. If he'd killed Englishmen to save the children of rebels, I think you'd feel quite differently about where the line is drawn in the sand. Our sands cannot shift.'

One of the ministers nodded his head slightly and Valerian began to wonder how many of these men Montfort had in his pocket. Montfort meant to take the high ground and argue from a philosophical standpoint. It would come down to philosophies against practicalities. Reality against theory. Honour against dishonour, and what constituted either.

'If that is all, the committee will deliberate,' the chairman said. 'Viscount St Just, you'll be informed of our decision as soon as it is made. It could be hours, or days.'

Valerian rose and nodded to the group. 'I thank you for your time, gentlemen.'

A guard came forwards to escort him from the room. He fought back his disappointment. He couldn't allow himself to think of going back to the tiny room. If he dwelled on it, he thought he might go mad. The precarious nature of his safety while at Newgate made it impossible to wander about the yards. Even with Beldon's presence, he felt it was too dangerous to risk his friend. It would be all too easy for one or both of them to fall prey to a subtle knife as they walked passed. He wouldn't allow the committee, most of all Montfort, to see how the thought of going back affected him. He didn't dare look back at Philippa and Beldon. He didn't have the mental fortitude left to manage that as well. More than he wanted daylight and sun and clean air, he wanted Philippa.

In the hall, there was a patter of heels purposefully clicking on the flagstones. Philippa's voice called out in its most imperious tone. 'Guard, I'll need a minute with the viscount.'

'I'm afraid I can't allow that. I have orders...' the guard stammered, clearly weighing the haughty woman in front of him against the orders of his supervisor at Newgate who was across town, tucked away in his office fleecing bribe money from unfortunate patrons.

'There's a room right here. I just want a moment,' Philippa said, gesturing to the small room off to her left. She didn't wait for the guard's approval. Instead, she took Valerian's hand and marched into the room. She slammed the door in the guard's face, hearing him protest and then Beldon's smooth tones reassuring him all would be well.

Philippa threw herself into his arms, her own arms going about his neck, and kissed him with all the emotion she owned. He met the kiss with his own intensity, his mouth pressing hard against hers, hungry and desperate, and yet somewhere in its depths was reassurance. In spite of all that had happened, their love still stood.

'Val, I've missed you,' Philippa gasped, touching his face as they drew apart, tracing the lines of his worry with her hands.

'You're well? And the baby?' His hand dropped to her waist, framing her stomach with his fingers as if he could feel the baby already.

'We're well. There won't be anything to see for a few months yet.' Philippa gave a tremulous laugh.

'I am so happy about it,' Valerian whispered. 'Promise me, you'll keep the child safe. Don't do anything foolish, Philippa, promise me.' His voice was urgent, desperate to wring a vow from her.

'I won't need to. You'll be free as soon as the committee makes their decision,' Philippa said brightly.

Valerian shook his head. 'I think Montfort will buy a trial.'

'Then I will go to Lucien. I have enough to sway him, I think,' Philippa said, trying to be confident against Valerian's dire words. She rapidly explained what she'd uncovered in the diaries.

Valerian's eyes filled with concern. 'Philippa, you

cannot toy with Lucien Canton. If you threaten him, it will be open war. Do not confront him alone. Take Beldon with you and the Watch if you must.'

The guard banged on the door, Beldon's charm having finally worn out. Philippa kissed him hard one last time. 'I love you, Val. Nothing will change that.'

Philippa clenched her fists in the folds of her skirt, using all her willpower not to chase after him or cry as the guard led him away. A terrible foreboding filled her as she watched Valerian stoically accept the handcuffs and was ushered down one of Whitehall's many secret hallways. If he didn't get out of Newgate tonight, he might not get out at all, at least not alive. It was time to act. In fact, she felt that she had little time to lose.

Chapter Twenty

Heavy booted footsteps pounded up the stone corridor of Newgate. Valerian heard them and was instantly on alert. It had only been four hours since the hearing. Surely they hadn't made a decision already? He rose from the cot, tense and ready. It was too soon for a decision and slightly too early for Beldon to come with a supper basket. But the footsteps were definitely for him. They came to a stop outside his heavy, barred door. The jangle of keys sounded and then a thick metal key clunked in the lock.

Valerian sprang behind the door. If Lucien had sent an assassin with a gun, he wouldn't get a clear shot. That was Valerian's greatest concern, that the assassin would come with a gun and he wouldn't have a chance to fight for himself. The door would open, a shot would be fired before he even knew who was there.

The door opened. A man dressed as a guard entered the room. Valerian didn't recognise him. He was not one of the usual men who watched his room. 'What do you want?' Valerian growled. The man was burly with a barrel chest and nose that looked as if it was used to being broken. He looked a menace.

'You're free to go. Your release is in my pocket if you're man enough to take it from me.' A blade flashed in his hand from a concealed sheath in his sleeve. The sharp edge glinted dangerously.

Valerian assessed the situation in an instant. The committee must have decided before Montfort could stand against them in full force. He was free, but Lucien couldn't allow that to happen so this man had been sent to silence him once and for all. His small knife was hidden in his pallet, so he had no weapon to counter the knife, except his own brute strength. The man clearly looked to outweigh him. His best defence would be to disarm the man and seize control of the weapon.

Valerian tensed into a fighter's position, ready to take the impact of the man's lunge. If the man wanted to fight, he'd have to make the first move. Valerian was not going to risk serious injury by launching himself at an armed combatant.

They circled each other in half-crouches, the man making jabbing feints with the blade, emphasising just how small the room was. 'I can walk all day,' Valerian taunted as they completed another circle of each other.

'Why don't you come and do what you've been paid to do? What's the going rate on killing viscounts these days? I hope it will be enough to start over in exile. Once Baron Pendennys arrives, you'll be caught.'

The man snarled, 'Then I better make short work of you.' He lunged, the knife making a downward slashing motion intended to catch Valerian in the shoulder. Valerian was ready for it, his arm going up in instant reflex and his hand gripping the wrist of the knife hand with the full force of his strength. Valerian grunted and used his power to push the man back to the wall, banging the knife hand against the stone, in hopes of shaking the knife free from his grip.

The man kicked out, catching Valerian in the shins, but the kick had very little impact since they were locked so closely together. Valerian gave a final pound and the knife clattered to the floor. He landed a jab to the man's stomach and dived for the blade.

His assailant was faster than he'd anticipated. He'd no sooner got his hand around the knife handle than the man jumped him from behind. He had no time to roll over and slash with the knife. He was effectively imprisoned underneath. A kidney punch caused him to cry out, followed by another. He could not lie there and do nothing.

The man's weight was formidable, but Valerian found the strength to heave himself up to his knees, slashing blindly with the knife to distract the man. He had some luck. The blade met with muscle and his attacker cried out, loosening his hold on Valerian long enough for Valerian to fling him off and regain his feet. He came up fast, ready to fight, ready to kill. The man rushed him, sensing his chance for victory slipping away.

Valerian felt a stinging sensation travel down his arm, cloth ripped. A red stain spread on the material. The bastard had another knife! He could see blood on the other man now, at his thigh where his blade had made contact. The man slashed at his face, Valerian reached out and grabbed the knife hand with his left. In the moment he held the assassin's blade at bay, he drove his own blade home. The man gasped and collapsed, hatred and disbelief frozen on his fading features. The fight was over.

'I guess I was man enough,' Valerian snarled, the rage of the fight starting to ebb from him. He straddled the man's form and rooted in his pocket for the release. He found it sealed and tied with a red ribbon. He tore it open, hardly daring to believe it was over.

'Val!' Beldon rushed into the room, dropping the dinner basket he carried. 'What's happened?'

'I'm free.' Valerian felt himself shudder from the shock. 'Now we can deal with Canton. He sent his man with the message. I wasn't supposed to leave here.' He drew a deep breath. 'Philippa won't have to do anything foolish.'

'I am afraid it's too late for that,' Beldon said, realisation starting to dawn. 'She doesn't know you're free. She's gone to see Canton, to bargain with him.'

Philippa faced Lucien Canton over the walnut desk in his town-house study. 'Lucien, I have come to bargain with you for Valerian's freedom.'

Lucien's mouth twisted into a sneer. 'Bargain or beg, my dear? I can't imagine what you have to bargain with. Your body, perhaps?' His gaze raked her form in a slow, deliberate perusal. 'If so, I am not interested in used goods.'

Philippa refused to be cowed by coarse innuendo. 'I have something better, I think. An even exchange. Your freedom for his.'

Lucien's eyes narrowed. 'Whatever are you talking about?' His voice protested innocence, but his narrow gaze suggested he was concerned.

Philippa took her courage in both hands. 'I am talking about how you plotted to kill Cambourne. There was no real accident in the mine. It was deliberately sabotaged and you planned it, right down to outlining it in your personal diary.'

'Do you have the books, then? It's quite intrepid of you to break into my home and steal from me, but anything for love, eh, Philippa?' Lucien said coldly. 'Still, your threat is empty and your bravado is desperate. St Just got in my way. I will not tolerate his interference. He is going to pay. It's too late to change that.

I expect any minute my hired assassin will be paying him a visit, if he hasn't already. The man's formidable. St Just doesn't stand a chance. The irony is that the committee dropped the charges. St Just's release is in my man's pocket. He may be dead already.' Lucien sighed with mock pity. 'But you, Philippa, I could still save and we can forget about your little foray into thievery.'

Lucien reached into the top drawer of his desk and drew out a sheaf of papers. 'This is from when I had a more optimistic outlook on our relationship. Perhaps I became cynical too soon? Now, I have a deal for you. This is a marriage contract. Marry me, sign over the minés and save your social respectability and your social standing. You will not be dragged down by Valerian's scandal. I doubt anyone will much care to have the political backing of a suspected traitor's wife. It would be a shame to see all your hard work with mining schools and mining reform fall into ignominy simply because you made a poor decision in marriage. We were friends once—I am confident we can be again.'

Philippa picked up the contract. 'You were never my friend.' She tore the contract in half and threw it on the desk. 'I would rather be dead than see myself married to the likes of you, since that's what you had planned all along.'

The rashness of her words was punctuated by the ominous click of a pistol's cocking motion. 'That can be arranged. Since you know about that little addendum to my plan, I am left with no choices, Philippa.' Lucien raised a small silver pistol from behind the desk. It was pointed at her. 'I had rather hoped this would come later instead of sooner.'

Philippa forced herself to breathe deeply and to stay calm. She couldn't think about the baby, about Valerian, or about Valerian's warning that she not confront Lucien alone. She could only allow herself to think about Lucien and what she could do to stay alive.

She managed a believable laugh. 'Are you going to shoot a woman in your town house and expect to get away with it? It's still daylight. You're usually cleverer than that. Besides, if I die, you can't find the diaries. Only I and one other know where they are.'

'I don't have to shoot you. I'd rather not. Murder is rather drastic.' Lucien waved the pistol towards a chair. 'Have a seat. I have another contract here. This one is a bill of sale between you and me. It's for the mines. The price is fair, at least for the record. You and I know what the real price is. That money will never show up in your bank account, but I will let you walk out of here.'

Philippa stared at the documents. She'd not thought to bring a weapon. She'd thought her threat would be enough.

'Here's a pen.' Lucien handed her the instrument, towering over her. 'I've been generous with you out of a sense of misplaced affection.'

Philippa's eyes narrowed. 'Your affection has never been misplaced.' Perhaps she ought to take the deal and live to fight another day. But then she thought of Beldon's words the time she'd suggested giving Lucien the mines. She thought of Valerian's honour and all that he'd risked over the years to live by his code. It gave her the strength to stand up, toe to toe with Lucien Canton.

'I won't sign the bill of sale. I won't give you permission to take what isn't yours. Nor will I give you permission to start a career of blackmail. This won't end until you possess every mining asset Cambourne ever owned. I see your game and I won't play.'

'You're beautiful in a temper, my dear. Perhaps there's another game you'd play to save your mortal soul?' Lucien whispered, his eyes going to her lips. 'I'd play that game with you.'

Philippa lowered her eyelids to hide her thoughts, trying not to flinch at Lucien's hands on her waist, trying not to think about the gun he held laxly in one hand as he began a lazy seduction. This was her chance, a chance to grab the gun, a chance to flee out of the door and into the street. If only she could make Lucien believe.

'Open your mouth, darling.' Lucien whispered, but they were not love words, they were commands. She did, trying to guess what he wanted. His kiss was rough, bruising against her mouth. Reflexively, her body tensed in resistance at the hard pressure of his member against her. He held her tightly, aroused by her instinctive struggle.

'Oh, yes, don't make it too easy,' he moaned, his eyes dangerous glints of malicious desire. 'I like a challenge.'

He had her against the edge of the desk, the hard wood biting into her back. Her resistance was real and it seemed to inflame him further. With one arm, he swept the desk clear of ledgers, laying the gun on the corner of the desk to force her on to the surface. Philippa saw it out of the corner of her eye, not daring to look at it fully lest she give away her intentions. She let him lay her back on the surface. The gun was closer now, her fingers could almost stretch out and claim it. She wriggled, hoping to inch closer to it.

Lucien's hips pressed into hers, grinding out his rising desire. She fought back the urge to give into tears. She'd been so foolish to think a man capable of Lucien's evil could be stopped by the threat of blackmail. That was his speciality, not hers.

His lips were on hers, hard and unrelenting, his body stretched over her, his hands in her hair, painfully pulling it free. She reached out her hand and found success. Philippa closed her hand over the gun and brought it up with a sickening thud against Lucien's head.

He jerked back howling, dizzy with surprise and pain. 'What the hell!' Philippa shoved with all her might, sending him toppling to the floor. She sprang up from the desk and ran for the door. But Lucien was not done.

He grabbed a handful of her skirt as she sprinted past. She tripped, half-falling, then half-running to put the sofa between them as a barrier. Lucien grabbed up a vase and threw it at her. Philippa screamed, ducking as crystal shattered against the wall.

Like a miracle, she heard someone call her name. She screamed again. This time the door burst open, cracking against the wall so hard it fell off its hinges. Valerian was there, followed by a half dozen members of the Watch, and Beldon.

'Stop where you are, sir!' the captain yelled. 'Is that the man?' He turned to Valerian for identification, who nodded. 'Mr Canton, you are under arrest for the murder of the Duke of Cambourne and for attempted blackmail.'

Lucien went rabid. 'You have no proof. Those are not easy accusations.'

'We have diaries, supplied by the Dowager Duchess of Cambourne, that are written in your hand, outlining your premeditation of the crime and your intention to swindle the Duchess out of her holdings, either through marriage or blackmail, and also including over-exaggerating charges of treason against Viscount St Just.'

Lucien paled. Then he roared and lunged for Philippa over the sofa. 'Bitch!' She was no match for his angry strength and she went down beneath him, the gun sliding out of her hand and beyond her reach.

She heard Valerian yelling, 'Get off her!' And then Lucien's crushing weight was lifted from her. Valerian and Lucien fell to the ground, wrestling, punching. They were too closely engaged for anyone to intervene. Valerian had the advantage, landing punch after punch, but, in one desperate move, Lucien had the gun.

Philippa screamed a warning. Valerian's arm reached out with lightning speed and grappled with the gun hand. But the gun was cocked and volatile. It fired and both men lay unmoving. 'Help me! Someone help me!' Philippa was down next to Valerian in an instant, shoving him away from Lucien's body. 'No, no, no, no.' There was blood everywhere, on his shirt, his face—she couldn't be sure it was not all his. 'Val, please wake up.'

'I'm awake,' Valerian groaned.

'Are you hurt?' She started searching his body through his clothes, frantic over what she might find.

'Miss, it's the other one,' the captain said quietly, motioning for men to join him at Lucien's still form. 'He took the bullet.' The captain shook his head. 'He's gone.'

Valerian struggled to sit up. 'Are you all right, Philippa?'

'Yes. Yes, we're both all right,' she said but she was shaking and she couldn't hold back her tears. It was all suddenly too much. Lucien had died in front of her. One moment, he'd been living among them; the next, he'd simply ceased to be. It could just have easily been Valerian. Valerian's arms were about her and he cradled her to him, murmuring reassurances.

The captain was efficient, but it still took the better part of the evening to wrap up loose ends and make statements. At nine o'clock the captain shut his notebook. 'We have all we need, my lord. Thank you for your patience. You may all go home. I'm sure it's been a very trying day. We will let you know if anything further is required.'

Philippa let Valerian lead her to his coach, which had stood waiting for them. The afternoon and early evening had been a blur of repeating stories and events. She was only just now able to shut out the horrors and appreciate the joys of the day. Valerian was free. The last threat that had stood in the way of their happiness had been removed.

She snuggled against Valerian's shoulder. 'What shall we do now? After all this excitement?'

Valerian looked down at her, a smile starting in his green eyes. 'We go home.'

'I've waited a long time to hear that.'

'Just as long as I've waited to say it, my love.' Valerian pressed a kiss to the top of her head and held her close. They might be days from Roseland, but Philippa knew she was home already.

Epilogue

1 January 1831

Valerian Inglemoore, the Viscount St Just, had a secret, a joyful secret that caused him to smile unceasingly as he stood with his wife and four-week-old son in front of the assembled congregation of St Justus's for the baptism of his child. He was desperately in love with his wife and she was in love with him.

That wasn't the secret. He doubted he could have kept his bliss hidden from anyone for long. He was all too aware that he wore his heart on his sleeve when it came to Philippa and his new family. Valerian's eyes flicked to the front row where Lilya and Constantine sat. In the span of a year, he'd become a husband and a father to two boys and one beautiful young woman preparing to take on London in the spring.

His life was full. But that wasn't the secret either.

A year ago on New Year's Eve, he'd silently vowed to court Philippa and win back her trust in him so that his life could be complete. That was his secret.

His resolution had been fulfilled, although not with ease. He and Philippa had done battle with the past and the present for the sake of their love. Now, there were no more secrets between them.

Philippa passed the baby to him, all blankets and dark hair in his arms. He passed the baby to Beldon, who stood as godfather to little Aidan Alexei. Beldon said the words easily and the ceremony was over.

There was mingling afterwards, everyone crowding the altar to get a good look at Roseland's new heir. Valerian watched Lilya and Beldon exchange a quiet look apart from the crowd, a knowing smile spreading across his face.

Philippa elbowed him gently. 'What are you thinking with that wicked grin on your face?'

'I am thinking that everyone deserves to be as happy we are.'

* * * * *

The Earl's
Forbidden Ward

For my niece, Rachel, who wanted to know how wars got started and actually listened when I explained it to her.

Chapter One

London—Spring 1832

Peyton Ramsden, fourth Earl of Dursley, was doing what he did best—technically superior, emotionally removed sex with his mistress of two years. Certain of her fulfilment, he gave a final thrust and efficiently withdrew to make a gentleman's finish in the sheets.

His mistress, the elegant Lydia Staunton, raised herself up on one arm, letting the white satin of the sheet slide provocatively down her hip. 'So, you're giving me my *congé*,' she said matter-of-factly.

'Yes, I am,' Peyton answered evenly. There was no need to dress up the conversation, although he'd planned to bring up the issue *after* he'd got out of bed. For a man who liked to keep his life organised into neat compartments, there was something inherently wrong about discussing business so soon after coupling, even if it was the business of sex.

'How did you know?' He hadn't spoken of it or dropped the slightest hint at ending their arrangement since he'd come up to town three days ago, although he'd made it plain at the beginning of their association that he had no intentions of sustaining their relationship beyond two years.

'It was worse than usual tonight.' Lydia could always be counted on to speak her mind.

Peyton fixed her with an arrogant stare, one eyebrow raised in challenge. 'I highly doubt that, *madame*.' If there was one area the Ramsden brothers excelled at, it was in the bedroom arts. They'd been schooled at an early age about how to please a woman, part of their father's training regimen for a gentleman.

Lydia fell back on the pillows, ennui punctuating her words. 'It's not *that*. It's *never* that. You know you're exquisite in the bedroom, Dursley. You don't need me to tell you your skills are unsurpassed.'

Dursley. He hated being a title to everyone, especially someone he'd shared conjugal relations with. Peyton rolled out of bed in a single fluid motion and strode across the room to the chair where his clothes waited. He picked up his shirt to put on. Perhaps he'd demand his next mistress call him 'Peyton'. And perhaps not. Forced intimacy wasn't true intimacy and he required honesty above all else.

'Well, thank goodness. For a moment I was

starting to doubt.' His tone conveyed the exact opposite. There was no misunderstanding the real message. The Earl of Dursley did not doubt himself in the least, in any aspect of his life.

Lydia sighed. 'Skills aren't everything, Dursley. It takes more than prowess in bed to be a good lover. Some day, you're going to have to feel something.'

This was an old discussion. Lydia had accused him of being detached more than once during their association. Tonight, Peyton chose to ignore the comment. Arguing at the end of their association would resolve nothing. He pulled on his trousers and shrugged into his coat. He walked to Lydia's dressing table and pulled a slim box from the inside pocket of his coat. He didn't need to tell Lydia what it was. She was experienced enough in these dealings to know the box contained an expensive parting gift; something she could choose to flaunt or sell, depending on her circumstances. He placed a calling card on top of the box.

'Peter Pennington, Viscount Wyndham, has suggested he is in the market. I offered him the lease to this house if you're amenable.' Lydia would know exactly what that meant. He'd found her another protector. Her financial security would not lapse in the wake of his exit.

'Bravo, very nice, Dursley. You've wrapped up all the loose ends in two sentences.' Lydia got out of bed and slipped her long arms into a silk robe, one of his many gifts to her over the years. She belted it at the waist. 'Tell me, do you ever get tired of being in control?' The words were not kind.

Ah, the usually unflappable Lydia was piqued. Peyton sensed it was time to make an expedient exit before a quarrel cast a pall over their parting. He understood her discontent. For all the physical pleasure he gave her, Lydia wanted something more from him, something he was unwilling to give. 'I know what you want, Lydia. Wyndham is better suited to give you the illusion of romance than I am.' He made a short bow in her direction. 'I wish you the best. Goodnight, my dear. I have other business to attend to before my evening is through. I will show myself out.'

Once outside in the cold evening, Peyton sent his coach home, choosing to walk instead. The night air was bracing and he suddenly found himself in possession of a burst of energy begging to be spent. It was just as well—a walk would give him time to think and there was plenty to think about. Giving Lydia her *congé* was only one of the situations he'd come up to town to resolve. The other item involved a summons from an old friend at Whitehall regarding a colleague who had recently passed away.

Peyton reached for his pocket watch and flipped it open. Nine a.m. That gave him a half an hour to make his nine-thirty meeting with Lord Brimley. It was Whitehall business they were to discuss. Brimley had made that clear in his letter. But they would discuss it at White's in a private room.

He had plenty of time to travel the few streets to St James's and White's Gentlemen's Club, but his pace increased none the less. There was a certain excitement in the prospect of the upcoming meeting and he'd acknowledged weeks ago he needed something to keep him occupied.

His youngest brother, Paine, and Paine's wife, Julia, had taken up residence at the family seat, deep in the idyllic heart of the Cotswolds, to await the birth of their first child not quite a year after their marriage. He was, of course, thrilled to have his brother under his roof. But the birth of Paine's son four weeks ago had made Peyton restless in a most uncomfortable way.

He adored his new nephew without question, having been shamelessly caught on numerous occasions in the nursery with the infant in his arms—a sight most of London would have been shocked to see, given his reputation towards sombre decorum. Yet, watching Paine and Julia together with their new son had filled him with disquiet and a sense that his life, for all his accomplishments, was incomplete in his thirty-eighth year.

Logically, the assumption that his life lacked something was ludicrous. He'd come into his title at the young age of twenty-three when he had years ahead of him to maximise the earldom's prosperity and take advantage of all the technological advances open to agriculture. Maximise them he had. While others struggled with outmoded notions of estate management and agricultural depression, Dursley thrived. It was no small thing to accept responsibility for the Dursley holdings and the people attached to them. His successes were their successes.

Additionally, he did his duty in Parliament, coming up to town when sessions needed him to lend his voice on weighty matters. And his devotion to country and king didn't end there. During the years following the Napoleonic Wars, he'd done his duty as a discreet diplomatic courier to Vienna when tensions over the future of the Balkans arose. He'd become a regular face in the drawing rooms of the New Europe in those days as nations negotiated new political boundaries and privileges.

Oh, no, although he was not one to need public acclaim for his efforts, he could personally acknowledge that his efforts had borne worthwhile fruits. His life had not been spent in idle pursuits of no account, but in the pursuit of building an empire that would far outlast his years on earth. A man could take pride in such achievement. Indeed, a man *should* take pride in such a life.

Which was why the internal unrest he'd suffered from lately was so distressing. It had sprung from nowhere and for no reason. Such an appearance was all the more disconcerting for a man of his ilk, who exerted control over all aspects of his life—demanded it, in fact. Imbalance was not a common or tolerated occurrence within his domain.

The façade of White's loomed across the street. Redemption waited inside. Soon, he'd appease the errant devils that plagued him and get his life back to normal.

He was expected. A footman whisked away his hat and outerwear while another one smartly led him upstairs to the private rooms. Brimley was already there. Peyton's anticipation grew. Brimley's early arrival suggested the man was anxious about the meeting.

Such concern seemed out of character for the context of the meeting. In his note to Peyton, Brimley had indicated simply that there were a few details to wrap up with Branscombe's passing. The only oddity was that Brimley had summoned him at all. He could count the times he'd met Sir Ralph Branscombe on one hand and still have fingers left over. If he remembered correctly, Branscombe had primarily been stationed in St Petersburg.

The footman opened the door to the luxuriously appointed room with its thick carpet and carved marble mantelpiece. The room would have done any grand home in Mayfair proud. But Peyton had scarcely a glance for the stately elegance of the décor.

Brimley rose from his chair by the fire and came

forward to greet him. 'Dursley, so good of you to come. What's it been? Two years, now?'

Peyton nodded. Brimley looked tired and careworn beyond his fifty years, but his memory was clearly still sharp if he could recall the last time Peyton had worked for him. 'Nearly two years,' Peyton affirmed, taking time to carefully study Brimley's features, searching for a reason for the weariness that plagued him.

Brimley seemed to sense Peyton's scrutiny. He waved a hand. 'Come and sit, Dursley. You're a lucky man to have missed the last two years, after all.'

Brimley pushed a hand through his greying hair. 'I was disappointed to see you go, but I understood you had estates to run. You couldn't be hotfooting it off to Vienna or wherever else at my beck and call. Now, I wonder if I shouldn't have bowed out, too. The Balkans and the Eastern Question are enough to drive any man insane. One wonders what we really won when Napoleon was defeated—a pile of war debt here at home and a handful of cocksure pocket-tyrants in the Far East stealing access to waterways.'

Peyton gave a short laugh. 'You don't fool me for a minute, Brimley. You love the intrigue of this new world.' He settled in his chair, relaxing into its depths. Ahhh. White's knew the value of a comfortable chair.

Brimley opened the humidor on the table next to him and selected a cheroot. He offered the cherry-wood box to Peyton. Peyton declined with a mild wave. 'Well, I suppose I do like some of the game,'

Brimley admitted, taking a long draw on the cheroot. 'But I don't like loose ends and that's what I've got with Branscombe's fiasco.'

'Fiasco?' Peyton felt his body tense. He certainly hadn't got that impression from Brimley's note. But then, Brimley was a master diplomat, never letting out more than he wanted anyone to know before he wanted them to know it.

'Branscombe had the bad taste to die while in possession of a list of Russian insurgents deemed dangerous by the Czar. Unfortunately, since his death, the list has not come to light. Our sources in St Petersburg are certain that the Russians have not found it. There's been no report of arrests or suspicious disappearances. However, we have not found it either.' Brimley gave a heavy sigh.

Peyton steepled his hands and studied the fire, digesting Brimley's news. He'd always known there was a fine line between espionage and diplomacy. Not every diplomat was a spy, of course. But some were. It seemed the mild-mannered Branscombe had crossed that line.

And why not? Diplomats had very little accountability to any authority once they were at their posts. Accounts of their deeds or decisions would take months to reach England, if at all. Often there was no time to waste in waiting for responses from home regarding how to proceed. One simply had to rely on instinct and do what one felt was best.

Peyton certainly understood the ease with which diplomacy and espionage could be mixed. What he didn't understand was why this particular list had Brimley edgy. He doubted Brimley was all that concerned about preserving the identity of Russian revolutionaries.

'What makes the list so important to us?' Peyton asked.

Brimley eyed him for a while. Peyton knew the man was weighing him up, assessing what could be told and what could be left out. 'This is strictly confidential, Dursley.'

Peyton smiled. Most of their conversations over the years had included that phrase. 'I assumed it would be.'

Brimley grimaced. 'An unstable Russia weakens Russia's power to influence Turkey and that's good for us. We need the waterway for our Indian trade routes.'

He was talking about the Dardanelle Straits, which Turkey controlled. A conquered Turkey, a Russian-controlled Turkey, would be an intolerable situation for Britain. Passage through the Dardanelles made it possible to cut weeks off the trip between London and Bombay, making passage around the dangerous African Horn unnecessary.

But this explanation would be commonplace to a man who'd been keeping up on current events. There was nothing confidential here. Such information was bandied about the House of Lords daily. Peyton shook his head. 'That's not good enough,

Brimley. I know all that already. How does the list influence Russia?'

Brimley seemed to concede. 'All right. It has come to my attention that Branscombe compiled the list on behalf of some ambitious and wealthy businessmen who would be glad to fund an internal rebellion to overthrow the Czar. In exchange, they are asking for guarantees from the new government to leave Turkey, and the Dardanelles, especially, alone.'

Peyton let out a low whistle. Foreign involvement in plotting revolution was serious business. He didn't need to be told Branscombe had been well paid by these men to make the necessary connections and compile the list. Even after the disastrous 1825 December uprising in Russia, secret revolutionary societies still abounded. The promise of cash for weapons and munitions probably appealed to the most organised groups.

But where there were secrets, there were traitors. The 1825 Decembrists had been betrayed to the Czar at the last minute and apparently Branscombe's intentions had met with the same fate. A suspicion crossed Peyton's mind. 'How did Branscombe die? I don't think you mentioned it.'

'For all intents and purposes, it was a natural death. He passed quietly in his sleep,' Brimley hedged.

'But you don't believe that, do you, old man?' Peyton pressed, not willing to be fobbed off. He didn't understand yet what his role in all this was to be, but he certainly wasn't going to commit himself without knowing all the details.

'Well, I only know what the doctors tell me. He was a thousand miles away in another country, after all. At this distance, I am heavily dependent on second-hand information,' Brimley prevaricated.

'I don't doubt the doctors told you exactly what you told me. But you suspect otherwise?'

'I only know the Russians knew he had made a list and what he intended to do with it. Which gave them a motive to put their best assassins on the case.'

Peyton recognised he wasn't going to get anything further from Brimley on that account. 'All right. We can leave his demise at that. The more burning question for me is what can I do here? I am not clear at all as to why you've contacted me. I hardly knew the man and I've only met him a few times.'

'The list is not in Russia. It's not at the British embassy in St Petersburg. If it's anywhere, it's in England.'

Peyton raised his eyebrows, encouraging Brimley to be more forthcoming. 'Yes?'

'The list is in England. As of today, a highly alert delegation from Russia is also on British soil.'

'So, we search the man's residences quickly.'

'We've tried that, but we've run into several stumbling blocks.' Brimley seemed discomfited. The man shifted in his chair. 'Precisely, four stumbling blocks in the form of Branscombe's daughters. The biggest stumbling block is his eldest daughter, Miss Tessa Branscombe.'

Peyton found the room had grown hot. His cravat seemed extraordinarily noose-like. Brimley's discomfiture was contagious and for good reason. He had his suspicions about where this conversation was headed.

'I want you to get close to the girls, Miss Branscombe particularly. I've arranged for a codicil to Branscombe's will to be drawn up regarding your ability to act as a guardian for the girls. With the exception of Miss Branscombe, the other three are all under eighteen. But they will all be under your guardianship. Once you've established the girls under your protection, you'll have access to the house. You can search it at will and in broad daylight without arousing their distrust.'

Peyton spread his hands out before him as if he were warding off an unseen blight. 'No, I will not play nursemaid to four silly females. What do I know about young girls in the schoolroom? I raised brothers. The condition of my unwed state alone would make the arrangement unseemly. I am a bachelor.' What Brimley suggested was not diplomacy at all, but babysitting in disguise.

'A bachelor with an impeccable reputation for honour and responsibility,' Brimley reminded him. 'Not to mention a formidable aunt in the Dowager Duchess Bridgerton.' Brimley meant Peyton's father's sister, Lily.

'Lady Bridgerton will be the perfect guide to help Miss Branscombe through the Season,' Brimley said, beaming over his thorough plan. 'And you'll be the perfect escort.'

Peyton gripped the arms of his chair. 'Wait, this is a new development. Why does Miss Branscombe need a Season?' He had no intention of doing the pretty. When he'd come up to London, he hadn't meant to stay longer than was necessary to take care of this 'small' issue with Brimley and settle things with Lydia. He was eager to return to his family in the country and his new nephew.

'Escorting her around town will give you a chance to gain her confidence. The more time you spend together, the more willing she might be to confide in you.' Brimley appeared untroubled about the breach of ethics the scheme demanded.

Peyton did not share the man's detachment. This was becoming more unpalatable all the time—a forged codicil to create an imaginary guardianship, and a veiled request to seduce the father's secrets from the daughter, smacked of dishonesty and double dealing.

Peyton got up from his chair and walked to the sideboard holding an array of brandies. He poured himself a glass and turned back to face Brimley. 'I won't do it merely to support the pockets of self-serving businessmen. You should have known I was the wrong man for the job.' He took a long sip of brandy, spearing Brimley with his eyes, letting him see the disdain in which he held Brimley's proposal.

'You'll be well paid,' Brimley said obtusely. 'I don't ask you to do this without reward.'

Peyton set the heavy tumbler down hard. 'There is no sum of gold that would entice me to flirt with an innocent young girl under false pretences and to betray her sisters at a vulnerable time in their lives.'

Brimley rose. 'I am not offering you gold, Dursley. We all know you've got more blunt than the rest of us. I am offering you lives.'

Brimley took a folded sheet of paper out of his coat pocket. 'Read it. British intelligence reports that the Russian army is preparing to mobilise against Turkey. It will be war by this time next year and British boys will be on the front lines. Internal instability in Mother Russia would be a powerful piece of leverage for our diplomats in St Petersburg to negotiate with. With the right persuasion, our diplomats will be able to halt the war before it begins.'

Peyton scanned the letter, weighing his options. But that was the irony—there were no options to weigh. He could not countenance the discomfort of four young girls against the lives of hundreds of soldiers. Neither could he countenance his own discontentment at escorting Sir Ralph Branscombe's daughter through the Season when it would prevent British soldiers from enduring far worse discomforts on the battlefield.

Peyton Ramsden, fourth Earl of Dursley, lifted his glass in a toast. 'Well, then, here's to king and country.' He drank a large swallow. It had been a hell of a night.

Chapter Two

Tessa Branscombe was doing what she did best: flouting convention intentionally and in some ways unintentionally as she ushered her three sisters through the busy markets of London. A basket hung from her arm full of prizes wrested from merchants who'd been cowed by her shrewd negotiations.

To Tessa's way of thinking, there was nothing inappropriate about the conduct of the outing. All four of them were dressed conservatively in sombre colours, although the period of half-mourning for their father had passed. Furthermore, they were escorted by the gallant Sergei Androvich, newly arrived from the Russian embassy.

If there was a glaring oddity about the outing, it concerned the place she'd chosen to take her sisters. She'd taken them to obtain greens and other foodstuffs that were usually obtained by a cook or housekeeper in a common marketplace. Tessa acknowledged this was not an errand polite society deemed appropriate for a lady of her station, and certainly not an appropriate outing for impressionable young girls. But while she acknowledged English society's outlook, she staunchly disagreed with it.

In Tessa's opinion, a tradition that prevented a girl from learning the intricacies of providing for a household's meals wasn't a very useful tradition and, thus, not deserving of her attention. So, here she was, a basket full of vegetables, a string of high-spirited sisters trailing behind her and the handsome delegate from the Russian embassy and old friend from St Petersburg, Sergei, beside her.

All in all, the little entourage made a strange picture in a marketplace not used to seeing a lady of quality amongst its customers, bargaining over prices with the tenacity of a fishwife on the docks. If merchants' jaws dropped in amazement as the little group passed, that was their problem. Tessa had a faultless escort in Sergei Androvich and that was as far as she was willing to bend for tradition's sake.

They passed a flower girl selling violets. Sergei tossed the girl a coin and snatched a bouquet, which he promptly presented to Tessa. He sketched an elegant leg in a playful, elaborate fashion that made her laugh. Her sisters gathered about her, giggling and clapping. Sergei dug out some more coins and presented each of them with their own posies of violets, to their great delight. Tessa pressed her nose to the gay bouquet and smiled. 'Thank you.'

'It is my pleasure. It's been too long since you smiled, Tess,' Sergei said softly in his perfect, but accented, English.

'I know.' Tessa met his blue gaze with her own, exchanging much with him in that moment. It had been a long nine months since her father's death. There had been the enormous effort of leaving St Petersburg, a place that had been their home for fourteen years. She'd grown up there and had left many friends behind. Then there had been the work of setting up a home in her father's little-used residence in London, a place Tessa had not seen since she was eight and her mother had been alive.

'I am so glad you're here, Sergei,' Tessa said sincerely. Sergei had arrived yesterday with the Russian delegation and she was glad of his company. London was foreign to her. She missed the familiar faces and pace of life in St Petersburg. 'How long will you be in London?'

'I am not sure, but at least until September,' Sergei replied. 'My work with the embassy won't be so arduous that I won't have time for you. We'll put a smile back on your face in no time.'

'You already have.' Tessa smiled again, slipping her free hand through the crook of Sergei's arm. She meant it, too. All she knew of London was through the Englishmen who'd been posted to the St Petersburg embassy. But Sergei was a familiar friend. The son of a Russian noble, Sergei had appeared at the Czar's royal court three years ago, looking to make his way in diplomatic circles. He'd been an instant success with his fluency in English, his education and his dashing blond good looks and blue eyes. It hadn't been long before he'd been assigned as a junior liaison between the British embassy and the Russian diplomats.

He'd become a fixture at the Branscombe home, talking over situations with her father and a natural friendship had sprung up between them, which extended to Tessa and the girls.

Tessa looked around at her sisters, busy admiring their posies. The simple gestures had brought them a moment of pleasure in their uncertain world. Seeing how happy the bouquets made them, she privately vowed it was time to start getting out more. London was full of sights to see, and, with Sergei here, it would be a perfect time to take in the attractions. For now, though, it was time to head home.

Sergei offered to hail a cab, but Tessa insisted the walk was good exercise.

Several streets later, they reached the neat row of town houses in Bloomsbury, a neighbourhood pre-ferred by a well-to-do intellectual set. The town houses ringed a well-kept key-garden for the resi-dents' private use and smartly dressed nannies pushed babies in prams up and down the park.

Overall, Tessa found it a pleasing area, quiet and

removed far enough from the hub-bub of the city and busier neighbourhoods for her tastes. She had no desire to call attention to herself. The last thing she wanted was interference in her life. All she wanted these days was to set up house, see to her sisters in her own fashion without society's intrusion and forget about the last tumultuous days in St Petersburg. She preferred remembering how life had been there before her father's death and the quiet terror that had stalked her afterwards.

The girls bounded up the front steps ahead of her, eager to get their violets in water. Sergei laughed at their enthusiasm. 'They're exuberant,' he said.

Tessa nodded. 'It's good for them. Will you come in and have tea? Mrs Hollister was making scones this morning.'

'It will be a perfect end to a perfect afternoon,' Sergei accepted.

Within moments, the perfection Sergei had spoken of evaporated. If Tessa had known what lay beyond the front door of her own home, she might not have gone in. No sooner had she and Sergei entered the hall than they were surrounded by her sisters, all talking excitedly at once. She caught only snatches of nonsensical phrases such as, 'A guest!', 'An earl', 'In the front room'.

Tessa clapped her hands for silence. 'One at a time, please!' She turned to Petra, her junior by five years. 'Petra, what is going on?'

Petra never got a chance to answer.

A masculine voice spoke with clipped, commanding tones from the doorway of the front room. 'I believe what the girls are trying to tell you is that the Earl of Dursley is waiting to be received.'

Tessa turned to her right. All her instincts were on alert at the sight of the imposing, dark-haired man. Her first impression was one of danger. This man was dangerous. Dangerous *and* powerful. His eyes were like cold sapphires. There was no warmth in them as they surveyed her and her sisters.

Her second reaction was to protect. Tessa stepped forward, adopting a cold hauteur of her own, the one she used when she had to inform an importuning guest her father wouldn't receive them. 'I don't believe we've met. Furthermore, I don't believe you have an appointment. I regret you've been waiting. However, I am not receiving today. I must ask you to leave.' She pasted on a polite smile at the last. She'd found in the years acting as her father's hostess that people often accepted bad news better when it came with a smile.

The man stepped forward, quirking a challenging eyebrow at her. 'You must be Miss Tessa Branscombe.'

Tessa's smile disappeared. The arrogance of this man was unprecedented. He'd come to her home unannounced, no doubt intimidated Mrs Hollister into being allowed to wait, and now refused to acknowledge her dismissal. She'd asked him to leave and he was ignoring her. Instead, he was carrying on with his visit as if she'd accepted his presence in her home.

Beside her, Sergei bristled. 'The lady has asked you to leave and come another day.'

The Earl turned his gaze on Sergei, as if noticing him for the first time. Tessa thought the gesture was intentionally done, meant to suggest that the Earl didn't feel Sergei was worthy of his particular notice. She doubted this earl in all his kingly arrogance overlooked anything or anyone.

'And you would be?'

'Count Sergei Androvich,' Sergei said with all the coldness of a Russian winter.

Tessa watched the blue eyes of the Earl become positively glacial. 'Ah, yes, the attaché with the newly arrived Russian delegation.' She was certain he was ignoring Sergei's title on purpose. In one sentence this man had demoted Sergei from Count to a mere attaché. Sergei had gone from a foreign peer worthy of being treated as an equal to nothing more than another man's clerk.

'I see you've heard of me.' Sergei summoned a modicum of aristocratic hauteur of his own.

'It is my business to be apprised of all the people and things related to the Misses Branscombe,' the Earl drawled elegantly.

What audacity! She didn't even know him and the man was arrogantly insinuating he had some claim to the intimacies of their lives. Tessa had had enough. The social temperature in the entrance hall was frigid. She wasn't going to let these two men, not even well-meaning Sergei, squabble over territorial rights when it wasn't even their home. It was hers, and right now her sisters were staring wide-eyed at her, expecting her to act as if it was.

'My lord, I must again request that you leave. This is a highly unexpected visit.' She gestured towards Sergei. 'As you can see, we've already got company.' Sergei gave the Earl a small triumphant half-smile.

'I heard you perfectly the first time, Miss Branscombe. However, I think you'll find time for me, once you hear why I've come.'

Was that a bit of condescension in his voice? Was he so certain of his news? Tessa placed her hands on her hips, her temper getting the better of her. 'Then tell me and get out.'

The Earl chuckled. 'Miss Branscombe, I am here to inform you that I am your guardian. A codicil to your father's will has placed you and your sisters under my protection.'

Like hell it had. Tessa stifled the urge to speak her mind. She was a diplomat's daughter and knew the importance of time and place. There would be nothing gained from erupting over the news. She needed more information before she could decide what to do and this overbearing male seemed to be the most immediate source to hand.

'I stand corrected, my lord. Won't you join us for tea?' Tessa said with great aplomb. She gestured to the drawing room and the group filed in.

He might have forced her to receive him, but she didn't have to like it. Round one to the Earl. She would not readily cede any more ground to him. He could take tea with them, but he wasn't getting a single bite of Mrs Hollister's scones.

Chapter Three

Tessa Branscombe hadn't *looked* like the kind of woman who caused trouble. When she'd come through the town-house door, Peyton's first reaction had been an entirely manly one at the sight of her. Brimley had not mentioned how stunning the eldest Miss Branscombe was. But Brimley was an old man.

Brimley had not mentioned the piles of pure gold curls that shone like a halo on her head, setting off the curve of her delicate jaw, or the cameo-like fragility of her ivory-skinned features. The woman was a walking incarnation of an angel, not to mention a properly dressed one. It would be a pleasure to see this young woman turned out in the more stylish, fashionable gowns of the *ton*.

His second reaction was that Brimley was getting soft if he'd had difficulty getting around this lovely chit with liquid-gold hair. He had every indication that her demeanour would match her beauty. Then she'd opened her mouth, her blue-almost-violet eyes flashing with irritation and Peyton understood with instant clarity what Brimley had implied.

The so-called angel had *dismissed* him, the Earl of Dursley. Out of hand, moreover. Peyton could not recall a time when he'd been so thoroughly given his *congé*. There was little he could have done aside from obliging her, which was out of the question, so he'd ignored her dismissal.

Fortunately, her escort made it easy for him to shift his attentions and now they were having tea— all six of them, including the Count and every one of Miss Branscombe's sisters. Miss Branscombe had made no move to send her sisters up to the school-room or wherever else they were supposed to go.

Peyton thought it was most unorthodox of her to let them sit in on this difficult meeting. To be fair, perhaps she meant to send them out of the room after tea, so he dutifully made small talk over two cups of tea—without cakes, he noted—waiting for an opportunity to continue with his business.

Over the third cup of tea, Peyton began to think Miss Branscombe had used the tea as a rather successful delaying tactic. He was growing thin on the patience a man needed for appreciating the girlish chatter that flowed about him. He now knew a copious amount of information about each of the Branscombe girls.

Petra, who was seventeen, had plied him with a veritable oratory regarding the differences between the horses she'd ridden in St Petersburg and the horses she'd seen here in England. He gathered she was as horse-mad as his brother Crispin had been at her age.

Eva was fifteen and gabbed incessantly about clothes and gowns, and how she liked to design her own dresses. The youngest was Anne, a shy ten-year-old who said nothing, but leaned against Tessa for comfort, staring at him with frightened wide blue eyes the entire time.

Miss Branscombe put down her tea cup during a lull in Eva's dissertation on the different qualities of silks and speared him with a sharp look. 'Well, my lord, we have had three cups of tea and you have not broached the reason behind your visit.'

Peyton set his cup down and met her challenge evenly. 'I've been waiting for you to send the girls out of the room. It is not the English custom to discuss business in front of children.'

Miss Branscombe visibly bristled. 'But it is *my* custom.'

'I do not wish my news to be unsettling to them. Sometimes, children are not mentally equipped to process information the same way adults are,' Peyton explained politely.

Miss Branscombe's fascinating eyes narrowed. 'My sisters are hardly children, as you've had a chance to ascertain. Petra and Eva are of ages where they should have a say in the direction of their destinies, and, while Annie is young, I must inform you that my father's death and all the changes of the past year have been most unsettling to her.'

Peyton's eyes flicked to the Count. 'And Count Androvich? Is he to remain as well?' Brimley had not suggested one of the Russian delegation would attach themselves so intimately to the Branscombe household. This was an unforeseen development and one Peyton didn't like in the least. He wanted Count Androvich dislodged. Hunting for the list would be difficult enough without the Count around. The man's presence begged the question of his motives. Was he here as a friend? He did seem quite protective of Miss Branscombe. Or was he using his association with the family to search for the list?

Thankfully, Miss Branscombe recognised he was giving her a victory by allowing her sisters to remain. She knew what she had to do to secure that victory. She nodded her angel's head at the Count. 'Sergei, we've taken up enough of your time today. I thank you for your escort to the market. I will not take up any more of your time. I can talk with Lord Dursley on my own.' Miss Branscombe rose and offered the Count her hand. Peyton silently congratulated her on the smoothness of her actions. There was no way the Count could refuse her polite invitation to exit the conversation without looking either obtuse or rude.

Miss Branscombe saw the Count to the door

and returned shortly, smoothing her demure skirts about her as she sat. 'Now, my lord, we can discuss your business.'

All four pairs of Branscombe-blue eyes fixed on him, waiting. Peyton brought out the papers and began. 'I have been informed that guardianship has passed to me upon your father's demise. That guardianship will last until each girl marries or turns twenty-five, at which point your trust funds shall be given into your individual care.'

Miss Branscombe assessed him shrewdly. 'You mentioned this permission was granted to you through a codicil to my father's will. But I assure you there was no codicil or mention of one in the will. I was there when it was read, we all were.' Her sisters nodded in affirmation.

Miss Branscombe continued, 'I have no reason to believe you and I certainly will not turn over control of my family and their modest fortunes to a man I do not know simply because he shows up on my doorstep with papers and a title.'

'It is regrettable that the codicil became separated from the other documents. It is fortunate that it's been recovered and placed in the right hands.' Peyton struggled for patience. He told himself he'd have been disappointed if the brassy Miss Branscombe had not been astute enough to see the possible flaws in his claim. He *should* appreciate that she was not easily hoodwinked. But the truth was, he didn't appreciate it in the least. It had been a long time since anyone had countermanded the Earl of Dursley. He'd quite forgotten what it was like.

'I understand your misgivings, Miss Branscombe. I assure you that I am the Earl of Dursley and I am, in the absence of any close living relations in your family, the man assigned to guide you and watch over you all. I have the most honourable of intentions.' And he did have honourable intentions for England—just not necessarily for the girls.

'I've never met you,' Miss Branscombe challenged. 'I am hard pressed to believe my father would have selected a guardian that we've never met. Quite frankly, it seems unlikely that he would have picked a man we didn't even know existed until this afternoon.'

Peyton nodded. 'I met your father on a few occasions in Vienna, but I never had the chance to journey north to St Petersburg.' At least this wasn't a lie, although the implications it hinted at—those of a relationship with Ralph Branscombe—were non-existent.

Peyton pushed the papers towards Miss Branscombe, since she hadn't moved to take them from the table. 'If you look at the papers, Miss Branscombe, you will see that they are in order. There is a letter of introduction that vouches for me. The codicil is there, as well as an outline of how my guardianship is to be managed.'

Forced to acknowledge the papers, Miss Branscombe picked them up and began to read. And read.

A weighty silence fell. Peyton could hear the mantel clock ticking off the minutes. The muffled sound of a passing carriage could be heard from the street and still Miss Branscombe read. At last, she looked up. Peyton thought he saw her hands tremble slightly, but she adroitly folded them and hid them in the lap of her skirt and he couldn't be sure.

'What do the papers say, Tess?' Petra asked in a quiet voice.

Miss Branscombe reached for Petra's hand. She was all calmness; the angel quality Peyton had seen in her earlier had returned. 'There's nothing for you to worry about, dear. Now, I need to speak with the Earl privately. Please take the girls upstairs.'

Anne whimpered next to Miss Branscombe and she bent to whisper reassurances to the little girl, gently nudging her towards Petra's outstretched arms. 'Annie, your dollies will be missing you. Perhaps you and Eva can try on the new dresses she made them,' Miss Branscombe cajoled. 'I'll be up in a while to see how they look and we can have a tea party.'

Peyton watched Miss Branscombe walk the three girls to the door, Petra shooting a last glance at her older sister, clearly worried. The scene was hard to take in. Seeing the sisters together reminded him all too acutely of life after his father had passed away, leaving him an earldom and two brothers to care for. But that was years past and he'd locked the feelings associated with those difficult days away deep inside himself long ago. He didn't want them resurrected. Nothing could come of them. They were best left alone, unexamined and unexplored.

When Miss Branscombe turned back to him, the angel was gone. She was all fire and rage. 'I will not stand for you or anyone splitting up this family. I have worked too hard keeping us together, too hard trying to give them stability.'

Peyton rose, since Miss Branscombe had no intention of sitting down. He strode to the window and drew back a lace panel to view the street below. 'I imagine the life of a diplomat is often trying for a woman. Moving about, making new friends, learning new customs must be an overwhelming task.'

'It is a difficult task for *anyone*,' Miss Branscombe promptly corrected. 'I have done it admirably and now I deserve my reward.'

'Which is what?' Peyton turned from his study of the street to watch Miss Branscombe.

'To be left alone with my sisters, to raise them where they will be safe,' she retorted sharply.

That got Peyton's attention. He veiled his reaction carefully. 'Were they not safe in St Petersburg?' Miss Branscombe seemed to hesitate. Interesting.

'Diplomacy in general is not always the safest of fields,' she answered vaguely.

Peyton nodded. He wondered—did she know about the list? Had something happened in St Petersburg to give her reason to fear for her own personal safety and that of her sisters? He couldn't ask her now. Such probing would seem too nosy. He'd have to file this away and remember to pursue it when the timing was better.

'I assure you, Miss Branscombe, that your fears are understandable and misplaced. I have no intention of swindling your fortunes out from under you. You are welcome to do a financial check on me. My solicitor has been instructed to be at your disposal. Additionally, I am not proposing that the family be split up. The girls are welcome to stay in London with you for the Season.' If he couldn't convince her of his reassurances, he'd be off to an awkward start in gaining her trust.

'We can decide, *together*, at the end of the Season where all of you should go next. I am prepared to make you welcome at Dursley Park until you're settled. My family is there,' Peyton offered. The last bit was spontaneous, perhaps motivated by guilt over the situation. His arrangement with Brimley did not require him to do anything for the girls.

Miss Branscombe appeared to visibly relax at the prospect. She nodded. 'Will your wife be joining us in London?'

'I am not married, Miss Branscombe. When I mentioned my family, I meant my two brothers, my brother's wife, their new child and my Cousin Beth.' Peyton held up a hand to ward off the protest he saw coming. 'I understand your hesitation. My Aunt Lily, the Dowager Duchess of Bridgerton, has agreed to sponsor you for the Season. Everything will be *comme il faut* and above reproach, I assure you.'

Miss Branscombe studied him for a long while. 'I do not desire a Season. Your aunt need not worry and neither need you. I am sure squiring around an unknown girl who is rather too old to be making a début is not high on your list of priorities.'

True, it wasn't. But that would not do. Peyton needed a reason to be in her company, to become a fixture in her life. 'Surely you wish to marry and settle down with a family of your own? A Season will enable you to meet people and get to know England all over again.'

'I've never known England,' Miss Branscombe said sharply.

'Still, if it's to be your home, you'll want to make friends,' Peyton argued. He'd never encountered a more obstinate female. His Aunt Lily was head-strong, but quite capable of seeing reason. His Cousin Beth was pleasantly compliant. But there was nothing reasonable or compliant about Tessa Brans-combe. He offered her a Season under the sponsor-ship of the revered Lady Bridgerton. No young lady he knew of would take such a gift lightly. Yet Miss Branscombe simply refused and kept pacing the carpet, intent on studying the pattern. Perhaps she was unaware of the honour he accorded her with such an offer.

Peyton played his ace. 'If you are unwilling to do it for yourself, I would encourage you to do it for your sisters. Petra should be out next year and Eva won't be far behind.'

That stopped her. She looked up. 'I will speak to them. Perhaps, for their sakes, I will consider it.'

Peyton nodded, knowing that was the closest to an acceptance he would get from her today. He couldn't push for too much too soon. He would have to instil his guardianship in gradual, subtle steps. It was clear from today's meeting that Miss Branscombe wouldn't take kindly to his outright assumption of authority. But there were definitely things that needed doing, starting with curbing inappropriate outings to the market and teas without cakes. It seemed that Tessa Branscombe intended for her sisters to grow up as wayward as she.

That would not play well amongst the *ton*. Her beauty and his reputation would only go so far in making the Branscombes acceptable. He knew how the *ton* worked and the Branscombes were fringe players at best in that world. Any mis-step from Tessa Branscombe would be magnified a hundred times over.

Peyton drew out his pocket watch. It was growing late. The visit had taken longer than he'd anticipated and he'd promised Aunt Lily he'd come for dinner after assessing the Branscombe situation.

'I appreciate your time, Miss Branscombe. I'll let you take the evening to help your sisters adjust to the news, although I want them reassured that all will be well. I do not wish to be wrongly painted as the ogre here. I will call with my aunt tomorrow in the afternoon so you can meet her and begin to make plans. It's early yet and the Season isn't fully underway for another two weeks. You needn't panic on that account.'

'I don't panic on any account, my lord,' Miss Branscombe informed him crisply.

The remark won a smile from him. 'I didn't mean to imply that you would. My apologies.'

Miss Branscombe was more than happy to help him find his way to the door. In the hall, Peyton felt the need to offer her a final assurance. 'All will be well, Miss Branscombe.'

She met his eyes evenly. 'I know it will be. I won't tolerate anything less.'

'Good evening, Miss Branscombe.' Peyton bowed over her hand, choosing to ignore her cold farewell.

Outside felt warm compared to the chill of Miss Branscombe's parting comments. Peyton's mind was already whirring with lists and plans in regards to the Branscombe girls before he got down the town-house steps. They would need additional staff and new gowns. The younger girls would need a governess to help with their studies. He suspected Miss Branscombe was overseeing that herself, but she'd be too busy once the Season started to plan lessons.

He stopped at the bottom of the steps to caution himself. It was best not to make too much of this guardian role. This was make believe. This was a role he was playing for his country in order to prevent a war. This was about recovering a list that could save the lives of British soldiers. His guardianship would terminate once the list was recovered. In all reality, his role wouldn't last past the Season, regardless of his offer to take them to Dursley Park. If Tessa Branscombe ever fully understood his role in all this, she would be glad to see him go, a thought that sat decidedly ill with Peyton for no logical reason.

Peyton tried to shrug off the feeling of disappointment. Most likely, that gladness would be reciprocal. The next time he saw Brimley, he would ring a peal over the man's head. The man had left out quite a lot about Tessa Branscombe when he'd outlined the mission, starting with her ethereal beauty and ending with her inconvenient streak of tenacity. Both attributes made Peyton Ramsden extraordinarily uncomfortable.

Chapter Four

Tessa climbed the stairs to the schoolroom, trying to decide how best to put the news to her sisters. A guardian was a completely unlooked-for development. All her protective instincts were on alert. She didn't like it in the least and not only because it curtailed her own freedom and plans. Such a development simply didn't make sense. Why would a codicil appear now? The Earl had implied she feared a swindle of their trust funds, but he was wrong there. She feared something worse than losing money.

Tessa shivered at the thought. It conjured up the disconcerting incidents that had occurred before they'd left St Petersburg. Their home had been broken into days after the funeral. She'd told Sergei, but even with his protection, she'd known she was being followed whenever she went out. She had hoped that distance would have quelled the subtle danger she'd begun to feel in Russia. The appearance of the Earl today suggested otherwise. They knew no one in England, but he'd certainly known them.

It seemed to be an eerie coincidence that after a month alone, they were beset with visitors. Sergei had arrived and now this unknown Earl was claiming guardianship. These newly developed circumstances begged the question: was this truly an accidental happenstance brought on by a quirk of fate, or were these men after something or someone? If the latter were true, it would be much easier to defend herself if she knew what their objective might be.

Tessa took a deep breath and pushed open the door, taking a moment to appreciate the rare tranquillity of seeing her sisters quietly engaged in activity. Eva sat with her embroidery. Petra pored over a beloved book of horses and Annie played quietly with her dolls. Then they spotted her at the door and questions erupted on all sides.

'Wait! Wait! One at a time,' Tessa said, moving to sit on the floor next to Annie.

Eva and Petra gathered around her. 'Well, is he or isn't he our guardian?' Petra asked pointedly.

Tessa opted for the direct approach. 'He has legal documents that proclaim him as such. Until I can prove otherwise, it seems we must abide by this development. I will meet his solicitor and look through the situation quite thoroughly, I assure you. I won't allow us to be taken advantage of.'

'When will we see him again? Is he going to live in the house with us?' Eva asked.

'Tomorrow and no,' Tessa responded. 'He will keep his own residence. His aunt will come with him tomorrow afternoon.' Tessa paused before adding the next bit of news. 'It seems that I am to have a Season, although I've told him I have no interest in such doings.'

Eva protested immediately. 'Oh, Tess, you *must* have a Season! Think of all the gowns and parties. You'll meet new people. You'll know how it's all done when it's Petra's turn and my turn.'

Tessa smiled thinly, thinking of the Earl's goad that she must be cognisant of her sisters' needs even if she would shun such an opportunity for herself. It was the argument of a traditionalist and it helped alleviate some of her suspicions about his appearance. It was exactly the sort of argument a real guardian would make, wanting to see his charges married off. A man on a different mission would hardly take an interest in such things. 'Of course, dear.' She patted Eva's hand, aware of Petra's gaze on her.

'The Earl is not married?' Petra asked, her natural intuition easily reading between the lines of what had and had not been said. 'Is that why his aunt is calling?'

Tessa nodded.

Eva gushed, 'He'll escort you everywhere, Tess. It will be like a fairy tale. He's what they call an "eligible *parti*".'

Tessa grimaced at the notion. Where had Eva

learned such a thing and so quickly after their arrival? She was growing up far too fast. Tessa tried to tamp down Eva's romantic notions. 'I have Sergei to act as an escort. I needn't rely on the Earl wholly, just because a set of papers made him guardian.'

Eva shook her head. 'Sergei will have to go home eventually. Besides, I thought the Earl was much more handsome than Sergei. He was so dark and mysterious.' That was saying a lot, considering Tessa knew that Eva harboured an adolescent infatuation with Sergei's blond Slavic good looks and courtly manners.

'I thought he was rather pompous and stuffy,' Petra argued.

Eva shot Petra a sly look. 'It's the perfect ones who have the most to hide.'

'Hush, girls,' Tessa scolded. She made a mental note to keep a closer eye on Eva's reading material.

'Will we stay in London with you, Tess?' Petra asked, returning to the subject at hand.

'Yes. I have the Earl's promise we are not to be parted.'

Petra nodded. 'Then perhaps his guardianship won't make that much difference and we'll be allowed to go on as we have been doing.'

Tessa smiled her assurances, hoping to convince her sisters that Petra was right and all would be well. Life would certainly be easier to manage if that was the case. Although she'd protested against the idea of a Season, and although she'd argued that Sergei would be a preferable escort, Tessa couldn't fully deny that the idea of spending an evening or two on the Earl's arm held some appeal. He'd been arrogant today, but beneath that arrogance she'd sensed compassion. He'd offered to keep the girls in London and to let her decide where they went after the Season. Tessa found such a mixture intriguing, and, in Eva's words, slightly mysterious.

Petra's idea of a *laissez-faire* guardian succumbed to reality at precisely eleven o'clock the next morning. The hypothesis that the Earl of Dursley would leave them be had hardly lasted fifteen hours, and they'd been asleep for eight of them.

Mrs Hollister arrived in the modest library Tessa used as her private office, nervous and out of sorts. 'Miss, there's visitors here to see you.'

Tessa looked up from her letters. The Earl wasn't expected to call until the afternoon. 'Did they say what they wanted?' It wasn't like the capable Mrs Hollister to be edgy.

'They say they're from the Earl of Dursley.'

Tessa frowned, trying to make sense of the arrivals. 'His solicitor, perhaps?' she mused out loud. It was the only explanation that made sense.

'No, miss. A maid and a footman,' Mrs Hollister breathed in alarm. 'I have them in the kitchen. I didn't know where to put them.'

'I'll see them at once. Send them up.' Tessa set aside her letters. 'I will see what they want.'

Tessa waited for them to appear, conscious of her choice to receive them in the library. Modest though it was, the room was done in dark woods and carried an aura of authority. Whatever their reason for being here, she wanted the message to be clear that she was mistress of this house. This was not their master's house.

Mrs Hollister returned with the unexpected arrivals and Tessa was immediately glad of her choice to stay in the library. She'd seen servants like these before—well-trained members of an exceptional noble household. In her experience, these types of servants had their own brand of haughtiness. She should have expected no less from Dursley's household.

'What is your business here?' Tessa asked, taking her seat behind the wide desk.

'The Earl of Dursley sent us. He said you were newly come to town and had need of staff, miss.' The maid was dressed as crisply as she spoke. She bobbed a curtsy at the end of her message.

'I appreciate his thoughtfulness, but he is incorrect in his assumptions. I do not require further staff. We keep an informal house here and Mrs Hollister sees ably to our needs.' Tessa took out a sheet of paper and dipped her quill in the inkwell. 'If you wouldn't mind waiting, I will pen a note to the Earl, explaining my position. I am sure Mrs Hollister will be happy to provide you with tea in the interim.'

The maid and footman exchanged anxious glances. The footman cleared his throat. Tessa stifled a sigh. Of course it wouldn't be that easy. She was starting to suspect that nothing regarding the Earl of Dursley would ever be easy.

'Excuse me, miss, I don't mean to be impertinent,' the footman began, 'but the Earl said you might not share his opinion on the issue and that we were to remain until his arrival this afternoon.'

Oh, that was very neatly done, Tessa fumed. She couldn't argue with them because they had no power with which to negotiate. All she could do was let them follow orders until Dursley arrived.

'I understand your predicament,' Tessa said tersely. 'You may make yourselves comfortable in the kitchen.'

They did more than make themselves comfortable. They made themselves *useful*.

When Tessa went down to check on the state of things shortly before Dursley's arrival, she was astonished at the amount of industry taking place. The footman had set about the business of polishing the silver and was now arranging it in the glass-fronted storage cabinet. In another corner of the large room, the maid was assisting Mrs Hollister with the ironing. A pile of freshly laundered sheets already lay folded on a work table in testament to their efforts. What was more, Mrs Hollister had lost the cowed look she'd sported upon their arrival and was chatting amiably with the girl while they worked.

Mrs Hollister spotted her at the doorway and excitedly waved her over. 'Miss Branscombe, Meg here knows a most effective recipe for getting food stains out of tablecloths.' Such first-name familiarity was a bad sign.

Tessa forced a smile. 'Lovely. Really, you didn't have to go to all this effort, Meg.'

Meg beamed, taking Tessa's comment as a compliment. Encouraged, Meg went on, 'Of course we did. You've hardly unpacked. Arthur discovered the silver and the dishes still in their packing crates in the cellar. I have no idea what you've been eating off since your arrival. We decided at once we had to set the kitchen to rights. Mrs Hollister is just one woman. She can't do everything.' Meg smiled again, no doubt convinced she'd said just the right thing to prove her and Arthur's efficiency.

Tessa reined in her temper. It wasn't Meg and Arthur's fault, after all. They were just doing what they'd been ordered to do. It was all Dursley's fault they were here at all. Still, it didn't help things that, while she'd been upstairs going over accounts, they'd been down here inventorying the household goods and deciding on their own she wasn't living grandly enough to suit them.

In the month they'd been in London, she'd made no move to unpack the household goods they'd brought from Russia or the items that were stored in the home for the infrequent times her father had come to London. She'd decided to keep life simple and unpack only the basics.

After all, she and her sisters had spent the prior months in mourning, travelling and living plainly during the journey. They knew no one in London and had no intention at this time of formal entertaining, although the house was big enough to do so. Tessa supposed there would come a time when they might offer salons and dinners, but not yet, not now when they were still adjusting to their circumstances.

Tessa didn't mind the practical nature of their lifestyle. Although, she had to privately admit that the sight of the well-polished silver service in the case looked magnificent and the elegant samovar she'd brought from Russia conjured up nostalgia for days past when they lived among the opulent surroundings of the St Petersburg court.

'The pieces look lovely, Arthur.'

'Thank you, miss. There's plenty more in the cellar. I saw the labels on the crates. I can begin work on them tomorrow.' Arthur rolled down his sleeves and put on his discarded coat bearing the Dursley livery in dark green and silver. 'Since the Earl is due in a few minutes, I'll post myself at the door for his arrival.'

It was said with perfunction and kindness. It was

clear from his tone he didn't mean to be high-handed. He only meant to please. Tessa hadn't the heart to remind Arthur she was sending him and Meg home with Dursley.

Tessa offered a few instructions to Mrs Hollister about serving tea and turned to go. She wanted to be ready in the drawing room when Dursley arrived.

'Miss Branscombe, don't be too hard on the Earl. He did what he thought was best. Meg and Arthur are good folk,' Mrs Hollister called after her. 'It was good to have the extra hands today.'

In all fairness, Tessa supposed it was a boon to Mrs Hollister to have the help. Running the kitchen alone for four girls was work enough for one person, not counting the laundry and other sundry chores that cropped up on most days. Tessa did her part, too.

She wasn't above shopping at the market or greengrocers or dusting furniture or changing sheets. After years of running her father's household, she'd learned how to do for herself. She didn't live an idle life while Mrs Hollister shouldered the lion's share of the chores. She saw to her sisters' lessons; when they weren't studying, she saw to it that they helped out around the house as well. She wanted her sisters to be prepared for whatever circumstances life threw at them.

Diplomats' daughters lived in an interesting half-world, not truly peers, but definitely a cut above the world of assistants, clerks and military officers. Some of her acquaintances married well, perhaps to a baron or a knight, and grabbed the bottom rungs of the peerage ladder. Others married merchants who'd engaged in lucrative import/export businesses. Others married clerks and assistants who had little in the way of money or family connections, but hoped to make their way in the diplomatic circles through hard work.

Now that she and her sisters were not part of that circle any longer, it was hard to know what kind of suitors they might encounter. Without their father, they were nothing more than four girls with only modest trust funds to recommend them and a respectable house in Bloomsbury. Tessa knew such dowries would limit suitors to the gentry. Dashing men with titles like Sergei Androvich would disappear from their palette of choices when the time came.

Tessa knew she should thank providence for the Earl of Dursley. His presence in their lives would provide a buffer from falling directly into obscurity. If she chose, she could use her Season to secure a match from among the *ton* and give her sisters a chance to make more advantageous matches than they could hope for otherwise.

Perhaps that was the very reason her father had chosen such a man to act as guardian. Such a rationale would explain much in regards to her father's actions in choosing Dursley. Maybe her father had seen a chance to give his daughters a leg up in the world in case of his untimely demise. That sparked another thought. The date on the codicil of the will had been six months before her father's death. A shiver went through Tessa. Maybe his demise hadn't been so untimely after all.

She was contemplating these new thoughts when Arthur announced Dursley's arrival with his aunt and ushered them into the drawing room.

The Earl nodded a dismissal to the footman with a proprietary ease that sat poorly with Tessa. Her earlier resentment over the Earl's high-handed assumptions flared.

'I hope Arthur and Meg have made themselves useful,' the Earl said after introductions, taking a seat in one of the chairs across from the sofa. Dursley looked immaculate and handsome in buff breeches and a blue coat. His presence filled the room, masculine and powerful. Tessa thought another kind of woman would be quite intimidated. As it was, she was merely annoyed.

'Yes, we must speak about that, my lord,' Tessa began bluntly. 'I do not recall asking for your assistance with my housekeeping needs.'

'None the less, I ascertained those needs during my visit yesterday and hastened to address them,' the Earl said easily, refusing to rise to an argument.

Tessa bristled at his smooth arrogance. He was quite sure of himself. He must walk over people's feelings on a regular basis to have acquired such a superior skill.

'I don't want them here.'

The Earl favoured her with a chilly smile. 'Ah, but, Miss Branscombe, it is my pleasure to have them here.'

'The pleasure is not shared,' Tessa shot back, momentarily forgetting the presence of the Earl's Aunt Lily in the other chair. The regally coiffed woman gave a discreet cough at the hot rejoinder. Tessa had the good sense to apologise. 'Pardon me, your Grace,' she said swiftly to the Dowager Duchess, sure to imply that the Earl was not included in the apology.

'Miss Branscombe, I think it would be wise to accept the offer of additional staff,' the Dowager offered. 'Life during the Season becomes hectic. One cannot see to all the little things as one usually might. The only way to survive is through competent staff. Additionally, it lends you an air of respectability, which, I dare say, you will need. Peyton tells me you went to the market on your own the other day. Those kinds of errands will have to stop or tongues will start to wag.'

Tessa studied the older woman. The Dowager Duchess was an attractive woman of middle years, blessed with stately height and a regal bearing. Her dark hair was streaked with the beginnings of grey, but it was unmistakably the same dark hair the Earl sported. The family resemblance ran strong between them. Tessa suspected the family tendency towards firmness ran strong as well. Aunt Lily showed all the signs of matching the Earl in forceful personality.

What the Earl's aunt said made sense and it was

hard to argue with the practical need for more staff, even if she had plenty to say about curbing outings to the market. Perhaps she could allow her pride to give way in this one matter. It served no purpose to turn away something she needed simply to spite the Earl. 'Perhaps you're right, your Grace. I will need the extra help in weeks to come.' Tessa turned to the Earl. 'I would prefer that you consult with me in the future before making decisions about my household.'

'I shall do my utmost to remember that.' The Earl nodded.

The rest of the visit passed more smoothly. The Earl's aunt was formidable, but likeable, with her straightforward opinions, and Tessa found her easy to get along with over tea. They talked about the upcoming Season and Lily's plans to get Tessa to a dressmaker post-haste the next afternoon. After tea, Tessa gave them a tour of the house, at Lily's request, including an introduction of her sisters. Lily wrung a gasp of sheer delight from Eva by announcing a visit to the dressmaker was in order for them as well as Tessa.

The Earl was silent, trailing the two women through the house without a word or comment. Tessa had half-expected him to be articulating lists of changes as they went. But he didn't have to say anything in order to make himself heard. Tessa's nerves were fully primed by the time she showed them the last room in the house, the small music room. It had seen little use and by the time they'd arrived there, she had begun to see the house through the Earl's eyes.

He didn't have to run a finger across the top of the pianoforte for her to be keenly aware of the thick layer of dust the instrument sported. He hadn't had to comment on the state of the faded striped curtains in the dining room for her to realise they might be outmoded. In her urge to settle into a quiet life, she had not noticed such things. To her, the house had been respectable, and for a middle-class family of some means, it probably was. Still, she found herself making subtle apologies as they returned to the sitting room.

'We've only been in town a month. We are still settling in,' she said. 'A good dusting will set quite a lot of it to rights.'

Lily smiled in sympathy. 'Whatever dusting and beeswax can't mend, Dursley's purse can. I can suggest several decorators to you.'

'My purse, you say?' The Earl cocked a challenging eyebrow at his aunt, who merely grinned.

'You're the guardian responsible for this house and its occupants, are you not, Dursley?' Lily had the audacity to wink at Tessa. The Earl's features clouded and Tessa fought back a laugh. She saw Lily's ploy in all its glory.

The scolding Lily had sent him was a subtle slap

on the wrists. If he was going to play lord of the manor by placing servants here without Tessa's approval and lay claim for the responsibility of the house, he would have to do so on all levels. Lily wasn't going to let him pick and choose which responsibilities he shouldered. He would shoulder them all or none of them.

'Aunt, make your plans with Miss Branscombe about tomorrow's outing. I need a word with Arthur before I go,' Dursley deftly excused himself.

'Thank you,' Tessa said after the Earl had left.

Lily waved such thanks away with her hand. 'It was nothing. My nephew can be stiff-necked at times, but he means well. Often, he has reasons for what he does that aren't always clear to us at the time. I have learned to trust him and you will too. Between us, we'll see you married and settled into a good situation by autumn. Dursley knows who would suit and who would not. He won't let you be snatched up by the wrong sorts.'

'I don't intend to marry,' Tessa said quickly. The sooner her new chaperon had that idea fixed in her mind, the better.

Lily patted her hand, dismissing the statement. 'That's what you say now. Wait and see. You can always change your mind.'

Dursley returned to escort his aunt to the carriage waiting at the kerb. As she was leaving, the Dowager Duchess said, 'Until tomorrow, Miss Branscombe. Thank you for a delightful afternoon.'

The Earl added his thanks. 'Good day, Miss Branscombe.'

'Good day, Lord Dursley,' Tessa said, trying out his name for the first time. It seemed silly to keep thinking him as 'the Earl'. He was going to be a fixture in their lives. She might as well give the fixture a name.

Chapter Five

Peyton sat with Brimley at White's, more relaxed than he had been the evening before. He felt much better now that Arthur was stationed at the Branscombe house. Anyone contemplating a break-in would think twice with a strapping man like Arthur on the premises. He told Brimley as much as they drank evening brandies in a quiet corner. The club was nearly empty; most people had headed out for the evening entertainments.

'I'll have a chance to look around tomorrow,' Peyton said. 'Aunt Lily is taking Miss Branscombe to the modiste's and the girls go to the park with Mrs Hollister in the afternoons.'

'Do you really think the list is here?' Brimley asked.

Peyton nodded. 'I think the sudden presence of certain Russians in the city confirms it. What other reason could there be for a diplomat of Count Androvich's background to be in London? Who better than a family friend to ferret out family secrets? After all, we're doing precisely the same thing, only we had to fabricate the family friend in me. The Czar had a legitimate one to send.'

'Maybe he could not bear to be parted from Miss Branscombe,' Brimley hypothesised. 'They are old friends.'

The idea that Count Androvich might carry a *tendre* for Miss Branscombe sat awkwardly with Peyton. 'It's hardly practical to wait until the object of one's affections journeys a thousand miles before declaring one's intentions.'

Brimley shrugged, enjoying the debate. 'Love isn't practical.'

Peyton laughed. 'Love isn't, but Miss Branscombe is, I assure you. I can't believe Miss Branscombe would waste her time on a trans-European romance. She would have settled the matter before she left St Petersburg.' The surety of his own declaration gave him pause. He'd thought as much about Tessa Branscombe as he had the location of the list lately, a sure testimony that she'd started to get under his skin. Such a feat was a novelty all of its own. He seldom allowed himself to be attracted to anyone so quickly. In this case, he wasn't convinced he'd 'allowed' anything to happen at all, it simply had.

He'd only known Tessa Branscombe for a couple of days, but he felt certain his analysis of her situation was correct. This transition point in her life would have been the perfect time to accept an offer from Androvich. She could have settled down with a wealthy count and avoided the turmoil of her recent upheaval.

But she had implied she hadn't felt safe in St Petersburg. His mind had chased that one elusive remark around his head after their first meeting, resulting in sending Arthur and Meg to the house as soon as possible in the morning. It had also resulted in drawing another conclusion—if Miss Branscombe didn't feel safe, she probably had a justifiable reason for it. Did she know about the list? More importantly, did the Russians think she knew about it? If they thought she was in personal possession of the list, the amount of danger she was in had just escalated exponentially.

The shopping expedition had turned out surprisingly pleasant. In spite of her original misgivings, Tessa had enjoyed herself greatly. Dursley's Aunt Lily was an intelligent and delightful companion. The two of them were loaded down with packages and chatting amiably when they entered the hall of Tessa's town house. Tessa set her purchases and her reticule on a small table in the hall and stilled suddenly.

'What is it, dear?' Lily asked, noting her distress.

Tessa shook her head, her panic starting to rise. It was happening again, the old fear she'd felt in Russia. 'I don't know. The house feels different. It feels unsettled, as if something isn't right.'

Lily smiled fondly. 'It's probably all the changes. Arthur and Meg have done a substantial amount of work in a short time. I can even see differences from before we left. I dare say the house is improved greatly.'

Tessa had to agree. Meg and Arthur had tirelessly devoted themselves to unpacking some of the crates from the cellar as well as the crates she'd brought from St Petersburg. She had not realised how incomplete the house had been until she'd seen the family's personal effects spread throughout the home and the rooms filled with furniture brought down from the attics.

There had certainly been a lot of changes, but those weren't what contributed to her sense of disquiet. The house felt disrupted from another's presence. Someone was here.

Tessa felt the gnawing fear start again in her stomach. She'd hoped to be done with such worry. Would the need to be constantly on guard ever be gone? She'd thought she'd beaten such fear since their arrival in London, but over the last few days the sense that she was being watched had returned, and now this. She reached for her reticule. She had her small gun inside. She went nowhere without it.

'Lily, if you would just wait for me in the drawing room, I'll have a look around.'

Lily looked at her strangely, but Tessa didn't care. At least her fears weren't misplaced. In St Petersburg she'd been right.

Tessa started upstairs slowly, her back against the

curving wall of the staircase as she went, making herself less visible if anyone was looking down. If there was an intruder, he would be upstairs. Anyone else would have heard them come in.

Tessa slipped the small gun from her reticule. She cocked the weapon, not doubting her instincts once. It was the perfect time to break in. Her sisters were on an outing to a nearby park with Mrs Hollister and Meg and Arthur were spending their afternoon off at Dursley House. There was no one around to notice the comings and goings of a stranger in the house.

She was five stairs from the top when she heard it: the sound of booted feet on the hardwood floor. She'd done a good job of hiding herself against the natural curvature of the staircase, but, reciprocally, she was blind to all else that moved above her. She could no more see who was coming down the stairs than they could see her.

Tessa had only seconds to think before the intruder was upon her. Her mind raced over her options. There was no chance someone coming down the stairs wouldn't see her as they passed. Her only choice was to seize the advantage.

Tessa boldly stepped out into the centre of the stairs, gun ready to fire. 'Stay where you are.'

She was not prepared for what happened next. Instead of obeying her command, the intruder flung himself at her, propelling them against the stair wall as opposed to tumbling down the steps. Tessa found herself most indecently pressed between the wall and the hard body of her attacker. Breasts met chest, her skirts met with the hard muscles of his thighs. She could barely breathe, let alone summon a scream. Her hand holding the gun was shackled against the wall by the intruder's iron grip.

Tessa struggled, but she was too closely imprisoned to land an effective kick. She tore her gaze from her trapped gun hand into the intruder's face. She found her voice. 'Dursley!'

'Miss Branscombe!' His shock was nearly as great as her own. In his amazement, he released her gun arm.

Tessa hadn't been ready for such freedom. The gun slipped from her weakened fingers and clattered down the steps. A misfire rang out. Instantly, Dursley surrounded her again with his body, this time as a protector. His arms bracketed her on either side, his body in full contact with hers, disregarding any compunction for propriety.

Tessa recognised the stance for what it was: the posture of a human shield. No one would be able to get close to her with such a force surrounding her. It was dark and safe in the confines of Dursley's protective circle. For a moment, Tessa let herself savour such a luxury. Then Dursley realised the only danger was the misfire of the gun.

The look he gave her was incredulous. 'The gun was loaded? The gun you pointed at me was *loaded*?'

Tessa looked up at him, his face very near hers. 'Of

course it was. I didn't know it was you. A lot of good an unloaded weapon would have done me.' She'd not noticed what a dark shade of blue his eyes were in their prior encounters. Then again, she'd not had the opportunity to appreciate them at such close proximity.

There were other things she was starting to 'appreciate' at this range, too, like the breadth of his shoulders and the firmness of his thighs, not to mention the supposed intimacy of their position on the stairs.

Any moment his Aunt Lily would determine it was safe to come out of the drawing room. Tessa could only imagine what kind of image she and the Earl would create to the unsuspecting onlooker who happened upon them. Tessa shifted, squirming a bit in the hopes of creating some distance between them. She immediately wished she hadn't moved. Her gyrations caused her hips to brush against Dursley in a highly improper manner. To her great embarrassment, she actually felt that most unmentionable part of him stir at the contact.

Dursley took a step back. 'A thousand pardons, Miss Branscombe,' he said with polite neutrality, as if they'd merely brushed past one another on the stairs at a ball.

Lily appeared at the bottom of the steps. 'Is everyone all right? Heavens, Dursley, is that you?'

'We're all right, Aunt,' Dursley assured her.

'Tessa thought she heard an intruder,' Lily called up.

'Did she?' Dursley shot Tessa a foreboding look. 'Do you have a lot of experience, then, in listening for intruders, Miss Branscombe? I find my curiosity is piqued as to why a young lady would feel it necessary to be armed with a gun in her own home.'

'No more so than my own curiosity, milord, as to why you were skulking about upstairs in my house,' Tessa replied coolly.

'Skulking, is it?' Dursley said in his most high-handed tone.

'Yes. Skulking,' Tessa insisted, moving down the stairs ahead of him, doing her best to match his haughtiness. But her cool exterior was a façade only. Inside, she was so jangled from the encounter that, after picking her gun up from the hall floor, she rang for tea before she realised all the staff was gone for the afternoon.

It wasn't until much later, after her sisters were asleep, that Tessa allowed her mind to consider the scene on the stairs. She sat at the desk in her private office, dwelling on those few moments. The most important concern on her mind was what Peyton—*Dursley*—had been doing upstairs. One of the consequences of the afternoon was that she was finding it difficult to think of him without wanting to use his first name. One could not brush up against a man's groin in such an intimate fashion and continue to think of him as a title. At least she couldn't.

Tessa marshalled her thoughts. She had to stay focused. What had he been doing here? It wasn't out of the realm of possibility that he'd come by to escort his aunt home from their shopping trip. Finding them still out, he'd decided to wait.

But waiting could be done quite nicely in the public rooms downstairs. There was no need to wait upstairs. Upstairs consisted of bedrooms, the school-room and her small office. Peyton—Dursley—had been properly appalled at her sisters' chatter over tea the first day. She doubted her sisters' bedrooms held any interest or allure to him. Never mind that it wasn't proper for gentlemen to go poking around young girls' bedchambers. And propriety mattered greatly to him. The only room that could hold any interest would be her office, and only then if he were looking for something.

Tessa gazed around the room. There was only a chair and a small bookcase, in addition to her desk. On the wall was a portrait of her father, newly hung by Arthur that morning. She couldn't imagine what Peyton thought he might find in here.

She huffed. There it was again—Peyton. She might as well give in. She would call him 'Peyton' in her mind. It could be her little secret. Tessa fiddled with a paperweight, studying the portrait of her father, which had been completed a few months before his death. In the painting he was elegantly posed, standing next to a table that contained a long scrolling document. She supposed the setting was to symbolise his diplomatic career, the scroll representing some kind of treaty or agreement he was so famous for.

She wondered what he might make of this afternoon. Her father had been an expert at reading people. What might he see that she'd missed? Something niggled at her about the encounter. At the actual time of its happening, her mind had been racing too much for the nuance to register. But now as she slowed it down in her head, pieces began to form. Peyton had not recognised her immediately. His instincts had not seen her. His instincts had seen danger. Had he thought she was an intruder? That raised a host of other questions, most prominently— why would he have suspected an intruder at a quiet house in a quiet neighbourhood?

The way he'd reacted indicated he'd expected the worst, for whatever reason. She'd never met a man with such lightning reflexes. He'd been on her before she could have even considered firing the gun. His skill was more than natural talent. That kind of reflex was carefully honed and acquired. She'd seen men with that kind of skill in the Czar's personal guard.

Once he'd recognised her, his demeanour had changed. He'd been all protection when the gun misfired. It was almost as if he'd thought the shot came from somewhere else. It clearly hadn't. But his reaction had been that of a bodyguard. If there had been another shot, his body would have taken the brunt of it. Surely such action was above and beyond a guardian's duty to his ward.

Then there had been that moment of mutual, acute awareness, the searing gaze of his hot eyes. How would she ever face him again without blushing? He and Lily had not stayed long once he'd been assured of her safety in the house. She'd been grateful. Her eyes had developed a fascination for glancing at certain male parts of his anatomy. Luckily, he hadn't seemed to notice. But she'd better get over the penchant for such behaviour quickly. He would be escorting her to the Broughtons' ball in three nights' time. *Where they would dance.* As her escort, he was obliged to dance with her once. The thought of being in such close proximity to Peyton's body again was unaccountably exciting.

Such emotions were unwise. Developing an infatuation over Peyton would cloud the real issue. Could she trust him? His actions suggested both yes and no. He'd been wandering around odd parts of her house while it was empty. He'd entered their lives without warning with only a misplaced codicil to recommend him. Those circumstances were highly suspect. Yet, he'd opted to protect her, which bespoke a message of trustworthiness and honour. Her own reaction to him had been one of security. In those moments on the stairs when she'd been surrounded by his body, she'd thought that here was a man who could share her burden.

She recognised her reaction was based solely on impulse. Tessa shook her head to clear it. No, she would not tell Peyton about her fears. Not yet. Not until she knew more about her situation and him. She'd thought there had been an intruder today, but it had only been Peyton. Her instincts might be off. If no one was following her, if it was all in her head, then there was nothing to tell him. He would ask for proof and right now she didn't have any.

The darker side of her conscience emerged, prodding her to more difficult hypotheses. All this assumed Peyton was on the side of good. Perhaps he was the source of her fears. He was the one new variable in her life these days, along with the arrival of Sergei's Russian delegation. The only difference was that she knew Sergei.

Tessa sighed in exasperation. There was so much she didn't know! What did she have that was worth all the trouble someone was potentially going through? Was Peyton connected to that? What did he know? Anything? Nothing? Everything? The only thing Tessa was sure of was that Peyton Ramsden and his exquisite body was dangerous to her in more than one way.

Aunt Lily had that dangerous look in her eye, Peyton noted over an excellent trifle. He'd agreed to dine with her simply because not to do so would be to immediately admit to hiding something. Damn Tessa Branscombe and her inconvenient gun. He'd hoped to avoid the complicated topic. To that end Peyton had now exhausted every subject of conversation he could think of.

But in the end, it was clear Aunt Lily could not be put off the scent.

Lily set down her spoon and fixed Peyton with her gaze. 'I think it's time you explained to me why Miss Branscombe carries a gun and apparently does not hesitate to use it. If I am to act as a sponsor for her, I want the truth, Nephew.'

Peyton dabbed his mouth with his napkin, gathering his thoughts. 'She's a woman on her own and quite alone. She's entitled to provide herself with protection.'

Lily gave him a long considering look. For a moment Peyton thought he might have succeeded in thwarting her. 'Let's try the question another way. Why were you upstairs in her house?'

Peyton sighed. 'There is concern that the Branscombe girls may have inadvertently brought some sensitive information with them from Russia.'

Lily raised her eyebrows in challenge. 'You're spying on those delightful girls and they know nothing? That is a bit different from what you told me two days ago when you asked me to take up their cause.'

'I'm not spying on them. I am protecting them from themselves and anyone else who might happen along,' Peyton clarified. Leave it to Lily to boil it all down to its simplest form.

'And who's protecting them from you?' she retorted. 'I assume they know nothing about your role or that they're even in the possession of this "sensitive information"?'

'I am of no danger to them, Aunt.'

'They're not really your wards, are they, Peyton?' She gave him a disapproving look that made him feel like a small boy again.

'Perhaps not legally, but I will do right by them. They'll have no reason to suspect otherwise.' He met Lily's gaze with a pointed one of his own. She nodded. The implicit message was clear. No one was to know. It was a compliment of sorts that he'd confessed as much as he had. But Lily had a right to know what she was getting into, at least to some extent. He did mean to see the girls taken care of.

Lily raised her glass. 'A toast, Peyton, to tangled webs and all that.'

Peyton knew it wasn't so much a toast his aunt offered as a warning. She understood the need for such subterfuge, but she didn't approve, not fully.

Chapter Six

'Peyton Ramsden's claim to being a guardian is a fraud,' Sergei Androvich spat angrily. The knife he'd been spinning on its handle clattered to the desk top of a private office in the Russian embassy.

The three men with him exchanged sharp looks with one another. They were older, more seasoned diplomats. Sergei felt the anxious undercurrents of their exchange. 'What?' he barked.

'We have no concrete proof of that,' Gromsky reminded him. 'We know only that he's done some diplomatic work before in Vienna. He hasn't done anything for the diplomatic corps for over two years now. He's a peer of the realm. If we go after him, we'll have to be very sure of ourselves and his level of involvement.'

'I agree. Still, I think what evidence we have suggests it is not a mere coincidence he's arrived in the Branscombe girls' lives. His actions suggest he has an agenda,' Ilanovich put in.

'That agenda is to push himself into their lives and to push you out, Sergei,' Vasilov said baldly. 'The whole reason you've been assigned to this mission is your connection to the Branscombe household, and he has now thrown that into question, whether he's acting the part of spy or not.'

'I haven't been pushed out,' Sergei said defensively, but that was indeed his main complaint. He'd thought it would be a simple matter of courting Tessa, wooing the list out of her if she knew where it was, or finding it and stealing it out from under her. Peyton Ramsden's presence had changed all that and quickly, too.

Ramsden was cleverly keeping Tessa too busy to see him. These last days, she'd been swamped with shopping, fittings, even a few visits to friends of Ramsden's aunt. There was suddenly no time for him, when just a few days ago she'd been so grateful for his escort to the market.

'I respectfully beg to differ,' Vasilov continued. 'You have indeed been pushed out. In the past three days, our watchers report Ramsden has been there three times. The other day, he came early to wait for Miss Branscombe and his aunt to come home from shopping. He was alone in the house. How many days have you been there since Ramsden showed up? Even when he's not there, his personally appointed servants are, while all we can do is hire men to watch from across the street.'

'I will tell Tessa our suspicions about Ramsden. I will do it tonight at the Broughtons' ball. She'll be furious and she'll evict him from their lives. You know what a shrew she can be,' Sergei said idly, unimpressed with the worries of old men.

They were alarmed with such a plan. 'No! You cannot tell her. She might tell Ramsden. It would be just like her to confront the scoundrel with her information. We can't have her raising a fuss and alerting all kinds of people. Besides, how can we explain to her why Ramsden would have been assigned to them without telling her about the list?' Gromsky argued.

'No, our original plan of action is still our best plan,' the third one, Ilanovich, said in reasonable tones. 'You must continue to court her as you did in St Petersburg. Win her trust.'

Vasilov gave Sergei a sly look. 'Perhaps it will be easier to court her here where she is far from the only home she's known. Perhaps nostalgia for St Petersburg will make your case stronger.' His tone suggested he had his doubts.

Sergei's eyes narrowed. He did not care for the man's insinuations that he'd failed to secure a marriage to Tessa before she left St Petersburg. Marriage would have made it much easier to keep her close and under surveillance until they found the list.

'I have no wish to be married to such an outspoken woman.' He twirled his ivory-handled knife again.

Vasilov's eyes gleamed. 'It wouldn't last long, only until death do you part and the Czar would not forget all that you sacrificed for your country. In the meanwhile, you could enjoy a beautiful woman in your bed.'

Tessa sat mannequin-still in front of the mirror, trying not to fuss while Lily's maid put the final pins into her coiffure. She was used to such attentions, of course. She'd dressed for several elaborate occasions in St Petersburg. But in the interim of her father's death and their travels, she'd conveniently forgotten how tedious an evening *toilette* could be. She had not realised just how much she'd come to enjoy the simple wardrobe of the past months.

This discomfort was all Peyton's fault. Naturally. Everything that had gone wrong could be laid at his door. Most recently, he could be blamed for the upheaval that had occurred that afternoon, trying to move her and her sisters to Lily's town house. Peyton had insisted she prepare for the ball at Lily's and that her sisters come along and spend the night.

She and Peyton had spent a large part of the morning arguing about it. Ostensibly, he'd argued that he wanted Lily on hand to help her dress and that he hadn't wanted to make the longer drive to Bloomsbury to pick her up. But Tessa was suspicious none the less. If they were gone, it would be all that much easier to search the house for whatever he thought was there. She'd countered that she'd been dressing for formal occasions for most of her adult life and had yet to appear naked at any of them. She'd also been quick to point out that the distance to Bloomsbury had not been great enough to keep him from darkening their doorstep the last three days.

The maid slid a final pin in and stepped back, letting Tessa take in the hairstyle with an uninter-rupted view. 'There, miss. You will steal all the gen-tlemen's hearts tonight!'

'Oh, Tess, you look lovely, like something from a fairy tale,' Eva breathed from the bed where all of her sisters were gathered, watching the spectacle of her getting ready.

Tessa turned her head in the mirror to study the pile of curls expertly arranged on top of her head. Some of the blame she'd laid at Peyton's door dissi-pated. The woman had done an excellent job. While the coiffure was securely pinned, her hair was by no means scraped up and back from her face. Instead, the pile of curls gave the appearance of being loosely done up, leaving a few trailing wisps to strategically frame her face. Tessa knew Eva and Petra could not have contrived to do better back at the house.

There was a scratch at the door. The maid went to answer it. She hurried back, followed by Lily. 'Dursley's coach has arrived, my dear.' Lily passed a narrow box to the maid. 'Stand up, Tessa, I am eager to see the gown.'

Tessa stood up and shook out her skirts for Lily's inspection, feeling self-conscious. Surely Lily would notice that the neckline was too low? Tessa couldn't resist a quick tug at the bodice. The gown was gorgeous, but indecent, no matter how much Eva raved it was the height of fashion.

'Stop fiddling,' Lily scolded, catching Tessa's tug. 'We're going to a ball, not a nunnery.' Lily stepped forward and tugged the bodice back into place. She stepped back to study the results. 'You look stunning. There will be a line of suitors coming to call tomorrow and the Season is not even in full swing.' Lily gestured towards the maid. 'The pearls will be just the thing.'

Before Tessa could resist, the maid clasped a strand of pearls about her neck and handed her ear-rings with matching pearl teardrops to fasten on her lobes.

'I can't possibly accept these,' Tessa began, but it was hard to protest in earnest when they completed her *toilette* so perfectly. Lily urged her over to the long standing-mirror and the sight of the woman in it conjured up a multitude of emotions in Tessa.

The woman in the mirror was positively lovely. The gown of eggshell on eggshell lace lent an ethereal aura to the ensemble. The pale yellow-ivory colouring of the gown was set off simply, but effectively, with narrow sky-blue ribbon at the bodice, hem and at the small puffed sleeves. Instead of ruining the fall of the lightweight fabric with fussy frills and bows, the modiste had used Tessa's height and a slightly fuller but unadorned skirt to show off the exquisite flow of the material.

Yes, the woman in the mirror was not only lovely, but proud. In spite of her complaints about the task of dressing for the evening, Tessa had to admit to herself that she had missed this. The woman in the mirror reminded her of what her life had consisted of in St Petersburg. She'd loved moving in the diplomatic circles, talking to people from all over Europe, sharing thoughts with intelligent individuals and doing so fluently in three languages. Her father's death had changed all that. She was no longer needed in those circles, but now Peyton Ramsden had given her a chance to make new connections.

'We must go. Dursley will be impatient,' Lily said, handing her a wrap of embroidered summer silk.

'I'll be just a moment. I want to say goodnight to my sisters.'

Tessa faced her sisters after Lily left the room. Even though she'd been to countless balls, the occasion felt momentous. In some ways it was. This was her first night among English society in London. She was doing this for all their futures, hers as well as theirs.

'Eva's right. You look beautiful, Tessa.' Petra took her gloved hand. 'We'll be all right here. This house is huge. We'll be so busy exploring we won't even know you're gone.'

'Make sure Annie is in bed soon and don't wait up. I don't know how long I'll be.' Tessa gave last-minute orders. She hugged them all, careful not to crush the gown.

'Oh, no, you're not getting rid of us that easily,' Eva said. 'We're walking you to the stairs. We want to see the Earl all tricked out.'

'Don't use slang, Eva,' Tessa chided automatically but she couldn't deny them their wish. At the top of the stairs she left them peering through the newel posts. She could hear Eva whisper in awe, 'He's so handsome.'

Privately, Tessa had to agree. The man waiting at the bottom of the steps, chatting with his aunt, was absolutely riveting in his masculine appeal. He wore the standard black evening apparel of a gentleman better than any man she'd yet encountered, and she'd encountered many in all shapes, sizes and ages.

The dark coat was well cut across his shoulders, showing off their breadth without giving the impression of being glued on. And the trousers... Well, recent experience had taught her she'd better not think about his trousers. Still, she stole a glance just to be sure that his legs were as long, his hips as lean, as she remembered them.

She was halfway down when he caught sight of her and looked up from his conversation. She was acutely aware of his gaze following her every step. There was no doubt that she had captured his full attention.

He was there to meet her at the bottom of the stairs. He took her hand and lifted it to his lips. 'Miss Branscombe, you certainly know how to light up a room.'

The Broughtons' ball was one of the first of the Season. The Royal Academy art exhibition in May, which was one of the highlights of the social whirl, wasn't for another week. But the Broughtons were close with the Home and Foreign Offices and wanted to be the first to entertain the Russian delegation. It was the perfect social occasion for Tessa to experience *ton*nish life in London.

The dancing was already underway by the time they gained the ballroom. The receiving line had been surprisingly long for an early Season ball and Peyton had had to stop several times and greet acquaintances. Lily had smiled and suggested slyly that Tessa had increased Peyton's popularity immensely.

There were countless introductions to be made in the ballroom as well since there were both Lily's and Peyton's circles of friends to greet. They slowly worked their way around the perimeter of the ballroom. They were deep in conversation with an acquaintance of Peyton's when Lady Broughton approached, the Russian delegation in tow.

Tessa stiffened involuntarily, her light grip on

Peyton's arm tightening. She recognised the men with Sergei: Gromsky, Vasilov and Ilanovich. She knew them from her father's work. They were considered dangerous men at court. It was widely known among the right circle of people that these men were by turn diplomats, spies and assassins when all else failed to render the anticipated results. That they had been sent to England lent credence to her fears—she was the cause of their arrival.

'Dursley, I want to introduce you and Miss Branscombe to our guests of honour tonight. I thought Miss Branscombe might enjoy seeing someone from her former home.' The hostess gestured to the three men behind her. 'Ambassadors Gromsky, Vasilov, Ilanovich and Count Androvich, this is the Earl of Dursley and Miss Tessa Branscombe, recently of St Petersburg.'

'Miss Branscombe and I are old friends. I spent much time at her father's house during his tenure at the Czar's court.' Sergei stepped forward and bowed low over her hand. 'It is a pleasure to see you again.' He shot a look at Peyton. 'It's a pleasure to see you again as well, Dursley.' Sergei's icy gaze met Peyton's searing stare. The tension in the little coterie escalated.

Lady Broughton looked overtly uncomfortable. 'I did not know you were already acquainted.' Her eyes moved noticeably between Peyton and Sergei.

Tessa moved in to alleviate the awkward moment, focusing her attention on the other ambassadors. She couldn't let them see her fear. If there was a chance they were here for other purposes, her nervousness would alert them to something more. 'How do you find London?' she asked smoothly in French, the language of the St Petersburg court.

After an appropriate interlude of small talk, during which Peyton and Sergei continued to glare at each other, the orchestra struck up a waltz.

'Miss Branscombe, may I have this dance?' Sergei asked.

Tessa accepted, although she could feel Peyton bristle beside her. In truth, she was oddly disappointed that it was Sergei leading her on to the floor and not Peyton. But she'd dance with anyone to get away from the other ambassadors, and Sergei was an old friend.

Sergei and she swung effortlessly into the pattern of dancers. They'd danced together often enough.

'Like old times?' Sergei asked with a smile.

Tessa gave a little laugh. 'A little. It seems surreal that you and I are dancing together a thousand miles from the dance floors we're used to.'

'Are you missing St Petersburg?' Sergei navigated them through the turn.

'Of course I miss it. Practically my whole life was spent there. But I don't miss the way it was at the last.' She didn't need to say more. Sergei knew to what she referred. There was comfort in knowing at least one person in London understood her worries.

'It could be that way again, Tessa,' Sergei whispered in her ear, drawing her close as they danced. 'I was wrong to let you leave St Petersburg without declaring my intentions. It was such a confusing time—your father's death, the break-in—I hardly knew what to do. Then you left early without saying goodbye. You must forgive me for letting you go.'

At one time, Sergei's proposal would have met with joyous acceptance from her. For over a year there had been an unspoken courtship of sorts between them in St Petersburg. During that time, she'd never been quite sure if his regular escort to social functions had indicated something more than friendship. She'd spent nights hoping that it did. She'd fancied herself in love with the dashing count. But tonight, that original attraction seemed diminished. That was probably Peyton's fault, too.

'It was a trying time for all of us. No one was thinking clearly,' Tessa responded evasively. The dance was coming to a close.

'Would you come outside with me? I'm in need of some fresh air.' Sergei directed them towards a door out on to the wide terrace.

'Ah, this is better.' Sergei took a deep breath. 'I find myself missing the sharp cold of Russia at times.' Sergei leaned back against the railing and gestured towards the ballroom. 'How is your guardian? Not too high-handed, I hope? Although that hope seems misplaced.'

Tessa chuckled. 'He's all right. He's very confident.'

'I don't see you tolerating such shenanigans,' Sergei offered shrewdly. 'I am surprised to see that you've accepted him at all and yet he's the one who has escorted you here. I would have, you know.'

She heard the hurt in Sergei's tone and felt guilty. It wasn't right to throw over her friendship with Sergei for the demands of a man she'd only known a short week.

'I checked all the paperwork. It seems legitimate. He and his Aunt Lily have decided I must have a Season. Lily hopes I'll catch a husband, but I am doing this for the girls. Petra will be out next year.'

Sergei gave a gentle smile, his voice intimate. 'You have no need to catch a husband. I would willingly marry you and take you back to St Petersburg where you belong. I should have done so long ago.' He reached for her gloved hand, making small circular movements on the back of her hand with his thumb. 'Just think, Tessa, we could marry here by special licence and spend the summer in London. Then, in the autumn, you could come home with me as my countess. The universe would be restored to its rightful order.'

Tessa studied Sergei closely. The offer held its degree of temptation. No more strange city, no more starting over and making new friends, no more uncertainty. Being with Sergei would solve a lot of problems. She would lead the life she knew, a life she was good at. Her sisters would have opportunities to marry well, thanks to Sergei's title and position. Never had he spoken of his feelings or intentions so plainly. Yet his gallant words seemed to lack a certain ring of truth. What reason did he have to play act, and with her of all people, his friend?

She was so wrapped up in her own internal thoughts she hadn't realised what Sergei was up to until it was too late to prevent it. He had her in his arms, his mouth on hers in a deep kiss, his tongue wet where it ran across her lips. The kiss was not entirely unpleasant, but certainly far too intimate for their surroundings. He was kissing her as if no one else could see. This was a kiss between lovers and it was disappointingly empty of all sensation. After her encounter with Peyton on the stairs, she rather thought there would be. But she felt nothing.

Tessa drew back, struggling to do so when Sergei seemed reluctant to let her establish a decent distance between them. 'Sergei…' she began.

He put a finger to her lips. 'Shh. Say nothing. Promise me you'll think about it.'

The bastard was kissing her as if no one else could walk out and see them, and she was doing a fair imitation of liking it. Peyton's fists curled at his side. Tessa's prolonged absence had prompted his hasty search. He'd been worried and here she was, playing kiss the count!

He'd not been oblivious to Tessa's well-concealed anxiety regarding the Russian delegation. He'd felt her grip tighten on his arm. She'd done admirably, making general conversation, but she'd been all too glad to escape to the dance floor with Sergei, a man she thought she could trust. Well, Peyton wasn't so sure about that. What kind of gentleman would take such liberties in a public place?

In hindsight, he should have anticipated such a manoeuvre. A woman far from home would be susceptible to the wiles of a fellow compatriot. It begged the question of what the Count was here for—was Brimley right and Sergei merely here to win his bride or was he part of something more sinister involving Ralph Branscombe's list?

Tessa suddenly gave a brief struggle, pushing at Sergei's chest. That was all the invitation Peyton needed to make his presence known. The cur thought to kiss her secrets out of her. Well, not when he was around. He was Tessa Branscombe's escort. If anyone was doing any kissing, it would be him.

Chapter Seven

Peyton strode towards Tessa and the Count, crossing the terrace in three strides. 'Miss Branscombe, I have been looking for you,' he said without preamble, situating himself between the two. 'Your absence from the ballroom has been duly noted.' He was gratified to see Tessa blush slightly.

'You may return inside at your leisure, Count Androvich. Miss Branscombe will return with me. It's almost time for the supper waltz, which is mine, I believe.' The Count's dislike for him was palpable as Peyton dismissed him. Peyton discreetly looped Tessa's arm through his and began retracing their steps, taking a certain amount of satisfaction in routing the Count. But his victory was short lived.

Beside him, Tessa bristled. 'How dare you treat Sergei with such disregard!'

Peyton stopped and turned to face her, careful to

keep his features and tone even. 'How dare *I*? How dare *he* treat you with such flagrant disregard for propriety! Can you imagine what would have happened if someone else had seen you? You would have been compromised beyond redemption and well on your way to marriage, whether you wanted it or not,' Peyton scolded in cold tones.

It would not serve to have her suspect the real motives behind his behaviour when he did not fully understand them himself. Jealousy was not a familiar emotion to him. It was too petty and beneath his notice, yet it was remarkably akin to the primal urge that had surged through him at the sight of her in Androvich's embrace.

Tessa was spoiling for a fight. 'Sergei has been my friend far longer than you've been my guardian. He has seen me through difficult times and stood by me. He deserves better.'

Her defence of the questionable Russian sat poorly with Peyton. '*You* deserve better, Miss Branscombe—no friend would play so carelessly with your virtue. I find that, of the three of us on the terrace, I was the only one watching out for your reputation. Come, our waltz is beginning.'

They resumed the short walk back into the ballroom. But the stiffness of Tessa's posture hinted she was not through with their conversation. Peyton guided her towards an open spot on the floor and set aside his own irritation in order to cajole her into good spirits. 'The interlude is behind us, Miss Branscombe. The waltz is my favourite dance. I wouldn't want to spoil it with a sour mood.'

'This discussion is not over,' she said resolutely as he placed a hand at the small of her back and took her other hand.

Peyton smiled tightly. 'The discussion *is* over. I am right and you are merely arguing because you're irritated that I am right.'

Tessa's blue-violet eyes sparked at that. Whatever rejoinder she had in mind was cut off by the opening strains of the waltz. She might have even left him on the dance floor if he hadn't had such a grip on her waist. As it was, she had no choice but to let him lead them into the patterns.

But Tessa was in no way defeated. Her eyes sparkled dangerously and her temper sizzled between them, a sharp contrast to the civilised steps of the dance. It soon became clear to Peyton that there was to be nothing civilised between them. The dance became a silent competition. The harder he tried to maintain the proper conventions, the harder Tessa pushed him to break them, using his gentleman's code against him. The distance between them shrank until he was forced to hold her tightly. The rapid pace of her steps forced him to greater speeds.

Peyton only fought back because he didn't like losing in any form and he avoided scandal like the plague. In truth, the temptation to hand her the victory was nearly overwhelming. He liked the feel of her body against his. The press of her breasts to his chest, as they whirled through a turn, was positively erotic. Then a miraculous transformation occurred. The speed of their dancing flushed her cheeks and the anger in her eyes faded to be replaced by something else that resembled pleasure.

The Fury had become an angel again. The combination of her pleasure and beauty was a stunning mixture. In spite of his vaunted self-control, Peyton felt his member stir at the sight and feel of her in his arms. Never had he wanted a dance to go on indefinitely. But he could have danced all night with Tessa Branscombe.

She was flushed and breathless when the music ended. Others swarmed passed them on the way into the supper room. Peyton was reluctant to give up the magic of the dance floor and quietly led her aside to an alcove where she could catch her breath and have a quiet moment apart from the crowd. Goodness knew he could use a moment, too, in order to let his growing arousal subside.

'What is this?' Tessa looked around their surroundings. 'We're alone.'

'Not entirely.' Peyton gestured to the throng just beyond them. The crowd was near, but, in their excitement to get to dinner, they were oblivious to anyone who had stepped out of the flow of foot traffic.

He was dismayed to see the exuberance fade from her face. The angel was gone.

'I see,' she said in a cool tone Peyton was coming to recognise all too well. 'You want the playing field levelled.' She gave a dramatic sigh. 'Very well, if you insist.'

Although Tessa was tall, she rose up on her toes to bridge their differences in height and kissed him full on the mouth.

The movement surprised him. Now he understood. She thought he was jealous of Sergei. His first reaction was protection. With a searching hand, Peyton groped successfully for the curtain that would shut off the alcove. His second reaction was to show her a thing or two about proper kissing.

She might have been bold enough to start it, but the kiss was no longer hers. Peyton took over, his tongue gently exploring the surface of her lips, testing her level of willingness. Her lips parted, and he deepened the kiss. With seductive skill, he caressed her tongue with his in slow circular strokes, allowing her to participate in this languid duel. He knew empirically this was the way women liked to be kissed. To prove his point, a small moan escaped her.

Her pleasure was potent. At the sound of her moan everything changed. The kiss was no longer an instructive lesson in technique. It was now a prelude to something much stronger. He had not meant to take things further. But possessing her mouth was no longer enough. He had one hand at the back of her neck and the other just below the underside of her breast. It was a mere adjustment of inches to cup the fullness of her breast in his palm, his thumbs reaching up to stroke her nipples through the cloth. She gasped in wanton delight and Peyton felt her knees buckle. He bore her backwards to the window seat and followed her down.

Her eyes were rich amethysts, dark with her desire, encouraging him onwards.

She wriggled beneath him, her untutored moves teasing his arousal where it lay heavy and obvious against her leg. Her movements indicated he was not in this alone. She was as aroused as he.

He *knew* what he wanted in that moment and it shocked the hell out of him. He'd never given in to such a burst of spontaneous passion before. Yet here he was, wanting to and even willing to ravish the beauty beneath him. This had to stop. Immediately. For a thousand reasons. Not the least being his honour as well as hers.

Peyton drew back with a hard breath. 'This is not the time or place. I must apologise.' He tugged at his waistcoat and extended a hand to help her rise. 'Are you all right, Miss Branscombe?'

'Yes,' Tessa replied curtly. 'And I think after *that*—' her eyes flicked towards the window seat '—you can call me Tessa.'

Her aplomb was laudable, Peyton thought, but his angel was unsteady on her feet, unsteady and beautiful, her golden hair loose about her face, her lips noticeably well kissed. Under no circumstance could she return to the ballroom looking like that. 'Wait here, I'll send Lily to you. You can tell her you're feeling out of sorts,' Peyton offered. It was the least he could do. His behaviour had been beyond the pale. He'd nearly seduced an innocent in an alcove as if he was a veritable rake. He needed time to sort things through, to make sense of his own feelings.

Peyton found Lily and discreetly sent her after Tessa. Lily would take Tessa home and send the carriage back for him. Peyton couldn't imagine riding home with Tessa just now, sitting across from her well-kissed lips and slightly tousled hair, knowing that he could do nothing for his aches or hers with Aunt Lily next to her. Right now he didn't need that form of exquisite torture. He needed distance. Secure in the knowledge that Tessa was taken care of, Peyton took himself off to a deserted library to await the return of his carriage.

The library was dark with the exception of a dim lamp on the fireplace mantel. Peyton found a long sofa and took the luxury of stretching out. Since dancing had resumed in the ballroom, no one was likely to come along.

Tessa Branscombe had turned his ordered world topsy turvy in a short time. He'd be more careful with what he wished for in the future. It seemed ages ago that he was bemoaning the fact that his life felt empty. Now, it practically burgeoned with activity.

Instead of smooth days, there was conflict. Tessa attempted to thwart his authority at every turn. Instead of predictability, there was now mystery everywhere he looked. He'd forgotten what that was like. Since he'd met Tessa, he'd been argued with, defied, held at gunpoint, soundly kissed and thoroughly aroused. It was no wonder his emotions were out of joint.

Peyton sighed in the near darkness. Riotous emotions were not what Brimley had hired him for. He'd been entrusted with uncovering a dangerous list for his government. He was getting nowhere with that. He suspected that wouldn't change until he'd acquired Tessa's full trust. Until then, he had no idea how much Tessa knew. Did she know there was a list? Did she fear the presence of the Russian delegation in town? What would she do if she had the list or found the list? Would she turn it over to the Russians?

A large part of Peyton hoped Tessa knew about the list. He very much feared a scenario in which Tessa accidentally uncovered the list among some family possessions and, unaware of its value, showed it to Count Androvich. Such a scenario was not so far-fetched. The Count was a family friend. It would be natural to go to him, to see him as a trusted confidant.

Tessa did know something, though. There had been the one reference she'd made the first day he'd called about her concern over safety. Tonight, the Russian delegation had unnerved her. There was the gun in her reticule and her perception that a disturbance in her home must be due to the presence of an intruder. The last had been most telling. Many women he knew would have concluded anything amiss was due to new items laid out by the servants or the general upheaval of the unpacking process. It would have been beyond the imaginings of these pampered women to conclude someone had been sneaking around. Yet Tessa had not bothered to think otherwise.

Not for the first time, Peyton wished he knew more about what had happened in St Petersburg. His best chance of finding out was to get close to Tessa and win her trust. Tonight's events indicated that might not be as hard to do as he'd originally thought. In spite of their stubborn quarrels, their passion boded surprisingly well. But Peyton was reluctant to use such techniques, especially when it was clear they both had something more than politics at stake. Lydia would laugh at the irony of it. Just when he needed his emotional detachment, it was being sorely tested.

The door to the library opened. Peyton thought to call out and make his presence known. When he realised who it was, he decided against it. Count Androvich and the two Russian ambassadors entered the dark room. Due to the gloom and the position of the sofa, they couldn't see him. They took seats in a cluster of chairs at the long library table running down the centre of the room. Peyton couldn't see them from there, but he could hear them, even with their lowered voices.

It was obvious they wanted their meeting to be private. Such a realisation increased the level of peril Peyton was in. They would not want to discover he'd lain there for the entire conversation. Peyton thought about the sharp, slender knife he carried under his trouser leg. He would not be unarmed if it came to a fight.

'We must make plans,' one of them said. Peyton thought it was Vasilov.

'Speak in French,' Gromsky insisted.

'Speak in English,' came a sharp retort. That was Androvich. 'If anyone overhears a foreign tongue, they'll know it was us. How many Russians speaking accented French would all be meeting together? If we speak in English, it will be less likely to pinpoint us. Even with accents, we could always blame other foreign nationals in town,' he reasoned.

The conversation went forward in English. Peyton was relieved. While he had a decent command of French, Peyton had yet to grasp the intricacies of the language in fast-paced conversations. It had been an eye-opener tonight to hear Tessa manage the tongue so effortlessly.

'I am making progress with Tessa Branscombe,' Androvich bragged. 'Tonight, I reminded her that I would gladly take her home with me in the autumn, that I would marry her and restore her to her rightful place in St Petersburg.'

'Is she amenable to that?' Gromsky asked.

Androvich snorted. 'Amenable? When has Tessa Branscombe been amenable to anything?'

'So you're saying she refused you?' Vasilov put in, a sneer evident in his voice.

Androvich's retort was quick and crisp. 'No, she has not refused. She is tempted, I think. But she is a woman and she wants to be wooed. Where is the romance in accepting right away? I know women. I will woo her and convince her this is the right course. She was infatuated with me once.'

'That was when we should have struck!' Vasilov said in hushed frustration. 'You let her get away when she was most vulnerable to us.'

'She left St Petersburg earlier than expected,' Androvich protested quickly.

'Now we have the Earl sniffing after her,' Vasilov continued his rant.

'He's not after her. He's after the list,' Androvich countered, his male pride hurt.

'It's starting to look that way,' Gromsky said, taking Androvich's side. 'New intelligence from a few embassies suggest he's highly accomplished and respected in diplomatic circles and not just for his overt negotiations. Rumour has it he once was a trusted member of the Filiki Eteria. Secret societies don't let outsiders in as a rule, and yet he was accepted.'

'I've told you, he's a fraud,' Androvich all but snarled.

Peyton was gratified to know that the Russian

team wasn't in the best of standing with each other. Those kinds of dynamics could be used against them if needed. Unfortunately, Peyton would have preferred to keep his identity a secret from the Russians a while longer.

'We need to treat him as if he's more than an ill-timed suitor.' Ilanovich spoke up for the first time. 'As I think we've suspected all along, he's been injected into this wild treasure hunt for the purpose of finding the list. You've got to get back into Miss Branscombe's good graces quickly.'

Vasilov began to plan. 'The best way to do that is to contain the Earl. We must act quickly. We cannot afford the Earl turning her head. Anyone looking at them on the dance floor tonight can't doubt their mutual attraction. More than a passionate flirtation, we cannot allow the Earl to fill her head with suspicions about you, Androvich. You must woo her and make it believable. If the Earl is nothing more than a love-struck guardian, he'll do the honourable thing and step aside once you make your intentions known. If not, then we'll know what his agenda is.'

'I doubt it. Stepping aside isn't in his vocabulary,' Androvich said derisively. 'If there's any stepping to be done, it will be me stepping over his dead body.'

'That can be arranged,' Gromsky said with more relish than Peyton would have liked.

'Yes…' Vasilov's tones entered the conversation,

contemplative. 'A dead earl would certainly make access to Miss Branscombe easier as long as it's done right. We don't want to cause an international incident.'

'If anyone does in the Earl, it will be me,' Androvich put in. 'He's insulted me one too many times.'

The conversation ended shortly after that. Peyton lay on the sofa, unmoving for what seemed like hours, making sure they were truly gone, that they'd had time to clear the hallway. There would be no explaining how he materialised in the hall if he walked out and they were still there.

Listening to one's own death being plotted was definitely high on the list of unpleasant experiences. There was no doubt that these ambassadors were hardened killers. The calm matter-of-fact discussion of who would live and who would die, who would be manipulated and who would be shoved aside, was quite unnerving. None the less, the conversation had been instructive. Peyton had confirmation both that Tessa was in the dark about the list and that Androvich was clearly the villain here, using their friendship to trap her. 'Not that you're much better,' Peyton's conscience reminded him. 'Ah, but I'm not going to kill anyone to do it,' he rejoined easily, although it didn't make him feel any better. He'd rather not have his motives listed in the same category as Androvich's.

Plans began to form in Peyton's mind. He would

talk to Brimley in the morning. Then he'd call for re-inforcements. He was going to need someone to watch his back on this and that's what brothers were for.

Chapter Eight

The particular brother in question, Crispin Ramsden, let the letter dangle from his long fingers as he sat back in his chair and studied the other two occupants of Dursley Park's private family sitting room. His younger brother, Paine, and his wife, Julia, stared at him expectantly. Julia gently rocked the infant in her arms. At least one of the room's occupants wasn't going to like the news.

'Well?' Paine said at long last. 'What has Peyton got to say for himself?'

'I am going up to London for a spell,' Crispin declared, trying to avoid the difficulty by not mentioning it at all.

Paine looked at him suspiciously and Crispin knew his ploy was about to fail. 'Is Peyton in trouble?'

'Can't a brother go up to town without there being trouble?'

'Yes, but it seems unlikely that you would go to the bother of facing London during the Season just to pay a social call on Peyton, who should be returning any day now,' Paine argued.

Crispin sighed and rose from his chair, taking up a position at the window overlooking the gardens. 'Julia, may I speak with my brother alone?' He knew he sounded harsh. Julia was hardly ever excluded from family issues. He adored his brother's wife. She was everything a man like Paine needed for balance in his life. But right now, he wanted the liberty of speaking freely, man to man. No matter how endearing a woman was, women had a way of squelching that ability.

'All right, tell me what's going on,' Paine said, staking out his own position at the fireplace mantel, arms crossed and slightly irritated over Crispin's manner.

Crispin passed the letter to Paine. 'It's all there.'

Paine took the missive and scanned it, a quizzical look crossing his brow. 'What's there? There's news of the city, a friend named Brimley, a mention at the end that he's lonely and thought you might like to come up to town since he's got to stay longer than anticipated. I am afraid I don't see the cause for alarm.'

'He's *lonely*. Have you ever known Peyton admit to being lonely?' Crispin pressed. 'He's in trouble and he's worried enough not to disclose it directly in his letter.'

'You got all that from a single line?' Paine's disbelief was evident.

'I know Peyton better than you do.' Crispin hadn't meant for it to come out so bluntly. Paine would be offended, but it was the truth. Paine had been away from the family for twelve years of exile over a duel in his wilder, younger days. He'd only recently returned. While the rift imposed by distance and time apart had been overcome by healthy doses of love, forgiveness and Julia's presence in their lives, there was still a significant amount of time unaccounted for in each other's lives. Crispin willingly admitted he didn't fully understand what Paine had been doing in India all those years, just as Crispin knew Paine had no concept of what Peyton had been up to.

'Is that why you banned Julia from the room? To insult me? To doubt my filial affections?' Paine was bristly. Crispin reminded himself to tread carefully. Paine was a new father who had been kept up all night with a colicky infant.

'Paine, I banned Julia from the room because I didn't want her to worry.'

'What's there to worry about? This nebulous "trouble" you think Peyton is in?'

'Exactly. Look, Paine, you don't know Brimley.'

'The man mentioned in the letter?'

'Yes. Brimley isn't just another politico haunting Whitehall and Parliament. He's an important player in the Home and Foreign Offices. If Brimley is mentioned in the letter along with being lonely, there's no questioning that something's up.'

'What does this Brimley have to do with Peyton?'

Crispin drew a deep breath. 'Once upon a time, not so long ago, Peyton worked for British interests in Vienna while I was in the military.' He let the information settle with Paine, letting him grasp its full import.

'My brother was a diplomat?' There was incredulity in Paine's tone.

Crispin nodded. Peyton had been a diplomat, sometimes acting in a grey area between diplomat and spy. 'I'll go up to London and see what's going on.' Perhaps the news would be enough to distract Paine from the rest of the news. He wasn't that fortunate.

Paine took a moment to consider the situation. 'I'll come with you.'

Crispin shook his head. 'No. You have Julia and the baby to think about. You can't leave her and you certainly can't bring her and the baby to the city.'

'I could just come for a while, a few days, to make sure everything's all right,' Paine argued.

'No, Peyton asked specifically that I come alone.' There. He'd said the worst of it. He knew Paine wouldn't like hearing it, but Peyton's instructions had been clear.

'Exactly where does he say I am not to come?' Paine said, scanning the letter again.

'He only names me in the letter,' Crispin said shortly.

Paine read the line Crispin referred to out loud. '"I

am lonely in the city. Crispin, you should come up for a visit and lend me your good company." I suppose in the special language you and Peyton have devised what that really means is "please leave Paine at home and let him worry from afar".'

Crispin smiled at his brother's acerbic tone. 'You're learning.'

'Well, you can't really expect me to wait here. I am a grown man. I can handle myself in a fight.'

Crispin's demeanour softened. He understood Paine's reluctance to be left out, but he could not capitulate to it. 'Peyton does not want to risk you.' He gave a dry chuckle. 'I'm expendable if there's a real danger. You're not. He would not risk widowing Julia and leaving your son fatherless. If his reluctance to have you come to town is not enough to prove the perilous nature of his circumstances, I don't know what is.' Crispin strode to the door of the room, clapping Paine on the shoulder as he passed by him. 'Hold the fort here in case we need to make a hasty retreat. I'll leave this afternoon. I can make a fair distance on horseback before dark.'

Up in his room, it only took Crispin a half-hour to pack. He liked to pretend that it was his military training and ability to live an unencumbered life that made packing so easy. He also pretended that he liked the freedom such a situation provided him. The reality was that his existence wasn't so much unencumbered as it was rootless and pointless. Watching

Paine and Julia with their son had driven that aspect home relentlessly over the past months.

Although Crispin deliberately eschewed London and all the mamas who thought snagging Dursley's brother a worthy prize, it would be a nice change from the stifling domesticity of Dursley Park and all the reminders of what he didn't have. Crispin threw a pair of fighting knives on to the bed, followed by a brace of pistols. In London he'd be useful.

'You say Crispin is coming?' Brimley asked confidentially over brandies at White's. 'Crispin will be useful. He's a good man in a fight.'

Peyton nodded, all too aware that meeting Brimley at White's was becoming a commonplace habit, a sure sign that the situation was nearing its zenith. He'd shared the Russians' conversation with Brimley. Brimley had concurred that bringing Crispin to town would offer the Branscombes and Peyton some extra protection. With luck, the Russians wouldn't see Crispin as an assistant, but merely as a brother who had come to town to enjoy the Season.

Crispin would be a good addition. He could act as a buffer between him and Lily, who had been furious over the events at the Broughtons' ball. One look at Tessa and she'd guessed exactly what had transpired. She'd given him a severe tongue-lashing the next day that had included a scolding for stealing kisses as well as a scolding for poor behaviour on the dance floor. What had he been thinking to pull her so close? Miss Branscombe had enough disadvantages—no fortune, no social connections—to overcome, without a dubious relationship with him. He was her guardian, for heaven's sake. He was supposed to help her avoid scandal, not court it.

Yes, the scolding had gone something like that, followed by Lily's assurances that she'd effectively scotched the budding rumours about the beautiful Tessa Branscombe, who had appeared from nowhere on the Earl's arm, spoke French and Russian fluently and had prior acquaintance with the four Russian men who'd arrived in town, particularly the young, dashing Count.

'What are you going to do about Miss Branscombe?' Brimley inquired, breaking in. 'Has she told you anything useful?'

This was the part Peyton detested the most: reporting to Brimley about his relationship with Tessa, as if it were nothing more than a negotiation process. His gentleman's code warred with his duty to his country. A gentleman didn't kiss and tell. But duty often demanded hard choices. Still, to say anything felt like a betrayal.

'She needs more time to become accustomed to me. We can't expect her to spill her secrets immediately,' Peyton said firmly, knowing this to be the truth. 'She does suspect trouble, though.' There was no harm in telling Brimley about the incident with the gun on the staircase.

Brimley raised his bushy grey brows at this. 'She is on the lookout for an interloper. That means this is likely not the first time she's feared one. We have to make her feel safe, Dursley.'

'I want to move her to my aunt's. Bloomsbury isn't secure enough for my taste.' Peyton spoke his plan out loud. He'd been thinking about it since the Broughtons' ball. 'She won't like it.'

'Well, make her like it. Sell it to her with a kiss if you have to,' Brimley rejoined sharply. 'I am sure women find you attractive, Dursley, with all your good looks and manners. Put them to use before the Russian competition does. My wife was going on at dinner recently about how handsome that Count Androvich is. We can't have him kissing her and manipulating the advantage of his so-called friendship.' Brimley took out his pocket watch. 'It's seven o'clock—don't you have somewhere to be?'

Peyton smiled thinly at the older man. To Brimley this was just another chess game. Usually Peyton respected that about him. Tonight, that quality seemed to have lost its lustre. He rose. 'Actually, I am supposed to look in on the Branscombe girls.' Not that he was looking forward to it. The girls had corralled him into spending an evening playing parlour games with them, since there wasn't a social event demanding his presence. Parlour games and a growing irritation with Brimley were just two signs as to how far Tessa Branscombe was getting under his skin.

Lamps burned in the front windows of the town house in Bloomsbury, throwing a welcoming light into the night. Peyton stepped down from the coach and sent his coachman off with instructions to return in two hours. There was no sense having the man wait in the cold when he could wait at a respectable nearby inn and stay warm.

Peyton stood on the pavement, surveying the house, reluctant to go in. He knew Tessa would balk at his suggestion about removing to Lily's. It might go over better if the request came from Aunt Lily.

He could understand Tessa's unwillingness. The house was respectable enough for women of their circumstance. More importantly, it was *hers*. He felt the same way about his property and his people. They were his—his to take care of, his to protect. It would take a legion to move him by force. Oh, yes, he understood very deeply what motivated Tessa's stubbornness. He was coming to realise that what appealed to him most about Tessa Branscombe was that, beneath her beauty and her quick-flaring temper, she was very like him.

The girls were thrilled to see him. He could hear Eva and Petra vying to see who would open the door for him. Fortunately, Arthur beat them to it and actually got to perform his job.

'Good evening, milord,' Arthur said, automatically reaching to take Peyton's coat and hat. '*Everyone* is here in the drawing room.'

Peyton took note of that and stiffened. 'Everyone' could only mean Count Androvich. 'How long has the Count been here?' he asked Arthur in low tones.

'A half-hour—he's been regaling the girls with his outing to the Tower today.'

Peyton pasted on a cool smile and entered the drawing room. Tessa sat next to Androvich on the sofa with Annie at her knee. Petra and Eva had resumed casual poses in the chairs. The domestic scene twisted Peyton's gut. Anyone else might see familial tranquillity at its finest, but he saw danger. Based on what he'd learned last night, Androvich could have a knife in Tessa's ribs before anyone was the wiser. The girls wouldn't last much longer after that. A throwing knife and a gun would put paid to them in short order.

Peyton shoved the morbid thought aside. Tessa was safe for the moment. Androvich didn't want Tessa dead yet. She would live as long as he was convinced she still had information he needed regarding the list. It was he whom Androvich had deadly intentions for.

Tessa looked up, aware he'd entered the room. 'I'm so glad you could make it. The girls are looking forward to a night of games.' She stood up and crossed the room to greet him. Peyton thought she seemed rather glad to have an excuse to leave Androvich's side.

'Can we start?' Eva asked impatiently. 'We have to pair up for teams.' Peyton caught a glimpse of mischief in Eva's eyes. She reminded him at times of Paine when he was younger. It had been the bane of his existence to keep Paine in line. He pitied the eligible bachelors when Eva came out. She'd keep everyone on their toes.

'I will partner Sergei,' she began. 'Tessa, you can be with Lord Dursley and Petra and Annie will be together.' Eva plopped down next to Count Androvich, who appeared to take the edict in good form. He was an excellent actor.

At least fate was on his side for the moment, Peyton thought, taking a chair next to Tessa. If he had to play parlour games, he might as well have Tessa for a partner.

They played charades, with enigmatic word descriptions, rather than acting out scenes. There was much laughing among the teams and even Tessa relaxed beside him, taking part in the game with zest. This was a side of Tessa Branscombe Peyton hadn't seen yet. It was intoxicating to watch Tessa among her family, her temper leashed, whatever fears she harboured momentarily restrained. The peace of the setting added to her beauty.

Did she understand how much of an illusion the evening was? Two representatives from two kings sat in her drawing room, playing charades with her sisters, acting as if they were her friends, people she could trust with her family, with her very life, all for the sake of a list. At least Peyton could say on his part that he wasn't acting. It made his conscience feel slightly better.

'Ah, this is just like those winter nights back in St Petersburg when we would sit by your father's fire and play games,' Androvich said after he and Eva won handily at charades. The girls looked at him enrapt, their faces dreamy with remembrances of better times, happier times. But Tessa looked down at her hands, refusing to meet Androvich's gaze. Peyton wondered about the awkwardness between Tessa and Androvich tonight.

As for himself, Peyton wanted to haul the Count outside and pummel some decency into him. No self-respecting gentleman would declare war on such unsuspecting girls. The girls thought he was their friend. Peyton had to stop right there. What did that make him? Meg entered with a tea tray, and saved him from too much speculation.

Peyton had been prepared to wait out the Count. He had no intentions of leaving the man alone in the house with Tessa. Fortunately, he didn't have to wait long. Perhaps the Count had sensed Tessa would not be receptive to whatever he wanted that night or perhaps the Count had another destination in mind to wind down the evening. After tea, Androvich took his very proper leave of the girls and Tessa.

'I would like to take all of you sightseeing tomorrow if your schedules are free,' Peyton offered to the room at large, but he looked at Tessa as he spoke. It had occurred to him during the course of the evening that the girls would want to see the sights of their new city. If he didn't take them, Androvich would. He could imagine all kinds of horrors that could befall young girls in the city with Androvich on watch.

His offer met with success. Even Annie seemed excited by the prospect. 'Please, Tessa?' Eva and Petra begged.

'Of course we can go,' Tessa acceded. 'Are you sure it's not too much trouble? We don't mean to interrupt your schedule. You must be very busy.'

'I would not have offered if I didn't mean it.' Peyton held her gaze over long until she was the one who looked away.

Quickly, Tessa said, 'If there's to be an outing, everyone needs to get to bed.' The order cleared the room efficiently and Peyton had what he'd wanted all night, a chance to be with Tessa alone.

He told himself it was for business purposes, but his body argued otherwise. The passion he'd tasted with her still lingered, coupled with an intensified desire to protect her from that snake Androvich. All night, his body had been teased by the mere proximity of her: the smell of lavender in her hair, the scent of soap, the clean smell of lemon and starch that hung about her clothes. The teasing didn't stop there.

The sound of her light laughter had been entrancing, the sight of her face lit with enjoyment had all combined into a potent elixir. Tessa Branscombe had definitely got to him. When he was with her, he could feel his objectivity slipping away, replaced by something subjective and primal.

'May I have a word with you before I go?' Peyton asked, all formal politeness, pleased that none of his inner longings flavoured his voice.

'Of course.' Tessa resumed her seat, habitually sweeping her skirts behind her as she sat.

'I couldn't help but notice that you seemed cool to the Count tonight. Is everything all right? He hasn't pressed you unduly since last night?'

Tessa gave a light chuckle. 'Playing the guardian, are you?'

'The gentleman,' Peyton corrected.

'Sergei is an old friend.' Tessa looked down at her hands. 'That's all last night was,' she added softly.

'You do not return his feelings?' Peyton probed.

'Not any longer. I do not see Sergei as more than a family friend. I fear his *tendre* for me has only developed out of loyalty to my father.'

'Is that all you fear?'

Tessa looked at him sharply. 'Whatever do you mean by such a question?'

'Well, I'm not the one carrying a gun in my reticule.'

Tessa stood up. 'Do not mistake one kiss in an alcove for more than it was. It does not grant you permission to snoop through my life. My business is mine alone. I am capable of taking care of myself and my sisters.'

Peyton rose to meet her, his own temper rising with hers. Lord, the woman was stubborn beyond all good sense. He knew instinctively that she would argue *ad nauseam*. He could think of nothing else to do except to take Brimley's advice and kiss her.

'One kiss might not qualify, but perhaps two will.' Tension sparked between them. Thank providence the Ramsden brothers counted kissing among their many accomplishments.

Chapter Nine

The girls were nearly giddy in their excitement over sightseeing the next morning as they gathered in the front room, fighting over a spot to look out the window and be the first to spy the Earl of Dursley. Tessa tried to share their enthusiasm. The sun was out and the prospect of seeing London under blue skies was quite tempting. But she'd rather see the sights without the pompous Earl of Dursley by her side.

The irritating man had had the audacity to kiss her not once, but twice. Once, she could countenance. The spirit of their dance had transmuted into energy that had needed an outlet, as unconventional as it was. There were multiple ways to explain what had passed between them in the alcove. Curiosity on her part—were all kisses as empty as Sergei's? Envy, maybe, on his part. He clearly had not approved of Sergei kissing her and she didn't believe his chagrin was solely motivated out of a need to adhere to the codes of propriety. But to kiss her twice? The earlier reasons simply hadn't applied to their kiss last night.

His kiss last night had been commanding, challenging, even, as if there was a hidden dare behind it. To her credit, or maybe not, she'd met that challenge, answering his kiss with a kiss of her own. Before she knew it, her back was against the wall, her hands were in his hair and they were both fully engaged.

How embarrassing! No one had ever kissed her in the manner Peyton had. Never had a kiss evoked such a flood of feelings. Simultaneously, she wanted to both give in, see where such abandon led, and to slap the arrogant Earl across the planes of his handsome face. How dare he make such presumptions! Possibly he wouldn't presume so much if she didn't give him leave.

Oblivious to the turmoil plaguing their older sister, the girls gave a squeal of delight as Peyton's carriage drew up to the kerb, the top pulled down in acquiescence to the good weather. He jumped down and headed towards their steps, looking well turned out in buff Inexpressibles and a blue morning coat for the outing.

With surprising little chaos, everyone was settled in the landau. Tessa sat facing forward with Eva and Annie, while Petra took the seat next to Peyton, who sat with his back to the driver. Tessa had originally thought the arrangement would be much more to her satisfaction. Sitting across from Peyton would somehow be less intimate to her way of thinking. There would be no chance for the natural contours of the road to jostle them into one another. There'd be no knees knocking, no shoulders brushing. But now there would be eye contact. She had not reckoned on how disconcerting it was to be the focus of his gaze.

'I thought we'd stop at the Tower of London first,' Peyton said as the carriage pulled into the street. Tessa hated how collected he sounded, as if their kiss hadn't happened, or, if it had, didn't matter. He had the unnerving ability to carry on as if nothing out of the ordinary had occurred. The nasty side of her posited a theory: maybe that kiss was not out of the ordinary. Maybe he kissed every woman he met. But that was hard to believe. The immaculately dressed, mannerly Earl did not strike her as one to engage in light dalliance.

Tessa spent the trip making small talk with Dursley, trying to pretend that he hadn't given her quite a thorough kissing on the last two occasions they had met. The trip to the Tower seemed endless, although, in reality, she supposed it hadn't taken all that long. Traffic was not that bad in the streets.

The coachman found a place at the kerb for them to get down, and Tessa was pleased to see that the girls remembered their manners, letting Peyton exit the carriage first in order to help them down.

When it was her turn, Peyton lingered over her

hand. 'Miss Branscombe, you look especially lovely today. Yellow becomes you.'

A wicked retort came to mind, but Tessa fought it off. Surely the daughter of a diplomat could do better? She opted for a more mundane but safer comment about the sun and the weather.

The Tower was an intimidating spectacle. Tessa had been eight when the family had left London, far too young to be out sightseeing. She was as new to the sights as her younger sisters. They were all suitably impressed and Peyton was a natural tour guide.

'The Tower has long been used in a variety of roles from a prison, a mint for the treasury, a home for jewels, and a garrison for soldiers. Up until last year, the Tower was even the home of a great menagerie of animals, including lions,' Peyton said.

'What happened to the animals?' Petra asked, concern evident in her voice. 'Surely they weren't killed?'

'No, not at all. The menagerie has been moved over to the zoo in Regent's Park,' Peyton allayed her concerns.

'Can we go there some time?' Annie asked shyly, surprising Tessa. Annie hadn't spoken directly to Peyton since his appearance in their lives.

To his credit, Peyton favoured the little girl with a rare smile. 'I will arrange it. Regent's Park is a lovely spot. There's boating and the gardens will be in full bloom. We can picnic and make a day of it.'

Annie beamed and Tessa was inexplicably moved by his kindness. She cocked her head beneath the brim of her hat and gave him a long, considering look. Peyton Ramsden was fast becoming the most complex man she'd ever met. His outward demeanour of urbane politeness gave him an aura of constant coolness, as if the world could not reach him with all of its busy, noisy messiness. However, that was not the sum of him. Beneath that well-cultivated surface lay a man with intense passions and mysterious depths, a man who intrigued her against her will. If their circumstances and stations in life were different, she might feel compelled to attract his attentions.

As it was, this was not the time to engage in a little romance. Nor would there ever be a right time. She had Sergei's feelings to consider. If she turned her attentions to the Earl so soon after she'd refused his proposal, Sergei would think Peyton was the reason for her rejection.

Then there were her concerns about potential danger to consider. True, there had been no other incidents to raise her suspicions since the day she'd mistaken Peyton for an intruder. Regardless, she couldn't help but feel that all was not as it should be. If there was anything amiss, she didn't want to drag Peyton into it. He'd gamely taken up his duties as a guardian and that was enough. Anything further would be an imposition.

Besides, nothing could come of such a flirtation than what had already occurred. Part of her thought this was the real reason. For all that her mind called him 'Peyton' and thought of him as a man, this man was a peer of the realm. The Earl of Dursley could not be expected to seriously consider courting a diplomat's daughter without any substantial monetary or social consequence to her name.

There would never be anything more than the kisses they'd already shared. And those, while quite stirring, had not been prompted by courtship or growing affection. They'd been brought on by the heat of conflict and the passions of the moment. She would be mistaken to construe them as anything else.

'Miss Branscombe, I do believe you've missed my fine dissertation on the armoury,' Peyton said drily at her side, a hand cupping her elbow to guide her through the crowd towards the exit.

'My apologies, I am sure it was riveting.'

'Apparently not as riveting as your wool-gathering. I will expect your full attention at the Jewel House.'

At the Jewel House, they gathered with other visitors on wooden benches to watch one of the daily ritual unveilings of the Crown Jewels. It was not terribly crowded, as it would be later in the day, but some jostling behind them drew Peyton's attention. Tessa could feel him tense beside her as he discreetly looked around for the source of the commotion.

'What is it?' Her own senses were on alert now.

'Do you recognise that man in the tan coat?' Peyton asked in a low voice. 'I seem to recall having seen him before, but I can't place him.'

Tessa studied the man covertly from beneath her hat. He was of middle years, a bit portly around the middle and dressed respectably in the clothing of a merchant. He didn't look menacing, but rather like a friendly father-figure, someone who might be a likeable neighbour. Tessa stiffened. It was probably nothing but a mere coincidence.

'He resembles a man who reads the news sheets on the bench by the garden near our home,' Tessa said softly. 'I can't say for sure if it's the same man. I've never approached him. I assumed he lived in the square with us. We haven't met many of our neighbours. Perhaps that's where you've seen him.' She added the last bit lightly, trying to hide her growing concern. It had only been the noise that had drawn Peyton's attention. Peyton had no reason to share her suspicions. She had to remain calm, lest she arouse his suspicions. He was already curious as to why she'd had a gun with her.

The girls gasped in appreciation, drawing her attention to the curtain, which was being pulled back to reveal the jewels of the monarchs. The group of people gave a collective gasp of awe at the opulence on display. An old woman came forward and stood next to the collection. She held her head high and began her recitation on the treasures. 'Ladies and gentlemen, behold the treasures of the ages,' she began in a pompous manner that made Tessa stifle a laugh. Peyton gently elbowed her and shot her a sideways glance that suggested he saw the humour in it, too.

Afterwards, Tessa looked around for the man in the tan coat. She caught sight of him exiting. He did not appear to be interested in the whereabouts of her group. Later, as they toured the rest of the exhibits, she saw him near them in some cases, but he did not attach himself to the group of people they moved with, nor did he seem to notice them at all. Her initial fears began to subside, but it was privately quite telling to her just how deep-seated her fears ran these days when she was alarmed by such an encounter. It wasn't a good sign that she was seeing danger everywhere.

The day progressed without incident. Peyton took them to Gunther's for ices and had them deposited at his Aunt Lily's town house promptly at four o'clock, so that Tessa had time to rest before the Ashmore rout that evening. Meg was already waiting at Aunt Lily's with Tessa's gown and the girls' things for spending the night.

The move had been accomplished so effortlessly that Tessa could hardly complain. Peyton's efficiency made it easy to let him handle the details and, for a change, it was nice to let someone else take care of things. 'Your management skills amaze me,' Tessa said as he handed her down from the landau. 'This could easily become habit forming.'

Peyton held her gaze for a long moment. 'I sincerely hope it does, Miss Branscombe.'

Tessa dressed carefully for the rout in an evening gown of a becoming shade of lavender that brought out the colour of her eyes. She was looking forward to the rout for far different reasons than she'd looked forward to the Broughtons' diplomats' ball. At the Broughtons', she had been excited about the idea of participating in a milieu she knew well and missed during the long months since her father's death. Tonight, the excitement that fluttered through her had very little to do with the venue and everything to do with a man.

Tonight, she'd be on Peyton's arm. He would dance with her. Perhaps they'd waltz again. She was almost certain they would. The thought of his hand at her waist sent a delightful shiver through her.

He might kiss her again if they could manage to be alone. When they were alone together, he behaved like an entirely different man than when they were surrounded by others. The neutral ambience of the sophisticated Earl would vanish in private, to be replaced by a man of an entirely different nature.

Meg popped her head into the room and announced the arrival of the carriage. Lily was already downstairs. Tessa said a quick goodnight to her sisters and sailed down to meet Peyton.

Peyton waited at the bottom of the stairs in the foyer, but he was not alone. Along with him and Aunt Lily was another man, equal in height to Peyton and with hair just as dark, although far longer. Her first thought was that Lily, still intent on seeing her engaged before the Season was out, was playing matchmaker.

A wave of disappointment rolled through Tessa. She'd thought to have Peyton all to herself. It was silly, really. At a ball one was never in great risk of being alone with their escort. The rules wouldn't allow her to dance with Peyton more than twice and they'd be surrounded by a crush of people all night long.

'Ah, Miss Branscombe,' Peyton said as she approached, firmly entrenched in his public role of the urbane Earl. 'Lovely as always, I see. Allow me to introduce you to my brother, Lord Crispin Ramsden.'

'It is a pleasure to finally meet you,' Crispin Ramsden said. 'I can see why my brother has found his time in the city extended beyond his original intentions.'

Up close there was no mistaking the resemblance. Crispin Ramsden physically aped his brother: dark hair, blue eyes, a commanding height and presence. But only a fool would miss the stark differences between them, Tessa thought. Crispin might be able to deliver a polite line, but he lacked Peyton's inherent ease in social situations.

There was a rough, wild quality to him that set

him apart from his elegant brother and from others, which became quickly apparent once they arrived at the Ashmores' rout. People gave Crispin a wide berth and might have avoided him altogether if it hadn't been for his brother's presence. Those mamas who did dare come forward for an introduction, daughters in tow, were sent scuttling back to their *chaise longues* with a sharp comment and dark look.

'Play nice, Cris,' Peyton warned in low tones after a fourth mama was routed. 'I'm going to waltz with Tessa now. Don't bite anyone until I get back.'

Tessa had waited all night for this. She'd been out on the dance floor with partners Lily had arranged and with several others who had voluntarily signed her card. None of them had equalled Peyton's grace.

'You're becoming quite the sensation, despite not having been on the town long,' Peyton commented as the music started.

'I don't mean to be,' Tessa said honestly.

'Why ever not? You're a beautiful woman, Tessa.'

She should have revelled in the compliment, but she hardly noticed it. He'd called her 'Tessa'. It was the first time. Of course, she'd given him sardonic liberty to do so after their kissing bout at the Broughtons', but it had been correctly 'Miss Branscombe' all day today.

'I like it when you use my name,' she said boldly. 'Since circumstances have required we spend so much time together, it seems ridiculous to do otherwise.' In truth, she was having difficulty recalling that Peyton had not always been a part of her life, which was a ludicrous sentiment given how little time she'd known him. If she thought about it too much, it was alarming how easily he'd woven himself into the pattern of their days.

'Perhaps you should call me Peyton, at least when we're alone, then,' he replied, swinging them expertly through a turn. 'It shall be our rule. We are indeed in an awkward position, are we not? Social protocol demands you call me "Dursley". But since we're practically living in each other's pockets, it seems far too formal.'

His eyes darkened and, for a moment, Tessa felt his gaze on her lips. With a slight pressure at her waist, he drew her infinitesimally closer to him. Her breath caught in expectation.

'I find that sometimes formalities can be used to build barriers between people and I don't want any barriers with us, Tessa.' His voice was deliciously low in her ear. 'You can come to me with anything, trust me with anything. I will be your bulwark, always.'

In spite of her warnings to herself not to get swept away in an entanglement with Peyton Ramsden, Tessa was losing the fight and gladly. It wasn't simply because he was a handsome man, although that could hardly be overlooked. She'd met handsome men before who were no more than their fair visages. Peyton was far deeper. Watching him with her sisters at the Tower, she'd begun to feel she could trust him. The time might come when he was the only one she could turn to, trust or not. Sergei was a foreign diplomat and a diplomat associated with the origin of the trouble. If there was difficulty, Sergei would be of little use to her. She'd need an Englishman. It felt good to know there was somewhere she could turn.

The invisible burden she'd been carrying for months lifted from her shoulders. She felt physically free in Peyton's arms as he waltzed her about the ballroom. She never guessed she'd have to test his resolve to stand as her bulwark so soon.

It took two carriages to transport them all back to the house in Bloomsbury the next day. Peyton and Crispin had decided to come along with Aunt Lily to see them home. Tessa had argued that it wasn't necessary. She was becoming acutely aware of the amount of trips Peyton and his family members were making between their rarefied homes in Mayfair and her neighbourhood. But Peyton had insisted, saying he wanted to show Crispin the area.

They pulled up to the kerb, more than a few heads peeking around lace curtains to peer out at the group. Tessa noticed immediately that the man from the Tower was reading his news sheets on the bench. She nodded discreetly to Peyton.

'I'll have a word with him for my own peace of

mind,' Peyton said. 'It can't hurt. If it's nothing, we're just being neighbourly.'

Tessa laughed at the thought of the Earl of Dursley being 'neighbourly'. Peyton shot her a teasing look. 'Can't I be neighbourly? He doesn't know I am an earl.'

Crispin laughed, too, unable to resist a chance to rib his brother. 'No, he'll think you're a duke instead. You might do better to tell him you're an earl.'

'Your faith in me is touching,' Peyton responded drily, but Tessa could tell he'd taken the teasing in good stride. She liked this Peyton quite a lot, the laughing, human, approachable Peyton.

Everyone clambered out of the carriages. Peyton and Crispin went across the street and she went up the steps to the house, her key in hand, Petra right behind her. Tessa unlocked the door and stepped across the threshold. Tessa took two steps and came to a shocked halt. She wavered, collapsing against the door jamb for support, mentally digesting the sight inside. The house was destroyed.

'What is it, Tess? Are you ill?' Petra made to move around her. Tessa flung out an arm in a protective reaction, barring Petra from the sight. 'No, don't come in. Get Peyton, quickly—we've been burgled.'

Chapter Ten

The conversation with the news sheet-reading neighbour was not going well. Instead of being happy to engage in friendly conversation, the man was proving to be taciturn, giving short, single-syllable answers. He was even quite defensive at one point, declaring, 'I can read my bloody news wherever I want. This is a free country.' After that rhetorical turning point in the conversation, Crispin had been ready to plant the man a facer and Peyton's own concerns about the man were heightened.

He hadn't wanted to say anything alarming to Tessa yesterday at the Tower. The damnable game he was playing for Brimley didn't allow him to. Tessa didn't know he knew something of her situation. To suddenly have misgivings about a stranger would be out of place. He couldn't have suspicions unless Tessa shared her suspicions with him first. She hadn't done so, although he could see that she was unnerved by the 'coincidence' of her supposed neighbour showing up at the Tower.

He had to win the stubborn woman's trust, not just for the sake of Brimley's game, but for his own male pride. He wanted to take on Tessa's burdens as his own, regardless of Brimley's dictates. She was in danger and the sooner he could openly convince her of that, the safer all of them would be. His mind ran ahead of itself. Once Tessa was acquitted of this deadly game with the Russians, he could devote himself to a different kind of game with her, a courtly one. But romance had no place between them right now while a more perilous game was afoot. He needed all his sharp-witted faculties to protect her.

A burst of activity on the steps across the street caught his attention. Peyton saw Petra run down the steps and stop briefly to say something to Lily, whose reaction was to gather Annie to her and clasp Eva's hand. He exchanged a quick glance with Crispin and was up and running.

'Lord Dursley! We've been robbed,' Petra gasped as soon as he was in earshot. Panic was never discreet and he could hardly blame the girl. But he wished she hadn't announced it so openly for anyone to hear.

Peyton bolted across the street, but not before he heard Crispin say in falsely polite tones to the would-be neighbour, 'It seems we have something else to talk about.'

Peyton bounded up the town-house steps, his protective instincts on full alert. Tessa was still inside. Did the woman have no sense? The intruder could still be there. At the threshold, Peyton bent swiftly and pulled the knife from his boot, a long, slender, lethal-looking blade. He found Tessa in the drawing room, her gun out. Apparently her thoughts had run along the same lines as his.

'It's just me, Tessa,' Peyton said in even tones before she was inclined to whirl around and point her gun at him. 'You should be outside until I can determine if the prowler has left the premises.'

'Peyton, my house has been destroyed.' Tessa turned to face him and he could see the struggle she waged not to fall apart.

He did not miss her use of his Christian name; while a part of him thrilled to the sound of it on her lips, he knew he'd trade that accomplishment to spare her this moment. He wanted to take her in his arms and conceal her from the sight of the carnage, but propriety would not allow such a liberty. All around them the drawing room lay in shambles. Furniture had been overturned, stuffing ripped from chair cushions, the fireplace mantel pulled loose, leaving the wall scarred where it had been mounted.

Those were the big items Peyton noticed immediately. There were smaller signs of devastation, too: a shattered vase, an overturned table, a shredded book. He imagined the rest of the house would look the same.

'Who would do such a thing?' Tessa sighed, kicking aside a ruined chair cushion.

Peyton had some very good ideas. The break-in told him two things—first, the intruder had been looking for something. That explained the wanton destruction of things like the mantel and the cushions. The intruder was seeking out a hiding place. The second was that the intruder also wanted to send a threatening message with his destruction. That explained the errant acts of violence, like the over-turned table and the shattered items that clearly weren't likely hiding places.

He wasn't ready to voice his thoughts to Tessa yet. He wanted to wait until he'd searched the whole house and seen the entire pattern of the prowler's destruction.

'Tessa, fetch your sisters. We need to get them off the pavement. Explain the situation to them. I am going upstairs to look around. We'll meet in the drawing room,' Peyton directed, starting up the stairs before Tessa could counter-plan.

Upstairs, the devastation was as complete as downstairs. Peyton drew a deep breath. In some ways what had been done upstairs was even worse because it involved the desecration of highly personal items. Clothing had been flung from wardrobes, beds had been torn apart. In Tessa's private office, papers had been thrown out of drawers. There was no choice now but to move Tessa and the girls to Aunt Lily's.

Downstairs in the drawing room, Peyton broke the

news to the Branscombe sisters. 'You cannot stay here. The mess alone is reason enough, even if there weren't concerns about the safety of this location. There's plenty of room at Aunt Lily's.' He studied their pale faces. The girls were trying hard not be overwhelmed by the situation, but they were clearly quite shaken and rightly so.

If he could give them something to do in order to stay busy and not dwell on the crisis, they would fare better. 'Aunt, if you could take the girls upstairs and have them gather up anything they want to bring, anything salvageable, we'll get packed up and get them settled at your place.'

Aunt Lily ushered the girls upstairs, but Tessa remained behind. 'We don't need to burden your aunt,' she protested. 'Once the mess is cleaned up, we can make do here. Within a few hours, the worst of this can be cleaned up,' she said bravely.

Peyton shook his head. He placed his hands on her shoulders. 'Supposing that were true, what would you do if the intruder came back? I have my doubts that the burglar found what he was looking for. If he did find it, he didn't find it right away. This prowler is dangerous, Tessa.'

'You're acting like this prowler isn't a common thief intent on a bit of jewellery.' Tessa tried to dismiss his concerns, but Peyton could hear the lie beneath her words. She didn't believe the statement any more than he did.

'You're exactly right. I don't believe for a minute that this break-in was conducted by an amateur looking for valuables to fence. Amateur thieves don't stick around to wreak havoc on furniture. The fewer signs there are that testify to a thief's presence, the better in most cases. But this thief wanted you to know that he'd been here. I don't believe this is the work of a regular burglar and neither do you.'

Peyton motioned with his eyes to the reticule hanging from her wrist. 'You carry a gun. You were expecting something like this and have been for quite some time.'

Crispin chose that moment to enter the room, preventing Tessa from responding to his charges. It was rather poor timing on his brother's part, Peyton thought. He needed Tessa to tell him what she knew, what she feared, and he'd given her a perfect opportunity.

'Your neighbour isn't very neighbourly,' Crispin said to Tessa sourly, flexing his fingers. 'I got him to warm up a bit, though. If he comes sneaking around again, we'll recognise him right away. He's missing a tooth and he'll be sporting a facer for a while.'

Tessa gasped. 'I am sure such violence was uncalled for.' She shot Crispin a scolding glance. 'My sisters and I have to live here among these people. I can't have you beating people up.'

'You won't be living here for a while,' Peyton

reminded her. 'Until this is settled, you'll be with Aunt Lily.'

Tessa shot him a withering look. 'I will decide what is best for me and my sisters.'

'I'm the guardian.' Peyton scowled. He could see Crispin's mouth working to suppress a smile. How dare she challenge him in front of his brother? On the other hand, he could understand how she felt. Her home had been violated and circumstances were now out of her control. It was natural to want to try to exert some influence on the direction of things.

Crispin intervened swiftly, his inappropriate inclination to laugh successfully suppressed. 'Has anything been taken?'

'Not that we can tell. But we haven't looked all that closely yet,' Tessa said, diverted from her brewing argument with Peyton.

'If you have an office of sorts, it would be a good idea to check there to see if family papers have been taken,' Crispin suggested.

Tessa nodded and took herself off up the stairs.

'Nice diversion,' Peyton said, watching Tessa sail off.

'I wasn't sure you wanted me to share my news in front of an audience.' Crispin shrugged.

'Tell me before anyone comes down.' Peyton shot a quick look at the staircase.

'The man isn't a neighbour. He claimed to live at

Number 4, but when I questioned a maid in the park afterwards, she said he couldn't possibly live at Number 4 since that house employed her to watch their two children.'

'What else did you learn?'

'After I roughed him up a bit, he said some foreign men with accents asked him to keep an eye on this place, wanting to know where the girls went, when they weren't home, when the servants were out, as they were today. Paid him in gold.'

Peyton nodded. It affirmed what he'd suspected. He wished he'd been more alert to the man earlier, and he would have been if Tessa had called it to his attention. It was becoming painfully obvious that he was limited in his capacity to protect her without full knowledge of the danger she was in. He would remedy that tonight. He could wait no longer. Tessa and he would have a long overdue discussion. The Russians were on the move.

Tessa kissed Annie and turned down the light in the spacious guest room at Aunt Lily's. Although there were several rooms and the girls could have had their own chambers, they'd elected to sleep together, at least for a few nights, until they could trust their security again.

Eva and Petra were snuggled together in the big four-poster bed. Annie was lodged on a wide couch at the foot of the bed.

'You all did so very well today,' Tessa told them, and they had. They'd gathered up their things and stoically driven over to Aunt Lily's, leaving the servants, who had arrived back before they left, to follow them, after securing the house. Even now, a few pieces of salvage from the house were strewn about the chamber. Among the items retrieved was the portrait of their father from Tessa's office. It was one of the few items left completely intact, even though it had been removed from the wall.

'It was good to have Dursley with us today,' Petra murmured from her blankets. 'I don't know what we would have done without him. And Lord Crispin, too,' she added sleepily.

'We would have managed just as we always have,' Tessa responded, hiding her hurt at the comment. Before Peyton had come along, her sisters had looked to her for guidance. How quickly their allegiance had shifted.

Eva propped herself up on one arm. 'I like Dursley immensely. Perhaps he could be your husband, Tess, if you'd stop quarrelling with him over every little thing. He thinks you're pretty. I could tell by the way he looked at you today.'

'You called him "Peyton",' Petra said. 'You like him, too, no matter how much the two of you fight.'

'Oh, yes,' Annie piped up. 'We could go on fabulous outings all the time. Do you think he'll still take us to the zoo?'

'I am sure he will. Now, go to sleep,' Tessa chided, glad the darkness hid the rising heat in her cheeks. She shut the door behind her. Perhaps it was a good sign that her sisters were focused on such silly things like a romance with Peyton Ramsden after the trying events of the day.

Tessa wished her mind was as easily diverted. But it had been awash with controversy. She was not looking forward to going downstairs and the impending interview. She had to speak to Peyton to thank him for his assistance and to remind him that she was capable of taking care of things. That was not all she needed to discuss with him. She should not delay in telling Peyton all she knew. It was time he understood the danger he'd inherited when he'd taken on their guardianship.

Maybe he'd already left and she could put the discussion off until morning. But, no, that was the coward's way out. Although him being gone was a distinct possibility, it was one she did not prefer. Better to be done with this tonight.

She found Peyton in Aunt Lily's study, a decidedly male domain done in dark woods and burgundy. The room had clearly belonged to her late husband. A fire burned in the fireplace, giving the imposing interior a more comforting feel.

'I wanted to thank you for today,' Tessa began. 'I hope I am not interrupting?' Peyton was behind the desk, writing and looking entirely at home in the masculine room.

'Not at all. I am glad you're here. We must talk.' Peyton rose and gestured to the sofa near the fireplace. 'Are the girls settled comfortably?' He kept up a gentle stream of small talk until they were seated. Tessa was immediately alert to the informality of their proximity. The edges of his roles were blurry tonight. Was he the polished Earl managing the business of his guardians, or the man who promised in seductive tones on the ballroom floor to be her bulwark?

'I meant it last night, Tessa, you can trust me. But I cannot help if there are things you are not telling me. Do you know why someone would want to break in to your home? Is there anything they could be looking for?'

'I don't know,' Tessa said, hesitating only slightly. It was the truth. She'd been grappling with the same thoughts all afternoon and with another dilemma: how much to tell Peyton? Tonight, here in the intimacy of the firelight, she wanted to follow her instincts and tell Peyton everything. The horrors of the day had illustrated poignantly that she could not face this alone, whatever it was.

But she'd never been good at relying on others. If she told Peyton, he would feel obliged to assist her, even if it meant putting himself at risk. That was unacceptable to her. Others shouldn't shoulder one's own responsibilities. Yet the temptation was overwhelming.

Peyton seemed to sense her dilemma. One of his hands curled over hers where it lay on her lap. He pressed it lightly. 'I've been in your situation before, Tessa,' he said quietly. 'You don't do well when circumstances don't bend to your will. I don't, either. When my father died unexpectedly, I was suddenly the Earl. I was young, not much older than you are now, and my brothers were about Eva's and Petra's ages. I wasn't ready to be the Earl, let alone be a father–brother figure to two rambunctious boys.

'People tried to make decisions for me. Aunt Lily's husband offered to take Crispin and Paine under his wing. Another distant cousin offered copious amounts of advice regarding how to invest the family fortune. They might all have been well meaning, but I would have none of it. Perhaps I feared that if I showed weakness, they'd for ever be assuming they could run roughshod over me, that I'd be Dursley in name only as opposed to deed.

'I can't say I was the easiest person to be around in those early days.' Peyton gave a chuckle. 'There's probably still quite a few people who think that. But I got the job done and successfully, too, even though there are some days I wonder if I might have gone about it a little bit better, more graciously. My autonomy was bought with the sacrifice of a few friendships.'

He'd voiced her sentiments precisely and Tessa was nearly undone by it. Maybe at last here was one person who *did* understand. And if he understood, he'd know how important it was that she not surrender all of her control to his will. Maybe, at last, she could trust someone enough to lay down her burden.

Tessa's eyes filled with tears. Perhaps it was the intimacy of the fire, the honesty of Peyton's disclosure, or the events of the day. It might have been all three of those combined. 'Peyton, would you do something for me?'

'Anything.'

She shouldn't have asked, but her emotions were running high. 'Make me feel safe, at least for a little while, like you did on the stairs.'

Chapter Eleven

Tessa moved in to his arms in one fluid motion or was it the other way around? Had he been the one to take Tessa in to his arms? The moment happened so rapidly, it was impossible to tell who did the moving. Regardless, the outcome was the same. Tessa was warm and invitingly soft against him. His arm was about her and she leaned against his chest as if she fit there, her golden head resting in the hollow of his shoulder.

He ran his hand up and down the length of her arm in a gentle, soothing gesture, but his body was well aware that he was not comforting a child. He was acutely aware of the breast that rose and fell against his side as she breathed. He was conscious of her hand where it lay on his thigh, more out of a need to simply be somewhere in their current posture than out of any seductive intention. But it did occur to him that her hand only had to move a few inches in order to come into extremely intimate contact with him. Certain parts of his body were becoming excited about that.

Peyton shifted slightly to manage his member's growing arousal. Did the vixen have any idea what she was asking? Did she have any idea how difficult it would be to offer her the comfort she was seeking without taking things too far?

It was not unreasonable for her to want the physical reassurance of strong arms after what had happened. Emotions ran high in circumstances like the ones they'd encountered today. It was greatly satisfying to know that she wanted him to be her comforter, that she hadn't sent off a note to Androvich seeking the reassurances of the Count's arms. Oh, yes, her need was understandable. That wasn't what made the situation difficult.

What made the situation difficult was that he knew better than to accede to her wishes. No gentleman ruined a lady, and certainly not a lady under his care. Taking advantage of his position in her life and the emotional duress she was under was most unfair. Only a cad of the lowest order would misuse his position in such a manner.

But logic compelled him just so far. All the arguments in the world about honour could not overcome one single fact that outweighed all other rationales. He wanted her with a single-minded possession that swept traditional considerations out of its wake.

Her emotions weren't the only ones to consider. His own feelings were quite piqued over the events of the afternoon. Well, 'feelings' might be a bit strong. Peyton didn't make a habit of having his feelings engaged in most situations. It would be more accurate to say his temper was fully engaged over the break-in. Yes, he felt more comfortable with that assessment. His temper had risen to the fore upon seeing the wreckage of Tessa's home and the subtle messages that had been left behind by the malicious intruder. None the less, the afternoon had stirred a primal urge in him that would not take kindly to being denied.

Next to him, Tessa sighed. 'This is nice. We're not quarrelling.' She gave a little laugh. 'Eva says you and I argue all the time.'

'Only because you disagree with me.' Peyton hazarded a little teasing, enjoying the peace of the moment.

'I do not,' Tessa said and then laughed again, catching her error. She pushed up from her position against him. He immediately missed the warmth of her body. 'You did that on purpose,' she scolded, mischief flirting in her eyes.

'No, I didn't,' Peyton answered before he could stop himself. He grinned. 'You've caught me at my own game.'

'So I have.' Tessa smiled back, utterly enchanting in the firelight. Her hair had come loose, curls randomly framing her face. She sat cross-legged facing him, her yellow skirts tucked about her. She looked entirely girlish. Her blue-violet eyes held his as they shared their little joke. The personal quality of the moment was heady.

Desire for her physically shook Peyton. He wanted this beautiful, brave angel right here, right now. Peyton could not recall a moment in his life when he'd felt so desperate to *be* with another human being. Peyton leaned towards her, a hand moving to cup the nape of her neck and guide her into his kiss. She came willingly.

She melted into his body, compliant and eager. There was no hesitation on her part and Peyton claimed her with his lips and his hands. The sofa could no longer hold them and they moved in one accord to the rug spread before the fireplace, a memento of one of his uncle's many exotic hunting expeditions. Peyton didn't much care at the moment except that it was soft and accommodated their needs.

He pushed the shoulders of Tessa's yellow gown down. His mouth found her breasts and sucked gently. Tessa arched against him in her newfound pleasure. He felt her hands reach up to tackle the fastenings of his shirt. They found success and Peyton shuddered at the contact of her palms against his own nipples, his own stimulation heightened by the idea that his own pleasure at her hands mirrored the pleasure he was giving her.

Tessa's hips pressed against his trousers, a moan of frustration escaping her at the limits allowed by the fabric between them. Peyton answered her with a kiss that claimed her mouth entirely, moving a hand to push up her skirts, searching out the core of her womanhood, determined to give her what satisfaction he could. Unerringly, his fingers found her sheltered pearl. She shuddered in her delight.

Intuitively, her hands grabbed at the front of his trousers, wanting to rectify the incompletion of the ecstasy that welled between them. He let her take him in her hand, her fingers exploring the hard, living length of his member.

Her eyes, wide and shining, stared into his face, reflecting her awe. 'Peyton, please. I want you to finish this, to find your own pleasure,' she whispered.

It was his undoing. The last thoughts of offering her pleasure while taking no further release for himself evaporated at the sound of his name on her lips as she made the most intimate of requests.

'Tessa?' His voice was hoarse. He was incapable of further speech. He hoped the questioning quality of his single word conveyed all that he meant it to. Was she certain of this next step? Did she understand he was willing to do this, wanted to, even needed to do this? That doing this placed her under his protection more firmly than she already legally was? All arguing aside, he was glad for it—he welcomed this addition to his life.

Her eyes were bright with the passion that drove her. 'Come into me, Peyton. Do not cheat us.'

Peyton. Us. The words were an aphrodisiac. Peyton took her lips in another searing kiss and brought himself into her, calling on all the skill he'd acquired in the beds of his mistresses, until she was as physically ready for him as she was mentally.

Beneath him, Tessa gasped at the sensation of his presence inside her. He felt her move, tentatively at first, looking for ways to meet him, to share this with him. He revelled in her need to participate. He should have known his Tessa would be no wilting, merely tolerant bedfellow. Peyton placed his hands on her hips and helped her find the rhythm.

Tessa's hips against his, the intimate joining of their bodies, her soft moans of delight, comprised a joy beyond imagining. Peyton hoped he would last long enough to show her the possible pleasures that existed between a man and a woman. Tessa writhed against him and he knew they were both close. He increased his pace, felt her own pleasure near. She cried out her achievement and Peyton's world exploded into a magnificent release.

He was drained, paradoxically sated and filled all at once. Peyton drew deep breaths, trying to reconcile the riot in his mind with the physical bliss that lulled him into drowsy placation in front of his aunt's fire. Against his shoulder, Tessa dozed, her golden hair sweeping his chest.

His body was completely at peace with what they'd done. Never had the act of sex been so fulfilling for both himself and his partner. What had transpired on his aunt's carpet was the physical pinnacle of human existence. Their bodies were designed to bring each other such pleasure. There was a tranquillity that came in being able to overcome the social constraints of their stations and situations and achieve such bliss.

Peyton wished his mind could accept such a natural rationalisation. But all his mind could comprehend was: sex in the study and not even his own study at that! He'd behaved scandalously. This was behaviour he had expected from his brothers in their wilder days. Paine and Crispin were perfectly capable of such shenanigans. Scandalised as his mind was, his brain couldn't decide on exactly what the scandal was. His gentleman's mind argued the scandal was that he'd taken a virginal young woman on the floor in front of a fire, not even bothering to do more than unbutton his trousers and push up her skirts—such actions were trademarks of how men took the whores against the walls in Covent Garden alleys.

A young woman of Tessa's background deserved a bed and fine sheets. Of course, the irony of such a conclusion was that a young woman of Tessa's background should not be inducted into love making at all without the benefit of a wedding ring.

She's twenty-two, for heaven's sake! the other

portion of his mind contended. She is capable of knowing her own mind and there was no doubt she was a consensual participant. You did nothing more than use the tools the situation put at your disposal.

Brimley would certainly applaud his actions. He'd done no more than what duty demanded. But something deep inside Peyton knew that he could not camouflage what had transpired with Tessa as merely 'duty'. Something in him would not let him paint their love making with such a superficial brush.

Tessa stirred, reminding Peyton they couldn't stay this way indefinitely. What they'd done in his aunt's study was risky. Crispin was out for the evening and Lily was gone as well, but there were still others in the house that could accidentally walk in on them: servants come to douse the fire or a sister who couldn't sleep.

Peyton gently dislodged Tessa and rose, taking time to adjust his clothing. His hands went to his trousers and his member roused a bit in remembrance of other hands that had recently passed that way.

He knelt down and took a moment to arrange Tessa's skirts and bodice decently before scooping her up in his arms. She made a mild protest that made him laugh. Of course his Tessa would protest, even though she was in no condition to walk to her chambers.

Peyton made the walk up the stairs to her bedroom and deposited her on the bed, taking time to remove her shoes and stockings. He pulled back the bedspread, debating whether or not he should try and get her into a nightgown. He didn't trust the reaction of his body and opted against it. He'd made the long walk with her in his arms—no easy feat—she could do her part and think what to tell the maid in the morning.

Peyton tucked the blanket about her. She reached for him in her sleep. 'No, Tessa,' Peyton said a quiet whisper. 'If I am going to get caught in your bed, I might as well have left us on the study floor and saved myself the effort. Sleep well.'

There was a chance she might rest well, if her current state was any indicator. There was no chance he would, Peyton reasoned. He had too much to think about and the night air on the way home would be bracing on the short walk back to Dursley House. He'd known what he was doing with Tessa. No matter how consensual their passion had been, there were still certain facts that had to be faced. He'd taken her innocence. His gentlemanly behaviour might have lapsed on the floor of the study, but he knew his responsibilities. When a gentleman took a young lady's innocence, there was only one acceptable reaction. Tomorrow would be a very busy day, starting with a visit to Lambeth Palace for a special licence and ending with a proposal.

The prospect actually filled him with satisfaction in spite of its precipitous nature. He'd not originally planned to marry Tessa Branscombe. He'd not planned to make love to her in his aunt's house, but he did not find the idea of marriage to her an un-palatable consequence. Peyton began to make lists in his head. He would propose over a quiet supper on the terrace of Dursley House before the dratted Academy Ball. He'd need roses, the ring from the vault, candles, the good champagne…

Tessa woke the next morning to brilliant rays of sunlight streaming through the windows of her room, the maid humming happily while she laid out clothes.

Tessa stretched, realising she was still in her dress. Then she remembered why. She had a vague recol-lection of Peyton carrying her to bed. But there was nothing vague about why he'd done so. That was very clear. Tessa wondered how quickly she could get rid of the maid. She devised a short errand and breathed a sigh of relief when the maid left the room to carry it out.

Oh, lord, what had she done? She was glad no one was there to see her embarrassment. She and Peyton had made love on the study floor. Strangely enough, that wasn't the embarrassing part. She'd not been ashamed of anything they'd done last night and that was still unswervingly true this morning. No, it wasn't the nakedness or the physical intimacy which caused her to blush. It was the motivations for it.

What must Peyton think of her? Did he think she'd seduced him? Tessa recalled her words—'make me feel safe'. Did he think that had been a ploy? A flirtation? This morning, she regretted the words. She had not meant them as any kind of coy game. She'd not suspected such words would lead them to the situation they found themselves in. But perhaps Peyton had taken them as such.

It was embarrassing to think Peyton might have taken pity on her. Surely that wasn't the case? Surely Peyton, with all his stiff-necked notions about propriety, didn't make a practice out of bedding young women on study floors because he pitied them?

No, that notion didn't fit at all. Tessa would have been relieved if it hadn't led to another notion. Peyton *was* a stickler for propriety. He was a gentleman of the highest order in both title and behaviour. She rather hoped such attitudes wouldn't lead to an embarrassing proposal. Peyton might feel compelled to make some kind of outlandish offer, all for the sake of her lost virginity.

She needed to make sure he didn't have a chance to do that. Today would be difficult to navigate. She would be with Peyton all day. The Royal Academy had its annual exhibit today and there was a ball afterwards to mark the opening. He would be by her side all day and all night. Fortunately, they'd be in very public venues and surrounded by people. With luck, there would be very little opportunity to hold a private conversation.

Tessa threw back the covers and began to strip out of her dress before her maid came back. Today would be a very demanding day.

* * *

'We can do it today,' Sergei Androvich said coldly from his seat at the table in the private withdrawing room of the Russian embassy. 'We could have done it last night if you'd allowed it.' He took a moment to fix Vasilov with a sneer, giving the man a taste of his own medicine. 'The Earl *walked* home alone in the late hours from his aunt's. It could have looked like footpads had simply stabbed him for his purse. We could have made it look like things turned rough when he tried to fight back and was outnumbered.'

'And I told you it would look too coincidental to have that happen on the same day the Branscombe house was burgled,' Vasilov retorted hotly. They'd been arguing about how best to eliminate the Earl for the last two days.

'Why is today any different?' Sergei said testily.

Gromsky intervened. 'Because, today it will be in public. Everyone will see. The man we've hired is supposed to look like a political radical. Everyone will think it is about his opposition to a bill in Parliament. No one will connect it to the Branscombe house. Best of all, we'll be there, all of us. Even those who might be aware of the reasons behind the Earl's involvement with the Branscombes won't be able to connect us to it. We'll be there, clearly talking with others and enjoying the occasion when the deed happens.'

Ilanovich turned to Sergei. 'After the Earl's

demise, Tessa will be ready to turn to you. She'll need comforting after the loss of the Earl.'

Sergei bristled at the implication. 'She does not love him.'

Vasilov chuckled. 'We'll see. I think you're losing your touch. But that's for another day. Today, we have an Earl to assassinate. It's all been arranged.' He looked at his pocket watch. 'Three hours until the curtain rises.'

Chapter Twelve

The courtyard of Somerset House, where the Royal Academy of Arts was located, was filled to near-capacity with people anticipating a grand social event of the Season. Up until now, the routs and balls had been modest events, growing ever more crowded, but today, the Season was on display in all its well-tailored finery.

Eva and Petra had argued without success to be allowed to come with them. They'd only accepted their fate once Peyton promised to bring them later in the Season on a quiet afternoon. In part, Tessa was glad to know they were at home, safe at Aunt Lily's. She had enough on her mind without trying to keep an eye on her two sisters. Most of her concentration was absorbed with the task of walking beside Peyton with her hand on his arm and pretending nothing had transpired between them. She took a small sense of pleasure from recognising that this was proving difficult for Peyton as well.

Certainly he did nothing that outwardly gave away the change between them. But privately, she knew he was behaving differently. She noticed the firmer grip he kept on her arm, the constancy of the light pressure of his hand at her back; little things that were not out of place to the outsider but were remarkable to her because she'd known him *before*. Tessa wondered if the rest of her life would be divided up that way—all the things that happened before Peyton and all the things that would happen after.

'Here we are. We've arrived at last,' Peyton said, leaning close to her ear in order to be heard over the crowd's conversations. 'The Great Room of Somerset House.' Peyton gestured to the enormous hall they'd entered. 'This is the most prestigious room in the exhibition. All the artists strive to have their work on display in this room.'

Tessa looked about her, taking in the overwhelming display of art. Not an inch of the high walls was left uncovered. Paintings of all sizes hung everywhere. 'It's nearly impossible to focus on just one!' Tessa exclaimed.

'There are other exhibition rooms, of course, that we can reach off this main room. Perhaps you'd like to start there?' Peyton offered. 'They might be less crowded.'

That would not do. Less crowded might provide an opportunity for a conversation she didn't want to have. 'No, this will be all right. I will accustom myself to the abundant display.' Tessa laughed, dissuading Peyton.

Lily and Crispin trailed behind them and the foursome made slow but steady progress about the room, taking time to admire the canvases and occasionally chat with friends.

Peyton turned out to be a well-informed escort on the subject of art, pointing out certain aspects to the artists' work. At John Constable's *Opening of Waterloo Bridge*, Peyton stopped for a while in front of the colourful painting, silently comparing it to a nearby Joseph Turner canvas depicting a seascape. He gave a short chuckle.

'What's so funny?' Tessa asked, following his gaze from one painting to the other.

'Joseph Turner has got the last word in on this, I think.' Tessa gave him a perplexed look and he hurried on to explain. 'Last year, there was some controversy between Constable and Turner. It seems that Constable took Turner's exhibition spot and hung his own painting in it, ousting Turner from the Great Room. This year, my friends associated with the Royal Academy told me that during the time period the artists can come in and touch up their paintings, Turner knew he'd hang his work next to Constable's, so at the last minute, he painted this yellow buoy into the canvas to steal attention away from Constable's colours.'

Behind them, Crispin snorted. 'What sissified nonsense, squabbling over where to hang a picture.'

Peyton shot him a quelling look. 'Cris, do try to appreciate the finer things.'

'I like that one over there, the one with the half-dressed, drunk lady in it.' Crispin tossed his head towards a picture entitled *The Swoon*. Peyton grimaced.

They moved through the room into another series of smaller chambers featuring other exhibits. They were examining a collection of Chinese art when Sergei Androvich found them.

'Tessa, I thought I might find you here today.'

Tessa fought the urge to cringe at Sergei's easy use of her name. True, he was a good family friend, but things were different here in England, her life was different and it struck her that his use of her first name was no longer appropriate. In all likelihood their friendship would end soon. She would not be marrying Sergei. She knew that now after her night with Peyton. Regardless of what that night meant, she knew that something magical was possible with the right man—whether or not Peyton was the right man, Sergei definitely wasn't. His kisses were empty of fire and Peyton had proved it didn't have to be that way. She looked about for any signs of the other ambassadors, relaxing slightly when she didn't see them in the vicinity.

As he stood beside her, Peyton's grip tightened. 'Count, how do you find our Academy?' He was all cool politeness.

'I suppose it is passable,' Sergei said with equal steel. 'It's not the Winter Palace. Tessa and I had a chance to survey the Imperial art collection on several occasions.'

'Perhaps your monarchs should spend more time and money on taking care of their people instead of scouring Europe for fine art. It's hard to eat paint, but I hear it burns well,' Crispin snarled, bluntly referring to the growing unrest between the Czar and the Russian populace. Tessa was all too aware of the volatile situation she'd left behind in St Petersburg. Building palaces and collecting art seemed like poor priorities when people were starving and the very social fabric of the country was on the brink of unravelling.

'Muzzle your dog, Dursley,' Sergei spat. 'I would willingly face you at twenty paces for the honour of Mother Russia.'

'Muzzle me yourself,' Crispin shot back, not willing to be ignored.

'Gentlemen, this will not do,' Lily swiftly put in, to Tessa's relief. 'Crispin, I want to look at that lovely Chinese statue over there. Come with me.'

'Tessa, my apologies,' Sergei said with a short bow as Lily led Crispin away.

Tessa smiled wanly.

'How are your sisters? I have not seen them since we played charades. That was a lovely evening,' Sergei said, taking a smoother conversational avenue.

'They are well. We've had a few—' Tessa began, but to her surprise Peyton cut her off.

'We've had a few outings,' he said swiftly. 'I've been showing the girls around town. We had a wonderful day at the Tower not long ago,' he added.

He was being pompous again, acting as if she couldn't speak for herself. Why didn't he want Sergei to know the truth? Why not tell Sergei about the house? When Sergei asked if he could show her some of the items on display in the next room, Tessa accepted, just to give Peyton a taste of her independence. He did *not* own her.

Peyton's gaze narrowed and she knew he saw the reason for her acceptance. She'd hoped she wouldn't be that transparent. 'I've been eager to see that display myself. I'll come, too,' he said evenly. He shifted his gaze to the Count, studying Sergei with an intensity that unnerved Tessa. She suddenly felt like a complete outsider. Under the veneer of this petty squabbling they were conducting over her, something else was going on between them.

The three of them made their way towards the other room. It was slightly more populated and there was not room to walk three abreast in many cases. Tessa felt Peyton slip behind them and her anxiety escalated. Something felt unnatural. Sergei was trying too hard to keep her with him. His grip on her arm was firm beyond politeness. When she tried to manoeuvre closer to Peyton, Sergei manoeuvred the situation otherwise. Something was dreadfully wrong, but what was it?

Tessa saw it all at once only because she'd turned her head behind her to say something to Peyton. A man dressed in a gentleman's clothes was moving swiftly through the crowd towards them—too swiftly, Tessa thought, for it to be natural movement in these close confines. Metal flashed in his hand, partly concealed by the cuff of his shirt.

Instinctively, she knew the man had set on her group as his target. Was the man after her? Her fear rose, but not for herself. If the man was after her, he'd have to get through Peyton first. Peyton was all that stood between her and the man advancing towards them. She cried out a warning. 'Peyton!'

The man charged, forced to hurry now that his attentions had been noticed. But her warning was enough to save Peyton from the brunt of it. He sidestepped, taking the slice of the knife in the side instead of in his vital organs. He crouched in reaction to the initial pain and came up with a knife of his own from some secret place on his person, the knife he'd had yesterday at the house.

Around her, women screamed. She heard her own voice call out for Crispin. She struggled against Sergei's iron grip as he forcibly restrained her and hauled her to safety. 'Let me go! Don't bother about me, help him!' she railed at Sergei. 'Please, go help him.' But Sergei did nothing.

'The bloody Englishman looks like he can take care of himself, Tessa.' He gave a low whistle at the sight of Peyton's blade slicing into the arm of the would-be attacker.

Out of reflex, Tessa turned her head into Sergei's shoulder at the sight of blood. She felt Sergei's arms about her, but she couldn't feel safe. These weren't Peyton's arms and they conveyed none of the strength of Peyton's embrace.

'You can look now,' Sergei said after long moments, disappointment peppering his tone. 'The guards have come to manage the situation. Quite the dangerous guardian you've acquired, Tessa. He carries a knife and apparently for good reason. Don't you think that's a little odd for a gentleman?'

Tessa lifted her head to see Crispin and three soldiers hired for the exhibition enter the fight. The soldiers inserted themselves between Peyton and the stranger so that Peyton could disengage and step back. After that, the man was easily subdued and led off, Crispin following close behind to mop up the details.

Tessa broke from Sergei's side and went straight to Peyton, pushing through the crowd of people gathered around him. She didn't care that people stared at her or that some murmured the beginnings of rumours: *That's the Branscombe girl, the one who danced so close to him, the one who speaks Russian. Did you hear her call him by his Christian name?* 'Excuse me, let me get him out of here,' she said in her most authoritative voice. It worked. Before long, she had Peyton outside and had summoned the carriage.

The carriage took an eternity to make its way to them in the courtyard. They seemed to be the centre of everyone's attention, but Tessa staunchly ignored the stares that came their way. Instead, she devoted herself to a quiet inspection of Peyton, who stood silent and stoic at her side. He didn't appear hurt, but that could be deceiving. This was not a man who would admit to injury, although she knew he had taken at least one cut.

The carriage pulled up and they climbed in. 'Are you badly hurt?' Tessa asked now that the crowds were behind them. She pushed aside his coat, searching for damage. She'd seen the knife slice his side and his coat was ripped.

Peyton snatched at her hands, trying to fend off her ministrations. 'Tessa, don't. I'll be all right.' But it was too late. She'd already discovered what Peyton wanted to hide. Her hands were wet when Peyton pulled them away, covered in his blood. In the dim carriage light it had been hard to see the blood against the dark blue pattern of his waistcoat. But on her hands, there was no mistaking it.

'Oh, God, Peyton.' Tessa felt herself tremble. She had to be strong at least until they got home.

'It's all right,' Peyton said, but he gritted his teeth as he said it and Tessa knew he was in pain now that the initial adrenalin rush from the fight was gone.

Tessa suffered a terrible pang of guilt. This was her fault. She was certain now that the attacker was meant for her. Why would anyone try to kill an earl? Yet, he'd almost been fatally wounded on her behalf. She shuddered to think what would have happened if she hadn't turned when she did, if she had called out her warning a second later. Peyton would be dead in her place. She had waited too long to tell her secrets and the man who'd made love to her had almost paid the ultimate price for her choice.

'I am so sorry, Peyton,' she whispered.

'Why?' Peyton studied her. 'It's not your fault.'

'But it is.' Tessa shook her head. 'That knife was meant for me. You were simply in the way. I am sure of it.'

There was no stopping Tessa Branscombe when she was determined. And she was determined to tell him everything. Peyton sighed, leaning back against the pillows of his big bed at Dursley House. At least she'd had the decency to wait until the doctor had cleaned his wound and bound it. But he could tell her impatience was getting the better of her. She paced the length of his room, oblivious to the fact that she was alone with a man in his private chambers.

But nothing mattered to her right now except her guilt.

Now that the moment of truth was here, and he was minutes away from having all the answers

Brimley wanted, he wanted to tell Tessa to stop. He wanted those answers, not just for Brimley and the British troops facing potential war, but for Tessa's own safety. Yet he knew there would come a time when Tessa would hate him for this. She would feel betrayed, and rightly so.

He should blurt out right now that he knew the knife attack was for him. He'd been accidentally privy to the Russians' scheme. Count Androvich didn't want her dead, Androvich wanted *him* dead. He had to be out of the way first in order to clear a more direct path to Tessa. Peyton had worried about just such an attempt once Androvich had shown up and started provoking Crispin. He'd thought the man might be angling for a duel. Then, when the Count had made the attempt to separate Tessa from him, Peyton's other suspicions had risen. The Count didn't want to take the chance that Tessa would be in the line of fire and become an accidental casualty.

There was no doubt in Peyton's mind that the attack had been meant for him alone. Tessa's warning had saved his life. But Tessa did not know that. She saw the situation only through the lens of what she did know. She knew only one thing: someone was after her, and so she blamed herself for his injury. Brimley would be overjoyed.

'Do you need water?' Tessa asked. 'Are you comfortable?'

'You would make a terrible nurse,' Peyton tried to tease. 'I have a slight knife wound, not a fever.'

'All right.' Tessa relented and came to sit on the side of the bed, her face earnest. 'You have to listen to me. You have to stay away from me. This is all my fault. Someone is after me and you could be killed if you stand in the way.'

Peyton raised a hand to her lips. 'Shh, Tess. Slow down, start at the beginning and let me be the judge of all that.'

And for once in her life, Tessa Branscombe did as she was told.

Chapter Thirteen

'After my father's funeral, our house was broken into, not unlike what has happened here, only with less damage,' Tessa began, trying to marshal her thoughts into some cohesive order. It had been so long since she'd shared any of this aloud. 'We lived in a prestigious neighbourhood in St Petersburg, one not troubled by common crime or criminals. I thought at the time how odd such an act was. It was so out of place for our surroundings. Such things did not happen.' Tessa pleated the coverlet between her fingers.

'Was anything taken?' Peyton asked.

Tessa shook her head. 'No. Just like the break-in here, nothing was missing, although, in both instances, the thief was obviously looking for something in earnest and there were items of value that could have been taken, but weren't.' Tessa thought of the few silver pieces in the kitchen cabinet that Arthur had so lovingly arranged and the brightly coloured Russian samovar. Those items would have fetched a good price, but the thief had left them behind.

Tessa continued with her story. 'Over the next few days I felt as if I were being watched every time I ventured from the house, which was quite often. There was a lot of business to wrap up at the embassy regarding my father. In some instances, I am quite sure I was followed, but I can't prove any of that.' She studied Peyton closely, watching for his reaction. 'You're the only person I've discussed this with since coming to London. Of course, I told Sergei about it in St Petersburg and he escorted me everywhere. After that, the feeling that I was being followed disappeared.'

Tessa regretted mentioned the last bit about Sergei. She could see Peyton's dislike for the man rise in his eyes. 'I know you don't care for him, but he acted as a good friend to us in a difficult time,' she scolded lightly.

'He was no friend to me today,' Peyton said coldly. 'The coward was more than happy to let me face the knife alone.'

Tessa bit her tongue. There were defences she could make for Sergei's choice: he was busy protecting her, it all happened too quickly. But she'd thought the same thing. Indeed, she'd urged Sergei to assist Peyton and Sergei had foregone the opportunity outright in a very blunt manner.

Tessa continued with her story. 'I felt it was best

we leave St Petersburg right away. We left quietly before the deadline I had put about in our social circles. I'm not sure Sergei has forgiven me for that small deception, but I think it was successful. There were no incidents on the road, nothing until here.'

'And the arrival of the Russian delegation,' Peyton added.

Tessa looked at him sharply. 'What are you implying? Those men were my father's colleagues. They'd worked together for years.'

Peyton struggled to sit up straighter against his pillows. 'That is exactly my implication. Who would know better if your father had secrets, diplomatic secrets, than the people he worked with most often? Besides, I've noticed they make you nervous.'

'Secrets?' Tessa questioned. 'I doubt that very much. My father was a most unassuming man. He was quiet and straightforward in his dealings. It was what made him so popular. People knew they could trust him, that he was there to do a job. He was not a man who had hidden agendas like so many of the others.' She was growing irate at Peyton's suggestion that her father might have been hiding something.

'It only takes one secret, Tessa,' Peyton said.

Tessa got up from the bed, no longer able to contain her agitation. She paced the length of the floor. 'All right, then, you tell me what you think is going on, since it's clear to me you see this in an entirely different light.'

Peyton recognised he was on very tenuous ground. Tessa was telling him all she knew, or at least all she thought she knew. But there were details he wanted. He had to ask his questions in a way that would help her expose those details without him appearing to be overly informed on a subject that he'd supposedly just heard about moments ago.

'Did your father ever talk with you about his work?'

'Always. He felt it helped me be a better hostess,' Tessa answered.

'What about anything unusual towards the end? Any new developments or people who had entered his circle?' Peyton probed carefully. He watched a certain amount of understanding dawn on Tessa.

'You think the people following me thought I knew something or had something in my possession that wasn't in the house when they broke in,' Tessa guessed, fitting the ideas together.

Peyton nodded. 'It makes sense. The item wasn't in the house, so they may have reasoned it was small enough to easily keep on one's person. Maybe they didn't know for sure that the item was a physical thing. Perhaps it was and still is some information they believe you remember. Perhaps, even, they followed you in the hope that you were going to retrieve it from somewhere. I am assuming most people were aware that your father kept you well educated.' He studied her, watching her mind work as her pacing slowed.

'So whoever is looking for this nebulous something believes I still have it?'

'Yes.' That was all Peyton could afford to say. It was positively killing him not to shout out that 'it' was a list of Russian revolutionaries willing to overthrow the Czar with the help of English pounds and arms.

'I wish I knew what it was.' Tessa sighed heavily. 'I don't think I have anything of use. All their terror is for nothing. No matter how much they frighten me, there's nothing I can do. If I knew what it was, I'd have some negotiating power.'

That truly frightened him. 'No!' Peyton sat up too far and winced. 'No,' he said in a softer, firmer voice, easing back on his pillows. 'Tessa, these men do not negotiate. They have ruined your home in two cities and have put you in personal danger. Promise me under no circumstance you will try to manage them.'

Tessa tossed her gold hair. 'That's an easy promise to give. I don't have any inkling as to who they might be.'

Peyton snorted. 'You're too intelligent to be that naïve, Tessa. You should look very closely at the Russian delegation and at Sergei Androvich before declaring them innocent. Whatever it is that you have, they are pursuing it actively and covertly.' He dared not go any further with what he shared, but he could not in good conscience keep Tessa unaware of the danger she put herself in every time she had contact with Androvich. He could at least put the idea into her mind.

'I have known Sergei for years!' Tessa protested. The rest of her tirade faded. Peyton didn't like the look on her face. 'That is precisely what Sergei said about you today.'

Peyton cocked a cool brow her direction. 'What did Count Androvich have to say that merits repeating?'

'He said I should not be so quick to trust you. Actually, what he said was "Quite the dangerous guardian you've acquired…carries a knife and apparently for good reason".'

Peyton tamped down his temper. There was no sense in letting his anger get the better of him, but that didn't change the fact that he wanted to show Androvich just how dangerous he could be. The fool was twisting the truth, creating doubt about him in Tessa's mind when the one Tessa ought to fear was Androvich himself.

'What is going on?' Tessa demanded from the window, hands on her hips as she faced him. 'I feel as if there is a game within a game being played out around me and I don't know all the rules. I will not stand for it.'

The door opened without warning and Crispin entered, picking up the conversation. 'Haven't you ever had two suitors fighting over you before? I would think a beautiful woman like you would know exactly what's going on.'

Peyton groaned, knowing the words Tessa would fling at him before she even spoke them.

Her blue-violet eyes flashed. She speared him with a stormy look. 'Is that what last night was? Some kind of gentleman's competition to get there first?' It was as bad as Peyton had expected. Really not the tone he wanted to set for his proposal. But what she said next chilled him entirely. 'Sergei was right. You are not to be trusted.' She pushed past Crispin and left the room, slamming the door behind her for good measure.

'What did I say?' Crispin said, pulling up a chair beside the bed.

'When are you going to think before you open your mouth?'

'What happened last night?'

'Nothing to comment on,' Peyton said, trying to push the issue aside, but Crispin noticed the briskness in his tone for what it was.

Crispin slapped his leg and hooted. 'You seduced her. At Aunt Lily's? In the study where I left you? This is grand. Is the rug as soft as it looks?'

Peyton tried to look more annoyed than embarrassed. His brother was the only one who could cut him down to size by painting his adventures for what they were. 'Really, Cris, a gentleman doesn't kiss and tell.' And, apparently, he wasn't going to propose either. He had the special licence, but it appeared that it would have to wait.

'You did more than kiss the delectable Miss Branscombe. This is so unlike you, Peyton. Wait until

I tell Paine. You've lectured us for years about a gentleman's responsibility.' Crispin gave a haughty pose and pointed a strict finger. 'Young ladies of good breeding are off limits. They're only for marrying. Taking the innocence of a young woman of good standing is tantamount to a marriage proposal.'

'I haven't broken any of my rules,' Peyton said, finally drawn into the argument. 'I do intend to marry her, if she'll have me.'

Crispin chuckled. 'I'd be more worried about the last part of that than the first. She was angry enough about you and Sergei competing over her. Can you imagine how she'll cut up if she finds out you've known about the list all along and that you're not really her guardian?' Crispin let out a low whistle.

Yes, he could imagine. It was a scene he preferred not to think about for many reasons. He hoped when the time came there would be a way to avoid the discussion altogether. 'We'll deal with that later. Now, help me up. I want to put my shirt on. We're going to see Brimley and you can tell me what you found out from the man with the knife,' Peyton said firmly. He refused to think of the aftermath this little episode would cause. Tessa would be beyond furious at his deception, but if they both lived through it, maybe there was a chance she'd forgive him.

She would *not* forgive Peyton for what he'd done! Tessa jabbed the needle mercilessly through the fabric of a small tapestry depicting the Nevsky Prospekt in St Petersburg. It wasn't going well. The river was crooked and the buildings looked wobbly. She had Aunt Lily's second-floor sitting room all to herself. Her sisters were gathered in the music room with a tutor Aunt Lily had hired.

It was just as well. She couldn't talk to anyone about the things on her mind. She couldn't tell Petra or Aunt Lily what had happened with Peyton. Unmarried women didn't go around making love to men who couldn't possibly wed them. It was a poor example to set for Petra, and Tessa feared Aunt Lily would think it a low attempt to take advantage of her nephew. Everyone knew the Earl of Dursley was fated to marry someone of high standing and enormous wealth. Like married like.

Even if there had been a chance, the ensuing scandal that had erupted from the attack at the Academy had scotched what hope there was. The *ton* had marked her as trouble. Their sympathies were with the Earl of Dursley, the poor man saddled with the Branscombe girls. How much could a man, even of Dursley's impeccable background, be able to reform what had taken years to instil? She'd heard those rumours, too.

At twenty-two she was nearly on the shelf. Such flagrant behaviour as dancing too close to a man and calling him by his Christian name assured her a place on that shelf. No man would want to marry a woman with those low tendencies. But what could be expected from her eccentric upbringing in foreign places and no mother to guide her? Tessa didn't mistake the last for genuine pity. Her circumstances were merely more grist for the gossip mill.

Most assuredly, Peyton would not consider aligning himself with a woman who fomented scandal on a grand scale. She could appreciate that reticence. He had his family to think of, an obligation he took seriously. His alliances affected all of them. He would not risk them by embracing more than guardianship with the Branscombes, and it was all Tessa's fault.

Knowing all that, Tessa still couldn't believe Peyton had done what he did just for the sake of competing with Sergei. He hadn't struck her as a man who felt anyone was worth competing with. Yet, Crispin's words made sense. The alternative was too horrific. If Sergei and Peyton weren't competing over her, then what was really going on? Was one of them right about the other? Was one of them capable of committing treachery of a magnitude she could not contemplate? Peyton and Sergei had both intimated as much about each other. If so, which one was it? Tessa made the cases in her mind.

Sergei was a long-time friend. He'd courted her and proposed to her, motivated, if not by love, then by honour. She was convinced Sergei felt he owed it to her father to take care of them the only way he knew how: through the security of marriage. Sergei had warned her about Peyton because he cared for her. To be fair, however, she needed to remember that her troubles in London hadn't started until the Russian delegation had arrived and she knew the dark reputations of the three men travelling with Sergei.

On the other hand, she could also say that her troubles had not started until Peyton appeared, coincidentally the first day Sergei had come to visit. That did not leave Peyton in a strong position. Peyton had blown into their lives like a thunderstorm, carving out a place in their family with his codicil and arrogance. Within days, he'd displaced Sergei as the main male in their little world. He'd put his servants in her home, he'd been making free of the upstairs rooms in her absence. He knew their schedules. He knew when they'd be out with Aunt Lily.

She had not thought of that before. Peyton would know the best times for a burglar to gain entrance to the house without any surprise residents being home. Her stomach twisted at the thought. Had Peyton planned the break-in? Her mind rallied in his defence. To what purpose? Peyton had known nothing about her circumstances until today. He had no motive. She immediately discarded the thought. But she couldn't discard the niggling notion that something about Peyton didn't ring true. Even if he couldn't be involved with her problems, he was dangerous.

Sergei's comment was strongly etched in her mind: 'He carries a knife and apparently for good reason.'

It wasn't the first time she'd seen the knife. He'd pulled it out at her house. It wasn't the first time either that he'd acted with such reflexes, if she counted that day on the stairs. Peyton Ramsden was not a soft earl accustomed to the easy life. He was a man with highly trained, potentially lethal skills. But to do what? Tessa shivered at the thought. She had been impetuous last night. It was unnerving to think she'd quite possibly slept with the enemy. Worse, she had liked it.

Chapter Fourteen

Sergei eyed the newly arrived folder on the embassy's conference table with ill-contained glee. Inside that folder lay the answers which would guide the next steps of their mission. More importantly, if those answers were what Sergei expected, he would be able to take a more aggressive approach where the quarrelsome Earl of Dursley was concerned.

It was all he could do to refrain from sneaking a peek inside while he waited for his comrades to arrive. Finally, there'd be some forward movement in their assignment to retrieve the list that had the Czar so concerned. He had not so much followed Tessa Branscombe to England as he had followed that list. It was here, somewhere, accidentally transported by Tessa Branscombe, whom he was increasingly sure had no idea what she'd done. While Sergei was certain Tessa had no idea the list existed, his comrades were not as convinced. But they hadn't seen first-hand what he'd seen. In the days he'd escorted her about St Petersburg, wrapping up her father's work, she'd not retrieved anything from a secret place, had not met clandestinely with anyone. Yet, the Czar had believed so strongly that she'd taken the list with her that he'd sent this coterie of ambassadors to ferret it out before it could be turned over to British officials.

The three others trickled in one by one, Vasilov being the last to arrive. 'This had better be informative considering the amount of money we paid to acquire it,' he groused, reaching for the dossier.

He reached inside. 'One sheet?' He pulled out the one piece of paper inside the leather folder and waved it. 'This is almost laughable.'

Sergei's hopes sank as Vasilov passed the sheet on to Gromsky. 'Not so laughable, it would seem,' Gromsky said.

'Our friend the Earl was not a close acquaintance of Ralph Branscombe. But he is a close acquaintance with a Whitehall conspiracy expert, Moreton Brimley.'

This got everyone's attention. They all knew who Brimley was. They'd met him at a few social occasions since their arrival. If there were plans afoot, Brimley would know.

Gromsky went on to read out from the page. 'While it cannot be empirically substantiated, it seems likely Peyton Ramsden is involved with

Brimley's latest project. Private sources informed me Ramsden had not expected to be in town very long. He certainly had not planned to join the Season. Socially being seen with a diplomat's daughter seems too much of a coincidence given that he's worked with Brimley extensively in the past and his original timetable for staying in town.'

'Aha!' Sergei said triumphantly. 'Our earlier suppositions were correct. He is indeed after the list, too. He's now a proven threat to Russian national security. We must move more quickly to eliminate him. No more relying on a third party to do our work. The attacker at the Academy was a poor excuse of an assassin.'

The three men exchanged glances. Gromsky coughed. 'Androvich is right. We've been less aggressive with the Earl because we haven't been sure of his role. That's weakened us.'

'I say we use a slow-acting poison like the one we used on Branscombe,' Ilanovich put in. 'Something we can slip in a glass of champagne at a ball and will take six or seven hours to work.'

Sergei humphed. 'I want to quietly run him through and dump him in the bushes somewhere.'

'Too much scandal,' Vasilov said. 'Ilanovich is right. Slow-acting poison would be very discreet. There'd be no scandal, no disrupting of an event. No hostess would be beside herself at thinking the Earl died in her ballroom or her rose bushes.' He shot

Sergei a withering look. 'We need to do it soon, before the invitations run out.'

There was no real fear of the invitations running out. There were plenty of circles they were welcome in, plenty of people in government who would gladly entertain foreign ambassadors and Sergei knew his own good looks had ensured a large level of interest, too. All the same, he knew what Vasilov meant. The Earl ran in lofty circles. Once the novelty of being the new Russian Count around town wore off, the invitations to events Dursley attended at the higher reaches of society would taper off. The chance to encounter Dursley would shrink, especially if Dursley put it about that there was a certain level of animosity between him and the Russians. Society would become a shield around Dursley.

So far, Dursley had thwarted him at every turn, subtly taking away access to Tessa and thus to the list. First, the man had insinuated himself into Tessa's life and taken time away from him. No longer could Sergei simply drop by and find Tessa able to receive him. Next, Dursley had physically removed her, putting her in his aunt's house. Even if there had been time to see her, now there was no place he could see her without being watched. Not that it mattered. She didn't know about the list, but she was the gateway to the Branscombe possessions.

Worst of all, it appeared Vasilov was right. Dursley was succeeding where Sergei himself had fallen short—the Earl was wooing Tessa with some success. She'd certainly been frightened for Dursley at the Academy. That moment in his arms, when Tessa had turned her head into his shoulder, he knew her fear for Dursley was far more than the sum of her friendly affections for him had ever been. To a man of Sergei's charms, such a realisation was quite lowering. He didn't love Tessa Branscombe, far from it, but it was a matter of male pride.

'Where are they today?' Ilanovich broke into Sergei's thoughts.

'The zoo in Regent's Park and then the Berrybourne rout tonight, to which we are invited. We'll need to be early. They'll probably move on to the Viscount St Just's private gala.'

'To which we're not invited,' Vasilov hastily put in.

'To which most of London is not invited,' Sergei corrected. 'It's a quiet supper for thirty to show off the Viscount's new rose breeds.'

'Gentlemen, please,' Gromsky put in. 'This bickering will not help. We'll be at the Berrybournes' early and see what can be arranged. Are they being followed today at the zoo?'

Sergei shook his head. 'No, there seems no point in it now that we know who all the players are. Tessa doesn't know about the list, so she's not manoeuvring to meet anyone about it, and she has nothing dangerous to tell Ramsden that he doesn't already know.'

'That's probably for the best,' Vasilov said slyly,

unable to resist one more jabbing remark. 'We're running out of people to enlist since Crispin Ramsden has decided the quickest route between questions and answers can be travelled with his fist. I had no idea how long it took a black eye to heal.'

'This is wonderful!' Eva flung her arms wide and spun a circle in the wide grass lawn of Regent's Park. 'The sun is out and the weather is perfect.'

Tessa smiled from her place on the large picnic blanket they'd spread out. She shared most of her sister's sentiment. This was a gorgeous day. She'd loved watching her sisters enjoy the sights of the zoo, especially Annie. Best of all, there had been no mishaps. They hadn't been followed. She could feel it. That knowledge alone had given her an enormous sense of freedom and well being. The only blight on that freedom was that she and Peyton had not talked since their stormy encounter.

More than ever, she felt she and Peyton were living two lives: the polite life they played out in front of society and her sisters, and the explosive, private life where nothing was quite clear beyond their intense physical attraction.

Even now, watching him play tag with Annie and Eva on the park lawn, Tessa was hard pressed to summon up her sinister thoughts about him with any validity. How could a man who was so good with children have such a dark side as the one her mind tried to accuse him of? He looked magnificent out there. He'd taken his coat off for tag and Tessa found the sight of him in only shirt and waistcoat physically compelling. Peyton Ramsden was a well-made man, a fact she'd had chances to verify on more than one occasion. He'd caught Annie and was swinging her around until the little girl couldn't stop laughing. An amazing feat considering he must have still been sore from the encounter with the knife at the Academy.

'He'll make a wonderful father,' Lily said, accurately interpreting the source of Tessa's wide smile.

Tessa quickly wiped the smile off her face, embarrassed to be caught so openly ogling the Earl. 'I am sure he will. It is good to hear Annie laugh and enjoy herself.'

The deflection wasn't good enough for Lily. Tessa was conscious of Lily's studious gaze. 'My nephew is a man of honour. He will always put family first. There are few things a person can bet on with any regular success, but that is one of them. In that, the two of you have much in common.'

'What a kind thing to say, thank you,' Tessa said as evasively as possible. 'I must remind you that I have no intentions of marrying.'

Lily only laughed. 'It seems you and Peyton have another item in common. That's what my nephew says, too, especially now that his brother has a new baby boy to ensure the estate is inherited by a close family member.'

Peyton returned to the blanket, carrying Annie on his back. 'I've found a rare, wild species that laughs when she's tickled.' Peyton dumped her on the blanket beside Tessa and Tessa picked up her cue. It was far easier tickling Annie than it was deciphering Lily's messages. Was the woman playing matchmaker, or testing the waters in terms of what Tessa's agenda was where her nephew was concerned? Surely Peyton had not told his aunt what had transpired between them? It was likely Lily wanted to be certain Peyton wasn't tainted by the rumours surrounding her. If Lily thought she held any ambitions where Peyton was concerned, the older woman would not hesitate to warn her off.

'There are ducks on the pond, Aunt Lily. I thought the girls might enjoy seeing them while Tessa and I talk a bit,' Peyton suggested.

Within moments, Lily had the three girls organised and headed towards the pond.

'There's a place that rents boats, too. I should have liked to have taken you out for a row, Tessa. It's a pretty venue for two. But sometimes such privacy is not possible with a family to look after.' Peyton waved an idle hand after the girls. 'Having the girls around reminds me of the days when Crispin and Paine were younger. Sometimes I thought I'd never have a quiet moment to myself.' Peyton shrugged, sobering a bit. 'Then there was a time when I had all the silence and privacy I wanted and I discovered I didn't like it as much as I thought.'

'It must have been hard to be the brother, the father and the Earl to them,' Tessa said.

Peyton reached for her hand. 'Yes, just as hard as it is to be guardian and lover to you, Tess. We have some unspecified roles between us. We would do best to settle them and clarify our positions. I had meant to speak to you the day of the Royal Academy show.'

Oh, oh. Tessa saw where this was headed. 'Peyton, if this is about what happened at your aunt's, you needn't worry.'

'Needn't worry?' Peyton looked appalled at her response. 'We may have made a child. We may have decided to launch a new being into this world. That cannot be dismissed.'

She had to handle this better. Lily had just told her how important family was to Peyton and she'd blithely ignored that in her opening argument to dissuade him out of a marriage proposal. Well, Peyton might be stubbornly loyal, but he was also practical. 'Let's not be hasty in our assumptions,' Tessa said. 'The odds are definitely against us.' This answer did not please him entirely, but he did seem somewhat flummoxed. Tessa plunged ahead.

'Peyton, I did not engage in what we did the other night out of any attempt to coerce a proposal from you. Marriage to you was the furthest thing from my mind.' *Oh, lord, that sounded even worse.* She should stop now. But Tessa found she couldn't. 'What I mean to say is that there are no obligations to be met on your part because there are no expectations on my part.' There, that sounded much more pleasing, much more as if they were equals in this.

Peyton's features were hard, unreadable as he studied her. 'Did you like what we did?' he asked quietly.

Tessa blushed, although she knew no one else had overheard. 'Yes, of course I liked it.'

'I did, too, and I find myself wanting to be with you again and again. Certainly, such a situation is tolerable only in marriage.' A glimmer of a smile played on Peyton's lips, giving him a look that bespoke sin and seduction. He was positively irresistible—not that she really wanted to resist at all. But her world was too complex to introduce another element into it at the moment. Beyond the physical satisfaction they'd found together, she wasn't entirely sure it was safe to link herself in such a way to Peyton for him or for her.

She shook her head. 'Peyton, my world is a dangerous place right now. You're wearing the evidence of that beneath your shirt. Someone is hunting me for reasons I can only speculate on. Until that situation is resolved, I cannot contemplate marriage.'

'What if the first situation is resolved? Would you consider marriage then?' Peyton asked casually.

'If it was for more than lustful reasons, Peyton,' she said. 'Lust is not a good standard for a marriage. We can have that without a wedding.'

The girls were coming back from the pond. 'I'll take that as a "yes", then, since I would not seek to demean you in any way,' Peyton said politely, 'and it seems that is the best answer I'm going to get from you today.'

'I wish it could be different,' Tessa offered tentatively. 'I'm not good for your reputation and I know it.'

'Let me be the judge of that, Tessa.'

'No, *listen*, Peyton. I regret the rumours that are circulating, but I can only be myself. That won't change, it can't change.' She would like to have explained more, but the girls would be within earshot shortly.

Peyton saw them, too, and spoke quickly. 'I need to apologise for Crispin's comment the other day. He was out of line and I wanted you to know that I had said nothing to him about us. You need never fear for your reputation with me.'

'I accept your apology. It was a difficult day for all of us.' She did accept it, what there was of it and what it covered. But it wasn't near enough to cover the entirety of their recent feud. It was interesting to note that he'd apologise for his brother's errant comments, but said nothing at all about his own comments, which had fanned the fire to start with—the implication that her father had been involved in something clandestine and unsavoury, that Sergei was no true friend.

It would have made her life much easier if he'd apologised for those remarks, too. Then she could have chalked them up as nothing more than male jealousy or emotions over the moment, over being stabbed on behalf of a woman who had not been entirely forthcoming about her situation in St Petersburg. Without an apology, those comments could not be discounted and swept aside. She had to consider them and with them the dark thoughts she'd had about Peyton himself.

The girls began picking up the picnic things, signalling the end of the outing, and the little group began the short walk to Peyton's carriage. Tessa slid a careful glance at Peyton. He was busy talking to Annie about the ducks. They were back in their other world now—their public world where they were Miss Branscombe and Lord Dursley, where their interaction and behaviour were limited by the circumspection of society. He would drop her off at his aunt's house in a half-hour and pick her up a few hours later for the Berrybourne ball where they would dance, drink champagne and pretend that everything was all right.

The word 'crush' seemed highly inadequate to describe the Berrybourne affair. Peyton thought 'squash', 'squeeze' or perhaps 'cram' would do more justice to the situation. The massive amount of attendees at the ball gave it an inelegant quality and Peyton was glad he had a legitimate engagement to move on to as he surveyed the ballroom, taking stock of the event.

Beside him, Tessa was beautiful and coolly accepting of her surroundings, no more pleased than he about the quality of the Berrybourne entertainment. The gown she wore tonight upstaged the other gorgeous gowns she'd worn on previous occasions. The gown was the iciest of blues, so pale that it appeared to be white until she moved and the gown picked up a hue of blue or on occasion even lavender. Every movement changed the viewer's understanding of the gown. To Peyton's eye, it was a most appreciative work of illusion, no doubt done to keep the wearer of the gown the centre of someone's attention.

Peyton thought the gown was succeeding admirably and he might have attributed Tessa's outward coolness to the qualities of the gown with its pale, ice tones except that he knew better. Tessa *was* playing it cool with him. She had refused his marriage offer because of what she felt was her complicated life and her refusal to drag him into it. Tonight, in the carriage, between the Berrybournes and the St Just supper, he would remove her concerns. The rumours would pass eventually, replaced by someone else's scandal.

After dropping Tessa and her sisters off from their outing, Peyton had gone straight to Brimley and demanded the right to tell Tessa at least some of what was going on around her. He'd argued on grounds of her own personal safety, her own ability to protect herself. At the very least, she had to know about Sergei Androvich. It was no longer enough for him to make suggestions about Androvich's character. Doing so simply made him look like a jealous man and Tessa did not take a jealous man's claims seriously, as she'd so aptly demonstrated.

Brimley had thought for a moment and agreed, within reason. She could know about the list and about Sergei. Those were the limits of Brimley's 'reason'. She could not know about Peyton's own involvement. Brimley feared it would drive her away.

The orchestra was playing a waltz. Peyton shot Tessa a dubious look. 'Do you think we dare?'

'I think we must or our hostess will be offended. Do you think it's safe?' Tessa said, looking around apprehensively at the hordes of people migrating to and from the dance floor.

Peyton immediately understood her concerns. Tessa was very courageous, braving a crowd of this magnitude after the incident at the Academy. It was hard to stop wondering who would come charging out of the crowd next with a knife or a gun. Suddenly everyone was a potential enemy. Peyton thought of the ever-present knife in his boot, which was under his trouser leg even now. For a professional, it would be easy for a knife to do damaging work here, courtesy of an accidental jostle in a crowd this size. Getting away wouldn't be as simple, which was why he felt fairly safe. But Tessa was still intimidated by the sea of people.

With as much protection as propriety would

allow, Peyton steered Tessa on to the dance floor and into a slow, careful waltz, all that the room allowed in its current overpopulated condition and just the right pace for a man who'd taken a knife wound in his side recently.

'There, see nothing untoward happened,' Peyton said as their dance came to a close. A footman walked past and offered them the last two glasses of champagne on his tray.

'That was fortuitous.' Peyton clinked his glass against hers. 'Who would've thought we'd get so lucky?'

'We're due for a little bit of luck.' Tessa gave a small laugh, her eyes sliding towards a movement in the crowd. 'Sergei's here with the other ambassadors,' she said quietly. 'They're standing by the French doors.'

'Hopefully the dolt won't have the bad manners to come over here after he failed to assist me.' Peyton's tone was light, but he knew what Tessa did not, at least not yet. The attempt at the Academy had been about an effort to kill him specifically. It would have been counter-productive for Sergei to fight against his own hired assassin. Peyton knew perfectly well why Sergei had acted as he had.

Peyton let his gaze wander to where Sergei stood. The other man raised his glass in a silent salute and drank, the gesture designed to encourage Peyton and

Tessa to do the same. Peyton gave a cool, assessing nod to the Russian and raised his own glass. The liquid slid towards his mouth, the fruity scent of it tangy in his nostrils, and the elusive presence of something sweet he couldn't place. At the last moment, Peyton brought the flute down, instincts on high alert.

His movements had arrested Tessa's own. She'd paused, the glass halfway to her lips, distracted by his gesture. Peyton rapidly reached for Tessa's hand, roughly jerking the glass away from her mouth. Some of the liquid splattered on her skirt. 'Stop, Tessa. Don't drink it,' Peyton warned in low tones.

Chapter Fifteen

'The champagne is poisoned,' Peyton said, leaning close to her ear. He did not care to be overheard. He didn't want a scene. He wanted only to get Tessa away from here and explain to her what danger they were in from Sergei, to convince her once and for all that Sergei Androvich was no friend of hers. Sergei was no friend of his. That had always been clear. But Peyton had expected their fight to be fought with covert blades. He had not anticipated Sergei would come after him with poison. That was traditionally a woman's weapon. Because he had not anticipated such a move, he couldn't be sure both glasses were tainted. His certainly was.

Beside him, Tessa trembled involuntarily, realising she still held a poisoned glass in her hand. Peyton moved to take it from her, but not soon enough. The fragile glass slipped from her shaking hand and shattered on the floor. Now, he'd never know if Sergei had tainted her glass, too. People around them turned in the direction of the noise.

It was definitely time to go. Peyton muttered a few excuses and took Tessa's arm, leading them through the crowd. He was careful to hang on to his remaining glass of champagne and to steer clear of Sergei. The longer it took the Russians to realise he'd left, the better. He wasn't sure what kind of poison Sergei had slipped him, so it was hard to gauge the reaction Sergei would be looking for—something immediate or perhaps a more latent effect that would take place hours from now.

In the hall, Peyton called for their things and sent for the carriage, trying to make their departure look ordinary. Peyton set his glass down and slipped Tessa's evening cloak around her shoulders, taking a moment to let his hands linger on her shoulders. 'Are you all right, my dear?' She was still shaking.

'Who would do such a thing?' Tessa breathed. 'What could I have that would cause someone to take such desperate measures?'

'I will tell you in the carriage,' Peyton said, close to her ear. He wanted to take her in his arms and reassure her all would be well. But words were all he could give her in this crowded venue. Such an embrace would not go unnoticed, especially with the *ton* on high alert to see what Tessa Branscombe would do next. Other actions would be less conspicuous, however. With his free hand, Peyton found Tessa's gloved fingers and gripped them tightly in the folds of her skirts, hidden from casual view.

She turned her head to the side. 'What do you know, Peyton?'

'Wait. Just wait,' he cautioned.

Waiting was not her strong suit. It seemed ages before they were settled to Peyton's satisfaction in the carriage. After he'd seen her situated, he'd taken time to tie a handkerchief over the top of his champagne glass before he'd let the coachman drive. But the delay had given Tessa time to transmute her horror over the episode into something sharp and useful.

Now that the initial shock had passed, she would not allow herself to wallow in the powerless sensation of being a victim. In the dim light of the carriage, she fingered her reticule and the familiar comfort of the gun inside. Tonight proved what an irrational type of comfort her little weapon actually was. Firepower was no protection against the silent threat of poison. All of the guns in the world would have failed her tonight if it had not been for Peyton's quick thinking.

I guess that makes him innocent, a little voice challenged in her head. Indeed, her mental accusations the other day seemed hugely misguided in light of what had happened. Villains didn't poison themselves. Neither did they attempt to protect the very people they were trying to betray.

Across from her, Peyton leaned back against his seat and fixed her with all his attention. At last, he was ready to talk, ready to give her the answers she craved. His presence filled the carriage and she was entirely aware of him. It was heady to think that she held the complete sum of such a man's attentions.

'Tessa, there are two things I shall tell you tonight. I'll tell you who is after you and why. I do not think you will like the answer, but you must believe me and you must keep this information in the strictest of confidences. If you cannot do these things, then I cannot tell you what I know.'

Tessa nodded slowly. 'That is a hard bargain to ask me to make when I don't know the merit of what I am trading for.'

Peyton chuckled. 'Spoken like a true diplomat's daughter. I would expect no less from you, Tessa. But I will ask for your pledge anyway. You know I hold you in the highest of regard. I would not trifle with you. Your pledge is well worth it.'

'Then it seems I have no choice.' Tessa held steady. Such a claim was bluff only. She'd never had a choice. Her curiosity would not allow such an opportunity to go by.

'There is a list that is said to have been in your father's possession. The list is of great value to the Czar. It contains the names of revolutionaries who are plotting to seize the throne.'

'Someone is after a list?' Tessa repeated. She tried

to search her mind for a reference her father might have made to something of the sort. Nothing. She shook her head. 'Are you sure? That doesn't sound like my father's usual line of work. Why would he be compiling a list for the Czar? He wasn't a Russian citizen.'

'He wasn't acting for the Czar. It is believed that he was acting on behalf of some British businessmen who were looking to fund a revolution in exchange for trade benefits and water rights when a new government came to power,' Peyton said quietly.

'That would be quite a dangerous proposition. Going against the Czar could mean the literal signing of your own death warrant—' Tessa broke off with a choked cry. 'You think that's what happened. Someone found out what my father was up to.'

'Not just "someone", Tessa. Sergei Androvich.' There it was, the second piece of information he'd promised to deliver. She didn't like it any more than she liked the first. The idea that her father used his position to sell information to private British citizens looking to further their own interests smacked of unethical behaviour at the highest level. Not once to her knowledge had her father ever engaged in anything of a questionable nature—no expensive gifts, no grandiose bribes, nothing. Now this threatened to taint his legacy.

If the list became known, his reputation would be tarnished. Her sisters would be devastated. Tessa could barely get her mind around the implications of

Peyton's first bit of information, let alone the second. Sergei had betrayed them.

In some ways, that was worse than the first piece of information, because she knew in her heart and her mind that this last bit was indisputably true. Too much made sense. There'd been no disturbing followers in St Petersburg once Sergei began accompanying her, because there'd been no need for that. The culprit was right there, legitimately attending her meetings as her escort. There'd been no problems in London until the Russian delegation had arrived. There had been Sergei's insistence that they marry.

Sergei had played the suitor very convincingly. He'd played the friend convincingly, too. She'd been all too glad to accept his friendship and let him into their lives. She'd had real affection for him, albeit a lukewarm one. How could she have been so foolish? Why hadn't she seen it? Was Peyton telling the truth? She wanted to dismiss the notion as ludicrous. Of course he was. What motives did he have for lying about Sergei? Yet, there were still things that were unclear to her.

'Peyton, how is it that you've come by this information?' Tessa asked with steely quietness. 'It seems odd that you would know so much that has been obscured from me.'

'You know I've done some diplomatic work in the past, Tessa. I mentioned to you that first day that I'd worked in Vienna. I have kept my connections. It was not hard to discover.' He leaned forward and grasped her hand. 'Tessa, I asked you to believe me. We are at a point where there can be no distrust between us. I need to know that you are fully with me. I can't have you running to Sergei. I need to know you'll support the decisions that need to be made.'

Tessa felt the intensity coursing through him in the simple power of his grip. 'What decisions?' she asked carefully.

'I want to send your sisters to Dursley Park with Crispin as escort. You and I need to find that list. We can't risk one of your sisters finding it accidentally or Sergei deciding to make one of them a target. I do not want to be in the position of bartering that list for Annie, Eva or Petra.'

Tessa nodded, seeing the wisdom of the choice. 'We'll do that.'

'Then you are in agreement? I have your trust, Tessa?'

Tessa bit her lip, feeling the magnitude of the commitment he asked from her. But, in truth, this last step was not as monumental as other decisions she'd already made with regard to Peyton. She'd given him her body, her passion and told him her secrets. In many ways, she'd already pledged what he asked now. 'Yes, Peyton. You have my trust.'

The carriage came to a halt and the coachman set down the steps. Peyton handed her out and Tessa was surprised to see they were nowhere near the St

Just address. Instead, the structure of Whitehall loomed in front of them. She looked quizzically at Peyton, who reached back inside the carriage for his carefully preserved glass of champagne.

'I want someone to look at this,' he said shortly. 'I have a hunch this might be the same poison that killed your father.'

Tessa blanched. Her world had taken a dark cast these days with poisons and assassins. 'My father died in his sleep.'

'With help,' Peyton commented. He took her hand and guided her faultlessly through the winding dark halls of Whitehall until they came to a door with a light shining beneath it.

Peyton opened it without ceremony. 'Brimley, I've brought you something,' he said without preamble, drawing her into the room with him.

The man in question lifted his gaze from the paperwork in front of him. 'You've brought me a girl?' he said drily.

'Brimley, this is Miss Tessa Branscombe. Surely you recognise her? What I've brought you is this glass of champagne. It smells off and I strongly believe it contains poison. You would be best placed to know if it's related to the substance that killed Ralph Branscombe.'

Brimley took the glass and sniffed. 'It's definitely not right, but I can't tell exactly what it is. I'll have some of our experts get back to you. Courtesy of our friends?'

Peyton nodded. 'Yes.'

'They must feel they have some growing influence if they can ensure you receive a tainted glass at a large affair without mishap,' Brimley commented, shooting a tight look at Tessa. 'You are completely with us, aren't you, Miss Branscombe? Not selling secrets to the enemy?'

Tessa bristled at the bald-faced comment. She edged closer to Peyton, her hand tightly wrapped in his. 'What are you suggesting, sir?' Tessa challenged.

A knowing smile creased Brimley's lips. 'Nothing at all, my dear. I can see that you're entirely with Peyton here and that's good enough for me.'

'Goodnight, Brimley,' Peyton offered tersely, cutting off further conversation.

'Were you protecting me back there?' Tessa asked, trying to keep up with Peyton's long-legged stride. She didn't dare fall behind. She'd never find her way out.

'Brimley doesn't go about among polite society much. His manners are a bit blunt for many,' Peyton said. He made a shushing motion with his hand and pulled them both against the wall.

Tessa stiffened, straining her ears to hear what he'd heard. She caught the sound of footsteps clicking in a nearby empty corridor.

In a quick motion, Peyton swept her behind him, pressing her to the wall. With his height and dark clothing, she was entirely obscured. A fact, she realised belatedly, she could not have claimed for herself. Her light-coloured evening gown would have stood out like a beacon. The footsteps neared and Tessa held her breath. Then they veered in a different direction and faded. She relaxed, feeling the warmth and strength of Peyton's back. Not for the first time, she was amazed at this man's willingness to place himself between her and danger. This incredible man was hers if she'd trust herself to claim him.

Tessa snaked her arms about his waist. 'Is he gone?'

'Yes. It was probably nothing more than a night watchman on his rounds. But it pays to be safe. The fewer people who know I paid a nocturnal visit here, the better.'

Tessa slid under his arm and came around front. 'There, this is much better.'

'Much better for what,' Peyton queried, not resisting when she put her arms around his neck.

'Much better for this,' Tessa said, stretching up on her toes and kissing him full on the mouth.

His arms were around her waist, he deepened the kiss. 'We have to go to St Just's,' he murmured.

'Do we? I'd rather go to your town house,' Tessa answered. From the feel of him through his trousers, she rather thought he'd prefer her option, too. This argument shouldn't be too hard to win.

'You are courting scandal, Tessa Branscombe,' Peyton whispered a warning, but she would have none of it.

She ran a hand down the length of him, exalting

in the power of his erection. 'The scandal is already a *fait accompli*. I might as well live up to it. Perhaps the carriage will do. I don't know if I can wait until we get home,' Tessa said breathlessly.

'The carriage is vastly overrated as a place to copulate,' Peyton ground out, his voice hoarse as his desire rose to dangerous levels under her attentions.

'As are the corridors of Whitehall, I am sure,' Tessa argued.

'Vixen.' But in the end, it was Peyton who led them to the carriage and gave the coachman orders to drive until he told him to stop.

Chapter Sixteen

Whatever the carriage lacked in convenience, it made up for in the exotic nature of the encounter. Peyton knelt on the carriage floor between her parted legs and pushed up her skirts. Tessa shivered deliciously as cold air met the moist warmth of her private juncture. This was positively forbidden territory and her body was awash with curiosity and sensation.

Peyton's hands massaged lightly at her thighs, fingers carefully brushing her curls, delighting in the little tremors they raised when they skimmed her woman's pearl. 'I love your passion, Tessa. Never hide it from me,' Peyton whispered, moving forward to take her lips with his. Peyton forged a trail of hot kisses down the bodice of her gown, to her waist and bared thighs below.

Tessa divined his intentions and gasped. But Peyton was gentle in his insistence. 'You'll like this,

Tess. Trust me.' Then he lowered his mouth to her, taking her most privately in the manner he'd earlier claimed her mouth and her breasts.

Whether it was the wicked decadence of their situation or the sheer magic of their intimacy, Tessa's senses were in utter thrall. She felt her hips lift, and pressed herself against Peyton's mouth, urging him to take her onwards to the place she knew waited just beyond this moment. She bucked once more and exploded, a completed cry escaping her.

Peyton fell back from her, his hair dishevelled, his evening clothes slightly wrinkled as he sat on the carriage floor, staring up at her. Tessa thought he'd never looked as handsome as he did now, his pleasure open in his eyes, his attentions entirely focused on her and not on his many responsibilities. Then she realised he had not had his pleasure.

'Is it possible for me to do that for you?' she asked.

'It is, but I'd prefer to wait and love you properly in my bed. We'll be at Dursley House shortly.'

On cue, the carriage lurched to a halt. Peyton lost his balance and laughed as he rolled against the seat.

'Oh, hurry and get up!' Tessa said, unable to restrain her laughter. 'What do you want your coachman to think?'

'I'm pretty sure he worked it out, Tessa.'

Tessa blushed. 'Is this a common occurrence, then?'

'Not for me, but I'm certain others have contrived similar proceedings.' Peyton was amused.

Tessa fluffed her skirts. 'We can at least pretend nothing happened.'

'I am sure that's what most people do,' Peyton said with mock severity as the carriage door opened.

They walked in stately propriety up the steps to Dursley House, although there was no one to see them at that time of night. They slipped inside and Tessa stifled a giggle. 'I don't think he suspected a thing. We're very good at pretending.'

Peyton laughed. 'Maybe he's very good at pretending, too.'

She liked this Peyton: playful, witty, so at ease. 'I like you this way,' Tessa said abruptly as they climbed the stairs.

'What way is that?' Peyton asked carefully.

'At ease,' Tessa said. 'Tonight, you're just a man.'

Peyton turned to look at her, his hand softly touching her cheek. 'Your man, Tess. Tonight, I'm just your man. I've waited a long time to just be someone's man.'

'Then I am honoured,' Tessa said, a bit choked by the honesty he put on display with his confession. Other men might make confessions of undying love and spout flowery praise, but such generic practices didn't suit this unique man.

Peyton drew her to him and cupped her cheek in his palm, his other hand at her waist, keeping her close against him. He gave her a sweet, deep kiss. 'I'll keep you safe, Tess, always.'

'We'll find the list, Peyton,' Tessa said fiercely.

'Shh. Don't mention such things tonight.' He reached a hand to her hair and pulled it loose. Tessa revelled in the feel of his strong hands in the loose tresses. His voice was low in her ear. 'Morning will come soon enough. Tonight, I want there to be nothing between us.'

She wanted that, too; understood better, perhaps, than he realized, just how much she wanted simply to be with him without the trappings of intrigue that had cast a pall over the potential of their relationship. She wanted to prove to herself that what she and Peyton had shared that night at Aunt Lily's was more than the product of adrenalin and crisis, that at its core there was something extraordinary and rare about what lay between them. Peyton took her hand and she let him lead her through the door to his bedchamber.

The chamber was dimly lit, the covers of the bed already turned down in anticipation of its occupant retiring. A robe lay on the bed, ready for Peyton. 'No valet?' Tessa asked lightly.

Peyton shook his head. 'I don't make a habit of having my servants wait up for me, especially when I don't know what time I'll be back. I am capable of undressing myself.'

'Makes it easier to sneak the ladies in, too, I'm sure,' Tessa joked. But Peyton didn't share her humour.

'You're the only one, Tessa. I am not in the practice of bringing my lovers home.' He grazed her cheek with his hand in a gentle, stroking motion. 'You're the only woman I want to have in this bed.'

Tessa swallowed. For a man like Peyton, who kept his emotions so heavily veiled, such a proclamation was quite possibly as close to the words 'I love you' as he would ever get. She wasn't sure how she felt about that. There was so much she couldn't promise him.

Peyton began working the fastenings at the back of her gown, his hands sure and competent at their duty. She revelled in the intimacy of his actions even as she rebelled against the sensations they aroused. What did she want from Peyton Ramsden? She wanted this night, she wanted this passion that surged between them. Did she dare want all that could follow? Could she allow herself to fall in love with all that Peyton Ramsden was and all that he was not? How could she ensure he wouldn't hate her for it in the end? The last thing she wanted was to ruin him.

Peyton pushed the gown and her chemise to the floor, the last of the fastenings undone. He placed a kiss on her bare shoulder, his hands moving to cup her breasts, thumbs gently tempting her nipples to pebble beneath their light strokes. It seemed her body knew the answer to that question already. It ached for Peyton and the pleasure it found with him. It knew instinctively that it could trust itself to him entirely. Her mind had only to follow.

She turned in his arms, reluctant to leave the pleasure of his hands on her breasts, but wanting to divest him of his clothes so they could move on in this passionate game of theirs. Peyton waylaid her efforts, scooping her up in his arms and carrying her to the bed. 'But…' she started to protest.

Peyton laid her down, his blue eyes glittering with desire. 'Shh, my dear. Tonight, you watch.'

Intuitively, Tessa found the idea strikingly titillating. Before, their passion had been confined by time and place, by layers of clothes subdued as best as circumstances allowed. Tessa unabashedly watched Peyton remove his jacket, his waistcoat, and finally his shirt, stud by careful stud laid aside deliberately in a small crystal dish on the bedside table. The anticipation of seeing Peyton's chest revealed heightened her desire. She'd seen his chest before, of course, the day he'd taken the knife wound, and she'd felt his bare skin beneath her hands the night they'd first made love, but this, seeing him deliberately disrobe for her, was entirely different. Tonight he was her lover, presenting himself to her in the most intimate of ways.

The shadowplay of darkness and light in the room displayed him superbly, limning the muscular perfection of his shoulders and chest, the sculpted form of his upper arms, and the tapered definition of his stomach. Peyton Ramsden sported not a single ounce of fat on his magnificent torso. Tessa wondered fleetingly if the women of the *ton* knew just how well made he was.

But Peyton was not done yet. His hands might have been concentrated on the task of disrobing, but his eyes were concentrated solely on her. His smouldering sapphire gaze did not leave her face as he bent briefly to remove his evening shoes. His hands skimmed the waist of his trousers and Tessa's breath caught. Within moments, Peyton had freed himself elegantly from his trousers and the small clothes he wore beneath. How he'd managed to do so with such grace, Tessa couldn't guess, but there was so much more to wonder at than the graceful mechanics of removing one's trousers.

Peyton was beautiful. There was no other word for it. Tessa had no idea how splendidly wrought a man could be. Without trousers, she could fully appreciate the length of his legs, the firm muscles in his thighs that spoke of long hours in the saddle, the leanness of his hips. And, of course, the great manly secret that lay at his core.

'Lay' wasn't precisely the word for it. Tessa could plainly see that it wasn't 'laying' about. Its length jutted out, begging to be recognised as its own unique entity.

'Peyton, you take my breath away,' Tessa whispered. 'I am entirely overwhelmed. I never imagined…'

He moved towards her. She could sense he was gratified by her words. 'I am glad it's only ever been imaginings. I want to be the first and only man you've seen naked.'

Tessa smiled in the darkness. Tonight such primal

claims carried a pleasing, erotic quality to them. Tonight, she wanted to be claimed, didn't want to fight for her position, didn't want to rail for acceptance as an equal.

'Come and claim me, Peyton.' She arched her back and reached for him, taking him in her arms and drawing him down to her, revelling in the feel of him as his weight covered her. She knew what to do. She parted her legs for him, taking pleasure at how easily he moved between them, how comfortable the intimacy of joining with him had become.

When he slid into her, it felt like the most natural of actions in the world. Her core was slick, enveloping his hot length as if welcoming a loved one home. She sighed her satisfaction and Peyton smiled knowingly above her. Then Peyton moved inside her and the pleasure began. All thoughts of comfort and rightness faded, replaced by intense feelings of primal delight. Tessa was not alone in her joy. Her cries of pleasure were matched by Peyton's own.

It was a heady discovery to realise that in wanting to surrender entirely to Peyton, she hadn't surrendered at all. What they'd achieved together in this bed hadn't been accomplished through the dominance of one person, but through mutual accommodation. They'd got their wish, Tessa thought sleepily. There'd been nothing between them tonight as they'd made love. There'd been only the shared desire to possess one another in the most complete way. And that had taken Tessa far beyond her wildest imaginings.

In her arms he was a god, immortal and strong. In her arms he could reach a place where he could set aside his burdens, where there was no longer a constant weighing of duty against pleasure, where he wasn't trading the lives of British soldiers for his personal desires, where there wasn't a list that would mark the end of the happiness he'd found with Tessa Branscombe.

In her arms he was the man he was supposed to be—her man. Peyton knew with a sharp clarity that one thing presupposed all else in the early dawn light. There would be no other woman who was Tessa's equal for him. *Ever.* She was the one woman who dared to challenge him, who dared to meet his passions, to unleash the real man he was. She was the one woman who loved him with all his conditions. She understood the duality of his existence, the Earl he needed to be, and the man he longed to be. She let him be both. Her very acceptance of his nature made him strong. She was the one woman who had not once tried to change him.

He recognised now how that had been Lydia's failing, the failing she had shared with all his other mistresses. He recognised how much he'd resented the attempt to mould him into a different man. No wonder he'd set a two-year limit on his arranged relationships. He wouldn't change, couldn't change. Then along came Tessa and it had not crossed her mind to change him because she couldn't fathom changing herself. She said as much at the park.

Too bad it couldn't last. The night had been amazing, fulfilling his wish to have nothing between them. But the morning, too, was fulfilling its promises of a less pleasing sort. Tomorrow had arrived and with it, the cares of the day. He needed to convince Tessa to send her sisters to safety. She'd agreed last night, but they'd not established a date of departure. He wanted them to leave immediately. He and Tessa needed to be free to search in earnest for the list.

It was something of a relief to have the list acknowledged between them. There was no more need for trying to pry information out of Tessa covertly, even though there hadn't been anything to pry. She'd known nothing about it. They could search openly and honestly for the list together.

But such an achievement had not been won lightly. Peyton knew it had cost Tessa greatly to accept that her father might not have been quite the man she'd believed him to be—a man with ethics above the norm—only to discover posthumously that those beliefs had been betrayed. Sometimes it was worse discovering it that way. He'd grown up thinking he'd understood his father, but he'd learned too late, when his father was no longer there to explain the truth to him, that his father had kept secrets, too, that life had not been precisely as it had appeared. Such realisations came with a price.

The other cost had been the rift between him and Tessa. She'd not taken his information well. He'd been lucky to get a second chance, but he was not fool enough to think she'd extend such courtesy again. Like him, Tessa valued honesty and straight-forwardness above all else. It seemed the height of irony that both of them should be drawn into a game that precluded direct disclosures.

He felt Tessa's warm hand slide to his groin, searching for him. She would find him hard and ready for one last bout of loving before they had to face the day's realities.

He was taking unrealistic chances there as well. Every time he made love with Tessa, he was tempting fate. Not once in any of his relationships had he elected not to do his duty and complete a gentle-man's finish in the sheets or to use sheaths. It was not fair to risk getting her with child, no matter how much the idea thrilled him. Such an occurrence would bind her to him without giving her a choice. At least it would if she was a conventional woman. Peyton wasn't sure what he feared most: Tessa marrying him for the sake of a ill-conceived child or Tessa refusing to marry him and taking the child off into a new life without him. He knew legally she wouldn't stand a chance if he pursued her. But he knew, too, that he could not bring her such pain if that was her choice.

Still, when Tessa's hand closed about his member, her delight at her discovery coming in a little gasp, Peyton could not refuse the chance to give himself over to the peace he knew would come, if only for a little while.

Afterwards, Tessa lay content in his arms, her head in its usual place against his shoulder. They'd been silent for quite some time, neither of them wishing to speak of the day ahead. But Peyton knew they could not put it off indefinitely.

Carefully, he ventured the topic that mattered to him most. 'Tess, I want to ask you something,' he began, easing into the conversation. She murmured her assent.

'I would like to send your sisters with Crispin to Durlsey Park immediately.'

Peyton felt Tessa shift beside him, moving to raise herself up on one arm. 'It's become that dangerous, hasn't it?' It was worded as a question, but she knew the answer already, he could see it in her eyes.

'Yes, it has. Until we recover the list, they are fair targets for Androvich and he won't hesitate to use them. I understand how hard it is for you to be separated from them. I promise they'll be safe. Crispin and Paine will protect them with their lives. Julia will love the company.'

Tessa nodded. 'I agree. We'll tell them after breakfast.'

Peyton smiled and reached to take her back in his arms. 'It's a good decision, Tessa. You'll be with them again as soon as we find the list.' He wished he could say as much for himself. When he imagined the reunion Tessa would have with her sisters at Dursley Park, he wondered if he'd be part of that, or if Tessa would have shunned him completely by that point, disgusted by his duplicity. He was tempted to tell her everything right then, throwing himself on her mercy in the hopes that she'd understand the weight he carried, the depth of what his decision required of him. But Tessa chose that moment to fling back the covers and rise, determined to dress and meet the day head on.

Tensions were high in Aunt Lily's drawing room two hours later. Everyone was gathered. They were only waiting for Crispin's arrival in order to begin. Little conversations flowed awkwardly, a clear testament to the strained atmosphere. There'd been no way to disguise the obvious: Tessa had spent the night at his town house. While Peyton had no worries about his staff's discretion in such a situation, it was clear from the stern eye Aunt Lily fixed him with that she wholeheartedly disapproved of the developing circumstances.

Peyton shifted infinitesimally in his seat. It was hard to act like the family patriarch with one's aunt shooting reproachful looks across the room. Lily's baleful stare made him feel like a toddler in leading strings who'd got caught stealing biscuits from the kitchen. It wasn't as if he was unaware of his culpability. He was a gentleman. He should have taken the high road and fought his urges, although he couldn't imagine how he would have succeeded. And he had tried, was still trying in fact, to do the right thing by Tessa. She had been the one to refuse him, after all. Of course, Peyton could hardly imagine explaining *that* to Aunt Lily: *I have asked her to marry me, Aunt, but she only wants to have sex with me.*

The door to the drawing room opened and Crispin slipped in, flashing a quick glance in Petra's direction before taking an unoccupied chair. Peyton cleared his throat for attention. It was time to get started.

The decision to go to Dursley Park was met with mixed emotions. Eva and Annie were thrilled at the prospect of a trip to the Cotswolds. Peyton painted grand pictures of the idyllic fields populated with stone walls and sheep, fresh air and places to run. The beauty of an English summer in the countryside could not be underestimated and the girls were enthralled. He tried to persuade Petra, too, with the promise of his excellent stables. The girl loved horses and at Dursley Park there were horses aplenty for any level of rider. But she was loyal to Tessa and clearly had misgivings about leaving her sister. Those misgivings were no doubt fuelled by Tessa's absence last night.

Crispin shot Petra a sharp look that Peyton

couldn't ignore. The two of them had been quiet in the wake of his announcement that they were to go to Dursley Park.

Peyton had noticed they'd exchanged looks ever since the conversation began.

'Crispin, do you have something to say?' Peyton barked. Petra immediately looked down at her hands, blushing. Lord help him if Crispin was even contemplating trifling with Petra Branscombe. The girl wasn't even out yet. It would give Tessa one more reason to kill him and Tessa would have plenty of reasons in the days to come. Right now, Peyton was enjoying the unity of Tessa agreeing with him. She'd stood beside him literally and figuratively, supporting his decision.

It wasn't Crispin that spoke. It was Petra. 'I want to know why we're to go to Dursley Park. We haven't been given a reason. It was my understanding that we were to be allowed to remain with Tessa for the Season.' As always, she was quiet and forthright. While soft spoken, there was no mistaking the directness of her question.

Peyton glanced at Tessa. It should be her decision how much her sisters were told. Tessa drew a deep breath.

'It has come to our attention that Father may have been in possession of a list that the Russian government wants returned. It has become something of a sticking point and we are not sure just how explosive the situation might become,' Tessa said carefully.

Eva cocked her head thoughtfully. 'Then it's good that Sergei is here. He can take care of everything and tell the others Father didn't have a list.'

Petra's gaze shot between Eva and Tessa. Peyton could see her keen intelligence working quickly. 'Sergei *is* the Russian government, isn't he, Tessa? That's why he's here. It's his mission to retrieve the list.'

Tessa nodded slowly. 'I believe so.'

Eva looked incredulous. 'He's not here to win you back, Tess? I thought he was here to court you.'

'It's what he wanted us to believe,' Petra said, a hard look in her eyes that belied her seventeen years. She shot a look at her sister. 'Oh, Tess, I am so sorry. He's treated you poorly, making you believe he was in love with you.'

Tessa dismissed the concern with a wave of her hand. 'I didn't harbour any affections for him beyond friendship. Any betrayal I feel is that of a friend. It's of no account. What does matter is that you are all safe, so Peyton and I can look for the list. Crispin will go with you.'

'And I will go with you,' Aunt Lily put in with good humour. 'Crispin won't last a day on the road with three girls.'

Peyton nodded his thanks. 'Your offer is much appreciated.' He wondered if Lily had the same concerns he did. He'd been so wrapped up in his own troubles he hadn't noticed the developments between Petra and Crispin.

'When do you think everyone can be ready to leave?' Peyton asked Lily.

'Tomorrow, if we hurry. I'll assign a maid to each of the girls to help with packing. I'll have the groom start readying the travelling coach. My secretary can spend the day closing up my calendar. There's no need to close up the house since Tessa will still be here.' Lily speared Peyton with a sharp look.

He would take Tessa to Dursley House with him as soon as Aunt Lily's travelling coach was out of sight. He wouldn't leave Tessa alone in a big house, an easy target for Androvich. Her safety far outweighed any social concerns for scandal. But Peyton knew there were certain battles he wouldn't win with Aunt Lily outright, so he tactfully kept his argument to himself. Better to do what he planned and argue with Aunt Lily after the fact. If she knew what he intended, she might choose to stay and right now he needed her to watch over Petra.

'Tomorrow it is, then,' Peyton said, standing up as if to signal that the meeting was over. He watched Tessa move towards her sisters, ushering them from the room. She would be absorbed with them today, but he was already counting the hours until dark and he would be able to claim her again. He wasn't sure how, but he'd find a way. He motioned to Crispin for a private word, his gaze fixed on Tessa, watching her sail out of the door of the drawing room with her charges. He ached for her already. The countdown till night had begun.

Chapter Seventeen

Sergei Androvich sipped his morning tea in the breakfast room of the Russian embassy, impassively listening to the latest report from one of the men they employed to keep an eye on Dursley.

'The aunt's travelling carriage left at dawn,' the man said. 'Looked like a veritable convoy with a luggage carriage, servants and outriders and everything.' There was a touch of awe in the man's voice. Sergei snorted. The last thing he needed was his own informants starting to respect the damned Dursley clan.

He pondered the information. Leaving in great style didn't suggest an act of stealth. He remembered Tessa's quiet flight from St Petersburg. *That* had been an act of stealth—amateur stealth, of course; Tessa didn't have his training in covert activities. Dursley did have training, on the other hand. Sergei did not doubt the Earl could effect a stealthy removal if he wanted to. It appeared that he hadn't wanted to, that secrecy wasn't the aim of the early morning departure.

Such an action could only mean one of two things. It might mean the girls had tired of the city in the summer—and, really, who wouldn't? Sergei couldn't imagine being in London without the allure of invitations to grand balls. London was hot and crowded, much warmer than St Petersburg. Perhaps the removal was just that—an escape to the cooler countryside. If so, that meant Tessa and Peyton hadn't found the list. It might also mean that Tessa didn't know about the list yet, but Sergei doubted it. At this point in the game, Peyton would recognise he would be better off if Tessa knew what to look for, even if it meant encountering her wrath.

The other thing the removal of Tessa's sisters might mean was the scenario Sergei feared most. They had found the list and were getting ready to act with the understanding that it was going to get dangerous. Sergei could not let that list fall into the hands of the British government. If people had to die to prevent that from happening, then so be it. Peyton would understand that, even if Tessa hadn't grasped such consequences yet.

'Let the carriage go,' Sergei said. 'They're likely off to enjoy the countryside. The people who matter are still in town. We must double our efforts to see what Dursley and Miss Branscombe are up to. Follow them and report on everything they do.'

Sergei tossed a bag of coins to the man. 'Share this with the others. Keep your eyes sharp. We don't want Dursley to spot you.'

Sergei dismissed the man and rubbed a hand over his face. He was getting tired of this. All he'd been able to do was watch and wait: *watch* Dursley steal Tessa's affections, *wait* for the list to come to light, instead of being able to search for it himself. Dursley was calling all the shots these days. Something had to change quickly. He had no doubt that Vasilov would be happy to report his failings to the Czar. Sergei had a lot at stake personally in the success of this mission to bring back the list before it could be used to destabilise the Russian throne. A promotion and money were on the line, both of which he desperately needed.

It was frustrating to be reduced to such a minimal role, but Sergei would wait for his moment. Dursley couldn't be perfect for ever and Sergei knew how to use the slightest slip to his advantage.

Tessa had not been to the house in Bloomsbury since the day she'd discovered the break-in. Returning now with Peyton, she could hardly reconcile the vision against how it had looked that day. The devastation had been minimised. She stood in the doorway to the front room, taking in the details. It was clear Peyton's servants had been hard at work to clear the debris and restore order. There was still work to be done. The walls would need new paint and paper. New furniture would need to be purchased to replace the articles that had been ruined beyond redemption. The ruined furniture had been removed and Tessa could see that all the rooms were considerably emptier in their absence.

'You've worked wonders,' Tessa commented as they wandered through the rooms, Peyton giving her time to assimilate the state of the house.

'It's not enough. There is more to be done and it will be done, Tessa. Your house will be restored,' Peyton said in a surprisingly fierce tone.

Tessa shook her head. 'Not with your money, Peyton. This is my house, my responsibility.'

'You are my responsibility, thus your house is my responsibility,' Peyton retorted.

'I am not your mistress, Peyton. I've come to you out of my own free will. I have no intention of being a kept woman.' Tessa stopped walking and faced him over the scarred piano in the music room. 'You don't *owe* me anything.' They'd been intimate too often without setting ground rules. Tessa regretted that right now. At the time she'd known better. She'd known Peyton would see a responsibility in their intimacy and yet so great had been her desire for him that she'd put aside the discussion for more immediate pleasures. Now that pigeon was coming home to roost.

Peyton's jaw tightened. Tessa stood her ground. They might as well get things sorted out once for and all. 'Tessa, I have no intention of making you my mistress. I had not thought to bring this up in such a manner, but the timing seems to have forced it.' Peyton held her gaze. 'I mean to discuss marriage with you. I know this is not an opportune time. There are issues that need to be resolved, but would you consider it? Once the Russian issue is settled to our satisfaction, would you do me the honour of being my wife?'

Tessa recognised immediately that this was perhaps the worst marriage proposal in the history of proposals. There were no flowers, no words of love, and no flattering protestations of great passion. But there was a sincerity that Tessa appreciated, a sincerity that could only come from Peyton. The last proposal she had received had carried with it all the trimmings a proposal should have. Sergei had proposed with flattering sentiments, grand promises of a life together and burgeoning affection. But the proposal had been wrapped in deceit. Events had revealed the proposal to be a fraud. This proposal, Peyton's proposal, was practical and real. He understood now was not the time for commitments, the future was too uncertain for that.

'Peyton, you are chivalrous to a fault with your offer. But you and I know that even if the Russian issue were resolved, it's not in your best interest to marry me. You mustn't feel obliged,' Tessa said gently. 'I do believe we've discussed this before at the park.'

'I am very persistent,' Peyton said staunchly.

'Yes. And I am very stubborn, which is why my answer remains the same.' Tessa gave him a soft smile. 'There is enough to worry about without throwing that into the mix.'

Tessa made to move on to another room, but Peyton grabbed her arm. 'Tessa, I need to know, do you have feelings for me? Do you harbour any serious affection for me?'

The question took her aback. She had not thought to ever see the confident, arrogant Earl of Dursley in a vulnerable moment. But that's what she saw when she met his blue gaze. She had not meant for him to take her refusal as doubt of her affections.

'I am quite undone by you, Peyton. My feelings for you are complex and overwhelming. I scarcely know what to make of them beyond the fact that they are more powerful than anything I've known,' Tessa said honestly. 'It's the truth, although I fear admitting it will only serve to inflate your substantial male ego,' she jested.

'It seems we are in accord then, Tessa, for I am quite overcome by you.' His gaze was searing, his touch on her arm electrifying. She saw the early signs of a seduction.

'Then we'd better find that list,' Tessa said, finding it necessary to break the rising tension of the moment. If this went on much longer, Peyton could have her up against a wall and she'd be making promises she didn't want to keep.

They'd come to the Bloomsbury house with the intention of following the thief's lead. Whoever had broken in had been quite certain the list was in the house. They hadn't found it. If it was here, then it was *still* here.

'I'll start in my office,' Tessa volunteered. 'The family papers seem a logical place to start.'

Peyton nodded his approval. 'I'll start in the kitchen. There's a chance there's a false bottom or something in one of the silver pieces that's been overlooked.'

Tessa mounted the stairs to her little office. Unlike the other rooms that had been tidied, this room had been left just as it had been. The thief had been quite thorough in this room. Papers had been thrown out of her desk. Her father's papers, which had been stacked in crates, had been upended and strewn on the floor. But in all likelihood, the thief hadn't had the time needed to comb through the individual files and look closely at the content of each.

Tessa sat on the floor and began sorting papers, making stacks and restoring order, scanning the papers carefully for references that might be of use. Occasionally, she could hear Peyton in the kitchen and the clink of silver. The humour of imagining the proper Earl of Dursley pottering around a kitchen brought a smile to her lips.

After two hours of work, Tessa leaned back on her hands and stretched. Her back was starting to hurt and her shoulder was stiff. The room was beginning to look more orderly. Mentally, she took stock of what she'd organised. In one pile, she had her personal letters and correspondence. There was nothing of note there. In another pile, there were household accounts and bills. Again, there was nothing of import. In a stack of her father's things was a social calendar full of his appointments. This held some promise and Tessa reached for it, eagerly flipping through the pages. But there was nothing present in the calendar other than appointments she'd already known about with people she already knew. Well, she could hardly expect her father to keep a secret list in a public place. It was unlikely that he would have written down in plain view, 'Meet with Russian revolutionaries to discuss munitions shipments'.

He might not have written it down in an obvious place, but Tessa was sure he had written it down somewhere. He had been a meticulous records keeper and had admitted on more than one occasion that if he didn't write things down, he'd get the details messed up. The list was somewhere. Carefully, Tessa stood up and began re-boxing the papers into the crates. The room looked substantially better when she was through.

Tessa looked around the room. It seemed barren without the portrait of her father on the wall. As soon as the house was fit for inhabiting again, she'd hang the portrait back up where it belonged. That decided, she went downstairs to see how Peyton was doing with the silver.

Peyton had long given up on the silver and had made his way into the cellar. When Tessa found him, he'd discarded his coat and waistcoat, preferring to work in shirtsleeves.

'That suits you,' Tessa said appreciatively, from the top of the stairs.

Peyton pried a lid off a crate. 'Help me bring this upstairs. It's too dark to really examine anything down here.'

Tessa made her way down the stairs and helped Peyton haul the contents up to the kitchen. They spread the items out on the long kitchen work-table. The items were in good condition and smelled of the wood chips Tessa had packed them in months ago. She picked up a *matryoshka* doll. 'This was a birthday present from my father when I was eighteen.' Tessa began untwisting the doll's different layers. 'He had placed a piece of jewellery inside each of the dolls,' she said wistfully. 'It was a perfect gift for a young girl who was so desperate to grow up. He needed a hostess and I wanted so badly to fill that role for him.' Tessa set each progressively smaller doll down in front of her in a line.

Peyton was staring at her inquisitively. 'What?'

'You've never said anything personal about your life in St Petersburg before. I've only ever heard about the robbery and your father's death.'

Tessa moved on to pick up a lacquer box with a painted scene of the Winter Palace on it. 'This was my mother's. Father gave it to her as an anniversary gift. There was jewellery inside, of course. It was the year before Annie was born. The year before my mother died.' Tessa opened the lid of the box. 'I keep a picture of my mother in here.' She handed the little miniature to Peyton. 'Father says I look like her.'

'You're the only mother Annie has known?' Peyton probed gently, handing the miniature back to Tessa.

'Yes. It was winter and the birth was too hard on my mother. She was too old for another child. I was twelve, Petra was seven and Eva was five. Mother herself was in her late thirties. It was just too much. The midwife put Annie in my arms and I've done the best I could ever since then. She was so tiny and no one thought she'd live. But I would have none of it. I wasn't about to lose her, too.' Tessa snapped the lid of the box shut. 'There's nothing here but memories, Peyton. These are my personal things. I packed them myself. If anything was hidden here, I would have found it before we left Russia.'

'It's all right to talk about the past, Tessa,' Peyton said, reaching a hand out to her. 'You shouldn't hide these beautiful things away and pretend they don't exist.'

Tessa shot him a wry look. 'Would this be the pot calling the kettle black, Peyton Ramsden? You're not the most forthcoming man I've ever met.'

'Learn from my mistake, my dear.' Peyton chuckled. 'After all, I have attained the august age of my late thirties. I'm a veritable temple of ancient wisdom. Trust me, I am better with people now. It's only been recently, since Paine's returned, that I've recognised the value of memories, of expressing my feelings to those I care about.'

Tessa looked dubious.

'Don't look at me like that. I am better. I don't run around professing emotions every second I feel them, but I've learned to be more careful with those I love.' Peyton gave a self-deprecating snort. 'My last mistress won't agree with that, but then I didn't love her.' Peyton paused. 'I am sorry, that was tactless. I don't know what prompted me to say that.'

'It's all right. When you make mistakes, it reminds me that you're human like the rest of us.' Tessa smiled.

'Did you find anything upstairs?' Peyton changed the subject.

Tessa shook her head. 'No. I had hoped to find hints, clues, maybe, that would allow us to reconstruct the list from original sources. I thought there might be references in a variety of letters or in his social calendar. But I saw nothing to support that.'

'Let's go back to Aunt Lily's and have some lunch. Then afterwards we can go through the few things you brought from the house. There might be something we've overlooked,' Peyton suggested.

Outside at the carriage the coachman leaned down

to speak privately with Peyton. His mouth was grim when he turned to Tessa. 'Our watcher is back. He's not on the bench, but my coachman said a man kept walking by watching the house.'

'Sergei is hoping we'll lead him to the list,' Tessa said tensely, taking her seat in the carriage.

'Yes. He doesn't know where the list is or how to get to it now that he's lost access to you. But chin up, my dear, as long as he needs us, he won't be harming us.'

'That's not funny, Peyton,' Tessa scolded, all too aware of the danger that lurked around them. She was more than glad that her sisters were safely away from harm.

Lunch was a short affair, mostly because Peyton had found other exquisite uses for strawberries besides eating them out of the bowl. Tessa found herself in bed, thoroughly loved and smelling of strawberries in the middle of the afternoon with a drowsy Peyton beside her.

'This is what Aunt Lily feared would happen,' Tessa said coyly, reaching for the last strawberry in the bowl.

'She only feared it would happen if she closed up the house and let me take you to Dursley House,' Peyton corrected. 'Now we can tell her honestly that her fears were for naught.'

Tessa laughed. 'Someone is going to find out. Servants talk.'

'Mine don't,' Peyton said.

Tessa sat up in bed. Peyton made to drag her back down. 'Where are you going? The damage is already done. We might as well stay in bed and enjoy ourselves.'

'I'm going to turn the portrait of my father around. It's like he's staring at us.' Tessa swung her legs out of bed and padded naked to the portrait she'd leaned against the wall days ago.

Peyton laughed at her.

'Have you ever made love in front of your parent's portrait? Don't laugh until you've tried it.' Tessa gave him a mock scolding.

'No, because I keep all my relatives in the art gallery where they belong. There's a reason all the big houses have galleries, you know. That way we can have sex—'

'Peyton, come here,' Tessa interrupted, all seriousness. She knelt down in front of the portrait.

'What is it, Tessa?' Peyton was beside her instantly.

She gave him a steady look. 'I know where the list is.'

Chapter Eighteen

'Is it painted into the portrait?' Peyton asked, taking a moment to retrieve her robe from the bed and grabbing a bedsheet for himself.

'No, I don't think so,' Tessa said, squinting at the long scroll depicted in the painting. 'I think this scroll is merely a clue.' Tessa struggled to turn the portrait around.

'Here, let me.' Peyton reached around her and easily turned the awkward object. The back of the portrait was sealed up in brown wrapping-style paper.

'I bet if we rip the paper backing off, the list will be inside,' Tessa said.

Peyton nodded and they began to rip the paper. They'd only torn back a few strips when Peyton halted them. 'Wait. Ripping paper works if the list is separate from the backing. But if the backing is the list itself, then we're ripping the list up as we go. Let me get my knife and then we can remove the backing as a whole piece instead of tearing into it like a Christmas present.'

Peyton grabbed his knife from his boot and began the laborious process of detaching the backing as a single large sheet of paper. Halfway through, he pulled back the paper, searching for signs of the list. 'The backing is blank. We're safe. You can rip away if you like, Tess.' Peyton sat back on his heels.

Tessa grinned and tore the remaining paper away. Sure enough, at the bottom corner of the portrait was a narrow, folded piece of paper. It hardly looked big enough to be the source of so much commotion. Tessa reached for it, feeling like a treasure hunter who'd just unearthed a chest of jewels. She unfolded the paper and a second piece fluttered out. She looked at Peyton, who picked up the second piece. For a while, they sat in silence, surveying their lists. At some point, it crossed Tessa's mind how ludicrous this must appear—two half-naked people in bedclothes sitting in front of a portrait they'd torn apart and reading small slips of paper.

'There are two lists,' Peyton said eventually. 'My list contains the names of the British businessmen who were interested in backing a revolutionary group. I am guessing that your list contains the revolutionaries who were willing to consider outside assistance?'

Tessa nodded and they exchanged papers. 'Do you know any of the businessmen on the list?' she asked.

Peyton shook his head. 'No. My brother, Paine, might. Do you recognise any of the Russian names?'

'Not really. One or two of them sound familiar, perhaps because they might have been named in a news article. But they're supposed to be secret societies. Publicity can hardly be what they want.' Tessa shrugged. 'It's amazing this was overlooked during the break-in. The thief was so close. The picture had been taken off the wall. The thief held the list in his hands and did not even realise it.'

'He was probably looking for a hidden safe. It's fairly common to hide a family safe behind a portrait. He removed the picture to see if there was a hidey-hole behind it. When there wasn't, he moved on to other possibilities,' Peyton explained.

'What do we do next, Peyton?' The thrill of finding the list was starting to fade as realities and next steps started to set in.

'We get the list to Brimley at Whitehall,' Peyton said, matter-of-factly.

Tessa fiddled with the tassel on the robe's belt. 'What do you suppose he will do with it?'

'He has intimated to me that British diplomats in Russia will be able to use the list as a bargaining tool. Britain wants to convince the Czar to keep the Dardanelle Straits open to British shipping.'

Tessa didn't like the sound of that. She sat up straighter. 'Your Brimley is going to sell the list to the Czar for water rights?'

'He might,' Peyton answered.

'Does that bother you? It bothers me quite a lot.' Tessa rose and began pacing away her agitation. 'We've risked our lives for this list. You've been stabbed and nearly poisoned. And for what? So that the list can be used as a death sentence for Russian revolutionaries. Your government is going to use this list to betray men.'

'Calm down, Tessa.' Peyton stood up. 'It's your government, too. You're as British as I am. This is about what's right for Britain. Those revolutionaries have committed themselves to treason against their king and they know the risks they run.'

'That's no answer at all, Peyton,' Tessa stormed. 'You could do something about that. You don't have to be the one to send them to their deaths.' Tessa stopped pacing at the window and drew back the curtain a bit to see the garden below. Her voice softened an increment. 'We were in St Petersburg in 1825, you know. I was about fifteen at the time. Later, once the leaders had been sentenced, we were invited to watch the executions. I didn't go. I couldn't bring myself to do it. My father went, of course, out of a show of loyalty to Nicholas I, the necessities of diplomatic relations and all that. This was not a rebellion of unorganised peasants. This was an internal rebellion that reached as high as the Czar's own military— smart, educated men who believed in freedom.'

'They were soldiers willing to die for their

beliefs,' Peyton put in from his side of the room. 'You can't shout "Constantine and Constitution" and not expect the Czar to do something about it.'

'Peyton, men were hanged from the ramparts of the Peter and Paul fortress,' Tessa protested. 'They weren't shot down in battle. They were marched out and put to death. It will happen again if you turn that list in. I can't believe you'd deign to be part of that.'

'If we don't turn this list in, Tessa, there will be war,' Peyton argued, exasperation evident in his tone. 'There are already Russian troops amassing for an attack on Turkey. Turkey will not survive a Russian assault without British assistance. If Britain does not ensure a Turkish victory, then we'll lose critical water rights. War means British troops will die, perhaps by the thousands.'

Tessa stared thoughtfully out of the window. These were the situations her father had grappled with during his career. She had never been quite so close, quite so instrumental to one of those decisions as she was now. In her hands literally was the power to decide who lived and who died. Did she let Peyton turn the list in and risk sending those Russian freedom fighters to their deaths, or did she dissuade him from his course and send British troops into Turkey for a war with no certain outcome?

If she chose the former, Britain could use the list as leverage for maintaining water rights, a few freedom fighters in exchange for safe passage to

India should Russia conquer Turkey. British troops could stay out of the conflict and let Turkey and Russia fight it out, knowing that British water rights were secure regardless of the outcome. If she chose the latter, nothing was certain. The freedom fighters would not be betrayed by her, but British trade could very well be jeopardised and there would be war, a war which Britain might win or lose.

Tessa desperately wished there was a way between her options that would allow her to prevent a war and yet protect the revolutionaries. She wished her duty was as clearly defined to her as Peyton's was to him. It would make this decision easier, more obvious. Peyton had lived his entire life in Britain. He understood his role and obligations as a British peer. But while she was born British, she hadn't lived a British life. She'd seen first-hand the need for reform in Russia, the oppressive practices of serfdom and the consequences of the outmoded government practised by Russia's Czars. She didn't want to trade freedom for water rights. Maybe she didn't have to after all.

'What if we give Brimley only one list?' Tessa began to hypothesise out loud. 'Give him the list of British investors. It's still something to negotiate with. He can promise the Czar he won't let those businessmen fund a revolutionary cause if the Czar promises water rights should Russia seize Turkey. The right diplomat could build a persuasive case. Czar Nicholas is putting down revolts all over the country. He'll be paranoid enough to take the threat of sponsorship seriously.' Hope began to grow in her as she outlined her argument.

Peyton stared at her thoughtfully, weighing, considering what she proposed. She knew he was thinking of his ability to keep his word, to keep his countrymen safe. 'What about the other list?' he asked.

'We burn it. We tell no one that it existed. We can claim my father's work wasn't as far along as people had been led to believe. He'd not yet had time to make the connections,' Tessa said ardently.

Peyton nodded. 'Those men will have the chance to live and die on their own.'

'It is the best we can do for them. Are we agreed, Peyton?' Tessa pressed. 'I want you to do this because it's the right thing to do, not because of your affections for me.'

'Yes. I will take the list of investors to Brimley. He will be disappointed it isn't more telling, but he'll see its uses none the less.' Peyton reached for his clothes and began to dress.

'You're going now? I'll come with you,' Tessa offered, striding towards her pile of discarded clothing.

Peyton shook his head. 'No. I want you to stay here. You'll be safer. There are servants downstairs who would come to your assistance. You can lock the doors. I won't risk you at the last moment when we're so close to being free from this cloud.'

His words gave her pause. 'Do you think it's all

that dangerous? The Russians don't know we have found the list.'

Peyton looked at her, a frighteningly serious look on his face. 'I am not as worried about getting to Whitehall as I am about getting home. We know we were followed this morning. There is a great likelihood that I'll be followed when I leave the house. I'll try to lose them, but, if not, they'll suspect something is up when they discover my destination is Whitehall.'

'Then meet Brimley somewhere else,' Tessa said shortly.

'It hardly matters if I go to Whitehall or White's, I'll be followed regardless. I'd rather go in the daylight. If anything is going to happen, I don't want any surprises in the dark.'

Tessa slipped her dress on over her head. 'I don't like this talk, Peyton. You sound as if you're not coming back.' She said the words briskly, but she couldn't keep the tears from forming in her eyes. She swiped at them, angry at herself for being a watering pot at such an inopportune moment. This was a moment for strength. 'Send a message and have Brimley come here. If he wants the list, he can come and get it.'

'That would be a dead giveaway,' Peyton argued softly, moving to take her in his arms. He was fully clothed now and Tessa could see by the set of his jaw that he would not be convinced from his path.

She laid her head against his chest, taking in the warmth of his body, its strength and power, while he laid out his instructions. 'I shouldn't be gone long, no longer than two hours. Hopefully, less. It will depend on traffic. Don't open the door for anyone for any reason. If I don't come back, make a run for the Cotswolds and Dursley Park. With luck, you'll catch up with Crispin on the road. You'll be safe.'

'You'll come back, Peyton,' Tessa said resolutely. 'We'll leave for the Cotswolds together.'

'Yes, we'll have to get out of town until Brimley can send the Russian delegation packing. I don't think Count Androvich will be pleased to discover he's been beaten.'

Tessa didn't wait for Peyton to set her apart from him. She stepped back from their embrace of her own accord, although it took all of her will to do so. All she wanted to do was to keep Peyton in her arms, safe. But Peyton needed her courage now. He didn't need a woman clinging to him. Her worry could prove to be a fatal distraction.

Peyton folded the list and tucked it inside his coat pocket. He slid his customary knife into his boot. 'I'll be back shortly, Tessa,' he said, his hand on the doorknob that would take him out of her bedroom.

'Peyton, I love you,' Tessa called after him as the door shut behind him.

Tessa sat quietly, straining her ears for the sound of the big front door shutting, signalling Peyton's complete exit from the house. She glanced at the clock to check the time. Five o'clock. By seven, this would all be over, she told herself. Perhaps earlier. In the meanwhile, she had to stay busy. She could pack. For them both.

Tessa threw herself into packing and tidying the room. A maid came in to light the evening fire and to offer to help. Tessa let her light the fire, but refused the help.

As the fire caught, Tessa fingered the second list. They'd agreed to burn it. She should do it now. But something held her back. Tessa tucked the list into her chemise. She would wait until Peyton was safe. Should anything happen to him, she might be able to use the list to free him. She had little else to use in place of a ransom. She would not trade these names for water rights, an issue that was volatile and ever changing, but she'd not hesitate to trade these names to save Peyton.

Tessa finished packing at half-past six. Peyton hadn't returned. She fought back the initial desire to panic. He'd said it could take up to two hours. Tessa picked up a book and tried to read, failing miserably. She put the book down and picked up her reticule with her gun inside and sat in the chair next to the fire. Peyton would walk through the door any moment and they would laugh together at her odd vigil, sitting in her chair with her gun.

By half-past seven Tessa had to draw the conclusion she'd avoided for so long. Peyton wasn't coming home.

Something had gone dreadfully wrong. She fingered the shape of her gun inside her reticule. The time for waiting had passed. Tessa scribbled a hasty note to Arthur at Dursley House. The time for action had come.

Peyton's worst fears had come to fruition. He stifled a groan in the darkness as consciousness returned to him, and with it the flood of events that had led to this. He'd left Lily's town house in his coach, alert to anyone who might be following him. Thanks to traffic, his coachman had eluded a couple of the followers, but Count Androvich had grown cleverer over the weeks. He had a network of watchers set up so that there was someone to take over for the others when they fell back. A few hundred yards from Whitehall, Peyton had felt he'd succeeded in losing the last of them. Neither he nor his coachman could see anyone of a suspicious nature in their wake. Peyton had quickly disembarked from the carriage and made his way to Brimley's office, feeling safer once he got inside the building.

As he'd expected, Brimley had been disappointed the list wasn't more detailed. Peyton had to argue far longer than he would have liked to get Brimley to see the merits of what he offered. 'This is the list I have,' Peyton had said. 'I have done what you've required of me.' It wasn't a lie. That was indeed the list he had. If Tessa had another list, well…

'Very well, Dursley. We had been led to believe

there might be something more informative, but this will do, as you've pointed out,' Brimley huffed.

Then chaos had broken out. The door of the little office had burst open and they were set upon by eight masked men. Peyton barely had time to draw his knife. To his horror, Brimley went down immediately, a victim of quiet knife work. It was him against eight. He understood instantly why the trackers had disappeared. Someone had gone directly to Count Androvich. His lengthy argument with Brimley had given Androvich time to put together his forces and make his attack.

Peyton fought them off, satisfied to note that he eliminated a few of them before the inevitable. When it came, it didn't come from the slice of a knife, but from a broken chair leg meeting the back of his head, no doubt courtesy of Sergei Androvich himself who had yet to fight fairly.

Peyton had no idea where he was now or how much time had passed. His head ached, his surroundings were dark, and the stone floor he lay on was cold and uncomfortable. If he had to guess, he was in a secret room in the Russian embassy. According to international law, that meant he was on Russian territory. It would be the safest place the Russians could take him without being caught by the British. He hoped Tessa had the good sense to follow his instructions and not come looking for him.

Peyton did some mental arithmetic in his aching

head. If Tessa got away, she'd reach Crispin on the road within a day and then it would take a day for Crispin to get back. If he could manage to stay alive for two more days, there might be some hope.

The door to his cell opened. Peyton squinted against the light that followed the men in. There were three of them. Peyton pulled himself up into a sitting position, his body protesting at the effort. 'What is the meaning of this? I am a peer of the realm,' he began. There was nothing like a little righteous indignation to get things started, and it was a good reminder to these men as to whom they were dealing with.

One of the men laughed, fingering an ivory-handled blade. As his eyes adjusted to the light, Peyton recognised Sergei Androvich. It was the first time they'd encountered one another since the incident with poisoned champagne.

Androvich sneered. 'This is a most unlooked-for circumstance. You could have saved us all immense amounts of trouble if you'd have drunk the champagne.'

Peyton took immediate measure of the comment. Androvich was a cornered animal. It had been the Count's job to eliminate him and the Count had failed in front of his countrymen. It was clear to Peyton that Androvich now had a personal agenda above and beyond the need to retrieve the list.

'You can't believe you'll get away with this,' Peyton said. 'I'm not an anonymous serf who could disappear without anyone noticing.'

Sergei scoffed at the warning. 'You may be surprised, Dursley. You're nothing here. British influence stops at my doorstep as does your extraordinary amount of luck, I'm afraid.'

That confirmed it. He was definitely in the embassy. 'What do you want with me?'

'We want the list.' Another spoke. Probably Vasilov. 'Your life for the list.'

'I don't have a list. I've given it to Brimley. I haven't any idea what Brimley might have done with it, and, now that Brimley is dead, you don't either.' Peyton hoped he carried off his charade with confidence.

Androvich snarled. 'Your bluff is a poor one. We've got Brimley's list, as useless as it is.'

'Then you've got all that I've got. We're even,' Peyton replied evenly.

'The list has been a wild goose chase the whole time,' Ilanovich said. 'It was never as important as we were led to believe. The list itself was just a bluff to scare the Czar. We should let the Earl go and get home. Our time here has been wasted.'

Vasilov looked ready to agree. Peyton thought he would agree to anything that showed Androvich poorly. He remembered the dissension in the group the night he'd overheard them in the library.

'No!' Androvich said in a forceful tone. 'Don't you see, there's not one list, but two. Ralph Branscombe was no fool. The lists aren't that useful separately. They're only powerful together. He's not telling you everything.'

It was Vasilov's turn to sneer. 'You're spinning fictions out of whole cloth now, Androvich. You're a desperate man. There's no proof there's two lists. Where would the second one be?'

Androvich fixed Peyton with an arrogant stare, daring Peyton to gainsay him. 'The second list is with Tessa Branscombe or on the road to the Cotswolds. She's in bed with the Earl in more ways than one.' Sergei fingered his knife blade maliciously. 'Isn't she, Dursley?'

The words chilled Peyton. He prayed Tessa had burnt the list already. He prayed she was gone from the city. He prayed a thousand things in those first seconds. He tried to think of a subterfuge that Sergei would swallow, that would steer him away from Tessa, that would keep him from tracking down Crispin and the girls. Above all else, Peyton had to keep his family safe. He had only one thing to barter with: his life.

'You're wrong, Androvich. Tessa and the girls don't have the second list. I'm the one who found them both. I had hoped to sell the other list privately on my own.'

'Perhaps you'll consider selling it privately to us in exchange for your life,' Gromsky put in. 'We can be very reasonable.'

'I won't tell you where it is.'

'Because you don't have it, because this is another lie,' Sergei said, stepping closer to Peyton, the knife blade glinting in the shadowed light. Peyton steeled his will not to flinch at the sight of the blade so near his face.

'He's lying to protect Tessa,' Sergei spat.

'I told you he was in love with her,' Vasilov said smugly.

'It hardly matters if this is about love or money. Men have been known to be highly motivated by both.' Gromsky eyed Peyton intently with a cruel glare. 'Shall I call the men and let them get on with it? I find I'm quite curious to see what the Earl of Dursley will do for love or money, aren't you, Androvich?'

Moments later two burly men entered the room. Peyton braced himself. During his time in diplomatic service, he'd been trained for this, although he'd never had to endure it. This would not be pleasant. One of the men ripped his shirt from him, not allowing him the dignity of removing it himself. The other clapped his wrists in iron cuffs and shackled him face-first to the wall.

'Start with twenty lashes and we'll see what he has to say,' he heard Androvich order.

Peyton gathered himself mentally and physically. He had what he wanted. He reminded himself of all his reasons for this sacrifice. The people he loved were protected. The girls were safe. He'd bought Tessa time to get to Crispin. Crispin would come. At last the pain obliterated his thoughts to just one: Tessa loves me. And that thought sustained him.

Chapter Nineteen

Tessa checked the little heart-shaped timepiece she had pinned to her gown. Ten o'clock in the morning. It had seemed an eternity had passed. She'd sat up most of the night, planning, plotting and hoping that at any time Peyton would come home and make her plans unnecessary. She took a final look in the mirror and carefully assessed her appearance.

She'd dressed smartly for this interview in a walking ensemble that had a military cut to it. The dark blue jacket was tapered to her waist and trimmed with braid. Beneath the jacket, she wore a high-collared white linen blouse. The matching dark blue skirt was cut to allow full, comfortable movement, giving the potentially severe outfit a soft, feminine appeal, too. She'd had the maid put her hair up beneath a small jaunty hat to complete the look.

Tessa picked up her reticule. She looked like a

woman paying a social call. She hoped that was what Sergei would see—a friend coming to call. She was betting heavily on the image. She had no idea how much Sergei suspected she knew, or how involved she was in the search for the list. She hoped he suspected her of nothing. It would make the interview easier. Tessa took a final look in the mirror. She was ready to go.

One of the footmen boldly tried to persuade her not to leave the house at the last minute. But she speared him with a silencing look. 'You all have instructions. You're to assist Lord Crispin when he arrives,' she said in a very controlled voice. Then she threw back her shoulders and walked to the waiting carriage and got in. Today she didn't care if anyone was following her. Today, she was going to the Russian embassy, a destination that would surprise anyone assigned to tracking her movements.

The embassy itself was a large, gracious building near Kensington Palace Gardens. The sunshine and the placid beauty of the gardens in full bloom beneath a blue sky made it difficult to believe she was in any real danger. Tessa gave the coachman a brief nod and sent him on his way. She mounted the steps to the columned building. She drew a deep breath and knocked on the door. There was no turning back. Her game was in motion.

'I am here to see Count Androvich,' she said with a sweet smile, extending a calling card to the man who answered the door. He bowed politely and took her card in.

Tessa held her breath. Surely Sergei would not refuse to see her? She waited and rehearsed her story.

The man returned and motioned her inside. 'The Count will see you.'

'Thank you,' Tessa said in Russian, much to the pleasure of the footman who gave off the smug impression that he was tired of hearing the harsh English tongue.

She was shown into a bright sitting room done in yellows and blues. The embassy's interior was quite impressive, extensively decorated with wainscoting and woodwork. Its regal interior fitted Sergei to perfection. He looked quite at home when he entered the room, immaculately dressed, his looks turned out to their best advantage. For a moment, he reminded Tessa of the young man she'd once held an infatuation for. In this bright and sunny room, it was hard to remember the dark game she'd come to play. But perhaps the setting had been orchestrated for just such an effect.

'Tessa! This is a surprise indeed. What brings you here?' Sergei bent gallantly over her hand, a mix of courtly elegance and the intimate informality of a friend. 'I thought you were angry with me after the commotion at the art gallery. I regret I've not had the chance to apologise. I have missed you. This is a big city and I know so few people. What brings you here?' He was her gallant friend of old once more, acting the part to its maximum.

'I am worried about Lord Dursley. He did not return last night,' Tessa began.

'Ah, your erstwhile guardian,' Sergei said with a modicum of regret in his voice. 'Surely, Tessa, you can't expect him to wait on you constantly? I don't mean to be indelicate, but perhaps he's taking a short holiday at his mistress's? I've heard Dursley keeps them.' He waved a hand in an attempt to play Peyton's friend. 'All men do, my dear. It's a fact of life. Do not be alarmed. I am sure he'll be around in a day or two.'

What could she say to that? She knew Sergei was lying. Peyton didn't have a mistress. He'd been with *her*. But she could not call Sergei a liar and tell him otherwise without exposing too much. The realities of the peril she was in at that very moment became very clear to her. Sergei was a smooth pretender. He was lying to her now. People lied to cover things up.

Sergei leaned forward and Tessa fought the urge to cringe. She could hardly stand being in the same room with the snake—a snake she'd once admired. 'Tessa, I am sorry if Dursley has let you down in any way. Perhaps he has led you to believe a certain understanding existed between the two of you? I would not want to see you hurt. But I am gratified that you felt you could come to me.' He reached for her hand but Tessa deftly evaded him, standing up to walk to the window. Her back was to Sergei. She used the moment to open her reticule.

Sergei was still talking. 'Tessa, I confess I still harbour hopes that you will consider my proposal. We have been friends for a long time and I can think of no greater joy than making you my wife.'

She could feel Sergei walking up behind her. Tessa whirled on him, her gun hidden in the folds of her skirt. 'It's time to cut line, Sergei. You've never been my friend or my father's.'

Her anger halted him, his arms spread at his side in supplication. 'Whatever can you mean, Tessa? Has Dursley confused you with his nonsense and jealousy?'

'You did not come to London to woo me. You came because you believed I was in possession of a certain list. You have schemed to have me followed, to have my house broken into and destroyed. In St Petersburg, you stayed close to me to spy on me. I came to you today because I think you've taken Peyton. You've already failed to do away with him twice. He's a menace to you and getting at the list.'

'Tessa, I am wounded by your accusations.' Sergei put a hand over his heart. 'If there have been attacks on Dursley, it is only because of the kind of man that he is.' Sergei gestured to the chair she'd vacated. 'If you would sit down and listen to me, I will tell you about the man Peyton Ramsden really is and then you can decide.'

Tessa eyed Sergei warily and took her seat. A tea

tray appeared on cue. Sergei smiled at her reluctance to accept any food. 'Suit yourself, my dear.' Sergei poured himself a cup. 'Now, as for Ramsden, he's not as perfect as he makes himself out to be. He works occasionally for the Foreign Office. In the 1820s, he spent time in Vienna, not all of it savoury. He's got a quiet reputation for knife work when the occasion arises. But then, we're not all saints. Perhaps we could forgive him for that.' Sergei paused.

'He met my father in Vienna. It's where they were first acquainted,' Tessa said with a touch of steel in her voice. She was not going to let Sergei think she knew nothing of Peyton's past.

Sergei gave a harsh laugh. 'No doubt that's the smallest lie he's told you. Did he actually say he'd *met* your father? He had *encountered* your father on maybe three occasions in Vienna at large state events. The most they'd ever exchanged were polite greetings.'

'My father appointed him as guardian, so surely you're mistaken about the depth of their association,' Tessa rebutted. But doubt was growing inside her. She had not thought of it at the time, but when she'd been looking through her father's papers, there'd been no mention of Peyton, not even as a social acquaintance.

Sergei held up a finger. 'My dear, wait here. I have something to show you.'

He returned in a few minutes and passed her a folder. 'I am not asking you to believe me. Believe the paperwork.' He spoke while Tessa read. She could feel her face paling. This couldn't be true. There had to be a trick. Peyton had been sent to find the list?

'The codicil to your father's will is a forgery, put together by British intelligence in order to place Ramsden into the centre of your lives. The hope being, of course, was that it would allow him access to the list. There is no real guardian, Tess. Your father made no provisions for you beyond the Bloomsbury house and the small dowries.'

'Are you telling me Peyton is a spy?' Tessa's mind reeled with the implications. If Sergei's claim was true, it would reshape the foundations of her relationship with Peyton. How much of their association was a lie? Was the passion a fraud, too? He'd seemed so honest, so upright with his concerns about propriety and her reputation. How could she have misjudged him? What was it Eva had said? It was the perfect ones who had the most to hide.

'Ah, Tess—"Peyton"?' Sergei clicked his tongue in a disappointing sound, picking up on her use of his first name. 'He has trifled with you after all. The man has no morals, insinuating himself into the lives of four girls, using his position and his looks to make promises he doesn't intend to keep.' Sergei shook his head. 'I will call him out for you, Tess. It would give me great pleasure to put a bullet through his black heart, or a sword if you'd prefer. You have only to say the word.'

Tessa's head swam. She put the folder down on the table next to the tea service. She had to be careful and not jump to hasty conclusions. Peyton had *lied*. No, that wasn't fair. He simply hadn't told her the entire truth. Were omissions lies? Why was she suddenly trying to redeem him in her mind? His place in their lives was a fictitious one. She no more knew the man she loved than she knew the truth about Sergei. If Peyton had lied about who he was, who was to say he hadn't also lied about Sergei? How was she to know who was her ally and who was not? Was Sergei the one she should have trusted all along?

Sergei spoke softly. 'That day at the Academy, I was only trying to protect you. I was trying to keep you away from Dursley, but he would not be shaken. I feared you'd be hurt accidentally in all the commotion.'

Tessa stood up. The interview had not gone the way she'd planned. She'd come to fight for Peyton. She'd come to rescue him and she'd ended up betraying herself instead. She'd expected an antagonistic Sergei. She'd been prepared to shoot him if needed. Instead, Sergei had been handsome, apologetic, reconciliatory even. And he'd shared information with her that had changed her plans entirely. 'Thank you, Sergei. I need to go home and think about all this. It comes as a great shock.'

'Are you going back to his aunt's house?' Sergei inquired in gentle tones.

Tessa shook her head. 'No. I think my time there is best ended. I'll go back to the Bloomsbury house. It will do.'

'I hope you don't think I had anything to do with that break-in.'

'I don't know what to think any more, Sergei,' Tessa said non-committally. She was starting to think it hardly mattered. Peyton had betrayed her and she was fast discovering how debilitating a broken heart could be.

They reached the front door of the embassy. Somewhere in the depths of the big building a dog whined. It caught Tessa's attention. 'Sounds like you have a stray dog,' she commented.

'Oh, I've discovered London is full of strays. There's always a bevy of them at the back door, waiting for kitchen scraps,' Sergei said lightly.

The dog yelped again. It was an odd yelp, rather human sounding. Tessa remembered something and shot Sergei a sideways glance. He'd kicked a dog once in her presence. His instinctive brutality had shocked her at the time. 'We had plenty of strays in St Petersburg, too. I don't recall you being so keen on kitchen scraps then.'

Sergei merely shrugged and held the door open for her. 'Thank you for coming, Tessa. I wish I had better news for you. I can see it's something of a blow.'

'I'll manage,' Tessa said, some of her calm and focus returning to her. Something wasn't right. Both Sergei and Peyton had lied to her. Sergei had lied to her that very day and then followed his lies with what Tessa supposed to be at least some truth about Peyton. But she was too intelligent to believe it was the entire truth about Peyton. The man who had made such exquisite love to her, who had worried so thoroughly for her sisters' safety, who had taken his duty to his country so seriously, could not be as corrupted as Sergei made him out to be.

The dog yelped again. Tessa cringed. 'Would you like me to take the mongrel home? I could do with some company in Bloomsbury.'

Sergei favoured her with a smile. 'I think I'll keep this one. Thank you all the same, my dear.'

Tessa started down the steps, preparing to hail a cab for the trip home. For the coachman's safety, she'd instructed him not to come back. If anything had happened to her, the Russians wouldn't allow the coachman to leave.

Sergei called to her, 'Tessa, there's one more thing I should tell you. I thought it best not to, I didn't want to hurt you more than necessary.'

There was concern etched on his face as Tessa retraced her steps. 'Bad news isn't like wine, Sergei. It doesn't get better with age.'

'Your Peyton was here. Yesterday evening. He said he had a list and that he wanted to sell it privately. Frankly, the list wasn't very impressive. I suspect there's another list somewhere that is much more valuable to Russia. I thought you should know, in case you run across anything in your father's papers. I don't know how Dursley found it. I am guessing he found it in the break-in and took it.'

The dog yelped again. Tessa studied Sergei. Her instincts were overriding her mental coolness. Sergei was an excellent liar with his cunning ability to create verisimilitude. But he'd told one lie too many. Peyton had been with her the night of the break-in, waltzing her about the floor, and he was not a man who sent others to do his job. Intuition warred with logic. Intuition won. Sergei was hiding something, wanting to build distrust and hatred. Why? It came to her in a flash: so that she'd turn away from Peyton. She'd not been wrong to come. Peyton was here.

She met Sergei on the top step and pushed him back to the wall. 'That's no dog you've got hidden away, Sergei. Peyton's here. If you value your life, you'll bring him up to me post-haste.'

Sergei's veneer of friendship vanished. His face was cold. 'That's a big threat without anything to back it up, Tessa. You're as poor a bluffer as he is. You forget yourself. Right now you're standing in my country. This is my house.'

'This is my gun.' Tessa pulled the weapon from the folds of her skirts and aimed it at Count Sergei Androvich point blank.

Chapter Twenty

Sergei was at heart a coward, self-preservation being his primary objective in all situations. His capitulation was quick and sure. 'I will take you to him—just put the gun away.'

'No. You weren't listening.' Tessa's hand on the gun never wavered. 'You send for him. I am going nowhere with you. I am not fool enough to let you lead me down into the secret bowels of this place. Let us step inside this door into the hall, you first. You send a footman for Peyton. He comes up alone with the footman only or you die the moment I see any other faces coming to your aid. Who cares if I am eventually overpowered—you're already dead,' she reminded him coldly, quelling any small tendency he might have to play the martyr. 'Do you understand? Are you ready to go inside?'

Sergei nodded, his fear palpable. Tessa prodded

him inside ahead of her, keeping the gun firmly in his back. Tessa hailed the first footman who crossed the hall. 'Tell him what you need, Sergei.'

Sergei did and Tessa added her own instructions in Russian, adding that he had only three minutes to get there and return with the prisoner before she fired on Sergei. The man's eyes widened, but he scampered off to do what he was told.

Tessa wasn't naïve enough to think she'd simply have her demands met and she could walk out with Peyton in tow. So far so good, but she had yet to see Peyton and she knew the Russians would not play fair. In spite of her instructions, they'd attempt to follow Peyton and the footman up. She wasn't convinced they were as enchanted with Sergei's life as he was. They might consider him expendable if it meant keeping Peyton.

Tessa checked her small timepiece. 'Two and a half minutes have elapsed. Is your footman fast? Do you think he cares enough about you to follow orders? Perhaps he's down there right now deciding you're expendable.' She had to keep Sergei on edge, frightened if possible. If she showed any weakness, any reticence to play her part, the ruse was up.

The banging on the door reverberated through Peyton's head with an intensity that caused him to cry out in spite of his intentions not to. He'd been doing a great deal of that lately in his struggle to cling to consciousness. The two big brutes were still in the chamber with him. If he recollected correctly, Gromsky and Vasilov were there, too, drinking tea and issuing instructions while the other two beat him to a bloody pulp. The brutes were resting for the time being, for which Peyton was thankful. His back was on fire from the lashing and the rest of him was chilled from the cold water thrown in his face to keep him awake.

He'd had too much time to take the measure of his captors. Vasilov had proven to be arrogant and quarrelsome. Sergei Androvich had proven to be much the same. It was Gromsky Peyton worried about most. He was the cool-headed one of the lot. There was a cruel streak that ran deep in him, as if he knew exactly how to break a man.

The door opened and Gromsky spoke in Russian to whoever had entered. Peyton couldn't see. Out of deference for his back, he was lying on his stomach. The exchange was short and rapid. The newcomer seemed agitated. Gromsky and Vasilov spoke briefly to one another. Without warning, Peyton felt himself being hoisted to his feet. He wasn't so far gone he couldn't rise on his own and, out of stubbornness, he resisted the assistance, awkwardly getting to his feet with his manacled hands.

'It seems someone is demanding to see you above stairs, Dursley. They promise to shoot Count Androvich if we don't produce you immediately,' Gromsky said, shoving him towards the agitated footman. 'Up you go, although Vasilov and I think it might be rather entertaining to see Androvich get shot. He's not exactly been an exemplary travelling companion.'

Peyton felt woozy from all the sudden movement. He steadied himself against the door jamb, trying to take it all in. Crispin must be here by some miracle. Peyton marshalled his strength. Crispin would need him to be alert and to aid in the fight to come. There were the five Russians, the two brutes and the three ambassadors. Who knew how many servants would come to anyone's aid? If he and Crispin acted fast enough, they might stand a chance. Peyton shivered involuntarily.

Gromsky gave an evil grin. 'Cold? When you get back we'll have a nice fire going that will warm you right up. Whoever is up there has asked that you come alone or they'll shoot Androvich anyway. But Vasilov and I will take our chances with Androvich's life. We'll follow you up shortly to help you back down.'

'We have to go, the clock is running,' the footman said nervously, tugging at Peyton.

Living or dying would happen upstairs, Peyton decided, dragging himself up the long flight of stone steps. He was not going back to that room and whatever fire torture Gromsky was arranging. He had complete faith in Crispin and in his own remaining strength, meagre as it was.

But it wasn't Crispin he saw when he crested the stairs. It was Tessa who held Sergei Androvich at gunpoint. The footman was obviously scared of her and Androvich looked as if he fully believed she'd shoot him without provocation. That was all well and good, but Peyton felt panic rise in his throat. How was he going to protect her in the condition he was in? What would happen when Vasilov and Gromsky came up the stairs and saw that it was her? Oh, God, he couldn't let Gromsky get his hands on Tessa. The foolish woman should have been halfway to the Cotswolds by now.

Peyton saw a glimmer of horror cross her face as she took in his appearance. He was aware how awful he must look, bloodied, bruised, shirtless, dirty from lying on the floor, his hands chained and she couldn't even see his back. *Don't give in to any emotion*, he silently willed her.

'I want to see him close up. Walk him over here to me,' Tessa commanded in her excellent Russian.

Peyton snarled as he neared Androvich. Given the opportunity, he'd not hesitate to wrap the chain of his manacles around the Count's neck. Androvich paled.

'Are you all right, Peyton?' Tessa asked.

'We have to get out of here now. The others won't wait below,' Peyton said in low, hoarse tones, his throat dry.

Tessa had neatly manoeuvred them both close to the front door and Peyton didn't want to lose that advantage. This would be their best chance. Hoping that Tessa would manage Androvich, Peyton turned on the footman with an elbow to the gut that bent him over double, giving Peyton a chance to get the length of chain from his manacles around the footman's neck. The man was tall and he struggled, but Peyton's will was stronger. The man collapsed at Peyton's feet.

'Good lord, you've killed him,' Androvich breathed in disbelief, too frightened at the speed at which it had all happened to do much of anything. 'Gromsky! Vasilov! Help me.'

His foolish cry was all the warning Peyton needed to know the other two had come up the stairs. 'Tessa, run,' Peyton said, bracing himself for a fight.

'They'll just come after us,' Tessa said firmly. 'We can't outrun them in the street.'

'Still, I think we should try,' Peyton advised. In his fear, Androvich made a stupid, sudden move and Tessa was ready for him, bringing the pistol butt down on his head. Androvich slumped to the ground.

'Good girl, we'll need that shot,' Peyton murmured. 'Shoot Gromsky if you have the choice.'

They backed to the door. It was clear now that Gromsky and Vasilov had weapons, guns of their own. They had not come unarmed. 'Put the gun down, Miss Branscombe,' Vasilov urged. 'We wouldn't want anyone being hurt accidentally.'

Peyton wondered what the odds were that they'd actually kill the two of them. There would be no chance of finding the list. Gromsky would lose the chance to torture him if he was dead.

Gromsky and Vasilov edged closer to them. Even if they made the door just two feet behind them, Peyton feared they'd be shot before they reached the street. Peyton wished he had his knife in his boot, but he'd lost the blade back at Brimley's office. He wished he'd taken the gun from Tessa. She had to shoot and he hated thinking that his Tessa had been placed in the position of doing murder, even if it was for a good cause.

Tessa pointed the gun evenly at Gromsky. 'It will be you that goes first,' she said in quite convincing tones.

'And you will go right afterwards,' he retorted.

'Maybe. But what does it matter? You'll be dead. That's all you have to think about.'

Goodness, his Tessa sounded like a professional, Peyton thought with admiration. Suddenly glass shattered to their right. Nervous, Vasilov fired in the direction of the sound. Tessa fired at Gromsky, hitting him in the knee. The man went down, his gun sliding away from him.

'Run!' Peyton flung open the door and pushed Tessa ahead of him, using his body as a shield in case Vasilov came after them.

They pounded down the embassy steps, Peyton stumbling as his strength ebbed. He could hear commotion behind them. Vasilov must be on the move. He heard a shot ring out and waited for the impact. But none came. Peyton turned back and saw Crispin standing over Vasilov's form.

'Where the hell did you come from?'

Crispin gave a cocky grin. 'I heard you were going to need a ride.' He loped up to them and gave a loud whistle.

Within moments, Lily's coach rounded the corner.

Tessa stared up at the coachman. 'I told you not to wait. Doesn't anyone listen to instructions around here?'

The coachman exchanged a glance with Crispin and made a quick nod. 'Just aping my betters, ma'am, just aping my betters.'

Peyton would have laughed at the sight of Tessa getting some of her own impudence back, but he hadn't the strength. 'Crispin…' he managed to choke out and then he was falling. He felt Crispin's arms take his weight, vaguely aware of Crispin and Tessa manoeuvring him inside the coach. He heard Tessa cry out at the sight of his back. 'Crispin, what have they done to him?'

Crispin was murmuring comfort words to Tessa. 'He'll be all right. I know what to do.'

Peyton was shivering again. He tried to cling to consciousness, but this time he couldn't win. The last thing he remembered was Tessa scolding him. 'Don't you leave me now, Peyton Ramsden, you've got some explaining to do.'

Laughter woke him along with the sound of feet running past his door, followed by an ineffectual 'hush'. Sunlight bathed his face. For a moment, Peyton wasn't sure where he was. A baby cried from somewhere in the house and then he knew. Miraculously, he was at Dursley Park in the master's chamber, his chamber. He stretched and groaned. Lucifer's balls, he was sore. His mind felt refreshed, as if he'd slept for ages. But his body did not match the vigour in his brain.

Peyton managed to get himself into an upright position, no mean feat considering he'd been sleeping on his stomach. He took a quick survey of himself. His torso was heavily bandaged and when he looked beneath the covers, he saw that he wore a pair of Paine's loose silk pants from India. Peyton ran a hand across his chin, feeling the stubble. He concluded there was at least four days' worth of beard there. He would have to shave immediately. He pushed a hand through his hair. And bathe.

He glanced around the room. It felt good to be here, but there was certainly a story to tell about how he'd arrived. He remembered none of it. His eyes lit on the chair in the big bay of windows and Peyton smiled. He knew who could tell him, when she woke up.

Tessa slept in the chair, oblivious to the sun on her face. Her head was nestled against one wing of the chair and her hair fell loose over the edge. She looked exquisitely beautiful as she slept. One would never imagine such a delicate beauty had stormed the Russian embassy—an army of one with a gun, all for him.

Peyton pushed himself out of bed and slowly walked towards her, cursing his stiff muscles at every step. He'd be damned if he would play the invalid. It simply wasn't in him. He could be sore in bed as well as out of it.

He hadn't meant to wake her. He'd merely wanted to watch her sleep. But she stirred, perhaps sensing his presence or the shadow his figure cast through the sunbeams. She opened her eyes and screamed in startled surprise.

'Shh, Tessa. It's just me,' Peyton said swiftly. He didn't want a room full of visitors just yet. Right now, he just wanted her. Peyton could feel his member rising at the sight of her lovely eyes. Wonderful, now the only part of his body not stiff was getting in on the act, too.

'What are you doing out of bed?'

'I'm sore, Tessa, not ill,' Peyton said. 'I wanted to see you.'

'I must look a sight,' Tessa said self-consciously, sliding a hand through her hair.

'You look lovely to me,' Peyton said, reaching for her hand to still it. 'You brought us here?'

'We couldn't stay in London. Gromsky was only wounded, not dead. I didn't feel safe in town. Crispin and I thought it was best to get you home, even if it meant three days on the road.' Tessa was up and moving. 'No more questions until you're sitting down.' She urged him back to the bed and Peyton let her. His little sojourn across the room had taken un-expected amounts of energy.

'And my prognosis?' Peyton asked once she had him settled to her satisfaction.

'You'll live. Crispin assures me you were never in danger of doing otherwise, but I had my concerns.' Tessa looked down at the bedspread, suddenly in-trigued by its textures. 'I had no idea how badly hurt you were when they brought you upstairs. I have no idea how you managed to fight beside me and get us out of the embassy.'

'There was no other choice, Tessa. When I came up those stairs, I'd already decided I wasn't going back down them. I was expecting Crispin. Then I saw you and I was scared out of my wits at the thought of Gromsky getting to you.' Peyton gave a short laugh. 'It seems irrational now, but at the time all I could think of was how was I going to protect you when I could hardly walk myself.'

'I don't need protection all the time, Peyton. I can take care of myself, you know.'

'I know.' Peyton reached for her hand and laced his fingers between hers. 'Still, when a man loves a woman the way I love you, Tess, it's hard to remember that.' He'd never told a woman he'd loved her before. He didn't expect Tessa to realise the import of his statement. But that was all right. He knew. 'I want to make love with you, Tess. I'm sure we can manage something if we're careful.'

Tessa's reaction wasn't the one he expected. She unlaced her hand and stood up, moving away from the bed. 'No. We can't pretend everything has been restored to normal. I have questions that need answers first. Starting with—why did you lie about being our guardian?'

The peace Peyton had felt vanished. Two thoughts hit him simultaneously: oh, hell, she knew, and, secondly, after all they'd been through, he could still lose her.

Chapter Twenty-One

It seemed he was making a habit of having awkward discussions in bed. First Lydia, and now this. Peyton much preferred to have this discussion in the estate office, behind his big desk, dressed in appropriate clothing.

'Why don't you tell me what you know?' Peyton began carefully. 'Did Count Androvich tell you that?'

'Androvich might be a consummate liar, but that doesn't mean everything he says is untrue,' Tessa countered. 'He says the codicil to the will is a forgery, compiled simply to give you access to our lives.' She fixed him with a sharp stare. 'You were sent to spy on us and you knew it.'

'I was sent to determine if there was a list.'

'You were sent to *get* the list,' Tessa inserted. 'By any means possible, too. Did you think pretty dresses, parties and trips to the zoo would be enough?

You've spent the last month maligning Count Androvich, but you're hardly any different.'

'I never plotted to have you harmed. I did not destroy your home or cause you to live in daily terror of being followed.' Peyton rose to the fight. 'I would say that makes me quite different.'

'You misled me and my sisters. You lied. You were never our guardian.'

'Not legally,' Peyton challenged, knowing Tessa would read between the lines. He'd been their guardian in all but name. He'd protected them. He'd whisked them to the safety of Aunt Lily's when needed. He'd taken them under his tutelage, given her a Season, a chance to make a good match and secure their futures.

'You had secret motives. Why didn't you just tell me?' Tessa retorted.

'Probably for the same reasons you didn't tell me.'

'I had no reason to trust you. I didn't know you and you were so arrogant, sending your servants to my house and re-ordering my life when I had it all under control,' Tessa argued.

'I had no reason to trust you, either, Tessa. You were stubborn and contrary from day one. You fought me over every little thing even when I was being nice. I had not planned to stay in the city very long, just long enough to answer Brimley's summons and break things off with my mistress, if you want to know the truth.'

'Is that why you kissed me at the Broughtons' ball? Because you were getting nowhere in your mission?'

Peyton's jaw worked. If the situation wasn't so dire, he'd politely remind her she had been the one to kiss him first. But this was not the time for humour. He knew what she meant. He'd been the one to prolong the kiss and turn the interaction into something more than what it had been intended to be.

He saw his actions through her eyes and was not pleased with the kind of man that image painted. 'No, Tessa. I never used our passion to manipulate you. I kissed you because I couldn't stand the thought of you kissing Androvich and not me. I wanted you and that complicated my life greatly. I still want you, Tess. But I find I'm a man of pride and I've already been rejected twice.'

Tessa swallowed. 'Then I must advise you not to ask me yet.'

That set off warning bells. What hadn't he done? What else had that blasted Androvich told her that was causing such doubt? Couldn't she see they belonged together?

The door to the bedroom burst open and they were immediately swarmed with family members. Peyton had always thought his chambers rather large, but filled with three girls, two brothers, a baby and sundry relatives, he was starting to reconsider 'large'.

'So much for my privacy,' Peyton joked as they all

pummelled him with questions. 'I'm better, really, I am quite well.' He held up his hands in mock surrender.

Tessa shot him a final look and took a cold form of mercy on him. 'Come on, girls, we have lessons and I think I promised you a treat this afternoon.'

'I'll help.' Julia and Tessa gathered the girls and ushered them from the room. Others took their cues and left Paine and Crispin to play the valets.

Tessa managed to avoid being alone with him for the next two days. It wasn't that hard to manoeuvre. They were constantly surrounded by large groups of people whenever they were together and the others made demands on their time. Not that Peyton begrudged anyone a moment of that time.

Summer was upon them and Dursley Park was showing to best advantage. It was a time for brothers and sisters. As his stamina returned, Peyton strolled the vast gardens of his home, catching sight occasionally of Tessa with her sisters, weaving daisy wreaths beneath the big trees of the parkland, or reading aloud from a book; sometimes he saw her with her head close to Petra's, talking quietly. He wondered if he was the source of their conversation.

He didn't stroll alone. These days, Paine or more often Crispin was with him. Paine was content at Dursley Park, content in his life as a father and husband. When they walked, Paine talked of his plans to return to London and his business ventures in the autumn.

But Crispin was unsettled. Peyton could palpably feel his brother's unrest as they walked. 'You never did tell me how it was that you came to be at the embassy that day,' Peyton asked casually as they strolled one afternoon.

'Tessa had sent Arthur out to find me immediately the evening you didn't return. The rest was luck. I didn't feel right leaving you in London and I had already started back. I was on the main road. It wasn't hard to meet up with Arthur. When I got to town, the coachman told me he'd dropped Tessa at the embassy that morning.'

'I owe you our lives, Crispin. I doubt Vasilov would have missed,' Peyton said, wondering if it was the shooting that weighed heavily on Crispin.

'I was glad to do it. You needn't feel as if you've forced me into taking first blood or any of that noble nonsense you're bound to think. I've killed before.'

'War is different, Crispin—'

'I'm not looking for absolution,' Crispin cut him off sharply.

'Then what's eating at you? We're all so happy here, but you're not.'

'I'll be going soon.'

It was so like Crispin to not say more than that. Peyton would have to drag every last ounce of information out of him. 'Where?'

'I don't know. Somewhere. Anywhere but here. Paine's got Julia and his son now. You'll be settling down with Tessa and all her sisters.' Crispin rolled his eyes at the thought of the Branscombe sisters taking up residence at Dursley Park.

'Well, Tessa has not accepted me yet,' Peyton said lightly.

'Cut up at you over the guardian fraud?'

'We knew it was coming. You warned me.' Peyton shrugged.

'Still, I'll be in the way. I'm not meant for such domesticity.'

'You could go to Farrier Hill. You could go to any of the estates you wanted. You could breed horses,' Peyton offered. 'And you're wrong about the domesticity, Cris. You just haven't found the right woman.'

'I'm a hard man to live with, Peyton. You of all people should know that, after living with me for thirty-five years.' Crispin laughed, his gaze going out to the fountain where Tessa and her sisters sat enjoying the warm weather.

Peyton divined his brother's thoughts. 'Is that another reason you're leaving?' He nodded in the direction of Petra Branscombe.

'She's too young for me,' was all Crispin would offer on the subject. 'I'm not nearly refined enough for her. What's your excuse? Surely you're refined enough for Tessa, intelligent enough, wealthy enough?'

Peyton studied the tableau at the fountain and shook his head. 'I wish I knew.'

'Why do you hesitate, Tess?' Petra asked as Eva and Annie drifted off to gather flowers. 'He's done nothing but follow you with his eyes all week. You cannot doubt his affections for you are real.'

Tessa scoffed at the statement. 'Real is something of a sticking point between us. I don't know what is real any more.'

Petra sighed and trailed her hand in the fountain basin. 'Are you still upset about the forged codicil? If it hadn't been for that, you never would have met him. Surely that's worth some forgiveness.' They had been discussing Peyton's perfidy all week, arguing the merits of the lies against the truths. Tessa was no closer to any answers.

'That's just it. I never would have met him. Girls like me aren't supposed to meet earls. The Earl of Dursley should marry someone of consequence.'

'You are someone of consequence, Tess. How could you believe otherwise? You speak three languages, you've given parties for diplomats from all over the world. You've run large households before. You'll be a perfect Countess.'

Tessa smiled wryly at her sister's assessment. 'You forget a few things. I have no title, no titled connections, and I come with the attendant scandal of being Ralph Branscombe's daughter.' The gossip had been bad enough before with the little criticisms of her behaviour. Now, she was at the heart of the Russian issue circulating through society.

Thanks to Sergei's petty-minded idea of revenge, she was being forced to wait and see how the rumours would affect her, and how they would affect Peyton. Tessa hesitated for Peyton's sake. In the absence of Dursley's power in town, Sergei and Gromsky had had free rein to do what they pleased. The scandal could be of monumental proportions.

Tessa could imagine how Sergei might construct his lies around the truth to shield the Russians from blame. Ralph Branscombe had concocted a list in the hopes of selling it to the highest bidder in hopes of fomenting rebellion in Russia. Put that way, her father's actions reeked of privateerism, not patriotism. She didn't want Peyton tied to such a scandal by marriage. He was too honourable a man. It would be the height of irony to see him brought low by such a scandal.

In her heart, she'd forgiven him for the initial deception. She might not have liked being the recipient, but she could understand the reasons for it and she respected his motives. Regardless of his deception, he'd never misrepresented his true character in their association. Inside his assumed role, he'd behaved with honour and treated her with respect and courtesy, even if that couldn't have been easy at times.

'You should let Dursley be the judge of that, Tess.

It's not fair for you to decide that the scandal super-
sedes his happiness,' Petra said.

'Then I'll wait and let him see what becomes of the
issue. I wouldn't want him to decide too precipitately.'

Petra stood up and brushed her skirts. 'Sometimes
you're too stubborn for your own good, Tess.'

Tessa's resistance was driving Peyton mad. After
two weeks of polite meetings and family dinners, he
had to do something. He needed an activity to take
his mind off waiting for Tessa. He appreciated she
needed time. He appreciated how her stubborn nature
must be working through everything. But in the
meanwhile, he lived with the mental torture of having
her near and not being able to touch her. During the
day he fantasised about catching her in an empty
room, taking her up against a wall and kissing her
senseless. At night, his fantasies took a far more
erotic track. Day or night, the result was the same.
He spent hours in a frustrating state of unrelieved
arousal. He would settle for a fight if that was all he
could have. Just anything but this polite aloofness she
favoured him with.

He was drinking port with Crispin when a perfect
outlet for his frustration offered itself. 'Did you see
the post today?' Crispin asked casually.

'Only briefly.' He had been finding it hard to con-
centrate on anything for long except Tessa.

'Count Androvich has been spreading unsavoury

rumours around the *ton* about the Branscombes. He's been suggesting that Tessa's father also possessed a list of Russian revolutionaries he intended to sell. The way Androvich tells it, Branscombe is a double-dealing bastard of the lowest order.'

Peyton fingered the stem of his glass. He didn't need Crispin to spell out the consequences. The deceased Ralph Branscombe didn't care what anyone did or said about his reputation, but the rumours could ruin Tessa and her sisters. Who would want to marry into a family tainted by a scandal of such a dishonourable nature? If he did not go up to London personally and put paid to those rumours, Sergei Androvich would have some modicum of revenge against Tessa. He probably hoped it would be enough to drive her from society's good graces.

Peyton stretched, testing his back. He would bear the scars from that horrible night the rest of his life. He'd be damned if Tessa would, too, although her scars would be of a different nature. He looked meaningfully at Crispin. 'It's time for retribution. How do you feel about a trip up to town?'

Tessa cursed her own stubborn pride for the hundredth time. She'd waited too long. She'd hesitated and Peyton was gone. She'd let him dangle without a word from her for two weeks and then he'd simply left. She'd woken up one morning to the news he had gone to London. When she'd asked how long he'd be gone, Julia had softly said, 'He didn't say.' That meant indefinitely. When she asked what he'd gone to town for, Julia and Paine had looked at each other and said again, 'He didn't say.'

But they knew. Tessa could sense it. He'd gone to town and she wasn't supposed to know why. She could imagine a myriad of things. Some of them were harmless explanations—he had business in Parliament. Other explanations were less so—he was bored in the country, he was picking out a new mistress, he was tired of waiting for her to decide. He'd said himself that he wouldn't ask a third time unless he was sure of her response. She'd done nothing to encourage that third time.

The irony was that she wanted to say yes. She'd decided that life without Peyton was not worth contemplating. If he was willing to live down the scandal, she would, too. Nothing mattered more than being together. In hindsight, she recognised she'd known that for a while now. She'd known it since the day she'd gone to the embassy and fought for Peyton in spite of Sergei's revelations. The revelations were a mixture of truths and lies, designed to drive her away from Peyton and into Sergei's confidence. But her heart had known a deeper truth that could not be thwarted that day, and Sergei's ploy had failed.

Tessa approached the big Dursley house, signalling the end of her afternoon walk. She screened her eyes against the sun, searching for a sign as she did every day, that Peyton had returned. It had been three weeks, and she needed him, wanted him.

There was no sign. She hadn't expected there to be. She told herself she couldn't realistically expect him back until after Parliament rose. She couldn't expect him for two more weeks at best. Perhaps she could write to him. Her pride was not greater than her need these days or her desire.

Tessa entered the wide hall. The big house was quiet. Her sisters were out with Lily. Tessa started up the stairs to her own room, surprised to meet Julia coming down the hallway. Julia usually rested this time of day while the baby slept.

'He's back,' Julia whispered in hushed tones. 'He's in the nursery.' She motioned to the stairs leading to the third floor.

Tessa shot her a look of gratitude. She didn't have to ask who Julia meant. She had not said much to Julia about her situation with Peyton, but the other woman seemed to divine much of her feelings.

Tessa hurried up the steps to the nursery, her heart in her throat. She had so much to tell him. At the nursery door all the thoughts, all the conversations she'd held with him in her head over the weeks, fled. The sight before her brought tears to her eyes in its simplicity and beauty. Of all the facets of Peyton Ramsden she'd seen, she'd yet to see this one.

Peyton stood at the nursery window dressed only

in his shirtsleeves, Julia's baby cradled confidently in his arms while he crooned a soft lullaby. The baby fussed a bit and he readjusted the little bundle, holding the baby up to the window. He began a recitation of all the things to be seen out of the window. 'There's the rose garden. There's the fountain. You'll like splashing in it when you're older. Maybe next summer, your mama will let you dangle your toes in it…'

She shouldn't be surprised. Peyton had been quite good with Annie. But a ten-year-old was different from an infant. He was going on about pony rides now and Tessa wiped quickly at her tears.

He turned from the window and caught her at it. 'Tessa?'

'Julia told me you were home. That you have news?' she said, ignoring the fact that he'd caught her at her tears. She'd forgotten how handsome he was. How had she managed to do that? There was something intoxicating about Peyton in a simple shirt and tight breeches.

'Yes, I do. It came to my attention that there were certain loose ends with the Russian issue that needed to be dealt with. I am happy to report that Count Androvich and Gromsky have been escorted off British soil with strict commands never to return. A letter regarding their conduct, which outlines their attempts to coerce a peer of the realm and terrorise an upstanding young lady, has been sent to the Czar. The Czar may have commissioned them. He may even have given them permission to act as they saw fit, but he cannot publicly ignore an outraged letter from a fellow monarch. Suffice it to say, they will not trouble us again.'

'And the rest of London society?' Tessa queried.

'Scandalised that the Count could behave in such a fashion,' Peyton affirmed. 'Your father's reputation and yours remain intact.'

Recognition dawned for Tessa. 'That is what you've spent three weeks doing? Fighting my dragons?'

'Our dragons,' Peyton corrected. The baby had dozed off and he moved to put him in the crib. 'It occurred to me that perhaps you feared the scandal, that it might be the reason you held yourself apart from me these last weeks. Has it, Tessa?' He wagged a finger at her. 'You should have told me. These last weeks have been torture, not knowing, always wanting you.'

'I know.' Tessa said simply. 'I had all these things I wanted to say to you, but now that you're here, all I want to do is kiss you.'

Peyton reached for her and pulled her close. 'That's all right with me.'

She sank into his embrace, her mouth easily finding his. She drank in all of him, the feel of his body hard against hers, the smell of his shirt, starch mixed with the sweet grassy smell of a man who'd ridden in the summer air.

The baby fussed in his cradle. Peyton broke the

kiss and went to tuck a blanket around it more securely. The child settled immediately with a coo.

'You're awfully good at that,' Tessa whispered, coming to stand behind him at the cradle. 'You'll make a wonderful father.'

Peyton turned slowly. 'Do I have reason to hope that will come to pass?'

Tessa took a steadying breath, unnerved by the devotion she saw in his eyes. Was ever a woman loved as much as she? In her stubbornness she had almost thrown this away. 'Yes.'

Peyton grinned. 'Then I guess the special licence I procured in London won't go to waste.'

'No, it won't, neither will a single minute of the rest of our lives.'

Dinner that night was a celebration both of Peyton's return and the announcement of their marriage. Afterwards, in Peyton's chamber was a celebration of a more private nature.

'I can see the babe already,' Peyton whispered huskily, kneeling before her chair as he undressed her, his hands rolling down her stockings.

'How?' Tessa said, knowing full well at six weeks her stomach was as flat as it had ever been.

Peyton's hands moved to her thin chemise and pushed it up over her breasts. He palmed them gently. 'Here. I can see it here in their fullness.' He leaned forward and stole a soft kiss. 'The prospect of my child suckling at the breast of the woman I love quite unmans me.' He slid his hand up the side of one breast.

Tessa gasped. She'd forgotten it was there.

'What is this?' Peyton asked, drawing back his hand. 'You carry paper in your chemise?' He unfolded the paper, his brows knitted together.

'I couldn't burn it until I knew you were safe,' Tessa said quickly.

'You had this with you at the embassy,' Peyton said, pieces starting to fit together. 'I thought you didn't want to risk these men.'

'Not for waterways. But I would have gladly given them up for you that day. And later, when it became clear Sergei would make a scandal of it, I thought crazily that I might sell the list to him as hush money if it would just get him to go home.'

'And now? Is there a reason to keep this list now?' Peyton asked huskily.

'No, the dragons are slain and by much nobler means.' Tessa reached for the paper and tossed it on to the grate where a little fire burned. It felt good to watch the slip of paper that had caused her so much trouble burn into oblivion. It could trouble them no more.

'Come to bed, Tessa,' Peyton whispered after a while. Later, as she climaxed in his arms, she knew with a certainty that the past was gone. With Peyton, everything had become fresh and new. The world was clean again.

Epilogue

A year and a half later

Peyton Ramsden, the fourth Earl of Dursley, was doing what he did best these days, juggling his twin boys on his legs while he attempted to eat. Already they'd managed to smear cake on his shirt, but he didn't care. Today was his fortieth birthday.

Beside him, Tessa laughed as the boys landed another forkful of icing on his lap. She dabbed at him with a napkin to no effect, but he appreciated the effort none the less.

Near him, Paine and Julia kept an eye on their son, now a strapping two-year-old, too squirmy for sitting on laps for long these days.

Further down the table, the Branscombe girls enjoyed the al fresco picnic with a few of their new friends from the area. Petra seemed quite taken with the squire's son, a nice boy who liked horses. Eva had been allowed to pin her hair up for the occasion. Annie was twelve now and chatting gaily to some girl friends her age.

Peyton knew he was blessed to be surrounded by so many family members. Only Crispin was absent, but he'd remembered the occasion with a letter, assuring Peyton he was doing well and a nebulous promise that he'd return later in the year.

Beneath the cloth covering the table, Peyton squeezed Tessa's hand, hoping the simple gesture conveyed all the joy he felt when he looked at her and their family.

Her eyes danced with mischief as she discreetly lifted his hand beneath the cloth to her stomach and leaned forward just for him to hear. 'I have a birthday present for you.'

Peyton smiled. 'Another? I thought I'd already got my present earlier today.' That morning, they'd locked the bedroom door and Peyton had engaged in something else he did well, making passionate love to his wife with every fibre of his being.

Tessa blushed. 'Well, this one won't arrive for another seven months.'

'It will give me time to put an extra order in for shirts.' Peyton reached around his messy boys and kissed her soundly on the mouth, not caring who might chance to see them. It was no secret he loved his wife. Neither was it a secret that, in his fortieth year, Peyton Ramsden had all he wanted and more. His life was complete.

* * * * *